TOUCH OF FIRE

"When I touched you, you melted for me," Iain said angrily. "Deny it if you dare."

It was his eyes that gave Caitlin pause, heated and intense, and glittering with an implacable resolve. Her own anger dissipated, and she shivered.

A distinct edge crept into his voice. "You know you've spoiled me for other women. For some strange reason, I want only . . . you."

He pulled off his shirt and flung it into a corner. Caitlin's eyes widened at the sight of his broad chest, the thatch of reddish hair across it; his arms knotted with muscles.

He wanted her. He really wanted her. The thought curled inside her and gradually expanded, bubbling up and intoxicating her. He wanted her—and she could not deny that she wanted him.

When he bent to her, she fell back on her elbows. His hands were pressed into the mattress on either side of her shoulders, supporting his weight, preventing her from slipping away. She closed her eyes when his head descended.

His warm breath caressed her cheek, and his lips brushed her skin. One kiss, she promised herself, only one kiss to last a lifetime; then she would put a stop to it.

But when his lips took hers in a ravishment of gentleness, there was no question that she would yield to temptation.

ELIZABETH THORNTON
HIGHLAND FIRE

PINNACLE BOOKS
WINDSOR PUBLISHING CORP.

DEDICATION

This one is for my husband, Forbes,
and for all those memorable holidays we spent on Deeside.

PINNACLE BOOKS are published by
Windsor Publishing Corp.
475 Park Avenue South
New York, NY 10016

First Printing: January, 1994

Printed in the United States of America

Chapter One

Deeside, the Highlands of Scotland, 1814

"Don't run away. I'm supposed to catch you. That is the object of the game, is it not? At least, that's what they told me."

The voice from the shadows was coolly amused. It was also cultured, English cultured, with that hint of arrogance the native-born Scot so detested. The leap of alarm which had set Caitlin's heart to thundering gradually subsided. She recognized the voice as belonging to her grandfather's nearest neighbor. As was his habit before he had taken up soldiering, Iain, Lord Randal, had come to his Scottish estates for the hunting season. On the morrow, he was due to return to his regiment. To her certain knowledge, his gentlemen friends had arranged a surprise party in his honor up at the house. Evidently, Lord Randal had become bored and had slipped away.

Sighing in frustration, cursing her ill luck, Caitlin turned slowly to face the man who had accosted her. In the split second that it took her to make the turn, she made a lightning decision. At all costs, she didn't want this man to know her identity. If he chose to, he could make a great deal of trouble for her. Better by far to pass herself off as a common cotter's lass.

Peering into the darkness, drawing the snood of her cloak forward to shield her face, she forced herself to speak calmly. "Lord Randal, what are ye doing here?"

As a delaying tactic, her riposte was hardly brilliant, but it gave her a moment or two to take stock of her position. The contraband whiskey was no longer in her possession, having been safely delivered not five minutes before to his lordship's deserted boathouse. She debated confessing that she was a smuggler and decided it was too risky. She could not be sure the whiskey was not destined for Lord Randal's servants. For all she knew, the Randal might take a dim view of smuggling. Then what reasonable explanation could she offer for trespassing on his estates at an hour when all decent women were safely cloistered in their homes?

He chuckled, and something in the sound brought a flutter of unease to the pit of Caitlin's stomach. "Lass, if you like elaborate games, I'm willing to indulge you. I think I get it. Are you supposed to be Little Red Riding Hood?"

Never having heard of Little Red Riding Hood, Caitlin was stymied. She presumed the Randal was making reference to some drama or other which he'd taken in when last in London. When he wasn't off soldiering in Spain, the Randal spent a good deal of his time in London and everyone on Deeside knew why.

In that Sodom of the south, Lord Randal was in his element. He was a sophisticate, a dandy who, if rumor was to be believed—and where Lord Randal was concerned, Caitlin accepted every scandalous tidbit as though it were gospel—fancied himself something of a ladies' man. With his blond good looks, he was a virile figure of a man in the English manner. Caitlin might have forgiven him that. What she could not forgive was that Lord Randal, the hereditary chief of her own clan, largely neglected his estates in Scotland except in the hunting season.

With good reason, they called him "the English laird." The Scottish strain in his blood was so diluted as to be almost nonexistent. Only his name and title were Scottish. In all other respects, the Randal was an English thoroughbred to the tips of his long fingers. Educated in England, he had vast holdings in Sussex. Deeside was merely his playground, a masculine preserve where he passed a few weeks every other year hunting and fishing in convivial masculine company. To the welfare of his tenants and cotters, the English laird hardly spared a thought.

Considerably fortified by her unpleasant reflections, Caitlin glared at the dark shadow which loomed over her. "I know nothing of Little Red Riding Hood," she snapped.

"Then permit me to enlighten you. She was almost gobbled up by a big bad wolf."

His reference to a wolf was more easily understood. Scotland's history was littered with men who had won that telling sobriquet—untamed, rapacious creatures who preyed on innocent victims, especially women. The Wolf of Badenoch came instantly to mind. Nervously transferring her wicker basket from one hand to the other she began to edge away.

He sighed theatrically. "Am I to take it that the chase is still on? Wouldn't you rather submit gracefully? This really isn't my style, you know. I'm too old, or perhaps my palate is too jaded for these titillating games. I prefer a more straightforward approach. You, me, bed."

Somehow the infuriated gasp came out as a girlish titter. Sheer nerves, of course, but the Randal wasn't to know it. He moved in closer. Though the darkness was so comprehensive little could be discerned, she knew that he was smiling. And she discerned something else. He had been drinking. For the first time since he had stumbled upon her, Caitlin began to experience real fear.

"Come here, little girl," he said.

His voice had taken on a different color. He was either as drunk as a lord, decided Caitlin, or falling asleep on his feet. "Why should I?" She stalled, girding herself for flight.

Dark or no dark, she saw the hand reaching for her and instinctively batted it away. "Don't touch me!"

There was a moment of silence; then he said in an altered tone, "I can almost believe that you mean it. But no. You must be one of Madame Rosa's girls, else why would you be playing hide-and-seek with me? Take off your cloak. I want to see what I've paid for."

When she lashed out at him, he laughed and captured her easily in his arms. With one flick of his wrist, he sent her basket flying. "I've caught you, fair and square," he said. "Now it's time to pay your forfeit."

He seized the hood of her cloak, preventing her from averting her head. His kiss was subtle, so subtle that Caitlin parted her lips without volition. The gentleness, where she had anticipated raw, masculine aggression, eased her panic. When the kiss was over, she had every confidence that she could persuade him to release her. Lord Randal was a rake, but to her knowledge, no one had ever accused him of rape. She held herself stiffly, waiting for him to be done with her.

When his lips left hers, she drew in a shuddering gulp

of air. Her mind hadn't been idle. She'd decided to tell him that she knew nothing of Madame Rosa and her girls. She was simply a country lass whom he had surprised when she was on her way to a tryst with her lover. Her thoughts backtracked. Madame Rosa and her girls? She didn't like the sound of that.

Murmuring "Sweet, so sweet," he took her lips again, cutting off her feeble protests. His hands slipped to her shoulders, then splayed out across her back, pressing her close to him. When they descended to cup her buttocks and lift her against his bulging groin, she let out a small, infuriated yelp.

"You're good. I'll give you that," he murmured, nipping at her earlobe. "I could almost believe this is real and not something bought and paid for. Forgive me, sweeting—that was crass. I'm not complaining. It's just . . ." His voice trailed to an unintelligible whisper as his kiss became more erotic, more demanding, and much too skillful for Caitlin's comfort.

In some small corner of her mind, she dispassionately allowed that the Randal was a master of seduction. The thought was not one she could hold. Distracted by the plethora of physical sensations which threatened to overwhelm her, she was going to faint. Her head was spinning; her knees were giving way; she was so hot, she might have been coming down with a fever. She couldn't help moving restlessly against him.

Summoning her wavering control, she raised one hand to push weakly against his shoulder. Capturing it, he brought it to his lips, kissing it passionately on the open palm.

"Tell me your name. I want to know your name."

She had to think before she answered him. "Why?"

He laughed softly. "Because, I want to warn the oth-

9

ers off. As long as you are here, you belong to me and no other. You're different. I can't explain it. And since my friends have generously agreed that I am to pay the shot, I'm allowing myself first pick."

Everything was beginning to come together in her mind with horrifying clarity—Madame Rosa and her girls; the game of hide-and-seek; something bought and paid for. Even his reference to Little Red Riding Hood was becoming excruciatingly clear—a scarlet woman or her name wasn't Caitlin Randal.

The irony of her situation was almost laughable. If this were happening in broad daylight, Lord Randal would never mistake her for a scarlet woman. He wouldn't give her a second look. There was nothing about her to attract the notice of a man of his voluptuous tastes—and much that would repel him. She was a confirmed spinster with no pretension to style or beauty. For a fleeting moment, she wished it were otherwise before she dismissed that thought as unworthy of her.

She balled her hand into a fist, but before she could strike out at him, the night erupted with the sounds of revelry. Half-clothed squealing nymphs, pursued by an equal number of bellowing, drunken satyrs bearing lanterns and torches in their hands, came charging into the copse in wild abandon.

"Oh, for God's sake!" Lord Randal, hands on hips, turned to face the unruly mob.

Caitlin, peeking from around his shoulder, let her jaw drop. Not nymphs and satyrs, she corrected herself, but young bucks and loose women bent on pleasure. Her ears burned from the ribald remarks that flew back and forth. Though she tried to look away, her eyes refused to obey the commands of her brain. Scantily clad girls, giggling coyly, were manhandled and unceremoniously thrown over broad shoulders as though they were the spoils of war. Some of the men, having run down their prey, went galloping off into the undergrowth like stampeding cattle.

Caitlin couldn't keep the fear from her voice. "Shouldn't you try to stop them?"

The Randal made a small snort of derision and glanced at her oddly before turning back to face the milling throng.

"Rand? Oho! You sly dog. Who have you there?" One of the male revelers staggered over and leered suggestively down at Caitlin. The nymph in his arms smiled in a languid way and stretched out one arm to curve it around Lord Randal's neck. Her invitation was graciously accepted. Caitlin had an impression that the kiss was open mouthed and carnal, and not at all like the kisses the Randal had bestowed on her. When the kiss lingered and the girl moaned, Caitlin's cheeks flamed scarlet. She would have dashed away if she had not been sure that doing so would only incite the males— she would not call them gentlemen—to give chase. By this time, she was positively cowering behind Lord Randal's broad back.

When the kiss ended, as if there had been no interruption, Lord Randal said easily, "This one is spoken for, John, but if that sample was anything to go by, you've caught yourself a rare one."

The girl made a *moue* of disappointment, and reached for him again. Laughing, he swatted her on the backside. "Later, perhaps, if I'm up to it," he said, winning a roar of approval from the man called John and two other young blades whose curiosity had drawn them over.

"Good Lord," exclaimed one, looking over the

Randal's shoulder, "never say that is one of Ma Rosa's girls?"

"She's no one o' us," disclaimed the nymph whom the Randal had newly kissed.

As he spun on his heel, Caitlin took several backward steps into the shadows. In her confusion, she let loose a torrent of Gaelic. He was on her in two strides, his hands reaching for the snood which concealed her face.

"Rand! What the devil has got into you?" The voice which prevented Lord Randal from exposing Caitlin to public view belonged to a young man on horseback. He was David Randal, cousin to the Randal and his junior by a number of years. His voice was rich with mirth. "Since when have you taken to ravishing innocent young virgins?"

Edging his way into the clearing, reaching down, he laid a restraining hand on the Randal's shoulder and spoke in an amused undertone. "If she is who I think she is, cousin, you'd best let her go. Touch her and you'll have the whole of Deeside out for our blood. Worse, you might find yourself shackled to the girl for life. Is that what you want?"

Lord Randal received the warning with a drowsy smile, a slight curl at the corners of his lips. As though debating with himself, he continued to finger the edges of Caitlin's snood. "Are you innocent, little mouse?" he asked whimsically.

David Randal's voice was less sanguine. "Rand, let her go."

Though Lord Randal addressed his cousin, his eyes remained on Caitlin, as if he would penetrate the shadows that hid her face. "I'd have the girl speak for herself. Sweeting, you see how it is. I'm a reasonable man.

Help me understand why you are trespassing on my lands at this hour of the night."

Caitlin faltered a little, then said in a rush, "If it please yer lordship, I was courtin' wi' my sweetheart."

"But it doesn't please me, sweet. Who is he, and why is it necessary to meet him in the dead of night?"

The Randal's face was so close to hers that Caitlin could feel his warm whiskey-soaked breath against her lips. When his hands closed around her shoulders, instinct held her motionless. Her mind was frantically groping for answers. The fingers on her shoulders tightened and Caitlin quickly got out, "Johnnie, his name is Johnnie. He is a sodger, a Gordon Highlander, and my da refused tae let him court me."

She sensed that her answer had not pleased the Randal and she was unsure whether or not it was in her favor. His hands suddenly released her and he stepped back.

"A soldier," he said. "Now that puts a different complexion on things. I'll not add to a soldier's burdens, no matter how great the temptation."

A few of Madam Rosa's girls, deciding that the little drama in progress was having a decidedly dampening effect on the party, chose that moment to liven things up. Squealing like banshees, they threw themselves on Lord Randal, endeavoring to carry him off. A moment later, Lord Randal and the girls were rolling on the ground.

David Randal made good use of the diversion. Reaching an arm down to Caitlin, he hauled her up, pillion-fashion, behind him. For her ears only, he bit out, "For God's sake, Caitlin, have you no sense? I warned you there was to be a party tonight."

Caitlin's reply was equally tart. "Your cousin is . . ."

13

Words failed her, and she finished lamely. "Just get me out of here, David."

Those sentiments were seconded by Lord Randal. He had dragged himself up to a sitting position, each arm draped around a squirming girl. A squirming amorous girl, Caitlin noted dourly. The light from the lanterns and torches illumined his features. In that moment, his strikingly handsome face looked almost boyish. "David," he said, "you can wipe that stupid grin off your face. There will be another time, another place, I promise you. Now get her out of here before I change my mind."

With a laugh and a cheery wave, David Randal dug in his spurs and decamped with alacrity.

Chapter Two

The rain was unrelenting, and dripped through the sodden tent like great gobs of melting wax. Outside, on both sides of the conflict, men were charging about, dragging hundreds of cannon into place for the morrow's battle. Cavalrymen were testing the mettle of their double-edged sabers or practicing the parry and slash which, God willing, would carry the day against Napoleon's lancers. In nearby cottages, up on the ridge, grimfaced surgeons were laying out their instruments in preparation for the grisly aftermath.

Inside the tent, the only light came from a sputtering candle. The two occupants, young men both, had donned their cloaks and sat in watery state amid the trodden rye. What could be seen of their red tunics and gold lace indicated that they were officers of a Scottish regiment—the Scots Greys. They were seated on folding chairs at a folding table—all army issue—and each was engrossed in his private thoughts.

Colonel Lord Randal, "Rand" to his intimates, stretched out his long legs. Idly observing the glutinous mud which adhered to the soles and sides of his boots, he frowned and wondered how he could introduce the subject on his mind without making himself sound like some green boy suffering from an incurable dose of calf love. It was no such thing. It was simply that with David's arrival, he had been given the perfect opportunity to clear up the mystery of the girl's identity. In the months since she had happened in his way, she continued to intrigue him. She was an enigma, and Rand hated enigmas.

He coughed. "I was wondering, David . . ."

"Yes?" David Randal, in his mid-twenties, and the younger of the two by a good five years, looked up with interest. His hair was dark and fell in disordered tendrils around a rather sensitive face.

Doggedly, Rand continued, "I was wondering . . . eh . . . how our mounts will weather the mud out there during tomorrow's battle?"

"Mmm." David nodded absently and lapsed once more into a reflective silence. Some minutes were to pass before he observed, "It's a matter of family pride and tradition."

"What is?"

"Us . . . here . . . serving with the Scots Greys. According to my father, there have been Randals serving with the Scots Greys since the founding of the regiment."

"True, but that was when the Randals really were Scottish. We are Englishmen, David, and I, for one, don't mind admitting it." Rand laughed and shook his head. "If I had known, when I first joined Wellington in Spain, that Scotland Forever was the regimental battle cry, I would have moved heaven and earth to serve with the Guards."

Smiling, David said, "You are more Scottish than you know, in spite of your cultured English accent."

"Am I?" murmured Rand quizzically.

"You are a Scottish peer, are you not, and the chief of Clan Randal? You can't get around that. You may not like it, Rand, but I'll wager there's a Highlander lurking somewhere inside that tough hide of yours. One day, you'll find out."

"I see what it is. You have been bewitched by that summer you spent at my place in the Highlands. Deeside will do that to you. Come to think of it, it did seem that you were in a bit of a daze a good deal of the time. I don't remember you joining in any of the entertainments I had laid on for my guests." Rand's smile deepened, and he went on easily, "Lazy days spent hunting and fishing with friends, and nights given over to the fair Cyrenes I had especially imported from Aberdeen." He let out a long sigh and slanted his cousin a questioning look.

David regarded Rand for a long moment. Gradually a wicked glint kindled in his eyes. "You are not going to get the girl's name out of me, Rand, so you can stow the charm."

"Did I ask for a name?"

"I know you. And we've had this conversation before." David was smiling.

So was Rand. "Did I really kick up a ruckus, later, when you refused to give me her name? I have no recollection of it."

"You were like a man demented. It took three of us to restrain you. Madam Rosa and her girls were so alarmed they locked themselves in one of the upstairs chambers. You certainly know how to put a dampener on a party, cousin."

A dryness had crept into Rand's tone. "Yes, well, if you remember it was my party, paid for out of my own pocket, even supposing my friends had kindly arranged the thing without my knowledge."

David's eyes were bright with laughter. "What else are friends for?"

Rand returned a mellow smile. "There never was a 'sodger' who was courting her, was there?"

Silence.

"And there were other things I should have questioned at the time. A country girl wouldn't have taken such pains to conceal her identity. This girl must be someone with a reputation to protect."

"You have a strange idea of country girls."

"And her accent—there was something odd there."

"Was there?" murmured David. "I didn't notice."

"Oh yes. If I had not been slightly inebriated, I would have spotted it at once."

"You were three sheets to the wind," retorted David, not mincing words.

Ignoring the taunt, Rand continued, "When she forgot to play her part, her English was as pure as yours or mine, allowing for the more melodious Highland inflection, of course."

"If you say so, Rand." David was enjoying himself enormously and didn't mind showing it.

"Were you her lover?"

"What?" David came abruptly upright.

"I said—"

"I know what you said. Good God, she's not that kind of girl. We were friends, nothing more."

"Every girl is that kind of girl."

"You don't know . . ." He stopped himself just in time. Pressing his lips together, he shook his head. At length, he laughed. "You devil! Look, I promised her on pain of death that I wouldn't reveal her name. Why do

18

you care? You haven't conducted yourself like a monk in the last several months. I'm perfectly aware that, at this very moment, the divine Lady Margaret is ensconced, at your expense, in a snug little house in Brussels awaiting your return. And when you were in Deeside, you showed not the slightest interest in cultivating the acquaintance of any of your neighbors."

Rand snorted. "If I didn't, I had good reason. I could not keep track of all the feuds that bedevil these Highlanders. Even our own clan is divided against itself."

"I never understood the genesis of that quarrel," said David carefully. "The Randals of Glenshiel hate our branch of the family. Why?"

"As far as I know, it all got started during the rebellion of forty-five. They fought for Prince Charlie. We came out in support of King George. The aftermath was inevitable. They were punished by the crown and we were rewarded."

"Is it true that the old boy—Glenshiel, is it?—would be the present chief of the clan if his father had not supported the Stuart cause?"

"Perfectly true. But that's not all. They were dispossessed of the title and estates which were thereupon handed over to our branch of the family."

David let out a long whistle. "Good God! No wonder Glenshiel hates the lot of us. I can almost feel sorry for him."

"I wouldn't waste any sympathy on that stiff-necked irascible old goat. He has done all right for himself, or he would not be a baronet today and the laird of a sizable piece of Deeside."

"Mmm. I think I get the picture."

"What?"

"Oh, merely that it sounds as though you and Glenshiel have had a few run-ins over the years."

"That's putting it mildly," retorted Rand and laughed. Almost as an afterthought, he murmured, "And those are the neighbors you accuse me of neglecting?"

Trying to stifle a smile and failing, David said, "I wondered when you would turn the conversation back to the girl. I'm beginning to think she has become an obsession with you."

Something flared in Rand's eyes and was quickly gone. His smile was faintly ironic. "You always were a romantic David. It's the mystery that intrigues me, not the girl. Frankly, I'm becoming bored with the subject."

"I'm glad to hear it."

"May I be permitted one last question before we send the girl to oblivion?" He didn't wait for an answer. "Where, exactly, did you first meet her?"

An unholy smile spread across David's face. "If you must know, I met her on the steps of Crathie church after Sunday services. You should have attended church more often, Rand."

After this, there was a lull in the conversation. The din outside the tent increased. Some shots were fired, but neither man gave any evidence of alarm. It had been going on intermittently for hours—men drying their carbines and firing practice shots. At dawn, on waking, they would go through the same motions before the battle was joined.

A trooper entered and set down an elaborately inlaid, wooden lap desk. He opened it carefully and removed a silver flask and two horn drinking cups. When he had withdrawn, Rand did the honors.

"Whiskey?" David looked from Rand to the cup in his hand. "Last I remembered, brandy was your tipple."

"Oh, this is a taste I acquired last summer when I spent my furlough in Scotland. It's the best that can be had, so I'm told." He put his nose to the drinking cup and sniffed. "It's good, but not on a par with the stuff I have in my cellars in Strathcairn. I never thought to ask what brand I was drinking."

"That," said David gravely, "was Deeside *uisge-beatha*."

"*Uisge*—what?"

"Homebrew and indisputably contraband."

Rand's brows rose. "Was it indeed? Well, there's not much I can do about that here." And, smiling, he gave the Gaelic toast. *"Slainte mhaith!"*

"Hypocrite! I'll drink to that, whatever it means."

David imbibed slowly, and without giving the appearance of doing so, made a study of his fair-haired companion. His cousin had a heroic look about him, the shade of some unknown Viking ancestor. To David, Rand had always seemed like a storybook character, someone larger than life. He was romanticizing, and knew it, but even knowing it, he still could not suppress the lingering hero worship that had got its start when he was a boy in short coats and Rand was a leggy adolescent. More times than he cared to remember, Rand had been held up to him by his father as a model, the paragon of every masculine virtue. Even the scrapes Rand had fallen into—his duels, his women—had only added to the glamour. If Rand had been a different kind of a boy, David would have ended up hating him. As it was, he admired his cousin enormously, and never more so than when Rand had forsworn his life of ease and pleasure-seeking to throw in his lot with Wellington.

They had been a grim four years. His own stint with the Scots Greys was of shorter duration, and he never would have joined the regiment if Rand, all unknowingly, had not exerted a powerful influence. It was a pity, he was thinking, that his own influence with Rand was almost negligible.

"Now that is what I call an enigmatic smile," said Rand.

"Was I smiling?"

"More or less. Share the joke."

"I was thinking how abysmally ignorant we both are about Scotland."

"What's to know? It's where the best hunting and fishing are to be found."

"There's more to Scotland than that!"

"Sorry. That was a facetious remark." Rand sank further into his chair until his neck lolled comfortably on the backrest. "Go on, David. I'm listening. What about Scotland?"

Now that he had Rand's full attention, David's confidence ebbed. "Well . . . you are the chief of Clan Randal. You must understand the problems better than I do."

"I'm sure I don't. Those matters relating to my duties as laird and chief are largely in the hands of my solicitors and factor. Besides, the only problem that concerns me at present is the one out there. Napoleon Bonaparte. I've given the last four years of my life to trying to solve it. With luck, after tomorrow, I can get back to the real business of living."

David leaned forward, bracing his elbows on his thighs, cupping his chin in both hands. "After this is over, what are you going to do, Rand?"

Shrugging negligently, Rand replied, "I haven't given it much thought. And you?"

"Oh, I'm going back to Scotland. I thought . . . I thought we might go together, and not just for the hunting and fishing."

Rand's look was shrewd, but not unkind. "It's that girl, isn't it? She's made a convert of you?"

"No . . . That is . . . we correspond."

"Do you indeed?" The smile on Rand's face was still in place, but the warmth had gone out of it.

David stared, then made a small sound of impatience. "For the last time, it's not what you think it is. The girl and I are friends, nothing more."

"And for the last time, I shall tell you that I could not care less what the girl is to you."

"Oh? Then I don't suppose you would be interested in what I was going to propose?"

"What were you going to propose?"

"That if you care to come to Scotland with me, I'd make it a point of introducing you to the girl. Without betraying her trust," he added for emphasis.

"You're on," Rand said at once, and they both laughed.

What they were thinking was that no one could predict who would survive the morrow's carnage.

At two o'clock of the afternoon, in the thick of battle, General Picton ordered his Scottish infantry forward to a line of holly hedges which concealed them from their advancing French counterparts. It was a tense moment. On his signal, they rose in formation and emptied three thousand muskets into enemy lines at point-blank range. The French were taken completely off guard and wavered. "Charge! Charge!" roared Picton, pressing his advantage. At that precise moment, an enemy bullet found its mark and Picton fell dead from his horse.

Sir William Ponsonby, commanding the Union Brigade, saw at once what was afoot. The order was given and the twelve hundred horse and men of the heavy cavalry began to get into position. Rand looked over his Scots Greys. They were a fearsome spectacle—row upon row of redcoats, with their distinctive bearskin hats with white plumes, and to a man mounted on immense white chargers.

As the shrill bugle call rang out, Rand transferred his saber to the ready position, up and forward over his mount's neck. The Greys broke into a walk and then a trot. "Don't fail me, Hotspur, don't fail me," he murmured and dug in his spurs as the bugle sounded the charge.

Their horses took the hedges like hunters and at full gallop, gathering momentum, charged down the incline to where the hand-to-hand fighting was going on. As they swept past their own infantry, some of Picton's kilted Highlanders, maddened by the death of their leader, reached for their stirrup leathers. Hoisting themselves up, they were carried into the thick of the fray as the Greys chased down the enemy.

The air reverberated with the sounds of bagpipes, bugles, cannon fire, and the earth-shattering thunder of a thousand hoofbeats. "Scotland forever!" The cry was taken up and rang out above the tumult. And then, another cry arose from the young Highlander who had attached himself to Rand's stirrup. "For Randal and for Scotland! For Randal and for Scotland!" A moment later, the French flank retreated in disorder under the crushing impact of the Greys, and the Highlander threw himself after them.

"For Randal and for Scotland!" Saber slashing, Rand roared the exultant battle cry. It stirred something in him, some latent pride in name and race that he had never before experienced, as though in this one moment in time, the honor of all the Randals in every generation resided in him.

By now all was pandemonium. Bonaparte's infantry was in full flight. Skirmishes and hand-to-hand combat were breaking out all over the field. And still the Greys pushed on, maddened by the French guns and the appalling slaughter they inflicted on their ranks. Like a frenzied mob, they ignored the bugle blast which sounded the recall.

Rand heard the bugle call and recognized the danger. Soon, the Greys would be cut off from their own lines. Officers were attempting to halt the stampede of their dragoons to no avail. One lightning glance over Rand's shoulder revealed David Randal forcing back his men with the flat of his saber. There was no time to ascertain whether or not David's ploy was successful. Digging in his spurs, Rand sent his mount flying to the head of the charge.

"Are you deaf? Obey the trumpet!" He was roaring at the top of his lungs as he tried to turn his men. "Retreat! Retreat! Else the French will have us in a vise."

As men reluctantly gave way and wheeled their mounts, they saw them—a horde of French lancers swinging down in a circle to cut off their retreat. Their powerful black horses were rested and straining at their bits. The huge grays were spent. The battle was unequal and men knew it. Ever afterward, the survivors of the coming confrontation would swear that for a second, a fraction of a second, a deathly, palpitating silence held men motionless before both sides gave the order to charge.

The shock of that charge was felt by appalled spectators as they watched from a ridge. The French lancers were deadly, and the Greys could hardly hold up their sabers to ward off their attacks. Then the red tunics of the Greys were swallowed up as the green-coated lancers ringed them in for the kill.

Unhorsed, his bearskin cap blown off his head by a burst of grapeshot, Rand fought like a madman. When his saber broke and he had emptied his pistol, he knew his time had come. As a lancer bore down upon him, he let out a blood-curdling roar, then yelled the ancient Randal battle cry.

That cry was answered by David Randal. Racing hell-for-leather up the corpse-strewn slope toward the French batteries, from low in the saddle, he took aim and fired. A lancer was blown off his horse's back and fell grotesquely into the churned-up mud.

Half-crouched over his mount, David reached down and grasped Rand's right arm. "Up!"

Rand needed no second bidding. He vaulted into the saddle behind his cousin. What the hell! he was thinking. We're all done for.

He was mistaken. A wave of Uxbridge's light dragoons attacked the French from the rear. As the way opened back to the British lines, men and horses found their second wind and sprang forward. Those who returned were welcomed with frenzied zeal.

Not a half-hour had passed since the start of the engagement. Less than half of the Greys had returned. The battle was a long way from over and already the field was littered with thousands of corpses. Rand's ex-

26

pression was grim. He was thinking of comrades whose faces were not among those riders who were dismounting around him.

"David!"

David Randal slipped from the saddle and fell on his knees in a heap. Rand jumped down and went to assist him. When he turned him over, he could see the spreading stain on the scarlet, mud-spattered tunic, see the rose-red droplets on his own white gauntlets and on the injured man's white breeches. For a moment, horror held him speechless.

"When did this happen?" He was signaling to orderlies to come and help him.

David's eyelashes were fluttering. "I took a bullet," he got out hoarsely, "when I turned back for you."

"Why did you do it?" Rand's throat was working. He could see that there was no hope, yet his mind refused to accept it. It couldn't end like this, not for David. He, Rand, was the real soldier. David was a poet. Rand was seasoned by years of active service. This was David's first major engagement. If there was any justice in this world, their positions would be reversed.

Gripped by remorse, Rand cradled the dying man in his arms. When he spoke next, his voice was a little steadier. "If you were not so confoundedly indisposed, as your commanding officer, I would be raking you over the coals. Why didn't you obey the trumpet?"

He looked up as an orderly approached. The man did not linger. With a sober look at Rand, shaking his head, he moved off to answer another call.

David's eyes focused on Rand's face. "I . . . did it for . . . Randal . . . and for Scotland."

"I wish I had never uttered that inane battle cry," Rand said, trying to make light of it.

The knowing half-smile in the chalk white face wrenched at Rand's heart. He had to bend down to catch David's next words. "The girl is . . . a Randal . . . a Randal of Glenshiel."

"Miss Randal of Glenshiel?"

David nodded, then a second or two later, "You'll go to her . . . take care of her?"

"We'll go together, just as we planned to do."

"Together? I wish . . ."

"What do you wish, David?"

For a long moment, David struggled to get the words out. "You'll go to her?" His voice was very faint. He closed his eyes and his head sank upon Rand's breast.

"I swear it!" Rand was never to know whether or not David heard his impassioned avowal.

Chapter Three

The English laird was coming into his own, and there was not a soul in that band of young men who lay in wait for him beneath the Feardar Bridge who would not have knocked him on the head if their leader had given the order. Twelve months had made a remarkable difference to the absent laird's credit among his cotters and tenants. There was a time when they viewed Lord Randal's comings and going with a tolerant eye. The laird went his way and they went theirs, much as they had done in his father's day. All that had changed.

A new factor had been set over them, Serle, a lowlander, and his ways were not their ways. He meant to dispossess them of their homes and livelihood. Strathcairn was now a hunting lodge, so he had informed them; and the thousands of acres of the estate—Deeside's finest woodlands and glens—were now a chase reserved for the pleasures of the English laird and his English guests.

Men returning from the wars had found their homes burned out and their families taking shelter in neighbors' byres and stables. Some were not so fortunate. They made their homes out in the open, like the Highland Gypsies. With the harvest in and winter fast approaching, men with families to feed were at their wits' end.

A young lad, a fledgling in the company of eagles, moved among the men, dispensing a welcome draught of *uisge-beatha* to ward off the chill night air. On his head he wore a bonnet with an eagle's feather. The green and blue plaid around his thin shoulders was pinned with a stag's-head pewter broach, proclaiming him a Gordon. As with every man present, tartan trews were molded to his limbs. Of them all, he was most truly the Celt—dark, small-boned and lithe, like the Highland ponies tethered to the rowans by the banks of the burn.

"Here's tae a warm Highland welcome tae his lairdship." Jamie MacGregor, a great redheaded fellow with dancing dark eyes, grinned and, throwing back his head, drank lustily from the proffered leather bottle.

Men laughed, but one voice cautioned, "There will be no bloodshed. Ye heard Daroch. Our purpose is to scare the *sassenach* awa'."

"We'll no scare the likes o' him," retorted MacGregor. "I've seen him in action, at Waterloo. Did I no tell ye? The man's a bloody hero. The bastard dinna ken what fear is. If we're wanting tae drive him awa', it will take more than the welcome we hae laid on for him. This is mere child's play."

There was a general muttering and grumbling, which quieted when young Gordon spoke up. "The man doesna lack sense, so ye hae oft told us, MacGregor. And this is only the beginning. The Randal may be fearless, but I doubt if his guests are all cut from the same plaid. If it's hunting they want, we'll gie it tae them, only they'll be the quarry and we'll be the stalkers."

No one disputed the boy's words. For one thing, he was only repeating what their leader, Daroch, had told them. For another, in spite of the paucity of his years, the boy's opinion carried weight. Theirs was a hard life, and even at the best of times, many a bairn went hungry to bed. Young Gordon had showed them a way to stave starvation from their doors. He had offered them shares in a thriving business venture. They were smugglers and dealt in contraband whiskey—Deeside *uisge-beatha*. It was a profitable business, as every man there could testify—if he was caught. There was little likelihood of that, however. Daroch's young kinsman not only knew the terrain like the back of his hand, he also had the uncanny knack of knowing when and where the patrols would strike.

Speculation about the lad was rife. Some said that he was Daroch's half brother, and he had been raised by the Gypsies until a year ago when Daroch learned of his existence. Others, observing his dark skin, shook their heads and vowed that the lad was in truth a Romany. What was known for certain was that Daroch watched over the youth like an eagle with its eaglet. When there was trouble, as there sometimes was, the men knew to look to young Gordon's safety first or they would bring Daroch's spleen down on their heads.

"I should hae stuck the bastard with my bayonet when I had the chance."

"When was that?" The boy was only half listening to the disgruntled young Highlander who had joined him to check on their tethered mounts.

"At Waterloo. God forgive me, he looked so braw, so much the Randal, I would hae followed him to the gates o' hell." MacGregor shook his head and would have said more if his eye had not been caught by the glisten

31

of something on the tips of the lad's lashes. Long, they were, and curling like a lass's.

"Ye were with the Gordon Highlanders?"

"Aye."

The boy moistened his lips. "The Randal had a cousin. David would be his name. He died at Waterloo. Would ye be knowing how it happened?"

Beardless, too. The lad was younger than he thought. "He saved the Randal. I saw it with my own eyes."

"What did ye see?"

"The young major. He turned back and plucked the Randal from under the lances o' the French cavalry. He was a brave man. How old are ye anyway?"

The boy's shoulders stiffened. "Old enough," he said, and threw out cockily, "And how old might ye be?"

"Eighteen," said MacGregor, grinning hugely. "Now that *is* old enough, as mony a bonnie lass between here and Aberdeen can tell ye. Can ye say as much?"

The boy's eyes flashed before he turned away to examine the girth on one of the ponies.

A hand fell heavily on MacGregor's broad shoulder. "Stop tormenting the lad." Todd Crombie was Daroch's gillie and second in command.

"Lad?" said MacGregor querulously. "He's only a bairn. He should be hame in his cradle. Tell me, is he weaned yet, for as sure as hell, he's no had his wick—"

"Enough!" roared Crombie, and his hand tightened around MacGregor's throat. "Mind yer tongue around the cub, or it will be Daroch ye answer to."

MacGregor, who had a temper of his own, and had the strength of three Todd Crombies by his own reckoning, was too surprised to throw off the older man. He was thinking that there was more to young Gordon than met the eye. He knew very little of the lad, having but

32

newly come home from the wars. One thing, however, was certain. Daroch and his gillie treated the lad as though he were a babe in swaddling clothes.

Shrugging out of Crombie's grasp, MacGregor rubbed his throat and went on doggedly, "Instead o' mollycoddling the lad, we should be arranging his baptism, makin' a man o' him, ye ken."

"And just what do ye mean by that?" Young Gordon's hackles were up.

MacGregor smiled easily. "Wenching, ye ignorant whelp. When next I go tae Ballater, ye are welcome tae come with me, or dinna ye like the lassies?"

"I like them well enough," mumbled the boy, and everyone laughed.

"Whisht!"

All heads came up as the muffled thud of hoofbeats approached. "By dand." The password was given, the Gordon motto, and then Daroch himself came thundering down the incline and sprang from his horse.

Even in that dim light, he cut an impressive figure. Youth, pride of race, and sheer devil-may-care audacity—every man there felt the pull of the young laird's magnetism. Given their druthers, they would have elected him to be chief of any clan they could name. Unfortunately, the chieftainship was always hereditary, and Douglas Gordon of Daroch belonged to one of the younger branches of the great house of Gordon. He was a laird, but he would never be chief.

"Up and at it, lads," he said. "Ye ken what to do." His glance roamed from face to face until it lit on his young kinsman. His eyes were twinkling. "Someone maun bide here tae look after the ponies," he said, and ignoring the lad's protests, led his men up the slope.

* * *

At that very moment, Rand was mounted on his huge bay, trailing the lights of his own carriage as it wended its way to the Feardar Bridge. He was glad of the exercise, glad to get out of the confines of his coach even when it meant that he was flanked by a detachment of troopers from the garrison at Braemar Castle.

The patron had halted him six miles east of the village. He had gathered that they were on the lookout for smugglers. A lone carriage, setting off at twilight, had roused their suspicions. He'd told them the truth, that he'd had every intention of staying a night or two at Inverey when he had received a garbled message from his factor warning him not to delay. Since tomorrow was the Sabbath and there could be no traveling the King's highways in Scotland during this hallowed day, he had decided to set out at once.

Whether or not he was believed was debatable. On balance, he thought not, which was why a detail of troopers was giving him escort to his own front doors. The arrangement suited him. A lone carriage traveling at dusk invited brigands to try their luck, whereas a troop of redcoats must give men pause.

The journey from Perth had been a long one, but far from boring. A man would have to be a philistine, Rand was thinking, if the Highlands of Scotland did not make some impression on him. And whatever else one might say about Scotland, and he could say plenty, it had the finest vistas of any he had seen in his life. The moors, the snow-capped mountains, the ancient forests in all the glory of their autumn colors, the lakes and rivers with waters so pure, so clear that one could see right down to their rocky beds, from Dunkeld over the pass to the Braes o' Mar—no one who had not seen it would credit that such stark beauty existed. Uncivilized was the word he wanted, but he did not mean it in a bad sense. Man had not made much of a mark on the Highlands and that was all to the good.

The weather had been fine, of course, and that had added to his pleasure. If it had rained, it would have been a different story. When it really rained in Scotland, one either packed one's bags and made tracks for England, or one built an ark.

He'd cracked that little joke with his good friend and host, John Murray of Inverey, with whom he'd planned to stay for a few days. John's face had not evinced a trace of amusement. That was the trouble with the Scots. They had no sense of humor. Dour. It was a Scots word but he comprehended it's meaning to a nicety. The Scots would be all right if only they would take themselves a little less seriously, enjoy life more.

This last thought led to another. David. Now, when it was too late, he wished he had taken the time to get to know his cousin better. After Waterloo, when he was back in England, he had paid a visit to David's father, hoping to find some answers. It was too soon. The old boy was immersed in grief. Rand had taken his leave knowing no more about his cousin than he had ever known. God, he hated regrets. They were such a waste.

This time, there would be no regrets. The girl had mattered to David, and he had given David his word. The thing was, he wasn't quite sure what had been on David's mind. A hundred times since, he had retraced that last conversation on the eve of battle. The girl. Scotland. He didn't know what to make of it all. He knew one thing. David had wanted him here, and for the present, that knowledge must suffice.

It was unfortunate that the girl was a Randal of Glenshiel. The feud would not be circumvented easily, though Rand was not overly pessimistic about bringing Glenshiel to heel, not when he had set his mind to it. According to his mother, the feud was something which Glenshiel, alone, perpetuated. Over the years, there had been overtures of friendship on his family's part, which the old boy had spurned with unbridled disdain. His family had not grieved overmuch at the loss of that friendship. In England, the Randals were great landowners, each successive English bride adding to the family's estates and coffers. As he had told David, only the name and title were Scottish. In all other respects, they were English to the bone. Yet, David had demonstrated a clear attachment to all things Scottish. That must be the girl's influence.

Suddenly, a small herd of red deer came leaping from the crags to cross the road, almost within touching distance. The startled horses plunged and reared, unhorsing two of the riders. Men cursed as they strained to bring their mounts under control. One horse got the bit between its teeth and bolted in the direction from which they had just come.

"Stupid beasts!" yelled one of the unhorsed troopers, shaking his fist at the tails of the departing deer.

By the time they had righted themselves, Rand's coach had disappeared into the gloom cast by the tall stands of pines flanking the road. Before long, they would have only the light of the moon to guide them.

"Let's push on," said Rand. "My coach has outstripped us." What he was thinking was that something must have startled those deer.

As if answering the question in his mind, the blast of a hunting horn pierced the silence. Almost simultaneously, up ahead, shots were fired and an unholy din broke out as though the hounds of hell had been let loose.

"Ambush!" yelled the captain of the dragoons, and men reached for their pistols and dug in their spurs, urging their mounts forward.

When they came out of the trees, they saw them—a dozen Highlanders, some on horseback, some on foot, milling around the coach. Rand was immediately struck with the impression that they were young men all, like a crowd of rowdy schoolboys up to some deviltry and enjoying themselves immensely.

"Redcoats!" The man on the box cried out the warning, and his comrade cracked the whip. The coach lurched, then took off like a rocket.

Before the dragoons could check their charge, a volley of shots whizzed over their heads. The thing was over before they could get their bearings. Highlanders leaped away over stone dikes and crags or were swallowed up in the trees. The troopers fired at random. Nothing moved. No one cried out.

"After the carriage!" On command, the dragoons rallied and went thundering off in pursuit.

Before long, Rand fell back. A moment later, he turned aside and, using the trees for cover, retraced his steps toward the Feardar Bridge. At length, in the shadow of two tall pines, he halted.

He was almost sure that no harm would come to his coachmen or the sole occupant of his carriage, who happened to be his valet. If the Highlanders had really wanted to hurt them, they would have made their shots count. This was mere mischief-making and on a par with the sport young bucks got up to when they were at a loose end, as he should know. Still, it was a dangerous game when firing pieces were involved, and if he was their target, as he presumed he must be, he meant to nip it in the bud.

His patience was rewarded. First, he saw shadows flitting across the road, then he heard laughter, subdued but recognizable for all that. Men were on the move, converging on the bridge. Keeping well out of sight, Rand closed the distance between them. It was no surprise to him when ponies were led out. They were in the middle of nowhere. Men must have some means of getting back to their homes.

More shots, this time coming from the direction of the river, then moments later the hunting horn sounded. The men on the ponies were jubilant.

"Right lads, it's done. Let's get the hell o' here," said one.

As the riders dispersed, Rand chose his quarry. He was in luck. The last to leave was a mere boy. He wasn't going to hurt him, not in any way that counted. If it proved necessary, however, he would box the lad's ears. That ought to loosen his tongue. And he aimed to do more than that. A boy of such tender years had no business meddling in men's affairs. When he was finished with him, the stripling would be glad to go back to playing with his toys.

Once she reached the open moor, Caitlin allowed her pony to have its head. Morder was Highland bred, sure footed and agile, which more than compensated for a lack of speed in this treacherous terrain. Even without the moon to light their steps, the mare could find her way to the shieling blindfolded. All Caitlin had to do was point her in the right direction.

It was only natural that her thoughts would dwell on David. According to Jamie MacGregor, the young major had saved his cousin's life at the cost of his own. She was not surprised at the manner of his death, and tried to take comfort from the conviction that there was no one David revered more than his cousin Rand.

She missed David. There were no words to describe her grief. He was the only person to whom she had dared unburden herself. They were both odd "men" out, David had once told her, preserving their little secrets from the world. It was this, more than anything, which had drawn them to each other.

So lost in thought was she, she grew careless. She was more than halfway home before she became conscious of being followed. She wasn't afraid, not at first. She'd half expected something of the sort. MacGregor was curious about her, or at least, he was curious about the lad he knew as "Dirk Gordon." The trouble with Jamie MacGregor was he was getting too big for his own boots. He had seen a bit of the world; he'd served with the Gordon Highlanders at Waterloo, and thought himself a cut above the lads who had never been out of the glen. He wasn't very good at taking orders and she wondered if it was because he was a MacGregor or because he'd risen to the rank of corporal in the British army.

She reined in the mare, turning in a half-circle. On the open moor, there was no cover to conceal her pursuer. Her first impression was that she was right. The rider the moon picked out was a big man, as MacGregor was big. She tsked under her breath and was opening her mouth to warn him off when she noticed something else. It was no Highland pony he was riding, but a great charger worthy of the proverbial young Lochinvar.

Fear tightened her hand on the reins, and her pony plunged sideways, tossing its head to protest the sudden pressure of the bit in its mouth. Recovering quickly, Caitlin wheeled her mount and whipped the reins across the mare's haunches, at the same time kicking her heels against its flanks. The pony shot forward. In a few leaping bounds, they were galloping hell-for-leather across the moor.

She did not think about what she was doing, where she was going. Instinct had taken over. Knowing that her pony could not outdistance the stranger's steed in a flat-out race, Caitlin had turned her mount's head downhill, toward the abandoned quarry. At this point, the moor changed character. There were obstacles to be got around—stunted trees clinging to the hillside, clumps of bramble bushes, gorse and broom, huge boulders and loose rocks—and all of them a menace to the unwary rider. It slowed her speed, but not so much as it slowed the speed of her pursuer.

When she gained the edge of the quarry, it took all of her willpower to draw rein and pause, giving him a clear view of her. This was the dangerous part, not for her but for the man who was so tenacious in his pursuit. If he came after her at any other point, both horse and rider would go plunging to their deaths over the edge of the quarry. Here, and only here, there was a scree slope. No horse could keep its footing on the loose scree, not even a Highland pony. Horse and rider would take a tumble, but not a fatal one.

She chose her moment with care; heard the man's violent curses, saw the whites of his mount's eyes and the taut muscles straining as it checked for each obstacle before she kicked in her heels. Three short steps and the little mare obediently vaulted the dense screen of brambles, landing with a soft thud on the narrow track on the opposite side. Caitlin's left hand tightened on the reins, swinging the mare's head up and around, checking her momentum. The mare reared up almost unseating her rider, then, finding her stride, she veered off to the left.

At any moment, Caitlin expected to hear her pursuer's cry of alarm as he took a tumble on the scree. Not a sound reached her ears except her own ragged breathing and the muffled pounding of her pony's hooves as they sent stones and heather flying in every direction. It was as though her pursuer had vanished into thin air.

Panicked, she leaned forward in the saddle, giving her mount free rein. It seemed to take them forever to reach the bottom of the quarry. Only a little way farther and they would come to the tree line. Once the pines swallowed them up, she would be safe.

He came at her with such speed, such stealth, that there was no time to take evasive action. The blow caught her squarely between the shoulders, and Caitlin went tumbling off the mare's back.

Dazed, winded, for a long moment she lay helplessly on a cushion of heather, blinking up at the stars. When she heard him dismounting, she made an effort to pull herself together. Ignoring her protesting muscles, she dragged herself to a sitting position and touched a hand to her aching head. Her cap was loose. As she scrambled to her feet, she pinned it securely to her hair, keeping one eye on her attacker. When she saw the quirt in his hand, she gasped and involuntarily reached for the dirk in her hose.

He advanced, she retreated, half-crouched over, keeping her face to him, shifting her dirk from one hand to the other as Daroch had taught her to do. It was all show. She did not know the first thing about hand-to-hand combat. Oh God, he was backing her into the quarry and there was nothing she could do about it.

Now that she had a closer look at him, she recognized him. His fair, sun-streaked hair was longer than she remembered. He moved like a predator, and that surprised her too. Lord Randal, for all his years with Wellington, was thought, in these parts, to be something of a dandy. He never traveled without a valet, and no one had ever seen him looking anything less than immaculate. It didn't seem possible that this awesome figure, twelve stones of outraged masculine virility, was the same handsome fop who made all the Deeside lassies' hearts beat just a little faster when he flashed them one of his slow grins, or made them an elegant leg. No one ever doubted that the Randal had an eye for the lassies. And she knew it more than most.

When he spoke, it was evident that his anger could hardly be contained. She could almost hear his teeth grinding together. "I thought you were party to an innocent prank," he said. "But I was wrong. You tried to murder me, up there." He jerked his head, indicating the top of the quarry. "You tried to trick me into jumping to my death. If I had not known about the quarry, at this moment I would be a dead man."

The violence in his eyes seemed to leap out at her. She opened her mouth, but no sound came. Her tongue clove to the roof of her mouth and she began to shake. This was not the man she remembered from the night he had caught her trespassing on his property, nor was he the man whose virtues David endlessly extolled. As David would have it, Rand was the flower of English manhood. To her furious charge that the Randal was not worthy to be chief of a great clan, David had replied with a chuckle that Rand was English bred and found

Highlanders with their blood feuds and vendettas a tad too uncivilized for his taste.

In that moment, as the Randal closed in upon her, it seemed the veneer of civilization, all his English breeding, had been stripped away. He was like a wild man, an offshoot of some Viking raider who centuries before had raped and pillaged his way along the shores of western Scotland.

It was unthinkable to use her dirk against him, not only because he was chief of Clan Randal, but also because he was David's cousin. Moreover, she was beginning to see that she had made a blunder by pulling a dagger on him. His eyes were trained on it. Nothing was more certain than that he was going to take it away from her. At the very least, he was going to break her arm. From the savage look on his face, he might well decide to use it to slit her throat.

When he lunged for her, she let out a yelp and, dodging away, went haring into the quarry. She didn't get very far before he caught up with her. Grabbing her by the scruff of the neck, he shook her with enough force to loosen every tooth in her jaws. One kick from his booted foot sent the dirk flying out of her grasp to fall harmlessly among a clump of heather.

Like a terrified, half-crazed wild thing, she went for him. She didn't wish to do him any harm, she just wanted to get away from him. With humiliating ease, he immobilized her. Kicking, arms flailing, she was dragged by the scruff of the neck and the seat of her trews to one of the many smooth-faced granite boulders which dotted the entrance to the quarry. Holding her face down, with one knee planted firmly in the small of her back, he brought the riding crop down smartly on the fleshiest part of her posterior.

The scream which erupted from the boy's throat at the first stroke was eminently gratifying to Rand's ears. The thought that the boy had tried to lure him to his death had unleashed a murderous rage. Nothing loath, Rand wielded the crop till the screams of pain and outrage had diminished to muffled snuffles and whimpers. When he was satisfied that he had whipped the boy into submission, he removed his knee from her back and straightened.

"And now," he said, tapping the crop threateningly against one booted leg, "we are going to talk. You, boy, are going to give me your name and the names of your comrades, or I shall give you more of the same. Do you understand?"

The boy rolled from the boulder onto his knees and stared wordlessly up at his captor. As Rand made a slow inspection of that pathetic, tear-streaked face with its huge frightened eyes glimmering with reproach and something else, something indefinable, against all logic, his anger softened and gradually melted away. He did not know what prompted him to stretch out a hand offering a belated comfort, he only knew he wanted to banish that hurt look from the boy's face.

He succeeded. Snarling, spitting in helpless fury, the boy cowered away. Rand edged closer.

"Look," he said, "perhaps I made a mistake. Perhaps you didn't realize the danger. I'm not really a hard man. I'll listen to what you have to say for yourself."

He did not know why it mattered to him, but suddenly he wanted to think well of the boy, wanted the boy to think well of him. Again, he stretched out his hand, but let it drop away when the boy began to tremble.

For a long moment, he simply stared at the lad, wondering how they were going to communicate. It was evident to him that the boy did not understand English. When he made a move to go down on his haunches, the boy sucked in his breath and touched a shaking hand to his cap as though reassuring himself that it was still in place.

Rand wondered about that cap. Not once in their struggles had it slipped from the lad's head. As he reached out a hand to pluck it off, he became aware of something else—shapes materializing out of the shadows, from the dim recesses of the quarry. Someone called out something in Gaelic, and the boy eagerly replied. A dog barked. Rand was debating what his next move should be when a roar went up and four burly men came charging out of the darkness and fell upon him.

He knew at once that his assailants were not bent on doing him a serious injury. They were not armed, nor were they disciplined. These were not the young men who had attacked his coach, but yokels, tinkers by the stench of them. Their aim was merely to subdue him or keep him away from the boy. It took very little effort on Rand's part to throw them off. Even so, by the time he managed to hold them at bay with his pistol, the boy was already making good his escape. One shrill whistle had brought the lad's pony to his hand, and within minutes, horse and rider were disappearing into the trees.

There was an interval when Rand might have got off one good shot. He never seriously considered it, not even when it occurred to him that the boy had made a fool of him. The boy's every move had been executed with forethought and precision from the moment he had become aware that Rand was in hot pursuit. The leap at the top of the quarry, this nest of foul-smelling vagrants, that hurt, frozen look, the delaying tactics—all designed to elude capture and punishment, whatever the cost to the man who hunted him.

Furious now that he had softened toward the boy, Rand rounded on the tinkers who had abetted his escape. Only the women remained, the men having judiciously melted away into the cavernous shadows. There was no satisfaction to be had here. They spoke only Gaelic, or so they let on, and though Rand did not know the language, he grasped their sentiments. Shaking their fists at him, gesturing, yelling, they made no bones about their contempt for the spectacle that had roused them from their beds—a grown man terrorizing a wee lad only half his size and weight.

Unable to exonerate himself, livid at losing his quarry, Rand mounted up. On that long, lonely ride to Strathcairn, he took comfort from the thought that it would be no great labor to discover the boy's identity. He already had some clues. The stag's-head broach and the tartan plaid were emblems of the Gordon clan. Unfortunately, there were as many Gordons in the northeast of Scotland as there were grains of sand in the links at Aberdeen. He would find him, Rand promised himself, and when he did, he would make young Gordon sorry that he was ever born.

Chapter Four

The ride to the shieling was sheer torture. Though Caitlin practically stood in her stirrups for most of the way, it was inevitable, given the rough terrain, that she would be jolted against the saddle from time to time. Whenever that happened, she let out a stream of curses that would have reddened the hardened ears of the fishwives of Aberdeen.

There were no words black enough or foul enough to describe the Randal. Only a monster would have used a poor defenseless boy so. She would not allow that there had been provocation. He would not listen to her, would not give her time to get her breath before he had set upon her and whipped her to within an inch of her life. And what galled her the most was that he had relished every minute of it. When she screamed, he had laughed. There ought to be a word to describe a man who enjoyed inflicting pain on his defenseless victims.

It would be days before she would be able to sit with any degree of comfort. And for what? They had not harmed anyone. Their target had been Lord Randal's trunks and boxes. So . . . all his lordship's fine clothes were dumped in the river Dee, and the dandy would be hard pressed for the next week or two to turn himself out with his usual sartorial elegance. Was that any reason to hunt a boy down and inflict the punishment she had been made to endure? Again, she would allow no excuses. Any sane, ordinary man would have apprised himself of the damage to his property before meting out justice. But there had not been the time for the Randal to ascertain the fate of his carriage as well as set out in pursuit of his assailants. He must have been lying in wait for them, must have seen through their stratagem and then singled her out, a mere boy, as the weak link in the chain.

It was a grave mistake, she reflected, to underestimate the English laird. She could almost hear David chuckling and whispering, "I told you so," and she could not prevent the old resentment rising up in her. David had always spoken of his cousin with such awe. He'd put him on a pedestal, and that had made her itch to topple him in the dust.

"What do you think of when you think of your cousin?" she had once asked David. She had been gazing at the mountains far off in the distance.

Without hesitation, he had replied, "Good fortune smiling. You know, all the planets in the right conjunction; signs and portents, and all of them favorable—that sort of thing."

"In other words, he's had a charmed life?"

"Everything has always come easily to Rand," he agreed.

"Mmm. Sounds like a prig."

This had startled a laugh out of him. "You are determined to dislike him." After a moment, he went on in a more serious tone, "I wish you had allowed me to invite him to come riding with us. He is not always in his cups and chasing after skirts."

But Caitlin couldn't see it. She'd come face to face with the Randal a time or two, and what she had seen she did not like. The man was an out and out roué. Not that he had given her so much as a second glance, except when he was in his cups. In point of fact, he had looked through her as if she were invisible.

It wasn't feminine pique, however, which prompted her antipathy. She knew his type. People like him, cosseted from the cradle, had no knowledge of the sufferings of lesser mortals, and if he did know, he was indifferent, as his methods in managing his estates proved. David had known nothing of recent events at Strathcairn, when the estate had been turned into a chase, and she wondered what arguments he would put forward in his cousin's defense if he could be with her now.

"There is no defense for the Randal," she told the back of her pony's head. "Everyone and everything must be subordinated to his pleasure. In all probability, he assumes that is how Providence has ordained things."

A mile from home, she dismounted. Her bottom was burning but not half as fiercely as her temper. As she hobbled through fords and navigated stone dikes, she eased the wound to her dignity by going over in her mind all the little "surprises" she had in store for the obnoxious English laird and his equally obnoxious English friends. One way or another, she would have her revenge for tonight's work.

Daroch was waiting for her at the bottom of the pasture. Even in her pain, she couldn't help smiling. She was thinking that there were a score of lassies from Ballater to the Braes o' Mar who would give their eye

49

teeth to have the young laird o' Daroch wait upon them. At two-and-twenty, he was the most eligible catch on Deeside, not counting the Randal, and Caitlin never counted the Randal if she could help it.

Douglas Gordon was a romantic figure in the Celtic mold—finally drawn features, dark hair, and eyes as gray as the waters of Loch Morlich. Caitlin had seen him only intermittently in the last number of years, and had come to know him as a friend only in the last several months. Daroch had spent a good part of his time in Aberdeen where he had received his education, first at the Grammar School, then at King's College. Having graduated from university, he had been in no hurry to return to the ancestral home.

Since Aberdeen wasn't so very far away, tales of young Daroch's duels and his fancy women had filtered back to Deeside. Shocking was the general verdict, and Daroch's credit had risen by several notches in the eyes of modest young maidens who ought to have known better.

Though Caitlin had a fondness for the young laird, she was never is any danger of losing her heart to him. He was too impetuous, too hotheaded. And reckless, as tonight's episode proved. It wasn't a desire to right wrongs that motivated Daroch to neglect his own estates and involve himself in the affairs of Lord Randal's tenants. It was the lure of danger. He enjoyed taking risks. Though Caitlin would never have admitted to it, there lurked at the back of her mind the picture of a youth who had yet to win his spurs. Daroch was only a year her senior, but she felt much older than he. The thought was a disloyal one, and she crushed it.

As she came up to him, he dismounted. "What kept you?" he asked softly.

She wasn't going to tell him everything, or he might take it into his head to pick a quarrel with the Randal. Daroch was very protective of her. He and David had never met, and she could not help thinking that David would not have approved her choice of friend.

"My pony picked up a stone in her shoe," she said at length.

"Is that all?" He sounded relieved. "There was no sign of the Randal and it occurred to me that a man of his abilities might have seen through our trap and set one of his own."

When they were alone, with no one to overhear them, they spoke the cultured English of the educated Scot. When they lapsed into Gaelic or broad Scots, it was done unthinkingly. Their language always suited the company in which they found themselves.

She didn't appreciate the inference that the Randal might be too clever for them. At the same time, she felt that Daroch should know the mettle of the man she regarded as the "arch enemy." Compromising, she said, "You were right. He was lying in wait for me, but I soon lost him. How did you fare with the coach?"

As they conversed, they walked their mounts toward a stone cottage which lay in a clearing in the dip of a small incline. Though Caitlin was one of the Randals of Glenshiel and lived on the estate, she did not live in the big house with her grandfather as did her beautiful cousin, Fiona. This two-roomed thatched dwelling was where she had been born and raised. It was enclosed by a dry-stone dike which was typical of the area. Both house and yard were as spanking as a new pin.

There was a time when Caitlin would have sold her soul for an invitation to join her grandfather's household. She and her mother had been virtual outcasts. In

51

the villages, people whispered about them behind their backs. Bastard was a word that Caitlin had come to know at a very tender age. On the death of her mother three years before, relenting, Glenshiel had finally issued the invitation that once would have made all the difference in the world to Caitlin. It had come too late.

"I never in all my life saw so many fine clothes," said Daroch. "Och, it was a terrible waste." He was laughing.

Caitlin led the way to the back of the cottage, to a lean-to which served as a stable. A huge deerhound, six feet from nose to tail, its head as high as Caitlin's waist, rose from its haunches and came forward to nuzzle her hand. By this time, Caitlin could hardly breathe without wincing. She did not see how she could take care of her pony without betraying herself.

"No one was hurt?" she asked.

"No. I'm thinking that the troopers recognized me. Well, they know there would be no more Deeside *uisge-beatha* for them if they arrested Douglas Gordon o' Daroch. Lass, you look as though you are fainting on your feet. Here, you go on inside and I'll finish up out here."

She tried not to sound too eager. "It has been a long night. You're sure you don't mind, Daroch?"

"What I mind," he said, taking the reins out of her hands, "is the danger to you on these nocturnal excursions. With the Randal in residence, the risks increase." Observing her flashing eyes, he went on soothingly, "No one is disparaging all that you have done, Caitlin. If it were not for you, there would be no smuggling and no money for bread to fill the mouths of the hungry children in our glen. I am aware of all that. But you are only a woman. These things are best left to men."

"For the longest time you thought in very truth that I was a lad." Her voice had risen, and the hound at her side growled.

"Aye. So I did. And we both know what happened when I discovered my error." His eyes were dancing.

Caitlin was glad of the dark to hide her blushes. The incorrigible Daroch had tried to have his way with her! In self-defense, she had blurted out that if he touched her he would be committing incest, or near enough to it. It was a terrible thing to say, especially when it was untrue, but he had caught her off guard, and it was the first thing that popped into her head.

Daroch had laughed away her fears. "Lass, if you are telling me that you are one of my late father's by-blows, you can save your breath. He was my stepfather. I thought everyone knew?"

She had known. It had simply slipped her mind. Daroch's real father was one of the Gordons of Fyvie. When he bent to her again, she had caught him a resounding blow with her fist.

Rubbing his cheek, he had backed away. "A simple 'no' would have sufficed," he'd said reproachfully.

From that moment on, they had become firm friends. Latterly, such as at the present moment, he was inclined to take a high hand.

"I shall decide if the risks to myself are too great," she told him.

"We shall talk more of this later," he said gently.

At any other time, she would have tried reasoning with him. She was too sore, too spent to waste her breath. "You may go to the devil," she told him, very much on her dignity. "And now, I'll say good night to you."

"Temper, temper!" he reproved, laughing, and began to unbuckle her pony's girth.

With her head held high and holding onto her hound's collar, she hobbled around the side of the house and dragged herself through the front door.

It took only a moment or two to light the lantern which was set on a table in the center of the room. Hanging onto the table for support, she breathed deeply. "Damn Lord Randal," she told her deer hound. "Damn Daroch, and damn all men in general!" Bocain, the deer hound, sensing that something was expected of her, whined in sympathy.

"Why is it men always underestimate a woman's faculties?"

The hound, who by this time had settled herself in her usual spot before the great stone fireplace, cocked her huge head and listened intently to each and every syllable which fell from her mistress's lips.

It seemed to take forever before Caitlin managed to disrobe. When she had washed the dark stain from her hands and face, and was down to bare skin, the transformation would have stunned the men who knew her as "Dirk Gordon." Her skin was milky white and made a dramatic contrast to the dark curtain of hair which fell to her waist. She was small-boned and slim, but there was nothing masculine in her svelte curves. Some women would have rigged themselves out to exploit that dark Celtic beauty. Caitlin was too unaware. In the morning, when she presented herself to the world as Miss Caitlin Randal, no one, not even the men who knew her as Dirk Gordon, would give her a second stare.

The next part, she knew, was going to be excruciating. Fortifying herself with a small medicinal dram of *uisge-beatha,* she liberally doused a cloth in the same potent medication, hesitated, then doused it some more before gingerly applying it to the most tender part of her anatomy. At the first burning touch, she sucked in several breaths in quick succession then moaned, low and long. So did the hound.

"His name is Lord Randal, Bocain," grated Caitlin, addressing the hound. "Remember that. He is the enemy. If I catch you flirting with him when my back is turned, it will be all up with you."

After donning her nightdress, she opened the shutters, as was her habit, and looked out. The view from her bedroom window was one of the best to be had in the whole of Deeside. Off to her right, she could just make out the lights of Lord Randal's place. Of all the residences in Deeside, Strathcairn was the grandest, a veritable fortified manse. But grander still, across the Dee, far off in the west, were the ancient peaks of Lochnagar. It was a view that her mother had never tired of in her last days. A fragment of a conversation came back to Caitlin.

"It reminds me of your father."

"What does?"

"Lochnagar."

"Why do you say that?"

"Oh . . . it's where we used to slip away and meet."

Caitlin had not pursued the subject. Her mother tired easily, and rarely finished a sentence in those days.

Now, as she looked out at Lochnagar, she shivered and turned away. As if sensing her mistress's mood, the hound padded silently from her place on the hearth, and entered the little bedroom. When no counter-command was given, Bocain crossed to the bed, then sat on her haunches before Caitlin, offering the comfort of one great, woolly paw. Caitlin couldn't help smiling.

"Sometimes I wonder if you really are a spirit. You always seem to sense my mood."

Kneeling on the floor, she brushed her hands along the silky beige coat, from ears to haunches. Bocain practically purred. "You are almost as big as my pony. It wasn't always so. When I first found you, you were no bigger than a squirrel."

Caitlin cast her mind back to that day. She had gone out gathering brambles for her mother, and had made for the very quarry that had been the scene of her whipping by Lord Randal only an hour or two ago. The juiciest brambles were always to be found along the rim of it. From below, had come such a commotion that she would have believed murder was being done.

Clutching her basket to her, she had raced down the path and stopped dead at the quarry entrance before the sight that had met her eyes. Tinkers and their dogs had tracked a badly injured deerhound to her lair and had finished her off. A tiny pup, no bigger than a squirrel, was mewling and snarling from a perch three feet above the ground. The dogs were about to start on her.

She supposed that the tinkers had backed off because they had known she was Glenshiel's granddaughter. The deerhound had gone wild, they told her sullenly, and could never be tamed now. It was the same for her last surviving pup. Caitlin didn't argue. Using her plaid to shield her hands from the pup's sharp teeth, she had captured it and had taken it home in her basket. It had taken months of patient nurturing to win the pup's trust. *Bocain*, her mother had called it, because at night, the hound had set up such a caterwauling that it seemed as if all the spirits from the nether world had come to visit them.

"Where did you come from?" Caitlin asked softly, gazing into the soulful brown eyes that gazed steadily back at her. There would never be an answer to that question now.

Rising, she made to take her dog back into the other room. She hesitated on the threshold, then glanced toward the lonely bed. That glance was enough for Bocain. She leapt onto the foot of the bed and made herself as small as she could manage. Sighing, laughing, Caitlin doused the candles and crawled in beside her.

When the lights in Caitlin's cottage winked out, a shadow detached itself from the dense foliage of a stand of pines and materialized into the shape of a man. Within minutes, he was striding along the track which led to the road to Crathie.

An hour was to pass before he had made himself comfortable at his own desk. Dipping his pen into the inkpot, he began to write. After the usual salutations, he went on:

> I have discovered enough about Glenshiel's granddaughter and the laird o' Daroch to have criminal charges laid against them. They are a wild lot. As for that other matter, I would say that the old feuds have not abated. Something is very far wrong here. If you have made up your mind to act, I suggest it be sooner rather than later. In the meanwhile, I shall see what I can find out.
>
> Your obedient servant . . .

Though the following day was the Sabbath, Caitlin was up at the crack of dawn. To her great surprise, she had enjoyed a comfortable night's rest. Her bottom still smarted, but only when she sat on it. She only hoped that the prayers during church services would be as long as ever they were. At the kirk at Crathie, the congregation always stood during prayers.

She dressed in her Sunday best. The frock she chose was plain, dark, and serviceable and made no pretension to fashion. Her shoes, stout leather brogues, were ideally suited for walking, as was proper. It was a three-mile hike to the church, yet only the infirm or the gentry escaped the minister's censure if they arrived in their gigs and carriages. For everyone else, the Sabbath must be observed to the letter.

Her mood had lightened considerably since the night before. She was thinking of the Randal sitting down to breakfast. What would he be wearing? Her imagination ran riot, picturing him wrapped in a moth-eaten blanket or outfitted in ill-fitting garments he had borrowed from his valet or perhaps one of his coachmen. A far cry from his usual skintight breeches and impeccable London tailoring. She very much doubted if the dandy would dare show his face in church that morning. He would be sulking in his manse, wondering what had become of his factor. They had sent Serle off to Aberdeen on a wild-goose chase—detestable man!

She was humming as she braided her hair, and giggling quietly to herself as she did her morning chores. There was little to do on the Sabbath, for it was regarded as a day of rest. There would be no cooking, no cleaning, no harvesting or any labor that was not absolutely essential, and that suited Caitlin fine.

Having eaten a breakfast of homemade bread and

jam, washed down with two cups of Glenshiel milk, she banked up the fire and took a last look around before preparing to set out. There was nothing luxurious in any of the furnishings, unless one counted the rugs which covered the flagstoned floors, adding a touch of color to what was essentially a Spartan interior. Caitlin and her mother had idled away the long winter evenings making those rugs from scraps of old plaids. There were no pictures on the walls, and no ornaments of any description. It was neat and clean and homely, and behind the doors of the presses were equally neat rows of jams, jellies, and chutneys; homemade potted meats and oatmeal puddings. In her cellar, there were apples from her own apple tree laid down for the winter, stone crocks filled with flour and oats, and vegetables culled from her own garden. This year, the harvest had been a good one.

Outside the cottage, off to the side, was a stack of peat, protected from the elements by a canvas tarpaulin. In the lean-to was fresh-mown hay and a barrel of oats to feed her pony. Water from her own mountain-fed spring filled the water troughs.

A woman on her own could never have managed all this. Caitlin was indebted to her grandfather for his care. Not that she wanted to be. Sometimes she wished she were more like her mother. Morag Randal would have starved before she would accept a helping hand from the father who had cast her out. There were occasions when they had come close to it.

On the death of her mother, Glenshiel had petitioned the courts to appoint him Caitlin's legal guardian. In an act of defiance, she had run off to Aberdeen. With no money of her own, no skills and no training, she had been reduced to finding employment as a menial. She had gone into service with a rich fish merchant's family and had found herself at the beck and call of every domestic in the house, from the tyranical, stern-faced butler on down the ranks to the pudding-faced scullery maid. From dawn till dusk, she seemed to spend all her time either filling up coal scuttles or emptying chamber pots. By the time her grandfather's agents had found her and had dragged her back to the Highlands of Deeside, some of the defiance had been knocked out of her. It wasn't so much the drudgery she objected to. She missed the scents and sights of the Highlands, especially the spectacle of its awesome mountain ranges.

Still, Glenshiel did not have everything his own way. She had learned a thing or two in her sojurn in Aberdeen: she had a powerful ally in Scots' Law, and she could name her own guardian, supposing she could find anyone to accept that burden. Unwilling to take that chance, Glenshiel had allowed her some say in the ordering of her own life. She was permitted to remain in her mother's house. At the same time, she was obliged to spend some part of each day with her grandfather, as a member of the family. Having by now reached her majority, Caitlin was free to choose her own course. The old rules no longer applied. It was only force of habit, she told herself, that made her continue as she was.

At the church door, mistress and hound parted company. Bocain made for her usual spot beside the stone dike, and Caitlin entered the narthex. The family pew was at the front of the sanctuary, facing Lord Randal's pew, with the pulpit and the communion table between them. Even in church, there was never any question of which families took pride of place in the valley. At one time, Caitlin and her mother had hidden themselves away behind one of the pillars at the rear. This was something that Glenshiel would no longer tolerate.

As she passed the rows of solemn-faced, silent worshipers, she could not help shaking her head in wonder. On the Sabbath, in their Sunday best, they were all decorum, herself included, as though the sermon on the mount was the rule by which they lived out their lives. On the morrow, religion would be forgotten as if it had never existed. In the Highlands of Scotland, feuding was a way of life.

One quick glance from beneath her lashes ascertained that all the members of her family were there before her. Her cousin, Fiona, and Aunt Charlotte looked as if they had just stepped out of the pages of Ackerman's Repository. Old Uncle Donald, with his faintly puzzled expression, nodded an absentminded greeting. Her grandfather's expression was as friendly as an eagle's. Caitlin returned his glower. Carefully, slowly, she lowered herself into place. When her eyes came to rest on the Randal's empty pew, she smiled a slow smile.

The beadle entered bearing the Bible and the congregation rose as one, standing respectfully at attention, eyes downcast. A few yards to the rear, sauntering down the aisle on the minister's right hand, came a latecomer, a young gentleman in full Highland dress. Without raising her head, Caitlin stole a quick look. Her first thought was that his kilt must have cost a fortune. She'd never seen better, and that was saying something. Only one kiltmaker could have tailored that one—George Hunter of Edinburgh's Lawnmarket.

Her next thought was that the man was built to wear the kilt. His lean hips rolled, giving the pleats just the right swing to reveal a glimpse of bare knee. Caitlin swallowed. Feeling herself blushing, she forced her eyes to move higher. There was no respite to be found there, for his short superfine jacket with its horn buttons hugged his manly form like a second skin. As he passed the pulpit, where he parted company with the minister, her eyes took in the whole of him. Golden, he was, like a tawny lion, or a Viking warrior.

Sudden comprehension brought her teeth snapping together. The feminine flutter in the pit of her stomach evaporated like flaming whiskey on a cloutie dumpling. The Randal had deliberately made a grand entrance, and they'd been caught gawking like a crowd of silly schoolboys.

As if to add insult to injury, on reaching his pew, the Randal raised one languid hand and said affably, addressing the congregation, "Please, don't stand on ceremony, not on my account. You may be seated," and thereupon, he seated himself.

Since the minister at that very moment had opened the Bible which had been set on the lectern, the Randal's suggestion was superfluous. Everyone sat down, and as though they had complied with his wishes, he smiled benevolently, allowing his eyes to roam over the sea of expectant faces.

Caitlin was almost sure he was mocking them all, showing his contempt for them. Or he was looking for someone. A frisson of apprehension brought a tremble to the fingers curled around her Bible.

When the service ended, the congregation filed out silently. It was on the steps of the church that neighbor greeted neighbor. Rand was well aware that no man would dream of absenting himself before the foremost person present, namely himself, had given him leave to do so, and knowing this, he took his time in studying each and every face. There was no sign of the boy, but there was one face he recognized, though he had never thought to see it again. It belonged to a redheaded young Highlander. He would get to that later.

Glenshiel was fidgeting, not knowing what to expect. When Rand attended church services, which he did rarely, he never lingered afterward, but left directly for Strathcairn. This time, things were different. This time, he had a duty to perform, and nothing on God's earth would make him shirk it.

Rand knew exactly what he was doing when he made directly for Glenshiel. In the past, he had avoided him as if the man had the plague. Now he knew a thing or two that gave him an advantage.

When he had arrived in Inverey, his first order of business with his friend, John Murray, had been to make himself conversant with the manners and modes prevailing in the Highlands. What he had learned had staggered him. It was like turning the clock back to feudal times. A chief was head of his clan. All other members of the clan were his vassals, owing him their loyalty as though they had sworn fealty to him. There was nothing in the law that compelled their allegiance. It was all in their heads, a relic of former times which persisted because of the relative isolation of the Highlands. Legislation enacted in Westminster counted for nothing here. In these parts, the chief was the law.

"Glenshiel," he said in greeting, and extended his right hand with the Clan Randal ring on his finger.

Glenshiel looked as though he would die on the spot from a fit of apoplexy. The buzz of conversation around them came to an abrupt halt as interested spectators waited for the explosion to occur. Rand never doubted the outcome for one moment. If Glenshiel insulted his chief here, before witnesses, he would become an outcast in the eyes of all members of Clan Randal. He did not think Glenshiel was so rash.

He was right. Though the old man's face turned purple with suppressed fury, he dutifully lifted the proffered hand to his lips and kissed the ring, then promptly dropped Rand's hand as if it were a live coal.

Rand suppressed a smile, but only barely. Since humbling the old boy, however tempting, played no part in his plans, he made haste to make himself agreeable. "Sir Alexander," he murmured, addressing the older man respectfully by his title, "I would be honored if you would make known to me the members of your family."

The rage in Glenshiel's eagle eye had faded to be replaced by a gleam of speculation. His glance fell on his beautiful granddaughter, Fiona, then lifted to Rand's face, and he bared his teeth in a smile. It was another lady he brought forward, however, to be presented first.

"Lord Randal, may I present my daughter-in-law, my late son's widow, Mistress Charlotte Randal?"

The lady's eyes were avidly curious. "Lord Randal, this is an unexpected honor. How is your dear mama? I had the pleasure of meeting her when I was last in . . ."

As the lady rattled on, Rand studied her covertly. So this is the girl's mother, he was thinking. At something over forty, Charlotte Randal was still a good-looking woman, though her figure tended to plumpness. Behind the girlish facade, he sensed a will of iron. She was a breed with which he was all too familiar—an ambitious mama who would stop at nothing, short of murder, to advance the interests of her fledgling. How on earth had David managed to escape her coils?

When the spate of chatter had come to an end, he answered politely and noncommittally, then looked inquiringly at Glenshiel.

"And my brother, Donald." said Glenshiel.

Behind wire-rimmed spectacles, faded blue eyes focused on Rand. "Is it the Randal I have the honor of addressing?"

"It is," replied Rand, taking stock of the elderly gentleman who bowed formally. The spectacles were slightly at odds with the impression Rand had taken of a gentleman who liked to be about and doing.

Donald Randal's smile seemed to be genuine, unlike Glenshiel's. "Well now, it's about time, I'm thinking. I never did hold with the feud, you know. Your branch of the family was no responsible for . . ."

"Not now, Donald, not now," said Glenshiel testily. His eyes had been scouring the faces around him. He brought his attention back to Rand and said, in the manner of a fisherman baiting his hook, "And this is my granddaughter, Fiona."

"Lord Randal," said the girl demurely, and curtsying, she lowered her lashes.

There was only one word to describe the beauty. She was sublime. During the service, he had noticed that most of the gentlemen could scarcely tear their eyes away. Her blond hair was a shade darker and curlier than his own, though not much of it could be seen for the flowery confection that he supposed was a lady's bonnet. Her lips were . . . provocative, as were the dimples that lurked in her cheeks. It didn't surprise him in the least that David had been drawn to this girl.

"Miss Randal," he said gravely, "my cousin, David, spoke of you often before his untimely death."

Her blue eyes widened. "Did he so?" she murmured;

65

then those beautiful blue orbs filled with moisture. "Poor David."

In these surroundings, there was no opportunity for private speech with Miss Randal. There would be other times, other places, Rand promised himself.

"Glenshiel," said Rand, his tone clipped and precise, "you will do me the honor of waiting upon me tomorrow morning."

This was a chief addressing his vassal. Glenshiel managed a stiff-necked bow. His reluctance was very evident.

Satisfied that he had achieved what he had set out to do, Rand turned on his heel and threaded his way through the crowd. He hadn't forgotten the face that he had never expected to see again.

His hand fell on the shoulder of the young Highlander who was in conversation with the dowdy young woman who had shared Glenshiel's pew. Rand had scarcely spared her a glance, nor did he now. In his mind, he had already summed her up as "the mouse." He had put her down as a serving woman, or some such thing, and it registered, though only vaguely, that he had seen her from time to time in the streets of Ballater.

"Well met, soldier," he said.

James MacGregor started; then a huge grin spread across his face. "Ye remembered me," he said.

"Of course," said Rand. "How could I forget you? You were the Highlander who latched onto my stirrup leathers in the cavalry charge at Waterloo. I never thought to see you alive again."

Rand was aware that, as he spoke, the mouse had slipped away, melting into the crowd. He put out his hand. "Randal is the name," he said.

"MacGregor . . . Jamie MacGregor," responded the Highlander as though in a daze. He was not unaware of the great honor in being singled out by so august a personage as the chief of Clan Randal.

"I'd be interested in hearing how you fared during the battle," said Rand. "I have a coach waiting, if you can spare the time?"

It so happened that MacGregor had all the time in the world. With every eye upon them, the two young gentlemen strode to his lordship's carriage. Caitlin's eyes, along with the eyes of every lady present, were trained on the swing of his lordship's kilt. The breeze ruffled the hem a fraction, and a collective sigh went up. She could not help wondering . . . but no, nice girls did not speculate about such things. The next blast of cold air did more than ruffle the hem of his lordship's kilt.

"Barefaced and bare-arsed," was Glenshiel's biting comment.

It was Meg Duguid, however, who expressed the general consensus. Meg kept the pie shop in Crathie. "Och, the bonnie lad!" she exclaimed. "The Randal is a true Highlander, and no mistaking."

In his first public appearance as chief of Clan Randal, there was no question that the English laird had made a favorable impression.

Chapter Five

For Caitlin, the Sabbath followed a familiar pattern, for it was then that she took her place as a member of Glenshiel's household, first publicly, at church services, and thereafter in the big house itself, as a member of the family. The big house wasn't really so very big by Deeside standards. Almost every other house of note in neighboring estates was grander, more opulent or simply of more historic interest. To Caitlin, as a child growing up, no other house had counted. If Holyrood Palace in all its magnificence had suddenly been transplanted to her own doorstep, it would not have made a jot of difference. The big house could only be the house in which her grandfather resided.

There were sixteen rooms on two floors, not including the attics. Over the years, the estate had changed hands many times, in common with other houses in the area, according to the vagaries of war. Glenshiel had bought the place from one of the Bissets of Abergeldie, having married a younger daughter to seal the bargain.

Caitlin often wondered about her grandmother and felt a good deal of sympathy every time she thought of her. Though it was true that Euphonia Bisset had died long before Caitlin was born, there was nothing in the house—no picture, no portrait, not a scrap of needlepoint—to show that it had ever been touched by a feminine hand. In almost every room, a plethora of glassy-eyed stags' heads gazed down from their perches on dark oak paneling. It was a bachelor establishment and put Caitlin in mind of a gentlemen's club. She really knew nothing of gentlemen's clubs, but she did not think any woman could be comfortable for long in those surroundings. And this wasn't a home. It was a mausoleum.

Glenshiel rarely mentioned his wife, but from the little her uncle had told her, Caitlin gathered that Euphonia Bisset had been something of a cipher and no match for the grim-faced, determined man who imposed his will on anyone of a weaker nature. There was no question in Caitlin's mind that her own mother had been a true daughter of Glenshiel. As she had heard tell, father and daughter could never be in the same room without fireworks erupting. Though Caitlin was aware that she was not made in her mother's mold, she knew enough about her grandfather to put on a bold front when the occasion demanded it.

On this occasion, little was required of her beyond her rapt attention. They were in the front parlor seated around a smoldering peat fire, and Charlotte Randal was dispensing tea and sweets. Glenshiel waved away the tea. He was intent on venting his spleen, and as long as he held the floor, no one would think of interrupting him. Caitlin sipped her tea in silence, remarking inwardly on the changes in her grandfather which had escaped her notice till the present moment.

Glenshiel was showing his years, she decided. His shock of white hair was thinning out; his skin was flushed, but whether from rage or from some other source was impossible to determine. The veins across his cheeks and on his nose stood out more redly. From time to time, he banged his walking cane against the floor, then winced as though the old injury to his leg was giving him pain. He was showing all of his eighty years, and that crept up on her so gradually, when it finally registered on her brain she was taken by surprise. As she watched him now, something moved in her chest, an odd tightening, and she felt herself swallowing.

"Does he not know," raged Glenshiel rhetorically, in a voice fit to waken the stags' heads on the walls, "that if it were not for an accident of history, I, Alexander Randal, would be the chief of Clan Randal? And he durst command me, aye command, tae wait on him on the morrow as if I were his vassal!"

Caitlin rarely took her grandfather's part. This was one occasion, however, when she found herself in complete sympathy with him and mildly annoyed when her great-uncle, whom she usually regarded as an ally, rushed in to the Randal's defense.

"It's no' the lad's fault that we were Jacobites in the forty-five," reasoned Donald Randal, fidgeting with the spectacles on his nose as he tried to bring his elder brother's face into focus. "Or that his branch o' the family supported the House o' Hanover. Ye maun remember, Sandy, that they were no' papists. It was a matter o' principle. The Randals o' Strathcairn would never support a papist claim to the throne."

Glenshiel's murderous glare was wasted on his near-sighted brother. "Were we papists?" he demanded softly.

"No, but—"

"And was our father the chief o' Clan Randal or was he not?"

"Aye. He was that, but—"

"Then the Randals o' Strathcairn owed their allegiance to him. When our father came out in support o' Bonnie Prince Charlie, every member o' the clan should hae done the same."

A stubborn set displaced Donald Randal's usually mild expression. "All I am saying is that the lad wasna even born. We, ourselves, were just bairns. It's no' his quarrel and it wasna ours. He is the chief of our clan, and to set yerself against him is worse than folly. It's . . . it's a stain on our family honor, that's what it is."

When the two elderly gentlemen paused to glare at each other, Charlotte Randal made haste to get a word in edgewise. The recital of ancient history left her unmoved. Ever since she had set eyes on Rand that morning, her mind had been toying with all the possibilities that his arrival in Deeside presented for the advancement of her daughter. Knowing that she had to tread carefully with her father-in-law, she remarked in a casual way, "You won't be the only one beating a path to Lord Randal's door."

"And just what do ye mean by that?" asked Glenshiel.

Charlotte took her time before selecting a buttershortbread from the tray of delicacies on the table by her elbow. Having taken a minuscule bite, she went on in the same careless way, "I heard it from Mrs. Noble. His lordship is fixed at Strathcairn for some time to come. He is young, eligible, and wealthy. It should not surprise you, Glenshiel, if all the leading families with daughters of marriageable age are falling over themselves to make his acquaintance."

"*A Dhia!* Is that all you women can think about— matrimony? I'd as lief make the acquaintance of an adder than humble myself for the likes o' that . . . that usurper."

Charlotte drew in a quick breath. "Would you so?" she said, and her voice was not quite steady. "Well, there are some of us who cannot afford the luxury of your pride. I am a widow. My dearest wish is to see my daughter settled before I depart this life. Naturally, I look to you, as Fiona's grandfather, to lend your support. You know yourself, Glenshiel, that there are few eligible young gentlemen in Deeside to whom you would be happy to see your granddaughter go—unless you think to encourage the attentions of Douglas Gordon?" This last threat was a brilliant stroke, as Charlotte well knew.

At the mention of Daroch's name, Glenshiel banged his cane upon the floor. "*A Dhia na gras,* give me patience. Are ye daft, woman? The Gordons o' Daroch are our sworn enemies. Are ye forgetting the ancient blood feud?"

"Daroch is no' o' their clan," remonstrated Donald Randal. "He was a stepson o' the former laird. Sure all the Gordons o' Daroch have died out. Their line has come to an end."

"He is still a Gordon. All the Gordons are o' the same ilk. They fought against us at Culloden."

"There are worse things than Gordons."

"Name me one." Glenshiel was never stuck for an answer.

Coughing, then slyly winking at Caitlin, Donald Randal jibed, "A Randal o' Strathcairn?"

Before Glenshiel could fire off another shot, Fiona flounced to her feet. She was pouting, but even that childish affectation did not detract from her beauty. Her eyes met Caitlin's and a silent message passed between the girls. Correctly interpreting that look, Fiona made an effort to compose herself before saying in a restrained way, "I don't wish to marry anyone, and if I did, it would not be Lord Randal. He is . . . he is too old for me."

"Nonsense!" Charlotte Randal pinned her daughter with a fierce glare, a portent of the retribution to follow when they were in private. "He cannot be much more than thirty or so, just the age when a man is ready for the responsibilities of marriage."

"But I don't wish—"

"Mother knows best, dear."

Answering Fiona's look of mute appeal, Caitlin said, "I understand that Lord Randal's mother has a girl all picked out for him." It wasn't exactly an untruth. David had once told her that the dowager threw eligible girls in her son's way with irritating regularity. The Randal had demonstrated not the slightest interest in them. As she well knew, his preference ran to the other sort of women.

"Then that's that," declared Glenshiel with so much satisfaction that Caitlin could not help smiling.

Charlotte had got the bit between her teeth, and she was not ready to let go. "There are always baseless rumors about men in high places. And even if this one were true, there has been no announcement of a betrothal. Mark my words—some girl with a little gumption is going to carry the day."

"Or some mother," murmured Caitlin, and Fiona giggled.

The snap of Charlotte's teeth could be heard clear across the room. "I might have known that you would incite Fiona to rebel against parental authority. You are not Fiona's guardian. Kindly remember that she has a mother. Sometimes, Caitlin, I think it is envy that motivates you."

Unbidden, there came to Caitlin's mind the memory of Fiona's tenth birthday. In those days, Caitlin saw very little of her cousin. Fiona's mother was a lowlander, from Edinburgh, where the family had taken up residence. From time to time, they came into Deeside for extended holidays. This had been one of those times. Since Caitlin rarely went near the big house, and Fiona was not allowed to roam the estate, the two girls knew each other only from a distance.

There was to be a party in honor of Fiona's birthday. Glenshiel, himself, came to the shieling to deliver the invitation. Caitlin was loath to go. In the first place, she was fifteen years old and considered her cousin a mere child. In the second place, she truly was envious. It seemed to her that Fiona, as the trueborn granddaughter, had everything. When she came into Deeside, she lived at the big house. She had so many pretty frocks in her clothes press it would have taken a month of Sundays before she could wear every one of them. Her looks, even at ten years old, were stunning.

Caitlin arrived at the party expecting to find a spoiled brat who would look down her nose at her "poor relation." What she found was a timid, solitary child who was terrified of putting a foot wrong. Charlotte was right in this—from that day forward, Caitlin had adopted the role of guardian to the younger girl, protecting her, as much as she was able, from the pernicious influence of a mother who was always finding fault.

"Caitlin hasna an envious bone in her body," declared Donald Randal staunchly.

Glenshiel brought the argument to a close by rapping

74

his cane on the floor. "It's no Fiona we should be thinking about, but Caitlin. Ye are going on for two-and-twenty. A woman must marry. Is there no one in Deeside who has taken your fancy, lass?"

Caitlin stared at her grandfather as though he had just asked her if she would like to become the queen of England.

"Well?"

She closed her mouth. "Like who, for instance?"

"How should I know? The Randal for one."

"The Randal?" Her laugh owed as much to astonishment as amusement. "What about the ancient feud? Our two families have been at daggers drawn since before I was born."

"Aye. The feud . . . Well now, ye have a point there." Glenshiel's grin wavered between sheepish and wolfish. "I'm a reasonable man. If the Randal were to marry into our family, I'd be willing tae let bygones be bygones."

Donald Randal snorted. "Ye mean the Randal has decided tae put his foot down. He wants an end tae the feud, and if ye try and thwart him, he'll turn every Randal against ye."

Glenshiel's jaw jutted, but he said mildly enough, "What do ye say, lass?"

"The Randal and me?" Caitlin's eyes were brimming with laughter. "Somehow, I just can't see it."

"And why not? Ye have a good head on your shoulders. I'll say one thing for your mammy—she saw to it that ye had a lady's education. If ye could only learn to curb that tongue, with the right clothes, ye'd be a taking wee thing." Bracing his weight against his cane, he leaned forward as if to emphasize his point. "Come home, lass. This is where ye belong, not in that bothy ye call home."

"I'm content with our arrangement."

"And if I am not?"

"You gave me your word, and I'm holding you to it."

"My word! My word! And what about your word tae me? Did ye no promise that ye would conduct yerself as a true daughter o' the house?" When Glenshiel became agitated, he tended to lapse into broad Scots.

Unsure of his meaning, Caitlin simply stared and Glenshiel continued in the same irascible vein, "Where were ye this morning when the Randal asked to be presented to the members of my family? I'll tell ye where ye were. Ye were skulkin' about, like a week timorous mole, terrified to see the light o' day. It would not have surprised me tae see ye diggin' a hole and disappearing down it."

Since this described exactly how Caitlin had felt that morning when surprised by the Randal on the church steps, she had no ready answer on the tip of her tongue. She was still humming and hawing when her aunt answered for her.

"Glenshiel, you're not seriously suggesting that Caitlin should set her cap at Lord Randal?"

"I don't see why not."

"No, you wouldn't!" Caution was thrown to the winds as Charlotte saw her hope of snaring the Randal for her daughter begin to fade. "Lord Randal will look higher than Caitlin for a wife."

"Now just what do ye mean by that?"

"Really," interrupted Caitlin, "there's no need for this. Why are you so obstinate, Grandfather? We all know what Aunt Charlotte is getting at." When Caitlin was agitated, as at the present moment, she sometimes forgot to address her grandfather as "Glenshiel."

"Spit it out, woman!"

"Very well. Though I've no wish to hurt anyone's feelings, least of all Caitlin's, you are forcing me to say what your own principles should tell you. Caitlin is not a true daughter of the house. She is base-born and everyone knows it."

The silence was profound. Glenshiel looked as though he had been struck by a thunderbolt. The color rushed out of his face, then rushed in again. It took a moment or two before he could find his breath, and when he did, his voice came out thin and reedy. "No one in his right mind would blame the lass for something she couldna help."

"You yourself abandoned her to that little croft. What else should people think?"

"That was her mother's doing."

"But—"

"Woman, hud yer tongue!" Glenshiel laboriously pulled himself to his feet. His eyebrows were down, clear evidence that his hackles were up. He glared at each person in turn. "My quarrel was with my daughter. If she had said the word, all would have been forgiven. Whisht, woman, do ye no ken that my own dearling wife, God rest her soul, was born on the wrong side o' the blanket? If that shocks ye, all I maun say is that ye've led a sheltered existence. Good God, where do ye suppose all these cadet branches o' the great clans got their start? They come frae bastard sons, that's what. Tell her Donald."

"That's very true," Donald Randal immediately responded, and rubbing his hands in evident relish, he began on a catalog which left barely one prominent family on the whole of Deeside untouched.

This recital was interrupted by the arrival of Glenshiel's physician, Dr. Innes, a dapper gentleman in his mid-to-late forties. Gentlemen of this age were always of particular interest to Caitlin, for she judged that her own father, if he lived, would be something over forty.

She had long ceased to wonder about Dr. Innes. He was a single man, whose devotion to his profession precluded, through choice, any interest in the opposite sex. As her grandfather had once put it, crudely if not succinctly, "The only bodies Innes is interested in are ailing and dead ones."

Glenshiel's words were borne out by the good doctor's opening remarks. "They got old Arthur Cameron last Thursday night, aye, and his relatives were in the watch-house keeping guard over him. They stole him from right under their noses." He spoke with relish.

"Who got Arthur Cameron?" asked Charlotte politely.

"The Resurrectionists, you know, graverobbers."

The cup and saucer in Charlotte's hand wobbled alarmingly, as did her voice. "This is sacrilegious! Why don't the authorities do something? People aren't safe even in their graves!"

More cautious now, the doctor responded, "They are trying, but our graverobbers are daredevil fellows and always one step ahead of them."

Glenshiel, seeing that the ladies would likely put a damper on the conversation, diplomatically suggested that a wee toddy might be more to the doctor's taste, and the three gentlemen quickly decamped for the library.

"Well!" exclaimed Charlotte, looking at the cup of tea she had newly poured out.

Fiona's thoughts still revolved around the conversation that had taken place before Dr. Innes had arrived. Looking at Caitlin, she said, "Grandfather said all would have been forgiven if your mother had only given the word. What I wish to know, Caitlin, is what is the word your mother refused to say?"

Two pairs of eyes were turned on Caitlin. "That," she said, and carefully licked a crumb of shortbread from her finger, "was the name of my father."

For the next several days, Rand was fully occupied in familiarizing himself with estate business. The damage to his property on the night of his arrival was only one small annoyance with which he had to contend. As one day followed another, it became alarmingly obvious that his factor had been lured away from Strathcairn for a purpose. In Serle's absence, mischiefmakers had run amuck.

Rand slammed down the decanter of amber liquid he had just unstoppered. "Puerile!" he told his companion distastefully.

John Murray's eye held a merry twinkle. In fifteen years of friendship, he had seldom seen Rand out of countenance. The spectacle tickled his fancy. "It's not whiskey?" he asked solicitously.

Murray had arrived from Inverey earlier in the day with the baggage and servants Rand had been forced to abandon when he had answered the urgent summons from his factor, a summons which had later proved to be counterfeit. With the arrival of the baggage, Rand was now attired in his usual sartorial elegance. Murray's costume of dark pantaloons and blue superfine coat was almost identical to his friend's.

"Need you ask?"

"Now this is serious," said Murray through his laughter.

"I don't happen to think this is funny," said Rand. He strode to the bellpull beside the fireplace and yanked on it. "Damn. I forgot. They've done something to the bells."

'They don't work?'

"Oh yes, they work. But they don't register the correct room."

"I don't think I follow you."

"It's simple. This is the library. The bell in the pantry, however, has just summoned a servant to attend me in my bedchamber. It's an infernal nuisance."

"Oh, quite."

Moving to the door, Rand flung it wide and bellowed for someone to bring him a fresh bottle of whiskey, preferably one that had arrived in the coach with Mr. Murray.

This was soon done, and both gentlemen were settled on either side of the blazing grate, each reverently nursing a tot glass of the finest vintage malt whiskey. When conversation resumed, it naturally turned to recent events in Strathcairn.

"These tricks remind me of the high jinks we used to get up to when we were undergraduates," murmured Murray at one point. "I don't think they had ever met with our like before at Oxford . . . a dozen of us or so, all fast friends from school days, and education the furthest thing from our minds. If we weren't thinking and talking about women, we were up to some deviltry or other. Laughing powder in the masters' pillows, sugar in the salt bins and vice versa; yes, and that was the least of it. When I think of the dueling we got up to, I wonder that any of us survived. Whatever happened to Parker?"

The next few minutes were taken up retracing the subsequent careers of their various friends. It was no surprise to Murray to learn that Rand had kept up with them all, or rather, everyone had kept up with Rand. As he remembered, it was Rand who had held the group together. It was Rand's friendship that each boy had felt himself privileged to enjoy. Nothing had changed in the intervening years.

A chance remark prompted him to say, "By the by, what was in the decanter?"

"Believe me, John, you don't want to know."

"Nasty!" said Murray, and choked back a laugh. Observing his friend's straight face, he said, "You are not forgetting, Rand, that we pulled the very same stunt on our tutor, old What's-his-face?"

"Dobson."

"Yes, old Dobson. And there was hell to pay. God, it was worth it! Shall I ever forget his expression when he discovered that what he was dispensing in the senior common room was not, as he supposed, his prize sherry?"

"I remember," said Rand noncommittally.

Grinning, Murray went on, "If Dobson could see you now, he would say it was a case of poetic justice. These pranks are scarcely hanging offenses, Rand. You should be laughing them off."

"And so I would if I thought that they would stop there. I am not forgetting, you see, the boy who tried to lure me to my death. That is a hanging offense."

81

"I understood you to say that you might have been mistaken there?"

"Possibly. I shall never know for sure. I went back to the quarry in daylight, did I mention it?"

"Yes. Something about a scree slope where the boy made his jump. Doesn't that let him off the hook?"

"It may, if he took that into account."

"I think he did."

In the process of bringing his glass to his lips, Rand's hand stilled. "How can you be so sure?"

Murray shrugged. "I'm not sure. But you are here. That must weigh in the boy's favor. Look here, Rand, you've no idea who he is?"

Rand smiled unpleasantly. "I've made inquiries."

"And?"

"And . . . I have reason to believe that he is kin to one of my neighbors whom I have yet to meet, Douglas Gordon."

"Daroch?"

"That's the one. Do you know of him?"

Murray made a sound that was not quite a laugh, not quite a snort. "The whole of Deeside knows of him. He fancies himself a Lothario. 'The bad boy of Deeside,' they call him. No woman is safe from him. My advice to you is to keep a close watch on your sisters when they come into Scotland."

"I think I know how to protect my sisters," said Rand dryly.

"What? Your reputation as a duelist? Rand, that was all of five years ago, before you went to Spain. You are quite the sobersides now. Besides, your reputation with foil and pistol won't deter Daroch, quite the reverse. He fights duels at the drop of a hat. All the Gordons of Daroch have been tarred with the same brush." To

Rand's questioning look he answered, "Their weakness for women has been their ruination."

"Point taken," said Rand. "At any rate, I have no desire to remove my family to Strathcairn until I can be sure there will be no repetition of the attack on my coach. And the only way I can be sure of that is to find the culprits and punish them or, at the very least, frighten them off."

"Hmm. Hence your determination to find the boy."

"Quite."

"What about the garrison at Braemar? Have you enlisted their help?"

"What can they do but stir up a hornets' nest?"

"True. To involve redcoats would forfeit you the good will of all your neighbors." There was an interval of silence before Murray went on, "You must have given some thought as to why you have been singled out in this way? Or are all your neighbors plagued with similar petty annoyances?"

Rand settled himself more comfortably into the depths of his high-backed armchair and allowed his thoughts to wander to two separate and unconnected conversations which had taken place in this very room. The first was with Jamie MacGregor after church services. The second was with his factor when Serle had returned from Aberdeen after a fruitless two days' wait for his master to appear.

Though both men had taken a different tack, the one respectfully reproachful, the other indignantly self-justifying, their views agreed in essentials. It seemed that Rand's desire to turn his estate into a chase had enraged the crofters who had been cleared from their homes. Rand was coming to see that his choice of factor had not been a happy one. Serle was a lowlander. He did not understand Highland sensibilities. Though he was an able administrator, he lacked tact. Nevertheless, Serle had acted on Rand's instructions, and Rand would permit no man to dictate how he would manage his estates. When that principle was understood and accepted, and only then, he might be willing to listen to the grievances of his tenants.

Rand rolled his head against the cool leather upholstery of his chairback and gazed at the blaze in the grate through drowsy, half-lidded eyes. "You know very well the answers to those questions, John."

"Aye. That I do."

Rand waited. When Murray said nothing, he smiled. "No words of advice? No caveats, John?"

Murray made a small sound of derision. "What would be the good of that? To my certain knowledge, you have never taken anyone's advice unless it was what you wanted to do in the first place."

"You're wrong, you know. Sometimes I do take advice, but only when I ask for it."

"Are you asking for my advice?"

"No."

"Fine," said Murray, and folded his lips together.

A log in the grate collapsed, sending sparks shooting up the chimney. The wind rattled the window panes. By and by, the clock on the mantel struck the hour. The silence lengthened.

Murray unfolded his lips. "What about the girl, Miss Randal?"

Rand pulled a long face. "I've exchanged no more than a few words with her. What can I say? She seems unexceptional."

"Do I detect a note of disappointment?"

Grinning, Rand countered, "Show me the woman who has never disappointed a man's hopes."

This observation got Murray started on a catalog of paramours and flirts who had played both gentlemen false over the years, provoking much raillery and good-natured laughter. By the time they had exhausted the subject, they were both in a mellow frame of mind.

"What about David?" asked Murray at one point. "Was he in love with the girl?"

Rand shook his head. "He denied it emphatically, and I have no reason to doubt him."

"Poor David." Murray let out a long sigh. "I wish I had taken the time to get to know him better when he was last here. He seemed such a good sort. I don't recall—did he ever go hunting with us, or fishing?

"On the odd occasion, but very infrequently."

"Ah, he was spending his time with Miss Randal, was he?"

Rand thought carefully before he answered. "So I presume. I think she was trying to make a convert of him."

"A convert? What does that mean?"

"A Scotsman!" answered Rand succinctly.

Murray's eyebrows rose. "And did she succeed?"

"I think she must have done. On the eve of Waterloo, his conversation was all of Scotland and her problems." Rand allowed himself a small smile. "In his own way, I think David was trying to convert me."

Murray allowed that thought to revolve in his mind. He was beginning to form a much clearer idea of why his friend had come to Scotland. It seemed that David had succeeded where he had failed. At long last, Rand's prejudices respecting Scotland were susceptible to change. Inwardly, he cursed the young Highlanders who had set upon Rand's coach. By that injudicious act, they had jeopardized all that David had achieved. Rand never allowed anyone to force his hand

Suddenly aware that he had come under Rand's scrutiny, he raised his glass and gave the Gaelic toast. *"Slainte mhaith,* good health to you."

After this, nothing was said until Rand topped up their glasses. "By the way, John, I'm indebted to you for your advice respecting Glenshiel, advice which I did solicit."

Murray looked perplexed. "What advice?"

" 'Act like the chief of Clan Randal,' you told me. And I did. And it worked. Glenshiel called on me yesterday morning."

"Did he, indeed! And?"

"We are hardly bosom friends, but at least we are on speaking terms."

"That's something!"

"Yes, isn't it? The feud is not turning out to be the insurmountable object I presumed it would be."

"So now you have the *entrée* into Glenshiel's household and access to Miss Randal?"

"Precisely," said Rand.

Chapter Six

Some days were to pass before Rand returned Glenshiel's call. It was not done without forethought. Having made it his business to find out that Glenshiel and Mr. Donald Randal would be in Ballater that morning, he ordered his horse to be saddled and brought round. He had invited John Murray to accompany him as a diversion for the mother while he sized up the girl, but Murray was obliged to spend the day with a married sister and her family who farmed at Aboyne, so Rand set off alone.

When he arrived at the house, his card was taken in hand by a buxom, goggle-eyed young maid who gave the impression that she had never seen such a thing. It came as no surprise to Rand when she told him, in response to his inquiry, that the gentlemen were not at home. His expression was so crestfallen, his manner so gentlemanly, that Maisie could not bear to see the young laird disappointed. It was her suggestion that, if he would be so kind as to wait in the library, she would take his card up to the ladies, though she did not think they were receiving visitors.

"Mrs. Randal and Miss Fiona," said Maisie artlessly, "are still in their beds."

"I don't mind waiting," said Rand, and flashed the maid a bold, potent smile which, she later confessed to Cook, made her clean forget what she was supposed to be doing until the Randal gently reminded her. Even then, she ascended the stairs as in a trance, and wandered about blindly until she was recalled to her duty by the card which was clutched, in a death grip, to her frantically beating heart.

In the interim, since this was the first time he had crossed Glenshiel's threshold, Rand was looking about him with interest. What he saw impressed him favorably, for here were no blighting portraits of former generations of Randals scowling down at their innocent descendants but a magnificent collection of prime stags' heads mounted on the walls.

Having studied the several specimens with the appreciation of the true connoisseur, Rand pushed open the door he assumed led into the library. Someone was there before him, the little mousy girl from the church, the one who had sat in Glenshiel's pew and whom he had taken for a serving woman. She was standing at one end of a long table strewn with papers and books. From time to time, she consulted these before making notations in the margins of the handwritten page she was perusing.

Silently, Rand watched her, studying her with far greater absorption than he had studied the stags' heads. He was thinking that if he had the dressing of the girl, he would never permit her to wear the drab grays she seemed to prefer. Her milky white skin and raven-black hair would show to better effect with clear, vibrant colors. Nor would he permit her to wear a style that was a good twenty years out of date. It wasn't that the plain round wool gown did not set off her womanly figure to

88

admiration. Rand could not find fault there. But it made her look too much the dowd, too unaware, too indifferent to what a male might find pleasing, as indeed did the thick plait of hair which dangled to her waist. It was as if the woman wished to efface her femininity. The thought gave rise to all sorts of interesting speculations.

She was humming some Scottish air under her breath. He did not know why he was smiling or why, having discovered his error, he did not simply slip away without disturbing her. As it was, with all the arrogance of one of his position and experience, he advanced upon the girl. "I beg your pardon," he said, "the maid told me I might wait in the library."

At the sound of his voice, Caitlin started. The pencil slipped from her fingers and Rand bent to retrieve it. That gave her a moment to get herself in hand. Even so, when he straightened, towering over her, the words on her lips died unsaid. She had never been so afraid in her life.

She wasn't plain, precisely, Rand decided, as his eyes made an unhurried assessment of each unremarkable feature. A dab of rouge to bring a little color to those high cheekbones, a little shaping to thin those straight black brows and the girl would be quite passable. He wouldn't do a thing to alter those intelligent gray eyes, unless it was to teach her to lower her lashes when a gentleman openly stared. As for her lips . . . Rand stopped there. He could feel his body tightening in the beginnings of sexual arousal.

Caitlin saw his eyes widen the moment before his lips curved, and the tension across her shoulder blades gradually relaxed. The Randal had not recognized her. That bemused expression denoted a pleasant train of thought. He seemed to be laughing at some private joke.

It was fortunate, Rand was thinking, that the girl could not see the pictures which flickered behind his eyes, else she would run screaming from the room. In his imagination, he was stripping her naked, unbinding her hair, lowering her to the table, watching her expressive eyes darken with awareness as he bent to her. He had never before experienced such a vividly intense response to any woman, and that it should be this little mouse of a girl who provoked it both amused him and filled him with awe.

Caitlin's thoughts had taken a different path. She observed his vacant smile and reflected that the Randal had plenty to laugh about. As far as he was concerned, the attack on his coach and the destruction of his property had been nothing more than a minor inconvenience. But how could they have known that his lordship had come into Scotland with not one carriage, as was his wont, but with three, and that two of those carriages had remained at Inverey while he had pressed on to Strathcairn?

He had turned the tables on them. Far from being made a laughingstock, he was being touted in the neighborhood as a great sport, a gentleman who wasn't above laughing at himself. His wearing of the kilt had been a masterly stroke, as had his subsequent refusal to permit the redcoats to track down his assailants. *Young bucks at a loose end are naturally attracted to mischief-making.* He had laughed it off to Meg Duguid when he had stopped in at her pie shop. Meg had passed his words along, and those who should have known better were completely won over by his lordship's winning manners.

It was all she could do not to snort like a horse. She'd had a taste of his lordship's winning manners, and her bottom still smarted from them.

"The library," she said pointedly, enunciating each syllable with careful precision, "is next door. This is Mr. Randal's office, Mr. Donald Randal, that is, and he is not here."

Humor and delight filled his eyes. He was smiling at her in a way she couldn't understand, studying her as though she were some exotic moth he had pinned to a card and which he could not for the life of him catalog.

"Your voice has a trace of mist in it, did you know? It makes a man think of mysteries and feminine secrets."

Her heart gave a great lurch. Mysteries and secrets? Oh God, he was onto her! No. That could not be it, or he would not be grinning like a Cheshire cat. Then what was he up to? With a supreme effort of will, she managed to say evenly, "Would you like me to show you where the library is? It wouldn't be any trouble."

His eyes captured hers in a compelling stare. The sensation was not unlike the one she had experienced when she had looked down from a great height, from one of the peaks of Lochnagar, and had frozen in terror, knowing that one misstep and she would fall to her doom.

"Your pencil," he said and held it out to her.

She gazed with unwavering intensity at the object in his hand, and slowly reached for it. As their fingers touched, she jerked as if an electric current had passed between them.

Rand could hardly credit the effect the girl had on him. The instant rush of desire was not new to him. Beautiful women who projected an aura of sensuality had been known to stir his blood almost as a matter of course. But this girl was not beautiful. There was no invitation in her unblinking stare, not a trace of the provocative seductress about her. Yet, he was too experienced to be mistaken. When their fingers had touched, something had leapt out at him. A sensible man, he was thinking, would be taking to his heels.

Abruptly moving away, he began to take stock of the room. On every available surface there were bundles of loose papers bound with tapes. He recognized the order amidst the apparent chaos.

"What are you, a scholar?"

"A scribe," she answered at once, grateful for his matter-of-fact tone. Her sense of relief was almost palpable. The queer light had faded from his eyes, and the threat in that predatory half-smile had been converted into something more pleasant. She inhaled lengthily several times and felt her heartbeat gradually return to normal. As the conviction took hold that her secret was still safe, her confidence returned in full force.

"What do you do, exactly?"

"I transcribe notes, verify facts, and so on."

He was leafing through the books and papers on the table. *"A History of the Leading Families in Deeside,"* he read, "by Donald Randal." His brows rose questioningly. "I take it Mr. Randal is the local historian?"

"Yes."

"Is he any good?"

"The best. His knowledge is prodigious. His memory is phenomenal."

"What are these?" He pointed to the bundles of manuscripts which littered the top of the sideboard and spilled over on to various tables set against the walls.

"Those are the histories of every family of any note that ever lived on Deeside."

"I presume that my family is represented here?"

"You presume correctly."

Something in her tone registered a discordant note.

He was holding a leather-bound volume in his hand, but he was looking at her. "Is Mr. Randal harmless?"

"Beg pardon?"

"Some families, some individuals," he amended, "might not take kindly to finding themselves in the pages of an unauthorized history."

"Such as yourself, for instance?" The words were not meant to be friendly, but even she was dismayed at the blatant challenge they conveyed. Before she could think of a way of softening them, he was edging one hip on to the table, leaning toward her with his arms negligently folded across his chest. She had to tip back her head to look up at him.

"What is it you think you know about me?" he asked.

For a moment, instinct held her silent. She was not quite sure that she trusted that cordial smile or the irrepressible twinkle that had leapt to life in his eyes. His next words reassured her.

"Look, there is something on your mind, and I would like to know what it is. I promise, I won't eat you."

For one moment more, she hesitated, then plunged into speech. There was no thought in her mind of castigating as if he were some guilty schoolboy. She meant to plead the cause of the tenants who had been cleared from their homes. The Randal had given her the perfect opening, and conscience compelled her to act, however reluctantly.

She began diffidently, but when he made no effort to help her, simply stared unblinkingly like a sphinx cast in stone, the words of supplication became more impassioned. To her ears, she was pleading for clemency for a group of people who had no means of seeking recourse for the wrongs done to them. To Rand's ears, she was lecturing him on his want of scruples.

In smiling, noncommittal silence, he listened as the husky tones made a long and extensive catalog of his failings. It seemed that every tenant who had been given notice to quit his lands—and he knew for a fact no more than a dozen families were involved—was a personal friend of this irate lady. She spoke of suffering and deprivation on a scale that equaled the Duke of Cumberland's barbarity in the aftermath of Culloden.

There was something in what she said, and if she had approached him in a more conciliatory manner, so Rand told himself, he might have revealed that he intended to redress any wrongs that had been done by his overzealous factor. Already, a beginning had been made.

What he would not tolerate was this blatant meddling in things which did not concern her. This hot-at-hand little spitfire was begging for a trimming, and he was just the one to administer it.

When she had run out of words, there was long pause. They stared at each other, she boldly, he cold-eyed. Caitlin was the first to look away.

He edged from the table and began to prowl around the room. Caitlin was holding herself in readiness, waiting for the storm to break. When it came, it wasn't the hurricane she had anticipated, but the chilling breath of a temperature suddenly turned frigid.

"I don't know where you learned your hurly-burly manners, nor do I care. Like the rest of you, they could stand to be improved. I see no reason why I should defend myself to the likes of you. What are you, a secretary? A governess?"

Though it was not easy, she managed to match his insolent tone. "Does it matter? It can make no difference to you."

He looked at her for a long moment, then said pleasantly, "Insubordination in an employee is usually rewarded by termination of said employee's services."

"And you, I presume, would have no compunction about lodging a complaint with my employer?"

"None whatsoever," he agreed affably.

Her smile was tight. "I am not an employee."

Slowly his eyes traversed her from the top of her smoothly coifed head to the toes of the little scuffed half-boots which peeped from beneath the hem of her gown. The pulse in her throat quickened to life, and she shifted uneasily beneath his stare. As if he held a mirror before her, she was blindingly conscious of every defect. Her complexion was too pale. Her eyes were too wide apart. Her gown was shabby and in urgent want of a press. Heat stole across her cheekbones, but in spite of her discomfort, she continued to stare doggedly into his face.

She knew what he was thinking. It was sheer bravado that forced the words past her lips. "The dowd and the dandy. How do you do, Lord Randal?" and she bobbed him an impertinent curtsy.

"Who are you?" he asked abruptly.

Smiling, she answered, "The poor relation. But you already worked that out, did you not?"

His nostrils flared and his eyes narrowed. After an interval, he inclined his head gravely. "I'm familiar with the breed. In my experience they are generally harmless, self-effacing creatures who earn their keep by making themselves useful. Once in a while, one comes across a tyrant, someone who is too big for her own boots, someone who has an exalted view of herself and her position. It happens in the best of families. Guilt is the currency of exchange in these situations—you know what I mean. Everyone is made to feel responsible for the misfortunes of poor Cousin Mary. And Cousin Mary trades on that guilt, I won't call it sympathy, because no one can sympathize with an ill-bred, *farouche* termagant who thinks herself above common decency. It's a grave mistake to indulge such a one, for she becomes insufferable, incorrigible and a bane to those of us who follow the rules of polite usage in society. If truth were told, everyone is probably wishing Cousin Mary at Jericho."

Not once during this long diatribe had he raised his voice. Caitlin was used to Glenshiel's ranting and raving. Lord Randal's softly spoken words carried a sting that far exceeded the pinpricks her grandfather had inflicted. Fortunately, she had a thick skin.

She found herself swallowing, but would not allow that his spite had hurt her, nor that it had been deserved. Someone had to stand up to the Randal and point out his obligations to his people. She might have known that so great a personage as a baron would not permit lesser mortals to challenge his iniquitous policies without some form of retaliation.

His perambulations had taken him full circle. In pent-up silence, she watched as he languidly propped himself against the table. His gaze was steady on hers. The icy crystals in his eyes gradually dissolved, and his lips quirked. "That's better," he said. "I think there may be hope for you yet."

It was the smile that goaded her beyond endurance. When she opened her mouth to answer him, he quickly interposed, "For God's sake don't say another word! I have no wish to annihilate you, but if you go on like this, you leave me no choice."

The sounds of feminine voices reached them, then doors slamming and Lord Randal's name called out in greeting. A moment later, the door opened to admit Charlotte Randal.

"Lord Randal, what on earth are you doing here?" Charlotte's eyes glittered with hostility as they came to rest on Caitlin.

Rand smiled in that easy way of his that Caitlin was heartily coming to detest, and he straightened, moving away from the table. "As to that, ma'am, I mistook this room for the library. No need to apologize for the delay. Mr. Randal's assistant kept me entertained. Do you know, it has just occurred to me that we have not been properly introduced?" The sleek, blond head was bent over Charlotte's hand, and her eyes softened at the graciousness of the gesture.

"Mr. Randal's assistant?" prompted Rand gently.

Charlotte was reluctant, but there was no way around it. "This is my niece, Caitlin Randal," she said brusquely. "Glenshiel's granddaughter and Fiona's cousin."

Close as she was to him, Caitlin could not miss the sudden tightening of his lips, the choked-off breath, the flare of shock in his eyes quickly brought under control.

"I don't know what she has been telling you," Charlotte went on archly, oblivious of the silent undercurrents, "but you mustn't imagine that Caitlin is obliged to assist her uncle. This is her choice. History is her passion, you see. When she and Donald get started, the rest of us almost expire from boredom. Caitlin, where are your manners? Make your curtsy to Lord Randal."

Caitlin bobbed a scant curtsy. After an infinitesimal pause, Rand bowed and Charlotte quickly took charge. With her fingers curled like talons around Rand's sleeve, she urged him to the door. "Refreshments are to be served in the parlor. Fiona will be down directly. My father-in-law will be so disappointed when he hears that he has missed you. Do you know, he was saying only yesterday—"

Rand interrupted her spate of chatter to turn back to Caitlin. "Miss Randal, do you want to come with us?"

Charlotte glared a warning at her niece, and Caitlin, who had not the least inclination to continue her quarrel with the Randal, immediately replied, "Perhaps some other time." She looked helplessly at the scattered papers on the table, then at Rand. "You see how it is, Lord Randal," and her eyes dared him to contradict her.

"Yes, I see how it is," he murmured, and left her with the chilling impression that he had said far more than those few bland words.

Rand was still smiling when he took a punctilious leave of the two ladies not half an hour later. The moment he turned his horse to the dirt track that led to his own property, however, his smile faded and his look became reflective.

It had come as no surprise to him when the fair Fiona had intimated that she had been introduced to his cousin on the steps of the church after Sunday services. It confirmed what David had told him. And if that were not enough to convince him he had the right girl, her obvious confusion in his presence had stilled every niggling doubt. She could hardly bear to look him in the eye. It was as though she were terrified that he was going to betray her to her mother. He could well imagine the effect on Charlotte Randal if she ever discovered that her innocent young daughter went gallivanting about the countryside in the dead of night. Having sisters of his own, Rand considered himself more sanguine. Girls might be young. They might be virgins. But they were anything but innocent.

Thoughts of Fiona led inexorably to thoughts of her incorrigible cousin. Here, Rand felt on firmer ground. David and Caitlin Randal? The idea was preposterous. That shrewish miss was indubitably not the stuff of which a young man's fancies were made.

As the recollection of the scene in that dusty, cluttered bookroom came back to him, Rand's expression hardened. No woman had ever spoken to him in such terms. From the time he was in short coats, females had pandered to him. He was used to yielding looks and sweet words, as was fitting in the softer sex.

He told himself that she was an officious busybody who would be better served employing her talents, such as they were, in caring for a husband and a brood of children. When he thought of the hapless gentleman who would one day find himself shackled to the fiery termagant, he could not help shuddering in sympathy. He knew her type. She was a managing female who must see to the ordering of everyone's life. Such a wife would not do for him.

His initial response to the girl, that rush of the senses, he now saw as an aberration, one of those odd tricks of nature which defied logic. To be forewarned was to be forearmed. He'd be damned if he'd permit a dowd with no claim to distinction to run rings around him. This hurly-burly slip of a girl with the air of a maiden aunt . . .

He gritted his teeth. Those damnable pictures were beginning to flicker behind his eyes again. He could not understand the girl's appeal unless it was because she was different. There wasn't an ounce of affectation in her. Dammit to hell, there wasn't an ounce of anything in her, neither beauty, nor address, nor breeding, nor style—nothing, in fact, to warrant any man's interest, and he was considered a connoisseur!

At this point, a small twinge of conscience pricked the bubble of his anger. The girl's position in her grandfather's household was extraordinary to say the least. The difference between Caitlin and Fiona was astounding when one considered that they were both Glenshiel's granddaughters. He had mentioned his perplexity in as inoffensive a manner as possible to Charlotte Randal.

Her response, an odd mixture of embarrassment and affront, had left him with as many questions as it had answered. "Do not be running away with the idea that Caitlin is an unpaid drudge," Charlotte had told him. "That girl has too much pride for her own good, yes, and Glenshiel lets her get away with it. If she were my daughter . . . but that is neither here nor there. Suffice it to say that Caitlin does as she pleases, and there is no correcting her."

He believed it. Still, deriding her as "the poor relation" was not well done of him. He wasn't sorry that he had taken her down a peg or two. Far from it. She had brought it on herself. But he regretted the manner of it. He couldn't remember the last time he had allowed anger to master him. It was one more annoyance to lay at Caitlin Randal's door.

Caitlin's reflections were no more comfortable than Rand's. From the moment her aunt had carried him off, her brain had teemed with a score of brilliant ripostes which would have cut the arrogant lord down to size. She was still furiously perfecting them a good half-hour later when she heard his step in the hall as he departed. Moments later, the door opened and Fiona slipped into the room.

The younger girl went on the attack immediately. "It was not very mannerly of you, Caitlin, to remain in here when we had company. Your place was in the parlor, taking tea with our guest. Lord Randal remarked upon it."

After one comprehensive glance, Caitlin grinned. "That bad, hmm?"

Fiona flopped down on the opposite chair. "It was painful," she agreed glumly. "Well, you know Mama. When she started extolling all my accomplishments, my *many* accomplishments, I wanted to crawl under the sofa. I almost did."

"I don't see why," Caitlin began loyally, then changed tactics when she caught Fiona's disbelieving look. "You are fated to be one of the beauties. Beauties don't need accomplishments."

"I thought you told me that beauty is as beauty does."

"Brat!" There was so much affection behind the word, no offense was given or taken. "That was an entirely different conversation. At that time, we were discussing character. Both beauty and accomplishments are adornments. Character is what counts.'"

"According to Daroch, I am deficient there too."

Caitlin's smile slipped a little. She was perfectly aware of her cousin's crush on their dashing neighbor and could not like it. As fond as Caitlin was of Daroch, she did not consider him an appropriate suitor for any girl, least of all her young cousin. Fiona's confidence was a fragile thing. When Daroch's interest waned, as it was bound to do, Fiona would be crushed.

Her voice betrayed nothing of her misgivings. "What does Daroch have to say about your character?"

"My lack of character," corrected Fiona. Her smile was overbright. "He says I am shallow and frivolous, with not a sensible thought in my head."

"Well! If that isn't the pot calling the kettle black, I don't know what is! Oh dear, that did not come out the way I meant it to. You are not shallow. If anything, you take things too seriously. And even if you were frivolous, which I don't allow, what of it? A girl who has not yet attained her eighteenth birthday has a right to be frivolous, and you may tell Daroch that I said so."

Fiona leaned her elbows on the table. Cupping her chin in both hands, she looked up at Caitlin with an arrested expression. "Were you ever frivolous, Caitlin? Somehow, I can't quite see it."

"What? Do you think I was born a confirmed spinster?"

A wicked light danced in Fiona's eyes. "In a word, yes."

"You *are* a horrid brat, and this time I mean it." Caitlin couldn't help chuckling. Fiona was ignorant of the double life she led, and she had no wish to enlighten her. Fiona looked up to her. Her opinions, her view of things carried weight with the younger girl. Though Caitlin had yet to think through all the implications of her position, she knew that she did not want Fiona to follow her own path.

Coming to herself, she said, "I'll have you know that in my salad days, my mother was wont to call me a flibbertigibbet and despaired of my ever keeping one sensible thought in my head."

Fiona laughed. "Were you ... were you happy as a child, Caitlin?"

"Sublimely happy. Does that surprise you?"

Fiona's eyes dropped away. "I beg your pardon. I did not mean . . . that is, I had no right . . ."

Breaking into this convoluted apology, Caitlin said gently, "My mother was a remarkable woman, and don't let anyone tell you differently. If she was bitter, I never knew it. To me, she seemed always gay and vivacious, except of course when her temper got the better of her. Then she was like a lioness. Strange to say, she never lost her temper with me, and I was thankful for it."

Though Fiona was silent, there was a question in her eyes, and Caitlin was moved to say, "As for my being a confirmed spinster, well now, my looks had something to say to that."

"You are pretty too!" To Caitlin's look of amused skepticism, Fiona returned hotly, "I am not the child you think I am. You don't wish to get married, that's what it is. I know you have too much sense to be swayed by anything Mama might say. Yet, there must be some reason for your antipathy to marriage, and I wish you would tell me what it is."

Fiona, Caitlin reflected, not for the first time, was sometimes too acute for comfort. She had come pretty close to divining the truth. Marriage had lost its allure since the day Caitlin had inadvertently overheard a conversation between some neighboring ladies who had come to offer their condolences on the death of her mother.

As though it were yesterday, she could hear the driving rain beating against the window panes. She had paused to compose herself before entering the front parlor. They were talking in hushed tones about her future, unaware that she was on the other side of the door.

103

Unlike Fiona, their confidence in Caitlin's ability to attach some eligible gentleman was negligible. It wasn't so much that she was born out of wedlock. What damned her chances in these ladies' eyes was the fact that her father could be anyone—a rapist, a felon, a murderer, or worse. Her bloodlines must always be called into question. Only one thing could mitigate the blot of her birth. Money. Glenshiel must be prepared to put down hard coin to secure a husband for his unfortunate granddaughter.

A shiver ran over her. She was too proud to accept a husband on those terms. Since she had no wish to debate the point with Fiona, nor to embark on a web of lies and half-truths, she said at length, "When you are older, I shall explain it to you."

Fiona compressed her lips, then burst out indignantly, "That is just the sort of remark Mama would make."

A laugh was startled out of Caitlin. Refusing to pursue this turn in the conversation, however, she said pointedly, "When I finish up here, why don't we walk down to the ford? The air will do us both good."

It seemed that Fiona would argue with her, but after a moment, she said meekly, "Fine. I shall see you later then." She was at the door before a thought struck her. "Lord Randal mentioned his cousin, David. He seemed to think that David and I had struck up a friendship."

"Oh?" Caitlin's voice was carefully neutral. "And what did you tell him?"

Fiona made a face. "You know Mama. I hardly got a word in edgewise. She made it sound as though David and I were fast friends."

Caitlin could well imagine that her aunt would seize on every little opening to advance Fiona's chances with Lord Randal.

"I tried to correct Mama a time or two, but it was impossible. I . . . I hope you don't mind?"

"Why should I mind?" Caitlin's look was artless.

"I thought, that is, I wondered if Lord Randal had confused us, since I scarcely knew David Randal. I won't question you, if you don't wish to confide in me. I just thought you should know." And with great dignity, Fiona swept from the room.

Chapter Seven

There were two Miss Randals of Glenshiel. Which one had been in David's mind when he had begged him to come into Scotland? This question occupied Rand's thoughts.

"It must be Miss Fiona," he mused aloud.

"I could not agree with you more," responded John Murray, in a bored tone. The subject of Miss Randal of Glenshiel was one that had been explored ad nauseam in his opinion.

The gentlemen were taking a last turn around the grounds before turning in for the night. For November, the weather had been splendid. No huntsman could have asked for better, and Murray was regretting that he could not linger at Strathcairn for many more days.

Across the river, the lights of Balmoral Castle could be seen, and close-by, the lights of the Mill of Balmoral. Even as Murray watched, the lights of the mill were extinguished, and he wondered what could be keeping Robertson, the miller, so late from his bed.

"Caitlin Randal and David? I just can't see it," said Rand.

"Frankly, neither can I." To Murray's way of thinking, Rand was creating problems where none existed. He had met both Miss Randals in the last weeks, and it was patently obvious to him that only one of them had the power to attract a gentleman of discriminating taste. Miss Fiona was a beauty. Her manners were delightful. Miss Caitlin, on the other hand, was a dowd whose manners verged on the deplorable.

They'd met the girl quite by chance outside the apothecary's shop in Ballater. As was to be expected, Rand's address was flawless. He made no impression on Miss Caitlin Randal. The girl had all the finesse of a frozen fish. Her dog, a monstrous creature, had shown more warmth. The hound had taken one look at Rand and had turned pure coquette. There was no other way to describe it. Eyelashes batting, whimpers indistinguishable from simpers, tongue lolling, the dog was a hilarious spectacle.

"Rand has this effect on females," Murray had said humorously, trying to crack the ice that encased the ill-favored old maid. He'd made to scratch the dog's ears, as Rand was doing, but the hound had suddenly turned nasty, and he'd quickly withdrawn his hand from those ferocious fangs.

"Upon my word! What's got into her?" he had asked, cautiously backing up a step or two.

"That dog," said Miss Randal, looking daggers at the object in question, "is as thick as a plank," and so saying, she'd turned on her heel and left them.

Murray shook his head as if to clear his thoughts of the provoking chit and gazed reflectively at his companion. Before Rand could continue with the boring subject of Miss Randal of Glenshiel, he adroitly changed the direction of their conversation. "I'm onto you Rand."

"Beg pardon?"

"The game we have bagged this week past? I know that most of it has been distributed to the tenants who were cleared from your lands."

"What of it?"

"Only this. It seems to me you would do well to allow them to return to their homes."

"I may yet, but not before certain parties have come to understand that there is a principle involved here."

"What principle is that?"

"That I will be master in my own house."

Murray understood. Rand was set on demonstrating to the young Highlanders who had waylaid his coach that such tactics could not persuade him to do their bidding. In point of fact, such tactics were more likely to achieve the opposite of what they intended.

"What of the boy? Are you any closer to finding him?"

Rand shook his head. "It's my guess that he went with Daroch to Aboyne. If I were in the boy's shoes, it's what I would do. He knows what will happen to him if ever I catch up to him."

Murray was thinking that if he were in the boy's shoes, he would not be satisfied until there was an ocean between himself and Rand. What he said was, "When is Daroch due to return?"

"No one seems to know."

"Aha! With that one, it has to be a woman."

Rand smiled and said quizzically, *"Cherchez la femme?* Yes, the ladies make fools of all us poor men, don't they?"

This observation led Murray to say playfully, "It's a braw, bricht, moonlicht nicht the nicht."

"Quite," said Rand, not even attempting to get his tongue around that old twister.

"A night when a young man's fancy turns to a bit of sport with the lassies," added Murray meaningfully.

"What?"

Murray let out a long sigh. "Rand," he said plaintively, "I am the first to admit that you are an excellent host. The hunting could not be better. Your chef is an artist, and that is no exaggeration. The small dinner parties with like-minded gentlemen, the conversation, the walks, the scenery, the splendid weather—you have arranged everything admirably."

Rand laughed.

"But where are the girls? Oh, don't misunderstand. I know there can be no repetition of the entertainments we indulged in when I was last here. No need to tell me that you are trying to establish your credit with your neighbors. But dash it all, Rand, we are two lonely bachelors with time on our hands. What's to stop us, if we behave discreetly, from enjoying the fleshpots of Deeside?"

"The fleshpots of Deeside?" repeated Rand, momentarily diverted. "To my knowledge, there are no fleshpots between here and Aberdeen."

"Now that is where you are wrong, my friend. I have it on excellent authority—"

"Whose authority?"

"That fellow you hired on as a groom or whatever."

"Jamie MacGregor?"

"Yes. He's the one. Mr. MacGregor was so kind as to put me in the way of a snug little change-house, a little off the beaten track, where the barmaids are not precisely barmaids, if you take my meaning."

When Rand said nothing to this, but merely smiled in a deprecating way, Murray burst out, "I knew it! You've fallen for the chit! Oh, don't try to gammon me, Rand!

Yesterday, all during church services, you were practically eating the girl with your eyes."

It was the truth. For a whole hour, he had scarcely been able to pry his eyes off her. He still could not see what the attraction was. She wasn't pretty. By no stretch of the imagination could she be called that. But "pretty" had long since come to bore him to tears. This girl was arresting. There was strength of character in her well-defined features. She had presence, or she would have, just as soon as someone knowledgeable took over the dressing of her. Her figure was perfection itself, and all her contriving with the shapeless plaid shawl had been unable to deceive his experienced eye.

It was madness to let his mind dwell on her like this. There could never be anything between himself and the girl. In the first place, he was not ready to shackle himself to only one woman, and with Caitlin Randal, it would have to be matrimony. In the second place, when that unhappy day arrived, he must choose a girl from his own milieu, someone who could preside gracefully over his various establishments. Caitlin could never fit into his world.

In the week since he had come upon her in her uncle's office, he had learned as much as he could about the girl's circumstances. What he had learned had convinced him that she was totally unsuitable. It wasn't only a question of her birth. He knew of many men who had married beneath them. But this girl was a law unto herself. She lived in her own cottage with only a hound for a chaperone. Her grandfather exercised not the slightest restraint upon her. She was a dowd. She was eccentric. No man in his right mind would give her a second look, and it irritated him that he was proving to be the exception.

Not that Caitlin had done anything to pique his interest. Far from it. On the few occasions they had come face to face, she had looked through him as if he were a plate-glass window. And when he had cornered her, forcing her to converse with him, she was abrupt to the point of rudeness. Completely reversing his former opinion, he decided that he envied the man who would take her to wife, for that man would have the schooling of her.

The pictures began to flicker behind his eyes. He was stripping her naked, but this time he was tumbling her over his lap and bringing the flat of his hand down smartly on her bare backside.

Observing Rand's odd smile, Murray's jaw dropped, and he exclaimed incredulously, "So it is true! You have fallen for the chit!"

Rand's brows rushed together. "Are you insane?" he demanded. "The woman is impossible! I would not have Caitlin Randal for all the flax in Flanders."

Murray's look of incredulity gradually changed to one of awe. A moment later, he burst out laughing. Between gasps and wheezes, he got out, "Who said anything about Caitlin Randal? It was her beautiful cousin I had in mind. So that's the way the wind blows! Oh Rand, this is rich! The dowd and the dandy! Who would believe it?"

Rand's blue eyes regarded his friend coolly. When the laughter was finally under control, he said calmly, "A snug little change-house where the barmaids are not precisely barmaids? I think that's a capital idea. I'll have my groom saddle our horses, shall I?" And he strode off in the direction of the stables, leaving Murray convulsed in a fresh bout of laughter.

* * *

111

Under cover of pulling her cap down to her eyebrows and fussily adjusting the plaid at her shoulders, Caitlin stole a sidelong glance at the young man who sat beside her on the box of the dogcart.

MacGregor was impatient. It showed in the way he kept flicking the reins and clicking his tongue to urge the little mare to a faster walk. There was something here that was not quite right, but she could not put her finger on it. Ever since they had left the Mill of Balmoral, where the miller had doled out a fresh supply of Deeside *uisge-beatha* to Daroch's little band of smugglers, MacGregor had been giving her odd looks. One might be excused for thinking that the young Highlander had been making inroads into one of the several wooden kegs which were concealed beneath the load of peat they were hauling. Caitlin knew he would not be such a fool. It was after the whiskey was delivered to its various destinations that the men stopped off at the nearest change-house to indulge in a wild bout of drinking. Not that she ever participated. Daroch was very strict on this point. Latterly, one of their group was always assigned to escort her as far as Crathie. From there, she made her own way home.

"Where is MacDougal?" she asked, careful to keep her voice in a lower register as befitted the part of the boy she was playing. "I understood Daroch to say that he was to come with us."

"Och, he's about somewhere," replied MacGregor, his eyes scanning the dense stands of pines which flanked the old drover road they were traveling. "He's acting as scout this time around. Be easy, young Dirk. No harm will come tae ye as long as ye hae Jamie MacGregor for company." After a pause, he laughed softly and added, "And if ye're a good wee lad, mayhap

112

there will be a treat in store for ye at the end o' the day."

Caitlin folded her arms and tightened her lips, unsure how to answer the strange remark. She was uneasy, but she still had no clue as to why this should be so. MacGregor was loyal to the band. He would not think of betraying them to the authorities. True, he had taken up employment with the Randal, but nobody held that against him. Since he had taken to providing fresh meat for the tables of his former tenants, Lord Randal's credit had risen dramatically. Even Daroch had been won over, delaying the campaign to drive off the English laird so long as he seemed to be in a benevolent humor. Only one person in the band had stood out against him: she had.

And she'd had no sound reason for doing it. What she feared was vague and not easily put into words. I'm not being petty, she assured herself. Actually it had nothing to do with the ferocious whipping the Randal had administered. Nor did it have anything to do with what Fiona had told her—that the Randal was curious about his cousin, David. She had nothing to fear there. It was true that she and David had kept their friendship a secret, but that was not a crime. They had done nothing wrong except flout the conventions. Unattached members of the opposite sex did not meet freely, unchaperoned, without causing a scandal.

Her mind slipped back in time to that glorious autumn when she and David had wandered the woods, where everything had seemed more vivid, and each day infinitely more precious because soon there would be no days left to them.

"Oh, David," she said involuntarily.

"What?"

113

She covered her blunder well. "Daroch," she said. "I was wondering what kept him so long in Aboyne?"

MacGregor gave a great shout of laughter and slapped her on the shoulder. "Ye're no that green!"

"His kinsman, the earl—"

"The Earl o' Aboyne is no' in Deeside at present. Laddie, do ye no' ken that Daroch has a wee ladybird tucked away in Aboyne? Aye, ye maun well stare! Och, he's a sad example tae the rest o' us."

"But . . . but what about Miss Fiona? He's courting her."

"So?"

When the boy made no answer to this, but stared in wooden silence, MacGregor patiently explained, "It wouldna do for Daroch to flaunt his fancy piece afore he is even affianced. And Aboyne is far enough away so that there's little chance o' Miss Fiona ever meetin' up wi' bonnie Mollie Fletcher. Dinna say I've shocked ye?" He grinned hugely.

Caitlin was incensed, not for her own sake but for her cousin's. It was all of a piece with what she knew about men. "Glenshiel will look higher for a match for his granddaughter than Daroch," she retorted. Suddenly straightening, she exclaimed, "Ye have taken the wrong turning, MacGregor."

"Nay, lad. This is the right road. Did ye no ken that we hae a new customer? The old change-house at Muik?"

"No one said anything to me."

"Ah, well, that's Daroch for ye. He doesna want an argument, nor does he want ye within a mile o' the garrison. And it's no likely we'll meet wi' redcoats on this road, now is it?"

The explanation soothed her uncertainties. More and

more of late, since penetrating her disguise, Daroch had contrived things so that the risks to her were minimal. While others of their band delivered the contraband to destinations all along the busy north road, she was sent across the river to the more isolated hamlets in the south. The writing was on the wall if this jaunt was anything to go by. This winding track was as busy as the streets of Aberdeen on the Sabbath during church services. Not a thing stirred. She very much feared that her adventuring days were coming to an end.

The old change-house, The Fair Maid as it was known, was ablaze with lights. At one time, the courtyard would have been choked with coaches and ostlers coming and going as they changed horses. Those days were a thing of the past, ever since the north road had gained in importance. There were plenty of horses about, but these were the mounts of the inn's customers.

"Where did they all come from?" asked Caitlin, looking first at the horses, then at the blaze of lights in the two-story building. "Nothing passed us on the road."

She was not unfamiliar with The Fair Maid, but had never had occasion to visit it so late in the day. At other times, it was practically deserted, and she often wondered how Graham, the proprietor, could afford to keep its doors open.

MacGregor jumped down and looked up at her with a slow grin. "There are back roads, then again, there are back roads; and there are some who would rather no' hae it known that they come tae The Fair Maid for,"—he laughed suggestively—"a wee dram."

The hairs on the back of her neck began to rise. "What manner of place is this?" Caitlin demanded.

Even as she spoke, the back door opened and three strapping lads in baize aprons advanced to the cart and began the process of unloading under MacGregor's direction. After a moment's hesitation, Caitlin jumped down lightly and went to assist them.

Each keg held twenty pints of whiskey. To these hardy Scots, this was a lightweight. They were used to clearing their fields of the backbreaking rocks their ploughs turned up in spring and autumn, rocks that formed the mile upon mile of dry-stone walls which were peculiar to Scotland.

When their business was concluded, Caitlin made to climb into the box. MacGregor forestalled her. She could see from the gleam in his eyes and by his viselike grip on her arm that there was no point in arguing. That did not stop her. She offered a few feeble excuses to explain why it was imperative that she head for home, but there was only so much she could do without attracting notice to herself. Finally, with an ill grace, she gave way.

"Did I no promise ye a wee treat?" MacGregor said jocularly. "Now, lad, it comes tae us all. Courage up, among other things." Snickering, he propelled her through the back door.

He was up to some deviltry, and she was beginning to have a fair idea of what it was. As though she were a condemned prisoner being led to the firing squad, she allowed him to guide her through the kitchens to the front of the building. Behind her frozen stare, she was calculating the odds, determining at what point she could make her escape.

There were three main public rooms, each one giving onto the next, and the place was crowded with patrons, a very mixed clientele, from the elegantly dressed merchant or squire to the coarser-clad farmer or tenant. The only kilt in sight belonged to the proprietor. The odd redcoat was glaringly in evidence. For a wild moment, her hopes rose. A few of the gentlemen were known to her, upright pillars of the community whose wives or sisters were sticklers for the proprieties. These gentlemen would not be caught patronizing a bawdy house, she thought.

But seeing the barmaids dashed her hopes. They were floating around in what appeared to be their underwear, flirting outrageously with the patrons, playfully slapping away hands that brazenly slipped inside gaping bodices or beneath skirts.

After that one shocking comprehensive glance around the room, Caitlin squared her shoulders and boldly swaggered after MacGregor as he strode to the counter. The order was given, and within moments, Caitlin was tightly clasping a glass with a double measure of whiskey in it.

"Get that down ye," said MacGregor, then with brusque kindness, "Now, laddie, there's no need tae look like that. The first time is, aye, a bit nerve-racking, but ye'll survive it, I promise ye. Look at me. Look at a' the fine lads around ye. And I willna desert ye. I'll be waitin' right outside the door."

With those few, sincere words, Caitlin's last lingering hope died. Bringing her glass to her lips, she took a long steadying swallow of the fiery liquid and promptly choked on it. MacGregor slapped her hard on the back. As she coughed and spluttered, a few interested spectators looked up.

"Och, it's his first time," explained MacGregor. "The lad has never had a woman afore, and him a Gordon.

Can ye believe it? He's as nervous as a raw recruit on the eve o' battle."

The spectators, young blades all, crowded a little closer. Though the corner was not well lit, Caitlin thought it prudent to avert her head. She was nervous, but she was also fuming, putting names to faces, wishing mothers could see their sons now and box their ears for patronizing such a low place.

"Who's goin' tae do the honors?" asked one.

"Doris," replied MacGregor, and gave a broad wink.

"Doris? That's a good choice. She has the patience o' Job. But are ye sure the laddie is up tae it?"

This was evidently a huge joke, Caitlin gathered from the guffaws which followed. She managed a weak smile.

"Doris," said MacGregor, with all the wisdom of his eighteen years, "could revive a man on his deathbed without blinkin' an eyelash. Where is she, by the bye? She was supposed to wait for us here."

"I saw her on the stairs not a minute ago," said one.

Another, a cut above the others, threw in, "Och, she'll be getting the place ready, you know, iron shackles and leather whips, birch rods and pulleys and so on." He nudged Caitlin with his elbow. "Or whatever your fancy happens to be."

Caitlin's complexion turned green.

"Now, now," remonstrated MacGregor, "dinna tease the lad." A thought struck him and his brows rose. "Iron shackles and leather whips, ye say? Good God! I had enough o' those in His Majesty's service. Tell me ye're hoaxin' me."

The speaker's voice dropped to a whisper. "They're there all right, but you have to ask for them particularly. No one ever does, except the English. But then, they're a queer lot." On this last observation, there was unanimous agreement.

MacGregor removed the glass from Caitlin's fingers and set it on the counter. As he spoke, he straightened the set of her jacket and adjusted her plaid. "This is my treat, so there's no need for siller to change hands. And if it's any comfort tae ye, ye should know that I've told Doris she maun be gentle wi' ye."

As the grinning men crowded around her and half pulled, half shoved her through the crush toward the stairs, Caitlin's plan to sneak away when MacGregor's attention was diverted drastically changed. These men were intent on seeing the thing through to its absurd conclusion.

She mounted the stairs in frozen silence, oblivious of the ribald advice and commentary of her newfound "friends." She wasn't panic-stricken, exactly. Doris was only a woman, and one whose prime motivation, one hoped, was mercenary. Caitlin's pockets were bulging with silver—her share of the night's work. In her mind's eye, she was forming a new plan. She did not see why she could not bribe Doris to say that the deed had been consummated. Then they could all go home happy.

At the top of the stairs, her steps faltered. Rough hands were laid on her, and she was shoved none too gently along a dark corridor to a door with a gleam of light peeping beneath it. As her trembling fingers closed around the doorknob, she looked pleadingly over her shoulder. Her grinning companions nodded and waved their encouragement.

Finally, when she made no move to push the door open, MacGregor said bracingly, "Now, lad, dinna turn craven on me. Just think on this. When ye leave that room, ye'll no longer be a lad but a man, in very truth."

Then he opened the door and thrust her over the threshold.

As the door closed softly behind her, Caitlin's eyes flew to the bed. There was a half-naked woman in it, reclining against the pillows. Her eyes were closed and she was breathing heavily, moving restlessly beneath the covers. Her face was painted. Her mane of red hair was of a color that nature could never have simulated. Yet, she was beautiful, alluring in an obvious way. Caitlin could not drag her eyes away. So this was what men really wanted in a woman, she thought, and stood there staring.

The woman began to heave and pant, and Caitlin frowned. When it came to her that Doris was in the throes of a respiratory attack, she took a quick step toward the bed, then froze in horror as a masculine head appeared from beneath the covers, a blond head with tousled locks, as though a woman had been combing her fingers through them.

Rand propped himself on one elbow and grinned sheepishly at the woman beside him. "It's no use, Nellie. This isn't going to work." There was laughter in his voice. "I think old age must be taking its toll. This has never happened to me before."

Suddenly his head whipped round, and his eyes flared at the sight of the intruder. Nellie said something in a commiserating tone, then sucked in her breath as she, too, became aware of the intruder.

"You!" exclaimed Rand and Caitlin simultaneously.

Caitlin felt as though someone had punched her in the stomach. A score of confusing impressions flashed through her brain. She wasn't thinking of her peril. In that awful moment of electrified silence, she experienced a betrayal so profound that she might have been the

120

personification of every wife who had ever caught her husband out in his infidelities.

She thought of Daroch and his ladybird tucked away in Aboyne, of MacGregor and his equally vile companions who thronged this cesspool of the devil. She thought of the iniquity of the double standard, the injustice of the restrictions men imposed on her sex; and her outrage could not be contained. Then the sight of the Randal and his alluring companion—something she could never be—made her want to weep.

Rand sat up straighter in the bed. Caitlin reacted instinctively. Like lightning, her hand snaked to her hose and her fingers closed around her dirk. At sight of the dagger in the boy's hand, Nellie screamed and quickly disappeared under the covers. Rand, mother-naked, dived for the floor, but not before the hilt of Caitlin's dagger had caught him a glancing blow to the shoulder. As he let out a roar of rage, Caitlin threw the door wide.

"Murder!" she screamed. "The Randal has murdered the poor wee lassie!" And she took off along the dark strip of corridor like a hare with the hounds at her heels. At her back, all hell broke loose. Caitlin's steps did not falter. She bolted down the stairs and flung herself out the front doors.

It took a moment or two for Rand to haul on his breeches, and more precious moments to calm the enraged spectators and reveal that Nellie was not murdered but suffering nothing worse than a fit of the vapors. By the time he sprinted out the front doors in only his shirt and breeches, he was practically breathing fire.

There was no sign of young Gordon. "Fifty guineas to the man who captures the lad," Rand roared out.

Word spread like wildfire. Before long, like cattle in a

thunderstorm, men stampeded out of the building and rushed off in every direction. A few of the more prudent ones had snatched lanterns from tables to light their steps.

"He meant to kill me," Rand said furiously, addressing MacGregor as he came up to him.

MacGregor looked stricken. "Ye maun be mistaken, Lord Randal. He's no' a bad lad. He didna even ken ye were there. The error was mine. It was Doris who was supposed to be waitin' for him. Aye, and she still is, for all I ken."

"Do you know him?" asked Rand sharply.

"In a manner o' speaking," MacGregor responded cautiously.

Before this promising line of questioning could be pursued, a shout went up. "He's in the river. The lad is in the river!"

Men quickly converged on the stone bridge and looked down into the murky depths of the Muick. All that could be seen from the light of their lanterns were the boy's bonnet and plaid floating on the surface.

"Poor wee wretch. He's surely downed," said someone.

Rand did not hesitate. He leapt onto the parapet. Hands reached for him to draw him back, but before they could grasp him, he had dived into the icy water.

Time was of the essence. The waters were too frigid for a man to survive for long. Ignoring the pleas of the spectators to save himself, Rand swam in ever-widening circles, gritting his teeth against cold and pain in his desperate search for the boy. Again and again he dived, but his hands encountered nothing but submerged branches and flotsam and jetsam. Time slipped away from him. So obsessed was he that even when he was foundering and men had jumped into the river to come to his aid, he tried to fight them off.

John Murray was the first to reach Rand. He had arrived late on the scene and was only mildly interested in what was going on until he discovered it was Rand who was in the water.

"For God's sake!" he said, evading a weak blow. "You'll have us both drowned if you don't give this up. No! I'll not leave you here to find a watery grave."

It was MacGregor who persuaded him. The young Highlander was thrashing about wildly. "I didna ken I couldna swim," he sputtered, and his head disappeared below the surface of the water.

There was nothing for it but to go to MacGregor's assistance. When they were hauled onto the bank, like fish gasping for air, Rand closed his eyes in torment. He would never find the boy alive now.

If anyone had spoken to him, he would have cried like a baby. No one did. The silence was fathoms deep. Men did not know where to look.

With legs drawn up to his chin and head bowed, Rand sat hunched over, trying to get a hold of his emotions. Inwardly, he was damning himself for giving chase. The boy was no coward. He should have known that young Gordon would take appalling risks to evade capture. By offering a reward, he had made escape for the boy virtually impossible. The boy's blood was on his head.

His teeth began to chatter and shudders wracked his body. Someone threw a plaid over his shoulders. Long minutes passed. He was not sure what made him raise his head, unless it was some sixth sense he had developed in his years of soldiering. His eyes scanned the opposite bank. Across the bridge, silhouetted against the lights streaming into the inn's courtyard, was a lone rider, a boy on his pony, poised for flight. As Rand watched, the boy raised one hand in salute.

Joy burst through Rand in waves, and he staggered to his feet. He had almost raised his hand to return the boy's greeting when an icy rage possessed him. Twice in one night, the boy had damn near been the death of him, first when he had thrown the dagger, and second when he, Rand, had dived into the icy river to save him. Worse by far, however, were the agonies he had been made to suffer in the last few minutes, believing that the boy had drowned. His fingers flexed, and he itched to feel them curled around young Gordon's throat.

Others turned to stare at what had caught the Randal's interest. When they saw the boy, a thunderous cheer went up, and somber faces broke into broad smiles. The harrowing drama that had just taken place had made them forget, momentarily, that the Randal had put a price on the boy's head.

When the boy wheeled his pony and rode off into the shadows, men looked to Rand for direction. For a moment, he stood there as if oblivious of his surroundings, then, shaking his head, smiling, he said, "The boy deserves his victory. He outwitted me fair and square. Shall we repair to The Fair whatever-it-is and console ourselves with a wee dram? Gentlemen, don't stint yourselves. Lord Randal is paying the shot."

As the crush of eager men moved en masse to cross the stone bridge, Rand hung back and brought MacGregor to his side with a look. "This is not the end of it," he said. "I want that boy, and no one and nothing is going to stand in my way."

MacGregor's heart sank. This was going to be a long night, and at the end of it, he was sure there would not even be a pony harnessed to his cart to drag him home to his weary bed.

Chapter Eight

That very night, when Murray had trooped off to bed, MacGregor came under a hail of questions respecting the boy who had been with him in the change-house. MacGregor was no coward, and he had his fair share of Highland pride. If Rand had raised his voice or had tried to intimidate him in any way, he would have been equal to the occasion. But his lordship's benevolent expression and affable manner completely unnerved him. He had a flash of *déjà vu;* two of his mates in the army of occupation had been dragged before the Randal and their own commanding officer on charges of rape and looting. They were lucky to have escaped with their lives.

He replied to Rand's questions in the vaguest of terms, not merely to save the boy's neck—indeed, MacGregor flashed a heartfelt prayer to the Deity that he wasn't standing in Dirk Gordon's brogues—but to protect them all. Smuggling was one thing. There was a certain glamour attached to it. Every man in Deeside was involved in it one way or another, even the rank and file in the garrison at Braemar. He did not think, however, that the Randal would be very forgiving if he ever discovered the identities of the highwaymen who had attacked his coach the night he had come into Deeside. Men had been transported to the colonies for less.

MacGregor was not a man who was prone to regrets, but he was now sorry that he had ever had a hand in that puerile misadventure with the Randal's coach. At the same time, he was thanking his lucky stars that Daroch had had the good sense to abandon their plan to make life difficult for the English laird. The Randal, he was thinking, was more than a match for the lot of them put together. Besides, he really admired the man. It was Serle, the factor, on whom they should have vented their spleen. He was the one who had cleared the cotters from their crofts. The Randal, after arriving on the scene, had clipped his factor's wings. A few of his cotters, by slow and devious means, were drifting back to their empty cottages, and their laird turned a blind eye to it. Oh yes, MacGregor was thinking, he truly admired the Randal, but at the moment he feared him more.

"So it amounts to this," said Rand in summation. "The boy's name is Dirk Gordon. He is Daroch's kinsman. You and he were delivering a load of . . . peat, and on the spur of the moment stopped in at The Fair Maid for a wee dram?"

MacGregor swallowed and his Adam's apple bobbed. "Aye."

"How often do you deliver peat?"

"Rarely! Hardly at all! Almost never!"

Rand smiled at the eager tone, but it wasn't the kind of smile that appealed to MacGregor. In an effort to recover the ground he thought he had lost, he began a long and involved explanation of how he had contracted to deliver peat to a number of change-houses all around Deeside. He concluded by saying, "When I came home frae the wars, it was all I could find to gie me a livin'."

This time Rand's smile was more natural. "Ah, yes. I wondered how long it would be before you harked back to the war, or to your old grandmother . . . or whatever."

"Sir?"

"MacGregor, you are an unconscionable rogue!"

MacGregor sensed that the ice had begun to melt, and he let out a telling sigh. "I'm no' sure I follow ye, sir."

"Never mind. I believe you. It was all a misunderstanding. The boy wandered into the wrong room and panicked. We shall let it go at that for the present, shall we?"

When MacGregor left Rand's study, those threatening words, "for the present," buzzed inside his head. He hardly knew what he was feeling. He was conscience stricken because it was he who had forcibly thrust young Gordon into the wrong room. He was annoyed because the lad had acted with all the aplomb of a hysterical virgin. But mostly, he was alarmed. If the Randal ever caught up with Dirk Gordon . . . MacGregor shuddered and resolved to find Daroch at once and tell him what was afoot.

For a long time after MacGregor had quit the room, Rand stared out at the avenue of oaks which graced the wide sweep of Strathcairn's drive. In that dim light just before dawn, the oaks had taken on a sinister aspect, had become grim and forbidding and infinitely menacing. The scene outside matched Rand's inner mood perfectly.

He was reflecting that MacGregor's story was reasonably truthful up to a point. By substituting the words "contraband whiskey" for "peat," Rand had a fair idea of what was going on. Having decided that MacGregor and the boy were smugglers, he concluded that Daroch, the boy's kinsman, whom he had yet to meet, was probably the leader. The boy was among those who had attacked his coach. It was reasonable to assume that Daroch and his fellow smugglers were in on that, too.

The smuggling was of no consequence to Rand. The attack on his coach, which he had once viewed as a minor irritation, was far more significant. On reflection, he absolved MacGregor and his cohorts from wishing him harm. The boy was a different matter.

For all his paucity of years, the boy was the real threat. Rand could not accept that he had panicked when he had walked into the wrong chamber. Dirk Gordon wanted his blood. The niggling doubt in Rand's mind had been quashed when the boy had calmly stood by while he, Rand, had almost foundered in a desperate bid to save him from drowning. What stuck in his craw was that last insult—the salute with which the boy had taunted him before making his escape.

Inconceivable as it seemed, Rand was forced to conclude that young Gordon was out for revenge. He had taken a whipping, and Rand must be punished for it. This was something Rand would not tolerate, not only for his own sake, but for those who were close to him. Very soon, his mother and sisters would be arriving in Deeside. Dirk Gordon must be stopped before matters got out of hand.

When he finally picked up the candle to light his steps to his bedchamber, he was thinking that it was more than time he made himself known to his neighbor, and he was willing to wager that Daroch had returned from his jaunt to Aboyne.

Caitlin thunked the teapot on the table and rattled the teacups. Daroch was absently picking at a dish of shortbread and gave no sign that he was aware of her displeasure.

Finally coming to himself, he said, "She refused to see me. I could hear her at the piano, but the maid said that Miss Fiona was not at home. Now why would she do such a thing?"

"You tell me." Caitlin's tone was decidedly unsympathetic. Seating herself, she studiously poured from a silver teapot.

Daroch accepted the cup and saucer from her hand, and threw her one of his coaxing grins. "I prefer strong tea. I don't suppose there's a wee dram to go in it?"

"I'm clean out of wee drams. Have another shortbread."

"What? Oh, thank you." It was beginning to register that he was no more in favor with Caitlin than he was with Fiona. Setting down his cup and saucer, he said, "Stop playing cat and mouse with me, Caitlin. Out with it. What have I done to annoy you?"

Caitlin looked him over as though he were a dead roach she had found under the last shortbread on her plate. "Mollie Fletcher," she said simply, succinctly, and with undisguised feminine scorn.

Daroch had the grace to blush. Quickly rallying, he said fiercely, "Mollie Fletcher can mean nothing to you! Besides, gently bred girls should know nothing of such things, let alone mention them."

"Ah, but you see, I am not gently bred, and"—she

130

broke off a piece of shortbread and nibbled daintily—
"and though Fiona most certainly is, I don't think she
sets much store by these fusty old precepts."

At the mention of Fiona's name, Daroch visibly
started and made to push back his chair. Bocain, who
was keeping a watchful eye on things from her favorite
spot on the hearth, rose slowly to her feet. Her lip was
curled, and the sound that issued from her throat resembled distant thunder.

"Don't make any sudden moves," advised Caitlin
conversationally, "or you may find yourself without a
finger, if not a hand. Good girl, Bocain. Down!" She
smiled her approval.

When Daroch sank back in his chair, the deerhound
resumed her former languorous pose. "That dog is a
menace," he said indignantly. "Why you allow her in
the house, I shall never understand."

"She's a pet, that's why."

"Bah!"

Caitlin's eyes twinkled. She and Daroch had had this
argument before. He was Master of the Deeside Hunt.
His foxhounds—vicious unpredictable creatures in
Caitlin's opinion—were kept under lock and key. His
hunting dogs were work dogs. The notion that someone
might wish to keep a dog as a pet was foreign to
Daroch, nor did he approve of it.

"Look here," he said, "you're not telling me that
Fiona knows anything about Mollie?"

"I don't see how she can *not* know. Glenshiel loses no
opportunity in blackening your character. Somehow, he
got wind of your little ladybird"—she spoke the last
word with relish—"and regaled us with the juicy details
over the dinner table." That wasn't quite true. It was
MacGregor who had given Caitlin the juicy details the

131

night they had stopped in at The Fair Maid. Her grandfather had alluded to Daroch's absence in broad hints. No fools the ladies, they had taken his point.

"But . . ." Daroch combed his fingers through his hair. "But . . . that means nothing at all, not to men of the world, and what's more, your grandfather knows it. From what I've heard, he was no saint in his youth."

Caitlin said nothing, and Daroch went on more desperately, "I am not responsible for spreading these rumors. Mollie belongs in my past. I haven't gone out of my way to look her up in almost a year."

When she still said nothing, Daroch ground his teeth. "You need not take that attitude with me. I am not betrothed to Fiona, nor am I like to be."

"Now that is the best news I have heard in many a long day." At the harsh, uncompromising tone, such a look crossed his face that Caitlin was momentarily thrown off stride. She opened her mouth to administer the tongue-lashing he so richly deserved, but something moved her to say instead, "You should not be surprised. Your reputation is scandalous. Do you wonder that I am not in favor of a match between you and my cousin?" Gentling her tone, she went on. "Fiona is very young, very innocent. Quite frankly, Daroch, it surprises me that you are taken with her."

His eyes flashed. "And what might you mean by that?"

Caitlin sat back in her chair and regarded him in a puzzled way. Before she could find the words to answer him, he burst out, "I thought, I hoped, that you of all people would put no stock in idle gossip. It seems that I was wrong."

"What else am I to think?"

His reply was fierce. "Is it too much to ask that you

judge me on what you have observed of my character? You think I am inconstant. You believe me to be a profligate. What makes you think so? Rumor and conjecture that have no basis in fact."

She blinked while her brain assimilated his words. It was true that rumor played a part in her assessment of Daroch's character, but there was a lot more to it than that. Indignantly, she exclaimed, "When you discovered I was not a lad but a female, you tried to have your way with me!"

A smile twitched his lips, and his eyes danced. "True, but at that time Fiona made no impression on me, and I was laboring under a misapprehension about you. A woman who dresses up as a boy and goes gallivanting around the countryside leaves herself open to that sort of insult. Yes, and this same specimen, who gets herself embroiled in an altercation in a common bawdy house, has no one to blame but herself if a gentleman assumes that she is any man's for the taking."

Caitlin sucked in an infuriated breath. "That's not fair!"

"Who said anything about 'fair'? I am merely trying to demonstrate that appearances can be misleading. I know you, so I put no credence in such things."

His words chastened her. Now that he had got her thinking about it, she was willing to admit he had a point. Her opinion of his character was largely based on the rumors which circulated. If she had to judge him solely on what she had observed, she would have been more than happy to encourage his attentions to Fiona.

She frowned, recalling that there was also the matter of his family's history. *All the Gordons of Daroch are tarred with the same brush.* It was almost a creed on Deeside. Daroch's father and uncle were notorious rakes in their own day. If she had not known her own mother better, Caitlin might have been persuaded that one of these gentlemen was her father. But she did know her mother, and Morag Randal would never have succumbed to the blandishments of a rake. For the first time, she began to question her prejudices respecting the Gordons of Daroch. A moment's reflection steadied her. In her uncle's bookroom, there was a tome containing evidence enough to convict the former lairds of Daroch of every vice ever invented. About the present laird, however, there was not a scrap.

She let out a long sigh and looked up at Daroch with an appealingly frank expression. "If you did not go to Aboyne to visit Mollie Fletcher, why did you go? It is not idle curiosity that prompts my question, Daroch. I care about Fiona. I don't wish to see her hurt. There is a mystery here, and it is in your interest to clear it up. You are absent for long stretches at a time. Where do you go? What do you get up to?"

His lips were tightly compressed, and a muscle flexed in his jaw. Lowering his eyes, shaking his head, he said, "I cannot tell you, so don't ask. Suffice it to say that it is *not* a woman."

After a lull in the conversation, Daroch said, "I had not meant to change the subject. Mind what I told you. There will be no more smuggling jaunts for you as long as the Randal is in residence. It's too dangerous. MacGregor says he'll be satisfied with nothing less than your head."

Caitlin could well believe it. "I should not have thrown my dirk at him," she said.

"What was in your mind? Were you trying to murder him?"

"Of course not! I aimed for the bedpost. How was I

134

to know he was going to leap out of bed and get in the way?"

Daroch's unexpected laughter brought her brows winging together. "Oh, Caitlin," he choked out, "a common bawdy house! I wish I had been there to see it! How do you manage to get into these scrapes?"

Caitlin's cheeks were burning. She had to force down the impulse to reveal MacGregor's part in the whole sorry debacle. MacGregor had meant well. But oh, she ached to box the young Highlander's ears.

Her train of thought was interrupted when Bocain's huge muzzle came off her forepaws. The hound cocked her head and pricked up her ears, then whined almost at the same moment they heard the whinny of a horse outside and the click of the garden gate. Setting down her cup and saucer, Caitlin went to investigate.

When she opened the door, she fell back a step. The Randal stood on the threshold. Every detail of the scene in The Fair Maid's upstairs bedchamber flashed into her head with mortifying clarity. He advanced, she retreated, one hand clutched to her heart.

"Good dog," said Rand, and obligingly scratched Bocain behind the ears. "No, you may not jump up on me. Down! Down, I say! Now stay!"

Having settled the hound, Rand's eyes moved to the young man who was staring at the deerhound with open-mouthed astonishment. Rand's first thought was amusing. *Lord Byron in tartan!* The young man, who had risen to his feet, might have stepped out of the pages of a Walter Scott novel. He was darkly good-looking in a romantically brooding way, and his immaculate English get-up of beige pantaloons and snug-fitting blue superfine was adorned by a voluminous Gordon plaid which was draped casually over one shoulder. Rand's subsequent thoughts were not so amusing. He was aware of a strange stillness in the atmosphere, as though the pair, suddenly exchanging eloquent, unspoken messages with their eyes, had just been caught out in something improper.

It was improper, Rand decided, as bile rose in his throat. In England, this kind of conduct would never be tolerated. Unattached males and females did not meet without a chaperone present.

When Caitlin made the introductions, he had the presence of mind to smile and offer a few pleasantries, but all the while his mind was functioning on another level, taking everything in. The cottage was as neat as a new pin. The furnishings were rustic. The only claim to elegance he could detect was the silver tea service and the fine porcelain set on the table. Caitlin and her guest had evidently shared a pot of tea. He wondered what else they had shared, and allowed his eyes to roam.

The door to the bedchamber stood ajar, affording him a glimpse of the made-up bed. The plain gray frock Caitlin was wearing was buttoned to her chin. Daroch's neckcloth could only have been tied with the aid of a valet. Rand understood about such things. He judged the young laird to be approximately the same age as Caitlin and far too young to be considered a serious suitor for the girl. By the time Rand accepted the chair Caitlin had indicated, his expression was considerably more agreeable.

Looking at Daroch, he said, "I've been trying to track you down for days."

"Oh?"

Rand smiled at the exaggerated show of unconcern. "Fiona suggested that I might find you here."

At the familiarity of his using Fiona's Christian name,

Daroch bristled, but before he could respond, Caitlin flashed him a warning look and quickly interposed, "May I offer you tea, Lord Randal?"

Rand inclined his head and forebore to grin when she bustled about, slamming doors and rattling drawers as she fetched him a cup and saucer and a silver tea spoon. So she knew about The Fair Maid, he thought. No doubt, she had heard about Nellie too. It had long ceased to amaze him that nice girls had their own methods of picking up all the salacious gossip going about. His own sisters were a case in point.

Caitlin's wrath did not unnerve him but rather amused him. It was a good sign.

"Mr. Gordon," he said finally, "I am anxious to trace a young relative of yours. Dirk Gordon is his name. Where may I find him?"

Daroch had been expecting the question. He was able to say easily, "Oh, Dirk never keeps me informed about his doings. He comes and goes as he pleases, that one."

"When did you last see him?"

"Before I left for Aboyne. Caitlin, did he say anything to you?"

Caitlin was studying the pattern on the rim of her teacup. The eyes she raised to Rand's were as clear a crystal prisms. "He said something about removing to his Gordon relatives in Fochabers." Fochabers was in the far north of Scotland, and miles away from Deeside.

"Ah," said Rand. "How convenient."

"Beg pardon?"

"I meant, of course, how inconvenient."

Caitlin slanted a sidelong look at Daroch.

Hastening to answer that unspoken plea, Daroch said, "See here, Lord Randal, if this has anything to do with the altercation that took place the other night in the change-house, I shall gladly pay for any damages that were incurred by my young cousin."

"What altercation?" asked Caitlin, trying to look innocent. Neither man spared her a glance.

Rand waved a hand negligently. "You misunderstand. I'm not asking for compensation. Why should I? No damage was done. No, I merely wish to assure myself that the young cub is unharmed. He's how old? Fourteen? Fifteen? I could not be easy in my conscience if I thought the lad was hiding out in the hills like some escaped convict." His winsome smile conveyed a hint of apology. "The other night I lost my temper. I put a price on his head. I've since gained a little perspective. After all, I myself was once a boy."

Into the silence, he said, "Miss Randal, this shortbread is delicious. My compliments to the cook."

Having achieved what he set out to do, namely to allay any fears that he was bent on revenging himself on young Gordon, Rand allowed the conversation to meander. He was waiting for the opportunity to be alone with Caitlin. When he realized that Daroch was suspicious and meant to frustrate his purpose, he resorted to subterfuge.

Exclaiming at the lateness of the hour, he made his excuses and left. Ten minutes later he was back. There was no sign of either Daroch or his horse.

Chapter Nine

Caitlin knew who was knocking on her door before she had even opened it. Her hound, which ought to have greeted the intrusion with fangs bared and hackles up, was thrashing the floor with her tail and panting like a broken-down bellows.

"I know you are in there, Caitlin. Please, open the door."

Her hand was on the bolt, but instinct held her motionless.

"One of my gloves must be on the floor. I thought I had it in my pocket." He rattled the locked door. "May I have it?"

The leather glove was down the side of the chair on which he had been sitting. Berating herself as all kinds of a fanciful fool, she unlocked the door.

"Thank you," he said as she handed him the glove, "and I have something of a particular nature I wish to say to you." Before she could prevent it she was swept inside and forced into a chair. Bocain was soon dealt with. Then Rand shut the door.

Moistening her lips, Caitlin said, "About Dirk Gordon . . ."

"I don't wish to think about that young jackanapes," said Rand.

Good. Neither did Caitlin. She watched him curiously as he took a few paces around the small room. Suddenly coming to a halt in front of her, he said abruptly, "What do you know about The Fair Maid?"

Plenty, but she wasn't going to tell him that. Choosing her words with care, as though she were charting a course through a treacherous Highland bog, she said cautiously, "I know that Dirk quarreled with you and that later you almost drowned trying to save him."

That part had been the most harrowing few minutes of one of the worst nights Caitlin had ever lived through. By giving the alarm after throwing her bonnet and plaid in the river, she had hoped to create a diversion so that she could slip away unseen. The Randal's precipitous action had stunned her. Her first thought had been that it was his relentless quest for revenge which had driven him to such lengths. But as she had observed it all, transfixed from the river bank, it came to her that he was desperately trying to save the boy. She had been on the point of giving herself up when he was dragged, on the point of exhaustion, from the treacherous waters.

Just thinking about it made her go weak at the knees. Tears stood on her lashes, and her voice cracked. "What you did was a very fine thing. The boy did not deserve . . ."

He stopped her words with the brush of his thumb on her lips. "I don't wish to speak about the boy." Holding her gaze steady, very gently, very seriously he said, "What else do you know about that night?"

A picture flashed into her mind of Lord Randal and

Nellie, the buxom wench whose bed he had shared, and her tears miraculously dried. Though she preserved a prim silence, the answer he was seeking could be read clearly on her face.

His lips quirked. "News travels fast," he said, and absorbed her faintly reproachful expression. "I understand I gained quite a reputation for myself when I was last in Deeside?"

His sudden swing from recent events to past history confused her. "Beg pardon?"

"Last year, when I came into Deeside for the hunting season." He waited a moment, then went on. "I believe I gained quite a reputation for myself."

Her chin lifted and the melting softness in her eyes hardened into ice. "Now why should you think so?"

"I was a soldier on furlough," he pointed out, "as were most of my companions. So, we shocked a few sensibilities. Perhaps there was the odd party which was a trifle on the wild side. I make no apology for it. I was a bachelor and need answer to no one for my conduct."

"In Deeside, we call a spade a spade." Her voice had risen by an octave. "Those were not parties. Those were orgies."

She was about to speak, then checked herself. A quick look up at him and caution gave way to a burning desire to wipe that aggravating twinkle from his eyes. "Naked nymphs pursued by drunken satyrs through the woods is hardly a party," she said indignantly.

"Oh, *that* party. Yes, I remember it fondly. Your cousin, Fiona, has been carrying tales, I presume?"

She looked at him blankly.

"She was there. Ah, I see from your face that the fair Fiona has been keeping secrets from you. Why don't you ask her about it?"

It took a moment or two for Caitlin to grasp that Lord Randal was under the misapprehension that it was her cousin he had caught trespassing on his estates on his last night of furlough.

Forcing her blushes to recede, she said in an odd little voice, "Fiona tells me everything." When she glanced up at him, his eyes were sparkling.

"I discovered something the other night at The Fair Maid," he said. "I discovered that my carousing days are over."

When she made no reply to this, he said in a more serious vein, "Don't tease your mind about the past. In the first place, my reputation is exaggerated. Good grief, I've been fighting a war for the last number of years. There's been little enough time to indulge in skirt-chasing. In the second place, it really isn't any of your business. What's done is done. Only the future need concern you."

His words were greeted by dumbfounded silence. Inwardly, Caitlin was retracing the path of their conversation from its inception, trying to discover why they seemed to be talking at cross-purposes. When she came out of the maze, she sucked in her breath and emitted a shocked gasp. The man was flirting with her.

Caitlin was no novice to the ways of gentlemen. Her mother had been her first tutor. Latterly, since she had taken up smuggling, she had received an education that few young women of her tender years could hope to possess. It was all done inadvertently, of course. It was shocking. It was also salutary. When ladies thought of flirting, they thought of hand-holding and stolen kisses and long, soulful looks. When men thought of flirting, they thought of bed. She'd learned that from the Randal the first time she had met him.

142

It came to her then that he had left his glove behind on purpose. She became excruciatingly aware of something else—the bed in the next room.

She moved quickly, darting away from him to stand by her hound. So that there could be no misunderstanding between them, she said pointedly, "I don't usually entertain strange gentlemen when I am alone. Daroch doesn't count. We have known each other since we were infants."

"Now that relieves my mind excessively; otherwise I might be forced to call him out."

Because he didn't want to frighten her, he closed the space between them slowly, in as casual a manner as he could manage. "Do I seem strange to you?" he asked whimsically. "That's not how you seem to me."

She moistened her lips. He didn't seem strange to her, but that was because David had talked endlessly about Rand. She knew more about him than he would wish her to know; more, perhaps, that was wise for her to know.

"No. Don't look like that. I would never do anything to hurt you. Look, give me your hand. I want to prove something to you, all right?"

For a long moment, she gazed at his open palm as though he were offering her a snake. "Give me your hand," he said sharply, and Caitlin automatically obeyed.

With great concentration, he slid his fingers between hers, separating them, fitting their palms together till not even a shadow could have slipped between them. "Tell me what you feel," he said softly.

She was unnerved by the contact. For long minutes, she stared at their joined hands in a kind of dumb stupor. Biting down on her lip, tearing her eyes away, she

143

lifted them to meet his. "What is it?" she asked hoarsely, sounding afraid and confused and desperately unsure of herself. "What's happening to me?"

"You wouldn't believe it if I told you. I can hardly believe it myself."

Rand had been raised from the cradle to cherish females, even the naughty ones. Chivalry was part of his code. It was so ingrained, he never had to think about it. But there was something more at work here, something deeper, something stronger. This girl aroused all the softer emotions in him. These were not new to him, but he had never experienced them with such shattering intensity.

It wasn't pity, Rand told himself. Having learned something of her circumstances, he applauded the pride that stiffened her spine. It was sheer bravado, of course, and that touched him, too. Though she would never admit it, she was as defenseless as a newborn lamb.

"Your bones are so delicate. You are so small . . . so fragile. I want only to protect you."

He wanted so much more than that. He wanted to make everything up to her. He wanted to lavish her with fine clothes and jewels, to place her in a setting where nothing ugly was allowed to exist, where nothing could ever hurt her again.

It was absurd. He hardly knew the girl. Then why did he feel that he had known her all his life?

The laugh he let out was not quite steady. "I don't believe I'm feeling this," he said. "Everything I thought I knew about relations between the sexes seems like so much hot air."

So much for Nellie, Rand was thinking, and all those beautiful high flyers with their practiced art. So much for the agreeable connection he had formed with Lady Margaret in the last year. This unawakened girl was lethal, a dangerous specimen, the confirmed bachelor's worst nightmare. There was no defense against her. A beautiful woman could always be replaced with another beauty. Passion was easily come by. This girl's appeal went beyond anything that could be explained. It wasn't general but particular. A hundred other men, a thousand, could have come upon her and walked away unscathed. Not he.

His eyes locked on hers, compelling her to willingness, and his hands splayed out, leisurely exploring the safe places on her body.

Though she was quaking like a jelly inside, something in the somber way he was looking at her allayed Caitlin's fears. She was still trying to find answers to his original question. She, too, thought she had known everything there was to know about relations between the sexes. No one had thought to tell her that logic counted for nothing when the very air between two people vibrated with some indefinable current.

"I feel . . ." She didn't know what she was feeling, she only knew that she liked his strong arms around her, liked his hands moving over her back, pressing her closer. "I feel . . ."

"I know," he said, and he brushed his smiling lips against the curve of her cheek. "Don't you think I'm afraid too?"

First kisses were special, and Rand was almost sure that this was Caitlin's first real kiss. It wasn't going to be chaste, but it wasn't going to be so carnal that she would be afraid to follow his lead when he wanted more than kisses from her. So he told himself.

She kissed him without a hint of awareness that she

145

was female to his male. Something in Rand's psyche took offense at this. Did she think he was a gelding? Had he made so little impression on her that she thought herself immune to him? It hardly seemed fair that while he spent his days and nights in a state of semiarousal, she should remain as cool as an iceberg. The devil she would! When this was over, she would know that as a specimen of virility, he was worthy of her utmost respect.

Caitlin wasn't completely lost to reason. Some remnant of feminine instinct warned her of impending doom. When he released her lips, she forced the words out. "If I give my d-dog the command, she will t-tear your throat out."

His hands held her face as he unhurriedly kissed her eyes, her nose, a small wisp of hair he discovered on her forehead. "Then give the command," he said, and moved in closer.

Her hair brushed the back of his fingers, that satinsoft ebony braid he ached to unbind and bury his face in. She didn't wear perfume, or none that he could discern. Instead she smelled of freshly laundered clothes dried in the open air, and her own scent, something dark and delectably female. As his senses became more acute, more aware of all the subtleties that made her different from any woman he had ever known, the seducer became the seduced.

Cupping her head with both hands, delicately, with all the skill he could command, which was considerable, he changed the texture of his kisses. Lips brushed and molded softly, broke apart, came together and clung. His fingers spread out against her jaw, applying a gentle pressure, separating her lips to the first tentative invasion of his tongue. The little betraying hiatus in her breathing sent his blood thundering through his veins.

Her hands were clutching his shoulders as though her head were spinning. Tearing her lips away, she said, "I think I'm going to faint."

"Good," he said, before he took her lips again.

Since she wasn't making any objections, he saw no reason for continuing with the subtlety. He kissed her the way he wanted to, angling her head back, taking her mouth voraciously, nipping at her bottom lip, aggressively thrusting his tongue between her teeth. She moaned and melted against him, circling his waist with both arms. With increasing abandon, passion feeding on passion, he edged her closer to surrender. The more she yielded, the more he wanted from her. He couldn't get close enough. His tongue drove into her mouth and began a wildly erotic rhythm that left them both gasping and greedy for more. When his control snapped, he was beyond caring.

Lost to reason, lost to his own code of honor, he began to tear at her clothes. Need such as he had never known hardened his body to the exploding point. She could have stopped him with a word. She was clinging to him helplessly, as though he were the one solid anchor in the storm that raged around them.

Her breasts were bare to him now. He didn't spare more than a moment to admire their lush contours. His mouth fastened ravenously on one taut dark crest and his hand slid to her bottom, lifting her in a crushing embrace against his hard groin.

Raw pleasure streaked through Caitlin, and she cried softly against his neck. It was too much. Using both hands, she brought his head up for her kiss.

They had both reckoned without the hound. Alternately snuffling and whimpering, Bocain suddenly threw back her head and let out a warning howl, then slowly rose on her haunches. Rand was the first to come to himself. On the second earsplitting howl, he forced himself to release Caitlin's lips. Fighting for breath, chests heaving, they stared at each other. They were both shocked, but his eyes registered something more, something between awe and delight.

He could take her so easily. Everything was in his favor. The cottage was isolated. There was a bed in the next room. Her deerhound wasn't much of an obstacle, or he would be a dead man by now. And the girl herself was willing. It would be so easy to press his advantage to the conclusion for which his whole body was fervently straining. Only one thing stopped him— the conviction that when it was over he would never be allowed to come within a country mile of Miss Caitlin Randal.

He saw her eyes darken with comprehension the moment before she jerked away. Capturing her by the shoulders, he held her immobile. "Don't move! Don't fight me! Don't you see, it's the worst thing you could do? Just"—he let out a breathy laugh and grinned crookedly—"just give me a moment to find my balance. Then I shall let you go."

Don't move? He wasn't to know it, but her legs were buckling under her. If he hadn't been holding her up she would have collapsed like a rag doll at his feet. Tears of mortification stung the backs of her eyes. How had he managed to rob her of the will to resist him? Hadn't she warned her cousin about men like this? He was too good-looking, too charming, too confident—and much too calm for her taste. His kisses, which left her feeling as though she had barely survived a hurricane, had made no appreciable difference to him. Even his neckcloth hadn't a wrinkle out of place.

Suddenly conscious of her own disarranged clothing, Caitlin gasped and began to fumble with the buttons on the bodice of her gown. He waited until she lifted her head.

Correctly reading her half-shamed, half-angry expression, holding her chin up with thumb and forefinger, he said gently, "I don't know how you do it, but you make me act in ways that are contrary to my own principles. I think I have the same effect on you."

Running his fingers across her hot cheeks, he then smoothed them into the tendrils of baby fine hair at her nape. Softly he said, "Now tell me what you feel."

Caitlin was not unmoved by that warmly intimate look. She felt the strongest urge to walk into his arms again, not for the breathless rapture he could give her, but for the security of having those powerful masculine arms wrapped around her. Trembling with a confusion of tumultuous emotions that were both unfamiliar and contradictory, she cried out, "I don't know what I feel, but I know this, I don't want to feel this way."

"Are you sure?"

"Yes! No! I don't know! You are deliberately confusing me! Why don't you tell me what you are feeling."

His eyes searched hers for a long interval, then flared. Shaking his head, smiling, he set her at arm's length and began to draw on his gauntlets. "There are going to be some changes around here," he said. "I think it's more proper if you remove in the interim to

149

your grandfather's house, don't you? If that doesn't suit, at the very least, I shall expect a chaperone in residence as soon as it may be arranged." He held up a hand to silence her protests. "Your hound is dismally inappropriate as a chaperone, as I have just proved. Frankly, Kate, I think your grandfather is grossly at fault here, allowing you all the liberties you enjoy. I am not cut from the same cloth as he, as you'll soon learn. You are not to receive Daroch again, is that understood? I don't care how innocent or how long standing that connection may be. And what goes for Daroch goes doubly for every male who is not related to you by ties of blood, including myself—*especially* myself."

Patting her cheek in an avuncular manner, he went on conversationally as he moved to the door. "Now where was I? Oh yes. I shall expect you to accept all invitations to dos and parties in the neighborhood. How will you learn to go on in society if you continue to make yourself a recluse? If your wardrobe is inadequate, as I suppose it must be, you have two choices. You may either appeal to your grandfather or I shall personally see to it. I think that about covers everything for the present. Are there any questions?"

His eyes were gleaming with laughter.

Her bosom was heaving. Passionately, she cried out, "I have no interest in learning how to go on in society. Furthermore, you have no right to tell me what to do."

"Ah, but you see, you just gave me that right, Kate, as well as a few others that I don't suppose have occurred to you yet. All in good time."

When she stared up at him in mute confusion, he swiftly kissed her. "As for what I am feeling," he said, "I feel like Adam in the Garden of Eden, having just been introduced to the woman who was created from one of his own ribs."

Chapter Ten

Caitlin acquired a chaperone. The lady was Jamie MacGregor's widowed mother. Though Mrs. MacGregor had made her home with her sister in Aberdeen, her heart was in the Highlands. She was looking for lodgings until she could find something more permanent.

"It's only temporary," MacGregor assured Caitlin. "She's no happy livin' wi' her sister, ye see. A' her life, she has lived on Deeside. She canna abide the lowlands."

It was after church services, and people were milling about on the steps of the church. Caitlin's eyes searched the crush for Lord Randal. He was in conversation with her uncle, or rather, her uncle was talking the Randal's ear off. She wondered if it had something to do with MacGregor's request.

"I'm used to living alone," demurred Caitlin, trying to sound gracious, feeling horribly churlish.

MacGregor's face fell. "Och, I shouldna hae asked ye. Dinna gie it another thought. Mayhap I'll find lodgings for her in Ballater. It's only that I wanted her near me, ye ken, and her so lonely an a'."

What could she say? Mrs. MacGregor could not lodge with her son in the bachelor quarters above Strathcairn's stables. Moreover, it was only for a week or two until more permanent arrangements could be made. Caitlin gave way gracefully. "I'd be delighted to have your mother stay with me, MacGregor. She was always kind to me when I was a girl."

Hardly were the words out of her mouth than MacGregor bounded away and returned almost immediately with his mother on his arm. No introductions were necessary. In her day, the Widow MacGregor had run the draper's shop in Ballater. She was as plump as a broody hen and, as Caitlin remembered, had a disposition to match, sometimes tyrannical, sometimes warm and motherly. Caitlin had always regarded the lady with the deepest respect. When Mrs. MacGregor raised her voice, even the village lads walked a little more softly.

Mrs. MacGregor's speech was a touch more refined than her son's. "I hardly like to ask so great a favor."

"It's no trouble," said Caitlin warmly. "Really, I shall be glad of the company."

Mrs. MacGregor's faintly anxious look gave way to a smile. "I know how to make myself useful. I'm good with a needle, and I'll help with the chores."

"Oh that won't be necessary," Caitlin began, then reconsidered when the anxious look returned to the older woman's face. There was no greater pride than that of a Highlander down on his or her luck. Anything that smacked of charity would cut to the quick. "To be perfectly frank," she said with a disarming smile, "I've been thinking it's time I did something about my wardrobe, but I scarcely know where to begin."

Now where had that thought come from? Frowning, she darted a quick look at Rand. Her frown deepened

153

as she trailed him with her eyes. He had one hand on her grandfather's shoulder and was directing him to his waiting carriage, all the while smiling affably. Rand helped Glenshiel to ascend the steps, then lightly jumped in after him, and the door was promptly closed upon them.

At dinner that evening, Glenshiel revealed the gist of the conversation that had taken place in his coach. The Randal, it appeared, was determined to demonstrate to the watching world that the breach between their two families was finally healed. As a beginning, Glenshiel and every member of his household were commanded to attend a ball to be held at Strathcairn House. The chief had spoken, and his word had the force of law.

Charlotte was in her element. As soon as the covers were removed and the whiskey brought out, she sent Fiona to her room to fetch back copies of *Ackerman's Repository*. Soon, in the downstairs front parlor, the ladies were engrossed in the glossy fashion plates, some of which were truly shocking to Caitlin's untutored eye. The necklines were too low. The waists were too high. There was an excess of bows and ruffles at the sleeves and hem. Most shocking of all were the flimsy swatches of gauze her aunt produced for their inspection. When she held them up to the candle she could see her hand through them.

Caitlin's consternation was a source of mirth to her aunt. These gowns were all the rage, she told her. In Edinburgh and London, no one gave them a second stare. And even in the Highlands, the ladies they were bound to encounter at the Randal's grand ball would be no provincial misses, but women of fashion.

"Who, for instance?" Caitlin wanted to know.

The names her aunt reeled off were not unknown to

Caitlin. These formed the upper crust of the Scottish nobility, most of whom had estates between Perth and Deeside. For the greater part of the year, they resided in their magnificent townhouses in Edinburgh or London. Like the Randal, they were more English than Scots.

Before long, Caitlin wandered off. She felt as though she had swallowed a great granite boulder. Snatching her plaid from a hook in the vestibule, she pushed through to the kitchens and out the back door. As she veered to the left, making for the stables, her deerhound detached itself from the shadows and trotted after her.

The familiar sounds and scents of leather and horses had an oddly calming effect. She found an empty stall and sat down on the fresh hay with her back against the wooden slats. Bocain sank down beside her and pressed one huge paw in her lap as though sensing that her mistress required a little coddling. Sighing, Caitlin angled her head back and closed her eyes.

This was how her uncle found her some time later. For a moment or two, he regarded her silently with a soft look in his eyes. At length he said, "So this is where ye are hiding yourself?"

Caitlin's eyes flew open. "Uncle Donald!" She pushed Bocain off her and scrambled to her feet. "I'm not hiding. I just wanted a quiet place to do some thinking."

"Aye. I thought as much. But no amount o' thinking is going to make a jot o' difference. Make up your mind to it, *graidh*, we must obey our chief."

"And if I don't, what can the Randal do to me?" Her tone was flippant.

His was serious. "Plenty, if he has a mind to. No. I'll no quarrel with ye. Just remember, this is not the lowlands. The chief has spoken and must be obeyed. If ye won't think o' yourself, think o' the rest o' us. The

Randal will hold your grandfather to account if ye dare flaunt his wishes. Lassie, is it the feud ye are thinking of?"

It wasn't the feud. It was the ball. It was meeting a class of people to whom bloodlines were everything. She would be an object of ridicule or scorn. It was the Randal and the way he had kissed her. She couldn't think of him now without wanting to burst into tears.

Swallowing, she led the way out of the stall. "It's not much of a feud if even Glenshiel kowtows to the Randal."

"Och, the feud was over and done with when your grandfather accepted his title from the crown, and well he knows it."

"He lost his chance to be chief. That must have rankled, especially when the new lairds were English bred."

Behind the thick lenses, the old eyes grew misty. "Aye, Glenshiel would have made a braw chief. Even so, it would all have come to Lord Randal in the end. He is the nearest male relative. It's time ye got used to the idea, Caitlin."

They stopped at one of the stalls to pet a big chestnut gelding. "You are still a handsome devil, Prince," Caitlin crooned, "in spite of your advanced years." The horse blew softly into her palm.

"Is Grandfather used to the idea?"

He had lost the thread of their conversation. "What?"

"Grandfather? What does he think of the Randal?"

"He has said very little, but I'll tell ye this. I know my brother. Chief or no chief, he would not cross the man's threshold if he did not respect him."

Caitlin looked skeptical, and he chuckled. "Glenshiel's roar is worse than his bite," he said with so fond an intonation that Caitlin smiled.

Donald Randal was devoted to his brother. Caitlin had always known it, but it was only as she became her uncle's assistant and transcribed his notes that she came to understand the depth and strength of that attachment. It went back to the bloody aftermath of Culloden when her great grandfather, the chief of Clan Randal, had met with a traitor's death. A month was to pass before government troops swept into Deeside on their murderous campaign of revenge.

Glenshiel, though a mere boy, had been out on the hills distributing food to the stragglers of the prince's defeated army, Randal men all, who dared not show their faces for fear of reprisal. Donald was alone with his mother when the redcoats had burst down their doors. When Glenshiel returned home, he found his mother brutally raped, his younger brother beaten senseless, and the three men who had perpetrated the crime in a drunken stupor in Strathcairn's great hall. He'd gone back to the hills to fetch help. When Donald came to himself, it was to hear the screams of the redcoats as they were castrated and then summarily hanged. After that, the family had hidden out in the hills until friends had spirited them away to Holland and safety.

That brutal event explained so much that she had not understood before. Donald Randal had never married. To her knowledge, there had never been a woman in his life. Peace and quiet were all that this gentle man required to pursue his scholarly interests. The highlight of his life was the occasional trip to Aberdeen or Edinburgh or such sundry places, to deliver a paper at one of the historical societies. He was also a great walker and could often be seen in all kinds of weathers tramping the hills.

As for Glenshiel, he had become the sole support of

his little family. As he grew to manhood, he saw that there was only one way to repair his family's fortunes. He took up arms for the crown. In time, he made his way back to Deeside. Some things, however, he could never reclaim. Strathcairn and the chieftainship were forever beyond his reach.

If Glenshiel, who feared no man, felt honor bound to accept the dictates of the Randal, Caitlin did not see how her puny will could prevail. She thought of something else. Donald Randal would be returning to the scene of that tragic episode in his young life. To her knowledge, he had never set foot in Strathcairn from that day to this. The thought made her vaguely ashamed.

"I'm proud to be a Randal of Glenshiel," she said, and linking her arm through her uncle's, she led the way back to the house.

As the carriage took the last turn on the road to Strathcairn, the house came into view. Every window blazed with lights. In one corner of the coach, Fiona chattered at an alarming rate. She was staring fixedly out the window, commenting excitedly on the long queue of carriages in the driveway, the groups of elegant ladies and gentlemen who descended from them. In the other corner of the coach, Caitlin calmly addressed desultory remarks to the other members of their little party. Beneath her tranquil exterior, however, she was quivering. Panic fluttered like a moth trapped within her, and her breathing was anything but regular.

It was too late to turn back. She fixed on that thought, trying to get a grip on herself. The worst thing that could happen was that people would cut her dead—she, an upstart and an interloper—for daring to enter their rarefied world. Before she could marshal her defenses, another thought, a poisonous barb, slipped into her mind. Worse by far was the fear that he would mock her and her pathetic attempts to pretty herself up. On the other hand, he might ignore her altogether. It was one thing for the Randal to pay her some attention when she was the only woman available, quite another when he was surrounded by beautiful, cultured sophisticates of his own class. Whether it was better to be mocked or ignored—just thinking about it made her shudder with dread.

That train of thought was mercifully cut short when the coach door was flung open by one of the Randal's immaculately liveried footmen. Donald Randal hung back momentarily, and Caitlin felt a twinge of remorse as it came to her that her uncle had far more to fear than she. He must enter Strathcairn's great hall and face the ghosts of his boyhood. Her own fears seemed petty in comparison.

Assuming a confidence she was far from feeling, to distract him, she casually laid her gloved fingers on his arm as she made to descend the carriage steps, then began a series of witty anecdotes on the trials and tribulations she had endured in preparing for her first ball. At least, she supposed they were amusing. The white tissue frock she was wearing, she told him, was her own creation, and she was still half-blinded from embroidering the row of tiny white thistles which adorned the edge of her bodice. Her hair—Mrs. MacGregor had dressed it for her—was a wonder of modern science, namely, paper and hot tongs and a gross of steel hairpins to keep the effects of gravity at bay. Her glowing complexion owed nothing to nature, but was rather the product of feminine invention—an oatmeal and lemon scrub, followed by a light dusting of corn flour.

It was something of a relief when Charlotte entered the conversation and regaled them with stories of her own girlhood vanities. Glenshiel soon caught on. Though he offered no comment, he chuckled in all the right places. In this way, they entered Strathcairn's great hall. As they joined the throng of guests who were slowly making their way to the reception line, Glenshiel positioned himself close to his brother. At the same time, he managed to draw Caitlin to his side.

His eyes swept over her, and for her ears only he whispered, "Lass, I'm proud o' ye, so proud o' ye."

Glenshiel wasn't given to flattery or flowery compliments. He was a typical Scot, distrustful of praise in all its manifestations. Caitlin felt herself swallowing, and her heart seemed to swell inside her chest like a hot-air balloon. She did not know it, but she held her head a little higher and her eyes shone with a new awareness.

This was as nothing, however, when her unwary gaze was caught and held by Rand's glittering stare. The worst thing that could happen to her was no longer of any interest. Rand's eyes told her so.

It was a gathering on the scale and grandeur of a bygone era. Glenshiel surveyed the crush of people, especially the gentlemen, with an appreciative eye. Kilts in the tartans of all the northeast clans were liberally represented—Gordon, Fraser, Farquharson, Murray, MacGregor, Forbes, and the Randal. Especially the Randal. The spectacle brought a small constriction to his chest. He could not remember the last time he had seen so many of the younger generation in their national dress. Trews and breeches were now a commonplace in the Highlands, so much so that one would never have known that the prohibition against Highland dress had long since been lifted. Only ancient relics such as himself had returned to the old modes. But not tonight. Tonight was a gala occasion in the Highland tradition. The Randal had done them all proud.

From his vantage point on the upstairs gallery, Glenshiel allowed his eyes to wander the interior of the great hall. It wasn't the same as in his father's day. The new lairds had refitted the place. It was grander, more opulent, more . . . "English" was the word he wanted. The paneling, the staircase, even the portraits on the walls, were different. It was just as well. When they had stepped through the door from the foyer, he could feel Donald brace himself for the terrible ordeal.

"I hardly recognize it," he'd said, and the tension had seemed to flow out of him.

Not so for himself. Glenshiel's memories were sharper, more vivid. His eyes were unerringly drawn upward to the massive wooden support that traversed the width of the hall. A silver chandelier with a thousand candles was suspended from it. He suppressed a shudder, recalling another time, when three men had been strung up and left to gasp out their dying breaths.

Resolutely putting that image from his mind, he searched the crowd for the figure of his host. The Randal was in conversation with the Duke of Atholl. Lords Aberdeen and Aboyne wandered over. Soon, they were joined by Huntly. Never, in Strathcairn's history, Glenshiel was thinking, had such exalted company graced its hallowed halls at one time. In the old days, this gathering of the flower of Highland nobility would have been highly suspect. Treason and rebellion would have been in the air. The constriction in his chest increased. It wasn't pride. It was regret. These days, the chiefs saw their role as landlords and men of business. Their conversation was all of profit and loss. The principles which had guided their fathers and their fathers' fathers were no longer of any interest. They were not guardians entrusted with the care of the land and all its people. Self-service was the new order of the day. The land and its people must be made to serve them.

An old era was passing and few seemed to lament its demise. At the rate these men of influence were going, in very short order, the Highlands would be barren of everything but sheep and game. The clearances on Atholl's estates were a scandal to all right-thinking men, and a foretaste of things to come. Didn't these men recognize that they, more than the English parliament, were the death knell of their own clans? Didn't they care? Highlanders cleared from their ancient lands were taking ship for the New World in droves. He wished with all his heart that he was thirty years younger. Then he would think nothing of taking on that coterie of powerful men whose heads were so intimately bent together. He wished he had an heir.

That thought sent his eyes searching the crush for Caitlin. He knew more regret but overlaid with an undeniable thread of pride. The lass had a head on her shoulders. She had heart. There was no one else to whom he cared to entrust the care of Glenshiel and its people. If things were different, if Strathcairn and its vast holdings still belonged to his branch of the family, if Caitlin were a boy . . .

His thoughts stopped there. Caitlin was illegitimate. Strathcairn and the chieftainship could never have passed to her, not even if she were a male.

"What are ye thinking?" Donald Randal had joined his brother at the balustrade.

Glenshiel's eyes narrowed as the Randal and his friend, Murray, approached Caitlin and bowed low over her hand. The fiddlers struck up for the "Dashing White Sergeant," and Caitlin, flanked by the two kilted gentlemen, made her way to the center of the floor to make up one of the sets.

"What I am thinking," said Glenshiel as to himself, "is that God works in mysterious ways to perform his perfect will."

"What?"

"I said that God helps them that help themselves."

The ball was only halfway over when it came to Rand that there were distinct disadvantages to being the host. His time was never his own. He needs must be agreeable to everyone, and have a particular care for those timid souls who looked as though they would bolt if someone glanced at them the wrong way. Next time, he promised himself, he would prevail upon Murray to do the honors. Then he would be free to follow his own inclinations.

From the corner of his eye, he glimpsed his hostess of the evening, Murray's married sister. She was beckoning him over. There was no doubt in his mind that Maria had a wallflower all picked out for him to partner in the dance. As a hostess, Maria was peerless. He knew that his mother would heartily endorse the way she shepherded his guests, just as surely as he knew his mother would reproach him for what he was about to do next.

Ignoring that raised hand as though he had never seen it, he let his eyes wander. When he caught sight of Caitlin, he made his move. It was like running an obstacle course. Circling the redheaded dasher who was making a beeline for him, the one who had pursued him relentlessly all evening, adroitly sidestepping those two august lords of the Gordon clan, Aberdeen and Aboyne, whose only interest was in getting up a game of cards, he stalked his quarry. Before she knew his game, he had her.

"A waltz?"

"I don't know how to waltz."

He loved the quaver in her voice. He wasn't going to give up his one chance to put his arms around her. "I'll teach you." Among other things, but they would get to that later.

She caught on quickly after one sweep of the dance floor. When he sensed that she was no longer counting her steps, he said softly, "Until I saw you arrive, I wasn't sure you would accept my invitation."

"I received no invitation."

"I distinctly remember—"

"What I received was a command, issued with all the authority of an oracle. 'Thus saith the chief of Clan Randal. The Lord hath spoken.' Yes, and as it was forcefully pointed out to me, hell hath no fury like a chieftain scorned."

"I presume from that smile on your face that you are not sorry I forced your hand?"

Her smile slipped a little. "I assure you, Lord Randal, no one forces me to do anything I don't wish to do."

He was too shrewd to contradict her. He thought of her chaperone, Mrs. MacGregor. His eyes absorbed the elegant gown and the modish coiffure, dark hair swept up in a coronet of curls, and he quickly dropped his lashes to veil his thoughts. When he saw the light of battle flare in her eyes, he sighed resignedly, knowing he had betrayed himself. Before she could launch them both into a full-scale war of wills, he tried to deflect her into a minor skirmish.

"You have already danced twice with the laird o' Daroch this evening. Dance with him again and you will have all the tongues wagging."

His ploy succeeded. Arrested, she stared up at him and promptly missed a step. When she had counted herself back into the tempo of the waltz, she took up where he had left off. "Why will tongues start to wag if I dance more than twice with Daroch?"

"I don't know. It's just one of those unwritten rules. Ladies may not partner the same gentleman for more than two dances. My mother dinned that precept into me before my first season."

"Pooh!" she scoffed. "These are English modes. We know nothing of that here."

Suddenly, the diversionary skirmish had all the makings of a full-fledged battle. Daroch had been hovering around Caitlin all evening. Rand remembered something else—the proprietary look in Daroch's eyes when he had come upon him in Caitlin's cottage. "What is Daroch to you, Caitlin?"

At the bluntness of the question, her eyes went very wide, then narrowed. "You are not thinking of picking a quarrel with Daroch over a dance?"

"If he insults one of my guests by dancing thrice with her, I most certainly will." The notion was not a serious one, but he could tell from her expression that she didn't know it.

Caitlin was thinking of pistols at ten paces. Daroch's temper was unpredictable. He was also a crack shot. She didn't know how skilled the Randal was with a pistol. "I won't dance with Daroch again," she said quickly. "You have my word on it."

She didn't like his lazy grin. It smacked too much of an opponent who had outmaneuvered her in a game of chess. Her move. "Do the rules governing dancing apply equally to men and women?"

He wasn't quite sure what the question meant, but he nodded just the same.

She rewarded him with a facsimile of his own lazy grin. "In that case, Lord Randal, look to your own conduct."

"What does that mean?"

"The lady with the red hair? The evening isn't halfway over and you have danced with her twice already."

The flippant remark on the tip of his tongue died unspoken when he observed a certain something in her eyes before she looked away. It wasn't jealousy. It was uncertainty. He had the strongest urge to kiss that look away.

Very seriously, he said, "Miss Burnett has all the grace and delicacy of Napoleon's Imperial Guard. Given half a chance, she sweeps everything before her. Twice now, she has attacked when I least expected it. If she comes within striking distance again, I promise you she is going to meet her Waterloo."

She shook her head and laughed. "Do you often express yourself in military terms? If you do, my lord, there must be few who understand you."

"I think you understand me well enough. I'd go so far as to say that words between us are almost superfluous."

He had not meant to seduce her in the middle of the dance floor, not for her sake but for his. He was wearing a kilt, for God's sake!

With his hand over the center of her back, he angled

166

her a little closer. His eyes held hers, willing her to read everything that was in his mind. Her breasts began to rise and fall rapidly. His breathing became shallow. The atmosphere between them was charged with sexual tension. Without volition, their steps slowed then halted altogether. She swayed toward him. His eyes dropped to her parted lips.

"Caitlin," he said. "Caitlin . . ."

Someone bumped into them, and the mood was shattered. Caitlin stepped back. He could see that she was completely disoriented. He wanted nothing more than to gather her in his arms and carry her to his bedchamber to finish what he had begun.

And she would let him! By jove, she would let him! This girl was in no condition to deny him anything.

Triumph flashed in his eyes as he reached for her and swung her into the dance. Where he led, she would follow. A man could not ask more of his woman than that.

By the time she sat down to supper, Caitlin's cheeks were flushed and her eyes were sparkling. She no longer felt out of place in this exalted company. No one had asked her point-blank about her father. She was Glenshiel's granddaughter. People were willing to let it go at that.

Daroch leaned over and snapped his fingers in front of her nose. "That's better. You have been lost in a dream these last five minutes. Where were you?"

She dimpled and shook her head. "Do you know, Daroch, I was dreading tonight?"

"Oh? Why?"

Sometimes Daroch's lack of sensibility could be exasperating. Didn't he know that she had felt like an impostor dressed up in her new finery? Couldn't he guess that even plain girls were prone to the sin of vanity? She'd feared that she would be a wallflower, and that the only gentlemen she could rely on to partner her in the dance were her male relatives. She had been sure that the Randal would be so busy fending off beauties that he would overlook her entirely. None of those things had happened. In point of fact, she'd had the time of her life.

Looking a question at him, she said hopefully, "I wasn't sure that my frock would pass muster."

Daroch's eyes swept over her indifferently. "You look fine to me. White suits you."

Caitlin thought of the long weary nights she and Mrs. MacGregor had labored over the most beautiful and delicate gown she had ever had in her possession, and she bit into the meat pastry on the end of her fork and chewed viciously.

Coming up at that moment, Fiona and her escort seated themselves on the opposite side of the table. Daroch's indifference evaporated. He fawned over Caitlin like the proverbial lovesick suitor. Fiona stared, then turned glowing eyes upon her companion. Caitlin's heart sank. When Daroch and Fiona were involved in one of their spats, it was best to give them a wide berth.

It was Daroch who made the opening gambit. As though suddenly conscious of the couple across the table, he said in a dangerously pleasant voice, "Mr. Haughton, is it not? We have met before."

Caitlin recognized the handsome young man as the new tenant of Balmoral Castle. His father, as she understood, would be joining him almost directly, as soon as he had attended to some business in London.

"Mr. Gordon, better known as Daroch, is it not?" There was a twinkle in Mr. Haughton's eyes.

Daroch took exception to that twinkle. "English, as I remember?"

Mr. Haughton glanced first at Fiona, then at Daroch. In a more considering tone, he said, "Yes, I am a true *sassenach*, I fear," and turning pointedly to Caitlin, he said, "Our host tells me you are a student of history, Miss Randal?"

"Lord Randal exaggerates. My interest is merely in stories about the past. Why do you ask?"

"My father, also, is something of an historian. He is fascinated by Deeside and all the myths and legends that surround the blood feuds which were once so prevalent here."

"Myths and legends?" repeated Caitlin, her brow wrinkling.

Daroch let out a laugh. "What Mr. Haughton means is that, in the retelling, truth has a way of becoming lost in what we accept as history." He looked pointedly at Fiona. "Not unlike gossip and rumor. It's human nature, one supposes, to want to embroider on a rather dull story to make it sound more interesting."

"That's it exactly," responded Mr. Haughton. "Well, just look at all the legends that have grown up around Bonnie Prince Charlie."

Fiona glared at Daroch. "Where there is smoke, there is fire," she declared, with all the force of a priestess delivering an oracle.

Mr. Haughton, unaware that two conversations were going forward simultaneously, nodded. "That's very true. However, sometimes the smoke becomes so dense that it obscures the fire."

"Or," said Daroch, his eyes boring into Fiona's,

169

"those with vested interests fan the smoke to blind the rest of us till we cannot see straight."

"Pooh!" exclaimed Fiona. "Who has vested interests?"

Mr. Haughton answered at once. "I myself would not put it so strongly. All I meant was that in the heat of battle, it's almost impossible to credit the enemy with any redeeming virtues, and afterward, one tends to justify one's own position." He laughed in a deprecating way. "Well, one only need look at England and Scotland. We each have our own version of what passes for history."

Caitlin, who had been following Mr. Haughton's train of thought attentively, gestured with her hand, cutting off Daroch's next remark. "Then how can fact be separated from fiction?" she asked. "The task would seem to be impossible." She was thinking of all the histories and biographies which littered her uncle's bookroom.

"No one said it was easy," replied Mr. Haughton. "My own father never accepts anything that is uncorroborated, that is, three sources are preferable to two. One source, on its own, must always be suspect." His eyes smiled into Caitlin's. "Miss Randal, I would consider it a great favor if you and I could get together at a more appropriate moment and compare notes."

Caitlin shook her head. "It is my uncle you should approach, Mr. Haughton. He is the real historian. I merely transcribe his notes. They're in the Gaelic, you see, and I translate for him."

No one was eating. Everyone's cutlery was laid aside. Daroch's eyes glanced into the faces of his companions and finally came to rest on Fiona. "That's the trouble with us Highlanders," he said. "We dwell too much on the past. It's the future that should concern us."

Fiona picked up her fork and speared several small

potato fritters on her plate. "As my Uncle Donald would be the first to tell you, Mr. Gordon, the past has a way of catching up with you."

"Not if we rewrite it," riposted Haughton, and everyone laughed.

Caitlin's mind was still assimilating that odd conversation when she and Fiona were restored to her aunt. One look at Charlotte Randal's face and she knew trouble was brewing.

"Have you no pride?" were her first words to her daughter. "Don't you care that people are talking about you?"

Fiona's head dipped. "Talking? About what?"

"You and Daroch."

"I've only danced with him once," protested Fiona.

Charlotte's voice rose. "That may be. But you are so transparent. Everyone can see that you've been hurt by the tales about him. You are making a spectacle of yourself."

"What tales?" Fiona studiously examined the toes of her dancing slippers.

Charlotte cast a surreptitious look over her shoulder. "We can't talk here," she said, and shepherded her charges to a vacant sofa against the window wall and bade them sit. She remained standing, glowering down at them.

"You know very well to what I refer. I'm talking about Daroch and his fancy women. They say he has one tucked away in every hamlet between here and Aberdeen."

"Daroch denies it. He says it's a pack of lies." Fiona's lip was trembling.

"Oh? Then tell me this. Where does he get to half the

171

time? He's certainly not here where he ought to be, looking after his estates."

"He visits friends," answered Fiona stubbornly. "He told me so."

"Then why are you at outs with him?"

When Fiona had nothing to say to this, Caitlin remarked, "It's my opinion that these rumors about Daroch are highly exaggerated, if, indeed, they have any basis in fact. And as for Fiona making a spectacle of herself, she did no such thing. On every side, I have heard her described as a credit to us all."

Her intervention gave her aunt's thoughts a new direction. "Credit is it? Then let me tell you, I gave you credit for more sense. I saw you on the dance floor with Lord Randal. He is toying with you. Matrimony is the furthest thing from his mind. If you are not careful, my girl, you'll find yourself embroiled in a scandal. Don't say I haven't warned you."

With these words, the evening was robbed of all its joy for Caitlin. Not for one moment had the thought of marriage to the Randal entered her head. She was Glenshiel's bastard granddaughter. The Randal was above her touch.

Truth to tell, since he had kissed her in the shieling, she had been living in a dream world. Her thoughts had dwelled on the feel of his strong arms about her and the heady pleasure of his kisses. She had not considered what the future might have in store for her.

She considered it now and saw at once that she was heading for disaster. She knew that he wanted her, and just as surely she knew that he would not be satisfied for long with mere kisses.

When Rand pounced on her for his third dance of the evening, he found her pleasant but evasive, and nothing he said could persuade her to partner him again. He watched her go with a faint smile, supposing, wrongly, that her grandfather had warned her against him.

Chapter Eleven

Silence, so long a silence on that narrow stretch of road that Rand was beginning to wonder if he had miscalculated. For more than three hours, he and Murray had patiently kept vigil on the road to The Fair Maid. Other men were posted at change-houses all along Deeside. They were lying in wait for Daroch and his band of smugglers.

Their orders were explicit. Only one person was of any interest, only one person must not escape their net, the boy, Dirk Gordon. Until he showed his face, they were to turn a blind eye to the smugglers and their commerce.

Rand had set everything in place with meticulous care. Having discovered that MacGregor was a smuggler, it had been no great labor to trace the source of the contraband whiskey. The still was hidden away in the mill of Balmoral, just across the river from his own place.

In an effort to allay any fears Daroch and his band might harbor, Rand had given out that he was returning to England to spend Christmas with his family. In point of fact, he had got no further than Murray's place at

174

Inverey. With him out of the picture, he had every hope that young Gordon would be tempted to leave his lair. When word came to him that the miller of Balmoral was enjoying one of his busiest days of the month, he knew it was time to act.

His horse shifted restlessly beneath him, and Rand patted the bay before dismounting and tethering the reins to the bare branch of a birch. He was chilled to the marrow. Not even the Randal plaid he had thrown over his riding cape gave much protection from the elements. The light sprinkling of snow which had begun to fall earlier gave no sign of slackening

Hunching his shoulders against the chill air, he cursed his ill luck for the sudden drop in the temperature. In all likelihood, the smugglers were home in their beds, or enjoying a dram or two of illegal Deeside *uisge-beatha* around a blazing fire. He said as much to his equally frozen companion who was stamping his feet to ward off the cold.

"You are far off there," said Murray. "With the weather changing, there is no telling when the drove roads will be passable. Your smugglers are a canny lot, I'll give you that. But they are reliable, and this is a crucial time for them. Every Scotsman worth his salt will want to restock his cellar for the New Year. It's our most celebrated festival, you see. If Daroch can't—or won't—deliver, there are plenty of others who will."

"Is there anyone on Deeside who isn't involved in smuggling?" asked Rand testily.

Murray laughed. "If there is, I don't know of him. Good God, no sensible man is going to pay the malt tax for inferior whiskey when he can have the best for a fraction of that price. Even your own cellars at

Strathcairn are well stocked, not to mention the garrison at Braemar."

"So I've discovered."

"Look here, Rand, I still think we should have pounced on them when they were loading up with the stuff."

"I'm not taking any chances. If they were armed and had put up a fight, anything might have happened."

"But—"

"What was that?" Rand's words were merely a diversionary tactic to end the argument. Murray could not be persuaded that Dirk Gordon had more lives than a cat. In a general mêlée, some were bound to get away. Dirk Gordon would be one of them. Rand had a sixth sense about such things, and he knew well enough that to get to the boy, he must first deal with Daroch and MacGregor. Those two would do everything in their power to shield the lad. Rand knew something else. Dirk Gordon must not suspect that it was he, Rand, who was closing in on him, or he would run to earth before they could act.

Suddenly, they heard it, the soft tread of horses hooves and the creak of wheels laboring through the snow. "Gee-up, Nell!" MacGregor's voice and the crack of the reins on the pony's rump. Shadows moved and a dogcart came into view.

"Damn!" said Rand under his breath. MacGregor was all alone on the box. Then where the devil was Dirk Gordon?

Caitlin fastened the shutters against the gathering storm and stood for a moment staring vacantly about the small room. Coming to a decision, she quickly crawled into bed. The silence was broken by the reassuring sounds of Mrs. MacGregor's soft snores coming from the spare bed in the kitchen alcove, and the occasional rattle of the window panes as a wind got up. The candle by her bed flickered. From time to time, Bocain shifted her position on the hearth in the next room and whimpered in her sleep. The door had been left ajar so that the heat from the only fireplace in the house could circulate to all corners.

There was no necessity for her restlessness, Caitlin assured herself. Daroch was well able to take care of himself. The Randal was miles away in England and not due back for another week at least. In this inclement weather, only smugglers were likely to be abroad. Decent folk were snug in their beds. Daroch could slip into Strathcairn's boathouse and slip away again before anyone was the wiser.

She could not help swallowing every time she thought about it. How had it come to this? It was her own fault. It was she and no other who had proposed this particular little "welcome" for the English laird when he had first come into Deeside. Knowing that he was an avid fisherman, she had willfully used a poker to poke holes in the bottom of the decrepit rowing boat which was housed in Strathcairn's boathouse. She's had visions of the Randal being made to look ridiculous when he launched his boat in shallow water and promptly sank in it. Only, the Randal hadn't used his boat to go fishing; he knew nothing of the holes she had cleverly plastered over with a mixture of peat and mud. There was no saying when the boat would next be used, or who would take it out. She was certain of one thing, though. It could not be launched till spring, when the river Dee was in full spate. She had not foreseen the delay. Just thinking about it made her go cold all over. What she had done wasn't a prank. It wasn't harmless like the other little "surprises" they had engineered for the Randal. This was criminal.

For weeks past, her conscience had troubled her. Daroch was supposed to have taken care of the matter for her, but every time she had asked him about it, he had put her off with excuses. He could not see the urgency. Fine, she'd told him, she would take care of it herself. That did it.

Tonight, he'd promised her. Tonight, with Lord Randal absent and half of Deeside at home anticipating delivery of their supply of contraband whiskey for the New Year, he would make a detour to the boathouse. When he left, the boat would be a wreck, and anyone seeing it would know it.

Her thoughts meandered. Finally, she dozed. Coming to herself with a start, she pulled herself up. The candle by her bed was sputtering in its holder. She glanced at the timepiece and judged that Daroch would have left the boathouse long since. It was done. Apart from the trifling matter of having to find a way to recompense Lord Randal for one wrecked boat, she could sleep with a clear conscience.

Dousing the candle, she settled herself against the pillows. All was dark. All was quiet. The minutes ticked by and still sleep eluded her. Sighing, flinging off the covers, she slipped from her bed. She made no sound as she donned her boy's clothes. Bocain, as silent as her mistress, waited alertly for the command. Though she was sorely tempted, Caitlin gave her hound the order to stay. Bocain was too easily recognized. Anyone seeing them together would make the connection instantly.

There was no moon to light her way. The snow,

which was beginning to fall with increasing vigor, muffled the sound of her pony's hoofbeats on the winding track.

At the boathouse, she found Daroch's horse and gig secured to a tethering ring at the side of the stone building. A fine hoar frost covered the pony's back and haunches. At Caitlin's approach, the beast tossed her head and stamped her hooves restlessly.

"Easy, girl." Caitlin calmed the frightened pony by stroking her neck. Something was very far wrong. "Daroch?" she whispered and pushed into the pitch black interior.

Almost at once, she stumbled and fell full length over something on the floor. Daroch groaned and Caitlin scrambled to her knees. "Daroch?"

Another groan and Caitlin pulled off her gloves and groped with her bare hands. His face was icy cold and there was a bump the size of an egg on one temple. The stench of whiskey was overpowering. She clucked her tongue impatiently and felt his limbs for broken bones. Her hands came away sticky. Blood, she thought, and fought to control her alarm.

Rand absently reined in his horse, allowing his two grooms to precede him through the gates to Strathcairn. He was lost in thought. So much for his stratagem to flush out young Gordon. At every change-house where he had set men to watch, he had been given the same story. The whiskey had been delivered sure enough, but not by anyone who resembled the boy's description.

Murray had received the news with something approaching relief. When he and Rand had parted company at the crossroads to go their separate ways, his farewell had been cheery in the extreme. Now Rand cursed under his breath. What did his friend imagine he would do to the boy when he caught up with him? He wasn't a brute. He would not hurt the lad in any way that counted. He would simply terrify young Gordon out of his wits before sending him on his way. It was a damn sight less than he deserved.

Shrugging off his disappointment, Rand allowed his mind to fill with thoughts of Caitlin. The grim line of his mouth softened when he recalled their last few encounters before he had ostensibly departed for England. Caitlin with a chaperone in tow! He couldn't help chuckling at the picture. And Mrs. MacGregor was formidable. Unshakable was a better description. Wherever Caitlin led, Mrs. MacGregor followed. Poor Kate. He wondered if he would ever dare reveal his part in securing Mrs. MacGregor's services. Probably not.

He didn't know why he was amused. Mrs. MacGregor allowed him no more liberties with her charge than she allowed the next fellow. Since the night of the ball, he had not managed to exchange more than two words alone with Caitlin. That wasn't all Mrs. MacGregor's doing. Caitlin was wary of him. Very wary. The girl knew when she was being stalked.

She wasn't expecting him to offer marriage. Truth to tell, the thought that he was blithely about to attach himself to one particular female, and such a female, shocked even himself. He wasn't thinking of their widely disparate backgrounds, though he was aware that, by anyone's standards, he was marrying beneath himself. No, what shocked him was his strange obsession with the girl.

He couldn't understand her fascination. She wasn't beautiful. She wasn't accomplished. She was a far cry from the sort of woman he had anticipated he would marry when that sad day finally arrived, as it must for all men in his position. He had to have her. It was as simple as that.

He knew he was a knave, but the thought that Caitlin expected him to offer her the position of mistress tickled his fancy. Caitlin as a man's kept plaything? He would have laughed out loud if he had not been swamped with the familiar flood of tenderness. The girl was a study in suppression. Her femininity, her vibrancy, her sensuality, her passion—he would be the one to bring them forth because he was the only one who had discerned what smoldered beneath the surface.

Just thinking about it made his body go hard with wanting. He shifted in the saddle and laughed without humor. He'd wanted to get his hands on her since the day he had so innocently walked in upon her in her uncle's study. She could rouse his passions by the merest gesture. When he recalled the bevy of beautiful women he had taken to his bed in his time, it seemed inconceivable that he should be burning to possess this dowd of a girl whose only claim to distinction was a streak of stubbornness that would shame a mule.

It would be a pleasure beyond imagining to be her lord and master. There would be fireworks, of course. Caitlin was too independent for her own good. He would not permit her to challenge him the way she challenged her grandfather. Not that he intended to ride roughshod over her. If she was wise, she would yield to him. If not . . . he shrugged carelessly.

The next pleasurable image to enter his head was Caitlin's expression when she finally understood what he intended for her future. The poor girl would be overwhelmed. She would know luxury on a scale she could not imagine. He would give her anything a woman could possibly desire, as well as teach her to desire a few things of which, as yet, she had little knowledge or experience. The thought made him smile.

It was one of the grooms who alerted him. From their right, close to the river, came the sounds of horses whinnying. All three riders reined in, and strained for a better look. The darkness was unrelenting and the flurries of snow had increased to almost blizzard conditions. Though Rand knew he was looking toward the boathouse, there was little he could make out. Motioning his companions to dismount, he cautiously advanced.

Two shadowy figures came out of the small building. One of them, a slight youth, was staggering as he tried to support the weight of his companion.

"Daroch," urged Caitlin, and she rested for a moment, catching her breath. "Just a few more steps. You can do it if you try. Please, Daroch, else you will freeze to death before we can get help."

She heard the click and froze like a terrified rabbit. It sounded remarkably like the cocking of a pistol. She peered into the darkness. When she heard the voice, the Randal's voice, she sagged with relief. He would take care of Daroch. It was only as the words registered that she began to think of her own peril.

"Well met, young Gordon," he said, and leveled his pistol straight at her heart.

In the Randal's bookroom, Caitlin perched on the edge of her chair, her face turned toward the blaze in the grate. Her garments were sodden and she was waiting for one of the stable boys to return with a change of clothes. Under the watchful eye of the burly young

Highlander who had been set to guard her, she raised the glass in her hand to her lips and swallowed convulsively.

So far, her luck had held. On that dismal ride to Strathcairn, there had been little time or opportunity for the Randal to question her. His first act had been to relieve her of the dirk concealed in her hose.

"What do you do, buy these things by the gross?" he had asked humorously, before tossing it into the river.

After that, his attention had focused on Daroch. She closed her eyes, thinking she would be eternally grateful for his presence of mind. He had stanched the bleeding on Daroch's leg, then wrapped him in his own plaid before laying him gently on the back of the cart.

At length, he had said, "It's an ugly wound but hardly fatal. I'd say that the laird o' Daroch is either suffering from concussion or is as drunk as a lord. How did it happen?"

His matter-of-fact tone relieved the worst of her fears. She deliberately mumbled her reply into the folds of her plaid. "He said something about tangling with a scythe, then falling and bumping his head on the edge of your boat."

His reply was swallowed by the wind, and there was no more conversation after that exchange. But there would be. She knew that as well as she knew her own name.

A shiver ran over her, and she took another small sip from her glass. The whiskey burned a path down her throat, but it made no appreciable difference to the cold which clutched at her heart. Her sins had finally caught up with her, and the reckoning would be severe if not downright painful.

The guard spoke to her. "Ye heard Lord Randal, lad. Get that whiskey down ye afore ye faint wi' the cold."

It was a nice voice, a kind voice, decided Caitlin, despite the fact that the young man was pointing a pistol at her. But that was Lord Randal's doing. His man was under orders to shoot her if she as much as blinked the wrong way. Meanwhile, Lord Randal and one of his lackeys were attending to Daroch's injuries in one of the upstairs bedchambers. There was no question of sending for Dr. Innes. They were well and truly snowed in.

A tap on the door momentarily diverted her guard's attention, and Caitlin took the opportunity to adjust her bonnet and plaid. She didn't know how long she could keep up the pretense that she was a boy, but she aimed to try until she was at her last prayers.

The guard returned with a set of boy's clothes. "Change, an' be quick about it," he said.

"Change?" She dared not ask him to turn his back. Her lower lip trembled.

Rab MacNair, the guard, shook his head. "Laddie, ye have not got a thing I have not seen afore now."

Caitlin did not doubt it. "I have to use the privy." It was no lie.

"What?"

"I have to go." To add weight to her words, she did a little jig where she sat and gazed up at him with huge, pleading eyes.

Rab felt like the veriest ogre. The lad looked to be no more than thirteen or fourteen, the same age as his own youngest brother. He could not see the necessity for these extreme measures, nor why Lord Randal should be so implacable. It was natural for young lads to get up to some mischief or other. In his experience, a good kick on the rear end or a cuff on the ear soon cured them of their high spirits. He could hardly believe that he was pointing a pistol at a poor, wee lad who had the look of a drowned puppy. He did not know what his own mother would say if she could see him now. If he knew her, she would cuff *him* on the ear. Still, it was not his mother who paid his wages.

Adopting his master's stern manner, he said, "Try anything and I'm warnin' ye, lad, I'll shoot." Waving his pistol, he motioned Caitlin to the door.

He used the kitchen lantern to light their way. Once outside, he indicated a clump of holly bushes. "Over there," he said.

Caitlin's jaw sagged. She wrung her hands. "But I want to use the privy," she cried out, torn between panic and acute embarrassment. She really had to go.

Rab sighed. The snow had obliterated the well-trodden path. He considered for a moment, then nodded his acquiescence.

Having availed herself of the facilities, Caitlin paused with a hand on the door, debating her next move. Daroch, she decided, could not be in better hands. For his welfare, she had no qualms. The same could not be said for herself. She had to get away before Strathcairn was completely cut off from the outside world. Her absence, once it became known, would cause a furor. Then there would be the devil to pay.

She heard the Randal's voice raised in anger. "Damn and blast you, MacNair. I thought I told you not to let the boy out of your sight?"

From the muffled sound of her guard's reply, she guessed he had turned to face the house. It was now or never.

She came rocketing out of the privy like an arrow released from a crossbow. With one lucky kick, she sent the lantern flying and used her momentum to do the same to MacNair. Darkness. She rolled to her side and came to her knees.

"Hold your fire!" The Randal's voice. Then, "Let him go. If he knows what's good for him, he'll turn back. Neither man nor beast can survive in this storm."

Holding her breath, she waited, straining her ears for the sound of footsteps. When she heard the door slam, she let out a panicked whimper. That one small sound was her undoing.

He came at her like a jungle cat bringing down its prey. The breath was knocked out of her. For long moments, she lay facedown in the snow, gasping for air. When powerful masculine hands flipped her over on her back, she cried out in fright.

"Who are you?"

Oh God, her hair had come loose, and he was ploughing his long fingers through it, separating each strand. He loomed over her like a shadow of doom. She had run her course.

"Rand," she cried softly, intuitively using the familiar name to soften the anger in him. "Rand, don't hurt me. I can explain."

At the sound of her voice, he stilled. When his fingers closed around her throat, she stopped breathing altogether. Hooking one hand into the collar of her shirt, he split it from throat to waist, separating the edges. Against her bared breasts, she could feel each snowflake as it melted against the heat of her skin. His hands touched her intimately, and she kicked out wildly, bucking against the press of his weight.

"Rand! No!"

His breathing was loud in her ears. "So it is you!"

186

The feral snarl that erupted from his throat had her flinching away in terror.

She was yanked to her feet and swung into his arms. The wind caught at her hair, fanning it about them both in a fragrant veil. She burrowed into him like a child seeking the protection of an older brother. The gesture wasn't a ploy. It wasn't a trick. It was something that came from the deepest reaches of her psyche, something she barely understood herself. She was helpless against his superior strength. That mute appeal failed to soften him.

With each step he took her fear increased. He was in the grip of some powerful emotion. She did not know what had provoked it, but she knew that it went far beyond her transgressions as Dirk Gordon.

When they entered the house, she turned her face into his throat, shamed that his servants should see her like this and recognize her. He barked out orders as he mounted the stairs.

"MacNair, lock up the house and get to your bed. Thompson, you are to relieve Graham at six o'clock. Forrest, if and when the storm abates, fetch the physician."

By the time they had entered what Caitlin grasped at once must be the Randal's bedchamber, her teeth were chattering and her skin was clammy. In her overwrought state, the sound of the heavy oak door as he kicked it shut made her think of the massive granite slabs that were used to protect graves from the deprivations of grave robbers.

When he dumped her in the center of the capacious fourposter, she made a vain effort to draw the edges of her shirt together. Her plaid was gone, but she could not remember what had happened to it. She had to force herself to look at him.

He leaned against the bedpost, arms folded, his heavy-lidded eyes roaming over her at will. In the warm glow of the candlelight, his blond hair glistened like gold. His features were carved as from marble. When his breathing became labored and audible, her eyes flared with feminine knowledge.

"Rand." It was a struggle to keep the fear from her voice. "If you touch me, I shall scream, and your servants will come bursting through that door."

He smiled at her naiveté. "You are wrong, lass. There is no one to hear you in this wing of the house, except perhaps your lover and the servant who is watching over him. And since Daroch is sleeping like a baby, and Graham is as deaf as a doorpost, your threat does not carry much force."

And then he calmly began to remove his neckcloth.

Chapter Twelve

Her curtain of dark hair fell riotously to her knees. Her skin was as white and unblemished as the snowflakes dashing in a wild dervish against the window panes. Through the torn edges of her shirt, the ripe globes of her breasts rose high and free, their dark crests begging for the touch of a man's lips. Her innocent eyes were shimmering like a Highland mist, gray, mysterious, and infinitely dangerous.

Oh no, she wasn't beautiful, thought Rand with uncharacteristic savagery, despising his need, the ache in his loins, her damnable allure. She might have been a priestess to the ancient cult of Bacchus. She was sensuality personified, and she was any man's for the taking. She must be. No decent woman would dress herself in boy's clothes and cavort about the countryside in the dead of night with only males for companions.

He was seeing things clearly for the first time—the freedoms she enjoyed, the isolated cottage, the lack of a chaperone, the dowd's disguise. Was it only at the witching hour that she turned into a wanton? He remembered something else—the girl his cousin, David, had

189

spirited away on Rand's last night of furlough before he had rejoined his regiment. He should have known it was she. Even then, she had cast her spell on him.

A red haze swam before his eyes. Bitterness welled up inside him. This was the woman he had hoped to make his wife? She had made a royal fool of him. Hell, he had made a royal fool of himself.

He threw his neckcloth to the floor and slipped out of his dark coat, letting it fall in a heap. Without haste, he started on the buttons of his shirt.

"It was you," he said. "You were the girl David rescued on my last night in Deeside?"

His words drove away the absurd suspicion that had begun to take root in her mind. He didn't sound like a man on the pont of ravishing a virgin. His voice was coldly polite, his expression haughty. He looked remarkably in control of himself.

Taking comfort from that thought, she concentrated on exonerating herself for a course of conduct which, by anyone's lights, must appear inexcusable. She nodded.

"Were you and David lovers? Had you arranged to meet when I was . . . otherwise occupied?"

"Don't be absurd," she gasped, outrage momentarily putting her fear to flight. "I was delivering whiskey to your empty boathouse."

One eyebrow quirked. "And you say that I am absurd?" He shook his head. "Are you saying you were involved in smuggling even then?" When she nodded, his eyes narrowed on her. "Yet, as far as I recall, you were not passing yourself off as a boy."

"You may believe that after so close an escape I learned my lesson. From that night on, when I was out smuggling, I adopted the role of a boy."

"What were you doing in the boathouse tonight?"

"We were trying to right . . ." Her voice was shaking so badly, she could hardly get the words out. Gathering the shreds of her control, she started over. "When you first came into Deeside, we set snares for you. You must know it by now."

"I do. Whiskey that was laced with turpentine; bells that summoned servants to the wrong chambers; candles made of soap; locked doors with no keys to them, and so on. Oh yes, I was well aware that a horde of mischievous children had been let loose in my house. Are you saying there was more?"

She nodded eagerly. "Yes. That's just it, you see. We assumed that you would go out in your boat. It's what you always do within a day or two of your arrival."

"And?"

Unable to hold that piercing stare, she raised her eyes to a point over his shoulder. "And so we . . . that is, I poked holes in the bottom of your boat but plastered them over so that you wouldn't know it until it was too late."

"I see. You meant me to drown. I wouldn't have, you know. I am an excellent swimmer."

"That's not it! How can you think such a thing? I only meant you to look ridiculous when your boat sank. It was more of a joke. There was no danger. The river was at its lowest ebb. But you didn't take your boat out. I had to do something, don't you see? In spring, when the snows start to melt in the hills and mountains, the river will be in full spate."

"Are you saying that tonight you and Daroch went to the boathouse to fix my boat?" He sounded faintly bored.

"In a manner of speaking," she said miserably.

191

"Go on. I'm listening."

"Daroch demolished it so that anyone would see at a glance that it could not float in the water. I'll pay for the damage," she added eagerly, hoping the offer would soften him.

"Oh, you'll pay, one way or another." He gave her a hard smile. "And that little episode at the quarry? How do you explain that?"

She coughed, then visibly swallowed. "There was a slope of loose scree where I jumped. I knew you were hard on my heels. You would have taken a tumble, but nothing very serious would have happened to you."

"And The Fair Maid? When you threw your dagger at me?"

"I was aiming for the bedpost, I swear it." Oh God, with every word, she could feel herself sinking deeper into a quagmire of her own making.

"And later, when I almost drowned trying to save you?"

She looked at him for a long moment with huge imploring eyes before she whispered brokenly, "Would you believe I was on the point of giving myself up when your friends dragged you from the water?"

"I would not. In fact, I think you were waiting to see the results of your handiwork."

"What does that mean?"

"You would not have lifted a finger to save me."

Her head jerked as though he had slapped her. Her nostrils were quivering. "What possible reason could I have for wishing you dead?"

"The feud. Revenge for everything your grandfather lost. Envy. Pride. Because I'm English. How the hell should I know?" He didn't really believe what he was saying. The thought that he might be softening enraged

192

him, and he lashed out at the bedpost in a fury of passion. She could spin her tissue of lies so skillfully that a man was tangled up in her gossamer threads before he could perceive he was well and truly caught.

Though she was far from panicking, she had a very healthy respect for the angry man who loomed over her. Her words tripped over each other in her haste to get them out. "You must believe me! The feud . . . none of that means anything to me, to any of us. It was your unfeeling treatment of your tenants! I don't know what we hoped to gain. We were warning you off, I suppose. But that is a far cry from wishing for your death. And later, when you restrained your factor's worst excesses and allowed your tenants to drift back to their crofts, we gave up any idea of punishing you. Oh God, why won't you believe me?"

He did believe her, but it hardly seemed to matter to him.

Misunderstanding his silence, she cried out, "Why should Daroch and I go to the boathouse tonight if not for the reason I've already given you? We did it for you! Can't you see that?"

At last they had come to the crux of the matter. Rand's eyes were very blue, very bright as they locked on hers. Behind that daunting stare he was reflecting that he had engineered things so that she was forced to accept Mrs. MacGregor as her chaperone. That must have been a difficult obstacle to circumvent. Where else could she tryst with her lover now that her cottage was out of bounds? His boathouse was deserted and conveniently located between Daroch's and Glenshiel's estates. Daroch was her lover. Hadn't he always suspected that there was something between them?

This, more than anything, was what had unleashed

the storm that raged inside him. Jealousy, pure and unadulterated. While she dangled him on a string, the young pup in the next chamber, whom he had doctored so solicitously only an hour before, had been keeping her bed warm. He, Rand, had misjudged her and she had connived at keep him in error. That look of wide-eyed innocence, the trembling whenever he touched her, the half-hearted refusals, those untutored embraces—all of it was a sham. He had thought to control her, and all the time, she had been controlling *him*.

His eyes flared in sudden comprehension. "Did you think I would offer you marriage?" he asked incredulously. "Was that your game? Is that why you led me on?" Something dark and ugly moved deep inside him, some hidden facet of his character, which he would examine later, goaded him to add, "Can you see yourself fitting into my world? Good God, girl, don't you think I know what I owe my name and family?"

"Marriage to you never once entered my head," she snapped.

His words had touched more than her vanity, more than her pride. He had struck at the deepest well of her femininity. Though he had said nothing that she had not said to herself a hundred times over, on his lips, the words had all the force of poisoned darts. She felt naked, defenseless, as transparent as crystal, with nowhere to hide herself.

Like a wounded animal seeking escape from a trap, she lashed out at him. "Don't you think I know what I owe myself? Your world holds no attraction for me. If I did think of marriage to you, it was only to pity the poor woman who would be your wife. I remember the orgies of former years. And I was there when you were bedding Nellie, as you must know."

The vivid recollection of that scene stirred a cauldron of emotions she ruthlessly pushed away. Tossing her mane of hair over her shoulders, unconscious of the tantalizing glimpse of exposed breast that peeked through the edges of her torn shirt, she went on scathingly, "I never led you on. If anything led you on, it was your own colossal conceit."

Her pride, her contempt, her outright denial that he had the power to affect her made him writhe inside. His eyes raked her coldly. Finally, with studied insolence, he returned to the business of unbuttoning his shirt. "You led me on in the only way that counts between a man and woman. When I touched you, you melted for me. Deny it if you dare."

It was his eyes that gave her pause, heated and intense and glittering with an implacable resolve. Her own anger melted away, and she shivered, whether with cold or apprehension she could not say. She sensed that the events of the night had knocked him off balance. What she could not accept, refused to accept, was where it seemed to be leading. Iain, Lord Randal, had never forced a woman in his life. There was no need. By all accounts, the Randal had only to crook his little finger and he had his pick of any woman he wanted. And he didn't want her. He had made that insultingly obvious. Then what was he up to?

If he was trying to frighten her, he was succeeding remarkably well. Rubbing her forehead with thumb and forefinger, she said crossly, "I'm horribly cold. My teeth are chattering. My head aches. I'm still waiting for that change of clothes you promised me. I think I'm coming down with a bad cause of pneumonia. Since I am a guest in your house, the least you can do is see to my comfort."

He was laughing, actually laughing at her. And his amusement was genuine, she could have sworn it.

"Good try," he said, "but it won't work. You knew it would come to this. You gave me to believe that I could have you. Do you want to know something amusing?" Suddenly, he did not sound amused. A distinct edge had crept into his voice. "You spoiled me for other women. Oh yes, I mean that quite sincerely. Nellie, since you brought her up, had as much effect on me as a dead fish. For some obscure reason, I want only . . . you."

He pulled off his shirt and flung it into a corner. Caitlin's tongue clove to the roof of her mouth and her eyes widened at the sight of broad shoulders, arms knotted with muscles, the thatch of coarse reddish gold hair across his powerful chest. The thread of a long silvery scar ran from one flat nipple to disappear below the waistband of his trousers. He was lean and hard, a prime specimen of masculinity.

He wanted her. He really wanted her. The thought curled inside her and gradually expanded, bubbling up, intoxicating her senses, warming her blood. He wanted her and she could not deny that she wanted him.

There was no question that she would yield to temptation. She wasn't thinking of right and wrong, of consequences.

When he bent to her, she fell back on her elbows. His hands were pressed into the mattress on either side of her shoulders, supporting his weight, preventing her from slipping away. She closed her eyes when his head descended.

His warm breath touched her cheek, his lips brushing over her skin. One kiss, she promised herself, only one kiss to last a lifetime, then she would put a stop to it. Then she would play the trump card she had been holding in reserve, and he would let her go. She didn't know why tears suddenly came to her eyes.

"Mo gaol orist," she said. "What time is it?"

He laughed softly. "No more talking. No more prevarication. It's time to pay the piper."

His lips took hers in a ravishment of gentleness, as though he were testing the waters. No other parts of their bodies were touching. He was waiting for something. His restraint wasn't what she wanted, needed. If she was going to allow herself only one kiss, she wanted more than this passionless embrace. Dropping her head back she parted her lips. He followed her, accepting the implicit invitation. His tongue pressed between her teeth. When she gave him access to what he wanted, he groaned and moved in closer.

One arm encircled her shoulders, pulling her hard against his chest, flattening her breasts, bare skin to bare skin. She spread her hands against the tensed muscles in his arms, and he immediately relaxed his hold. When his hand curved around one lush breast, his thumb grazing the distended nipple to a painful arousal, Caitlin tore her lips away. "This has gone far enough," she got out thickly.

He didn't give her time to think, to say the words to stop him. "No," he murmured, and kissed her again. This time, he held nothing back. He was ravenous, starving for her, his senses suffering from the deprivation of several months of self-imposed celibacy. He couldn't turn back now. His kiss implored her not to put him to the test.

He savored her mouth, nipping, licking, penetrating with his tongue until her neck lolled against the crook of his arm, giving him access to her throat and breasts. Her nipples were stiff and swollen, peeking up at him like succulent berries. He milked them with his mouth, working first one then the other with his teeth and tongue to drive her pleasure higher. She whimpered and brought up one knee to ease the ache he had started in her loins.

Rand recognized that involuntary feminine gesture and the blood began to pound in his ears. His hand slipped inside her damp shirt, divesting her of it and her jacket in one smooth movement. With his lips pressed fiercely to hers to stifle any belated protests, he turned to her trews. Shoving them down over her slender hips, lifting her effortlessly, he tugged them over her ankles and dropped them on the floor.

Caitlin shuddered, lost in a realm where no logic existed. Pleasure such as she had never known seemed to burn away every conscious thought, every feminine inhibition. He rained wild kisses over her face and throat, then worked on the aching peaks of her breasts as he had done before, nipping, licking, feeding on her engorged flesh.

When he was sure he had reduced her to mindlessness, he pulled back to look at her. He watched his hand caress the smooth line of her shapely legs, watched her belly quiver as his fingers splayed out and slid higher to encompass the creamy globe of one breast.

"Look at me," he commanded.

When she raised those fans of dark lashes and gazed up at him with desire-drenched eyes, he smiled knowingly and allowed his fingers to dip to the dark nest between her legs. His fingers slid over her, separating, probing, barely penetrating. She moaned and lifted her hips slightly, offering herself to him.

Mine, he exulted, and he knew that he would never give her up to any man. In spite of everything, he still wanted her. But how different were his feelings now. Before he had found her with Daroch, he had wanted to cherish her, protect her, shield her. Jealousy had unleashed another side of his nature, something dark and primitive that he had not previously known existed. He had never felt this way about any woman.

His fingers pressed into the folds of her femininity, discovering her wetness. She was ready for him, and this excited him more. She whimpered, and made to draw her legs away but he followed, stilling her movements with the press of one powerful leg. He knew that he would explode if he didn't release himself from the confines of his trousers. His hands went to the buttons of his waistband and deftly undid them.

The press of that hard, silky shaft against her thigh jerked Caitlin from the sensual fog that clouded her mind. Her eyes slid to the swollen sex that sprang up from the bush of fiery curls at his groin, and her legs tightened against him.

"No, you can't—we mustn't," she whispered.

Rand groaned. She had turned skittish on him at the worst possible moment. He had to have her. He ached to spread her glorious legs and bury himself deep inside her. He came up on his knees and reached for her.

"What is it, love?" he asked hoarsely. He could hardly breathe, let alone talk, but he knew he had to soothe her fears. "I'm a big man. I know it. But your body will soon adapt to the fit of mine. There's nothing to fear."

She made no move to stop him when he carefully insinuated one hand between her legs. The slick heat at the junction of her thighs drew him like a bee to nectar.

Her sweet scent inflamed him past bearing. His chest was rising and falling; his breathing was harsh. He groaned when his fingers found her.

"Rand, I—" She cried out, but his kiss washed the words from her tongue, and his fingers worked her rhythmically, robbing her of coherent thought.

He eased her legs apart and knelt between them. She was so tight, so small, he knew he was going to hurt her. "I won't hurt you," he lied, soothing her in the age-old way of a man with his mate. "And if my seed takes, I won't abandon you. I'll take care of everything."

She reacted to the threat of pregnancy as if he had immersed her in a bath of icy cold water. She gasped and spluttered and slapped his hands away. She was so humiliated, she wanted to burst into tears.

Sexual frustration was beginning to work on his temper. "Now what have I done?" he demanded roughly.

In that moment, she truly hated him. He knew nothing of the slurs and slanders she had been made to endure. The blot of illegitimacy had followed her all her life. That he would father a bastard child on her without a ripple of conscience! That he would wish such a thing on an innocent child! She would rather die an old maid or enter a nunnery.

His hands were feathering over her shoulders and arms, gentling her, easing her misgivings. If she did not act soon, she would become a mindless quivering jelly.

Praying that she had not left it till too late, she frantically searched her mind for some way of averting what seemed inevitable. He kissed her again, and in sheer desperation, she blurted out the same blatant untruth she had once offered Daroch.

"Didn't anyone tell you? Surely you must have

guessed? You are my brother. I am your sister. We have the same father."

Her outburst stunned him. Rand sat back on his heels, and Caitlin quickly retreated to the headboard. Hugging her knees, using her hair to cloak her nakedness, she stared at him wide-eyed.

"You're lying," he said at last, and reached for her.

She let out a terrified yelp. Grabbing for one of the pillows, she slapped it into his outstretched arms. "It's the truth, and if you would only think about it, you would see it too."

He was shaking his head, smiling. "Caitlin, you wretch! I know my father. If what you say is true, he would have made provision for you in his will, and as his executor, I would have known it."

She looked away. She didn't want to deceive him, but he wasn't ready to give up yet.

"I know nothing of that!" she said. "I'm only relating to you what I've managed to piece together." She was practically sitting on top of the headboard. One of his long hands shackled her ankle. "You are my half brother. At least have the decency to listen to what I have to say."

"Hell and damnation!" He let her go and rolled to his feet. She had found the perfect way to kill his desire. He didn't believe her, but she had planted a small seed of doubt.

He adjusted his trousers and stalked to the large mahogany wardrobe between the long windows, in which he rummaged for his dressing gown. Having donned it over his trousers, he returned to the bed. In his hands, he held a white linen shirt. "Cover yourself," he said brusquely, and tossed the garment to her.

Keeping a watchful eye on him, she quickly donned

her makeshift nightgown and slipped beneath the covers. Rand sat at the edge of the bed.

"Well? I'm listening. What did you manage to piece together?"

For a moment her mind refused to function. When he absently began running the backs of his fingers along her arms, she unglued her tongue. "Your father was in the habit of coming into Deeside every year for the hunting season. Your mother rarely accompanied him."

"I'm aware of that. But he did not come alone. He kept open house. Many of his friends came to Strathcairn for the hunting and fishing. The man who fathered you might just as easily be one of them."

She groped in her mind for a plausible explanation. "I've thought of that. But my mother must have had a pressing reason to keep the identity of my father a secret. Don't forget, the feud between our two families really counted for something in those days. My grandfather would have killed my mother if he had thought a Randal of Strathcairn had dishonored her."

His expression was thunderous. "My father was a faithful husband. He loved my mother. In his younger days, he may have been a bit of a rake—wild. He would have been the first to admit it. But from the moment he set eyes on my mother, he became a reformed character. He never looked at another woman."

"Pooh! That's what they all say!"

They glared at each other. Rand's frown gradually dissolved, and he threw back his head and laughed. "You conniving little witch!" he exclaimed. "You are doing this on purpose, trying to confuse me. Well, it won't work. If you had truly believed I was your brother, you would not have responded to me the way you did."

She had the grace to look shamefaced. Her voice was so small as to be almost inaudible. "I didn't want to. I couldn't seem to help myself."

He cursed long and fluently, but made no move to touch her. When he sprang to his feet, she cowered beneath the covers. "Damn you!" he said. "Damn you, Caitlin!"

With the covers up to her chin, she watched him warily as he strode to the fireplace. He used the iron tongs to bank up the fire with great lumps of coal. He was mumbling under his breath.

"What are you doing?" she asked cautiously.

He gave her a long look over his shoulder. "What does it look like? Since you are a guest in my house, I am seeing to your comfort."

"Oh." She'd won. Then why did she feel so miserable?

"Is there anything else I can get you. Something to eat? Something to drink?" One hand was on the doorknob.

She shook her head. She couldn't believe how easy it had been to put him off.

Interpreting that look correctly, he said, "I don't accept what you have just told me, but now is not the time to enter into a debate. After a good night's rest, we shall both be in a better frame of mind to discuss it." He opened the door.

"Rand?"

"Mmm?"

"Promise me you won't say anything to anyone about what I've just told you. If my grandfather ever got to hear about it, there's no saying what he would do."

203

"You have my promise—oh, not for your grandfather's sake but for my mother's. Do you suppose I want something like this to get back to her?"

For a moment her expression was stricken. He nodded. "Yes, you hadn't thought of that, had you, when you sprang your little surprise on me? Caitlin, if this is a blatant untruth—"

"I told you, it's what I've pieced together. I can't swear to it on a stack of Bibles." Again, he made to quit the room. "Rand?"

"What is it now?"

"You . . . you wouldn't have forced yourself on me, would you?"

He flushed scarlet and stuttered before he got out, "Don't be a simpleton! If you had told me 'no' and could have made me believe it, it would have gone no further than a kiss."

When the door closed behind him, there was a lump in her throat. Though her ruse had succeeded, she felt no sense of relief, no sense of triumph. She grieved as if she had suffered an unspeakable loss. It was finally over. She could see that now. The Randal wanted her, but not enough to marry her.

Sighing, she turned her head into the pillow. *Did you think I would offer you marriage? Can you see yourself fitting into my world? Good God, girl, don't you think I know what I owe my name and family?* His words pounded inside her head, over and over, like a blacksmith's hammer striking the anvil.

He would keep his distance now. It was for the best. Then that secret part of her which never obeyed the commands of her brain would cease entertaining flights of fancy respecting the high and mighty chief of clan Randal.

For a long while, she dwelled on Rand's words and the insulting way he had flung them at her. By degrees, self-pity gave way to a slow simmering anger. By the time she pounded her pillow and composed herself for sleep, she was thinking, Marry him? I'd as lief marry a toad!

On the other side of the door, Rand hesitated, torn between storming back into the room to have it out with her, and finding a quiet place where he could reflect in private. The minx had given him a lot to think about.

He delayed for no more than a moment or two. The corridors and great hall were cold, drafty places at the best of times. He looked in on Daroch, but did not linger when he ascertained that the youth was sleeping peacefully. He debated about rousing one of the servants to prepare a bedchamber for him. Thinking better of it, he descended the stairs and made for his bookroom.

Flinging himself down in the leather armchair flanking the grate, the one Caitlin had occupied earlier, he stretched out his long legs and gazed morosely into the embers of the fire. In a long night where one jolt had followed hard upon another, that last disclosure had been the most astonishing one of all.

He and Caitlin brother and sister? The idea was preposterous. Then why would she throw such an obvious fiction in his teeth? The more he thought about it, the less he liked the answers that came to him. And how to disprove it? That was the rub.

He awakened to such a thundering that he first thought he was leading his Scots Greys in a cavalry charge. Blinking back sleep, rolling his neck to ease his cramped muscles, he pulled himself out of the armchair. Light streamed through the windows. The storm had subsided and the fresh fall of snow reflected the pale wintry sunshine to a crystal brilliancy.

The thundering came again. Yawning, stretching, Rand went to investigate. When he reached the great hall, two manservants were hauling back the bolts on the massive front doors. His housekeeper, Mrs. Fleming, was standing well back, wringing her hands.

The doors opened. There was a heart-stopping roar; then a great beast of prey came bounding over the threshold, followed by a crush of angry Highlanders brandishing clubs and knives. Mrs. Fleming shrieked and fell to her knees in mortal terror. The deerhound checked her momentum at this odd behavior then continued on, hurling herself at her quarry.

"Down, Bocain!" Rand's commanding tone had the desired effect. Caitlin's deerhound sank to her haunches. Tongue lolling, she gazed adoringly up at him.

The great hall was filling up with men, most of whom were Glenshiel's gillies or tenants. Rand's few retainers were roughly herded into a corner, where three Highlanders stood guard over them with raised clubs. Finally, the laird of Glenshiel himself appeared, leaning heavily on his walking staff. His eyes were shooting sparks, and his lips were pulled back in a bestial snarl as he advanced on Rand.

When they were toe to toe, he hissed, "My granddaughter is missing. Caitlin's hound has led us to your door. Where is she?"

Feeling the disadvantage of his position, Rand tightened the belt on his robe. "You need not take that tone of voice with me. When I explain the circumstances that brought your granddaughter to my house, you will, one hopes, give her the beating she so richly deserves."

"I don't doubt it. Will that be before or after I put a ball in your black heart, yer lordship?"

"What is it? Why all the ruckus?"

All eyes turned to the gallery. Daroch, in borrowed nightshirt, with Gordon plaid draped negligently over his shoulders, leaned against one of the oak columns. There was a dazed look about him.

Glenshiel's face was an ugly shade of purple. He wheezed, he spluttered, then struggled to draw air through his teeth and into his lungs. "What kind o' orgy have I stumbled upon?" he whispered; then he roared, "Caitlin? Where are ye, lass?" And to Bocain, "Find her!"

The housekeeper, still on her knees, broke into a fit of uncontrollable weeping. "Och the poor lass, the poor wee lass. And to think I slept through it all."

"Oh, for God's sake!" Rand pressed one hand to his eyes and fought to control his temper.

The deerhound lurched to her feet and loped away. At Glenshiel's signal, two of his men went after her, drawing wicked-looking dirks from their hose as they stealthily climbed the stairs. Some minutes were to pass before they reappeared.

"We found her," shouted one from the gallery. "She was in one o' the bedchambers. Dinna fash yersel', Glenshiel. The lass is no the worse for wear."

At the ill-chosen expression, Glenshiel winced.

Seeing that reaction, the Highlander on the gallery hastened to reassure his laird. "Twa beds hae been slept

207

in, but there's nae doubt about who's bed the lass shared. The Randal is yer man."

Glenshiel's hand whitened around his staff. His teeth ground together. Glaring at Rand, he said, "It would seem, yer lordship, that ye are goin' to a weddin'!"

Chapter Thirteen

It was to be a grand wedding in the traditional Highland manner. Though it was a press-gang affair and everyone knew it, there was no unseemly haste. There was no need. No one was going anywhere. From the Braes o' Mar to the village of Ballater, the glen was completely cut off by the storm, a little world unto itself.

The banns were published in church for the specified three weeks before the event. As the whole parish was invited to witness the ceremony, and the church could hold only a fraction of that number, Glenshiel graciously decided that his granddaughter should be married from his own house.

By and large, no one reproached the principal characters or even hinted at misconduct. Those in the know, with a sly wink and nod, rather congratulated Glenshiel in stealing a march on the unsuspecting *sassenach*. The wily old fox had cleverly snagged a matrimonial prize for his granddaughter, a girl whose virtue was unquestionable. And he'd done more. The Randal clan, soon to be reunited, must once again be in ascendancy in Deeside. The regrettable English strain could only benefit from a fresh infusion of vigorous Scottish blood. The future looked rosy indeed. Rand, hearing the good-natured raillery, took it in good part. Caitlin shrank into herself.

In the weeks preceding the wedding, there wasn't a female in the parish who was idle. The ladies outdid themselves in preparing a banquet for the *ceilidh* which was to follow the religious service. At Glenshiel House, the pace was frenetic. Charlotte Randal rose to the occasion with commendable zeal. She deployed her army of servants like a general at the commencement of a major battle. Rugs and drapes were beaten and hung on washing lines to air; every wooden floor was scoured with sand, then scrupulously swept. Chandeliers were let down and dismantled, then washed and carefully reassembled. Silver, crystal, porcelain—everything was cleaned and minutely examined before being put away. Even the stags' heads in the great hall came in for their fair share of attention. A detail of maids, especially employed for the grand occasion, set to work. With hard-bristled brushes, they routed years of ingrained grime and dirt till the stags' coats shone like satin.

In the midst of so much activity and excitement, Caitlin forced herself to put a good face on things. Not surprisingly, since the night she had been discovered in Rand's house, she had taken up residence with her grandfather. She wasn't a prisoner exactly, but she was well guarded. Even a visit to the outside privy required the presence of a chaperone. As for Rand, she saw him only at church services, when they were hedged about by hordes of people. She was coming to think that he was deliberately avoiding her. What Caitlin could not guess was that Glenshiel, distrusting his granddaughter's frame of mind, had warned Rand off. The days for courting were over, he told him. There would be no private little *tête à tête* with his granddaughter until the ink had dried on their marriage lines.

As the days passed and the wedding preparations went forward without interruption, Caitlin's mind became more and more frozen. She didn't know what to think, what to expect. The Randal had promised to take care of everything. He didn't want to marry her. He had told her so in no uncertain terms. She would not fit into his world, he had told her. He was highly conscious of what he owed his name and family. His words, the insulting way he had uttered them, were burned into her brain. At every hour, she expected to be summoned to her grandfather's presence to be informed that the Randal had cried off. It was what she wanted to hear. Somehow, she would find the strength to weather the mortification and ensuing scandal. What she did not think she could bear, what her pride could not endure, was marriage to a man whose hand had been forced by circumstances.

For most of the time, she seemed to be weighed down by an immense lassitude. She couldn't think for herself. To make decisions even about trivial things was beyond her. It was her aunt who decided that her grandmother's wedding gown would do very well for Caitlin if it was made over into something simpler, in the current mode. When Fiona suggested that Caitlin's long hair should be dressed *à la grecque*, Caitlin readily agreed. Only her grandfather's timely intervention at the urging of the maid prevented Fiona from wielding the shears. Caitlin could not have cared less. Mrs. MacGregor supplied the wedding bouquets, an assortment of dried wildflowers with the traditional white heather for luck. Whatever was suggested found favor with Caitlin.

As the wedding day drew nearer, everything became

211

more unreal to her. At the bridal tea, when the ladies came to view the wedding presents, she presided with grace and charm but afterward could never remember who had spoken to her or what had been said. She dutifully stitched her bridal clothes till her eyes teared and her fingers curled with cramp, but she was hardly conscious of what she made. On the day of her wedding, when she rose from her bed, she moved as a sleepwalker.

The piper on the gallery gave a mighty blast on his pipes. A moment later the jaunty strains of a Highland air rang out and Caitlin slowly descended the staircase on her grandfather's arm. In their wake came the bridesmaid, Fiona, in pale peach organdy. In one hand, she clasped her posy of dried flowers, with the other, she carefully steered the train of the bride's gown.

Rand, resplendent in full Highland dress, watched their progress as if mesmerized. He could not seem to find his breath. The lustrous white taffeta was a dramatic contrast to his bride's dark coloring. It also did something wonderful for her figure. Above the low, square-cut bodice, the swell of her full breasts rose, soft and womanly. Her skin was translucent, her features as fine and as lovely as an Egyptian cameo. Her delicately rose-tinted lips were parted as though she, too, had difficulty drawing her next breath. Her hair, caught back in a silver net, gave her the look of a medieval madonna. He willed her to raise her eyes and look at him. One look into that carefully averted gaze, and he would know his fate.

If she hadn't wanted the marriage to take place, she should have made her protests long before now. She'd had all of three weeks. In that time, she had been as cloistered as a nun. He couldn't get near her, not until they were to be joined in holy wedlock. He didn't know what she was thinking. It still wasn't too late to call the whole thing off. She could feign sickness, or simply refuse to go through with it. If all else failed, she could tell that cock-and-bull story which she'd told him.

He couldn't accept that she was his sister. He would have known it. And if she were, he would not have been plagued these last three weeks by the agony of unsated desire. During the daylight hours, he'd flung himself into a frenzy of activity, trying to wear himself out. At night, he'd tossed and turned on his lonely bed, aching from wanting her, tormented by thoughts of tasting her, pleasuring her, burying himself deep inside her. If she were his sister, he wouldn't have had such carnal thoughts. Why wouldn't she look at him? Had her grandfather browbeaten her into submission?

His thoughts circled, adding to his confusion. He was remembering that never-to-be-forgotten morning three weeks before when Caitlin was rudely dragged from his bed and hauled before her grandfather. He had wanted to murder Glenshiel and his minions. The old man had gone on the rampage, shaming her. Rand had listened in stunned silence for only a moment or two before putting a stop to it.

"That's enough!" His voice had thundered through the cavernous hall, setting the overhead chandelier to humming, and men had looked away from the icy challenge in his stare.

Stripping off his dressing robe, he had draped it over Caitlin's shivering form and had pulled her gently into the shelter of his arms. As she wept copious tears against his bare chest, over her bowed head, he had flayed

Glenshiel with his eyes. "She is innocent of any wrong-doing," he stormed. "If you have something to say, say it to me."

"Ye'll wed with her?"

Rand didn't have to think twice about his answer. "I'll do whatever is necessary to protect her from scandal."

Glenshiel had regarded him somberly for a long interval, as though this answer was not quite what he wanted. His wily old eyes flicked to the gallery, where Daroch was stationed. "There is another solution," he said, almost baiting Rand.

Rand's voice was dangerously soft. "Over my dead body. I mean that sincerely. She'll have me, or she'll have no man."

The wily gleam in Glenshiel's eyes had warmed to something suspiciously like humor. "I believe ye."

Caitlin had recovered sufficiently to begin a tearful explanation of the night's events. Rand cut her off without a qualm. "Lass, no one gives a damn about what brought you here. Look at you. Look at me." When she raised her beautiful stricken eyes to his, he nodded. "Yes. We are compromised. There's no getting round it." He brushed his fingers against her lips, silencing her protests. "Leave everything to me. All right?"

With the inevitability of marriage hanging over their heads, he was sure that she would retract her outrageous assertion about their blood tie. Before Glenshiel carried her off, he contrived a few moments alone with her. "Tell me it isn't true," he said.

In a fierce little voice, she replied, "You know we cannot wed. That is my final word on it. Do something before it's too late."

It still wasn't too late. She had only to say the word

214

and the whole thing would blow up in their faces like an exploding artillery shell.

When her fingers closed around his, he chafed them gently to ease their tension. Finally, she raised her eyes to his. They were as cold as her hands.

The last note of the pipes echoed through the hall. Through stiff lips, she whispered, "I was counting on you to find a way out of this impossible fix we are in. You promised me you would take care of everything."

Equally stiff, Rand hissed. "What would you have had me do? I'll have no man say I shirked my duty. You were found naked in my bed. Do you suppose anyone will believe we are brother and sister after that?"

Caitlin bit down on her lip. The black-robed cleric looked askance from one to the other. In mounting impatience the guests began to shuffle their feet.

Glenshiel fixed the priest with his eagle eye. "It's a weddin' or a hangin'. Take your pick," he said.

Shuddering, the priest began on the familiar liturgy.

The next few hours were like no wedding reception Rand had ever attended. Dancing, dining, and drinking on an unprecedented scale—that was the order of the day. Though he stood up for several dances with Caitlin, the energetic country reels and strathspeys did not lend themselves to conversation, not when the music was provided by Deeside's finest—three stalwart pipers who tried to outdo themselves in raising the roof by the sheer power of their lungs.

Shaking his head, Rand watched from the stairs as a dozen kilted gentlemen took to the floor. The famous sword dance was about to get under way. No ladies participated, for this was a war dance.

"I hope it's not prophetic." Rand's humorous words were addressed to Glenshiel who had come to stand beside him at the balustrade.

Glenshiel's answer was drowned out by the skirl of the pipes. Smiling, he made to move away but Rand forestalled him. "And now, Glenshiel, we shall have that conversation you promised me."

Taking Glenshiel's elbow in a firm clasp, Rand steered him along the edges of the dance floor till he came to a door he recognized. Pushing it open, he bade Glenshiel enter the little parlor.

Sighing, Glenshiel limped to a brocade sofa and lowered himself onto it. His expression was resigned as he gazed up at the younger man. "I could do with a wee dram," he said hopefully.

"And you shall have it just as soon you tell me what I wish to know."

When he had last met with Glenshiel in this very room, there had been solicitors present. Their time had been fully occupied in arranging marriage settlements, dowries, and the disposal of property. In passing, when the solicitor's attention was diverted, Rand had broached the subject of Caitlin's paternity, and Glenshiel had promised to answer his questions at a more appropriate time.

"Ye'll be wantin' to know who Caitlin's father was."

"I do."

"And as I told ye, I would only be guessing. Morag, my daughter, never revealed the name o' the man who had dishonored her." He mumbled indistinctly, then continued, "I dinna want any o' this to get back to Caitlin."

"I shall be the judge of that."

Glenshiel's eyes flashed. Rand absorbed the fire in them, but his own will never wavered. At length,

Glenshiel let out a sigh. "I trust ye. God alone knows why, but I trust ye." Irritably he said, "Well, dinna stand there like a great glowerin' mountain. Ye're givin' me a crick in the neck. Sit yerself down and I'll tell ye what ye wish to know."

When Rand obliged, Glenshiel said grimly, "Caitlin is a Gordon. Her mother was dark, but no as dark as the Gordons. Ye have only to look at the lass—her gray eyes, her fine bones, the way she moves. Och, I canna explain it. Ye'll just have tae take my word for it."

Rand breathed deeply. He felt as though a millstone had been removed from around his neck. "Who?" he gently prompted.

"I was a fool for not seeing it at once. She despised him, ye see, the laird o' Daroch. When he asked for her hand in marriage, I refused him."

Rand straightened in his chair. "Are you saying that Daroch's father is Caitlin's father?"

"What? No, no, ye misunderstand. Daroch's uncle was the elder brother. He was the laird then. But they were all tarred with the same brush. Profligates. Womanizers. Deeside was scandalized with their goings-on. Aye, has anything changed? Young Daroch takes after the spear side o' his family. He's mad if he thinks I'll countenance a match between him and Fiona."

Rand fastened on the one thing that held any interest for him. "If she despised him, it hardly seems likely that he is Caitlin's father."

"He wanted her. He took her. It's the only thing that makes sense."

Leaning back in his chair, Rand absently laced his fingers together. "What exactly did your daughter tell you?"

"She refused to say anything. I suppose she was

ashamed. I would have killed him if I had not been spared the trouble. He was killed in a duel before it all came out."

This was not what Rand had hoped to hear. There was too much conjecture and not enough hard evidence. He could not conceal his frustration. "Dammit, man, I am no nearer to knowing the name of my wife's father than ever I was. It could be anyone."

"Who for instance?"

Rand could not bring himself to mention his own father by name, especially as he considered him innocent of wrongdoing. In a more roundabout way, he referred to the possibility of visitors in the area. Though he broached the subject as diplomatically as possible, Glenshiel took affront.

"My daughter was a good lass. She was proud. If ye had known her, ye would know what I mean. If a man did not like her well enough to put a wedding ring on her finger, she would have none of him. Daroch raped her, I tell ye."

A period of silence followed as Rand digested Glenshiel's words. There was such pain in the older man's eyes that he was almost tempted to give up. If the matter had not been of such crucial significance to himself, he would have stopped right there.

"Surely," he said diffidently, "later, after the duel, your daughter would have confided in you? What had she to lose? She had nothing to fear from the man who had abused her. What reason was there to preserve her silence?"

"Shame. Pride." The words were barely audible. Glenshiel stirred and lifted his gaze to meet Rand's. "Does it really matter? It's all over and done with. If I had believed, truly believed, that Caitlin's bloodlines

218

meant a straw to ye, I would not have forced this marriage upon ye."

"You didn't force this marriage upon me," Rand snapped. "No man forces me to do what I don't wish to do."

Glenshiel chuckled. "I'm glad I did not misjudge my man. Ye'll do very nicely."

Rand folded his arms across his chest and surveyed his companion for a long interval. At length, he said, "You seem very pleased with this turn in events, Glenshiel. Yet, you must be aware that my own reputation is hardly spotless."

"What are ye saying?"

"You know what I mean. You chose me over Daroch, and I want to know why."

Glenshiel's brows met in a frown. "Do ye think, man, that I give a fig for your title and wealth? Is that what ye think?"

"I don't know what I think."

"Then allow me to put ye straight about a few things. Naturally, I was aware of your reputation—the wild parties at Strathcairn; your jaunt to The Fair Maid. But man, that wasna the stretch o' your ambitions. Ye were a soldier. Ye were no idle fop squandering your inheritance in gaming and wenching. And in the last little while, ye have conducted yourself with all the propriety o' a man in holy orders. And I know why. Aye, I think ye will do very well for my wee lass."

"It may surprise you to know," Rand tossed out sarcastically, "that your 'wee lass' does not share your opinion."

Glenshiel stared, then brayed uproariously. Finally, he got out, "Och, ye have only yourself to blame. Aye, she'll know about the wenching. Well, every man and his dog knows about it. But it's more than that. Ye turned your tenants out o' their crofts. Ye are English bred. Ye scorned the very things she holds dear—the land and our way of living. Sure the lass would not come to ye willingly, and well I knew it. It will take her a wee while afore she admits that she wed the right man."

Rand raised his eyebrow skeptically. "You think I am the right man?"

"I do. I've watched ye since ye returned to Deeside. No, that's not precisely true. I've watched ye since I became aware that your eye was on my wee lass. Now that surprised me, ye being the Randal and having your pick of any woman, so to speak."

"So to speak," said Rand dryly.

"It occurred to me that ye had eyes in your head. Ye saw something in the lass that few others have the wit to see. She's generous. She's loyal. She's affectionate—"

"Not to mention rash to a fault, stubborn, and intractable," Rand threw in, half in earnest, half flippantly.

Glenshiel blinked, then smiled. "Aye, as you say, rash, stubborn, and intractable. But ye took her measure and soon had her dancing to your tune." He emitted another low chuckle. "Mrs. MacGregor was a masterly stroke. I cannot think why I never thought o' such a stratagem. And as for inveigling her into female finery and taking her place in society"—he shook his head— "she would not do as much for me."

Rand frowned. "You should have put your foot down long before now. She has been too long indulged; she enjoys too many freedoms. It was the height of folly—" Suddenly conscious of the heat in his voice, he broke off and compressed his lips.

In contrast to Rand's tone, Glenshiel's was mild. "Ah,

well, we all know that Caitlin has a mind o' her own. But never mind that now. It was something else I wished to say to ye."

As though to emphasize his point, he leaned forward, bracing his weight on his cane. "My wee lass has been too much alone. She feels things too deeply, takes things too much to heart. She is afraid o' life, afraid o' getting hurt." Satisfied with what he read in Rand's intent look, he unconsciously relaxed his grip on his cane. "Ye say she is indulged to the point of folly. In some respects, mayhap ye are right. I did what was necessary to keep my granddaughter with me. In other respects, however, ye are far off."

Inhaling deeply, he said, "I want her to be happy. I want her to experience the best life has to offer. I want her married to a man who will appreciate her, not some useless popinjay who thinks he is conferring a great favor by taking her off my hands. As ye well know, Caitlin is no a pauper. Half of everything I own will be hers. She is well dowered. Anytime this last while, I could have arranged a match for her. I was waiting for the right man to come along."

"Caitlin might have had something to say to that."

"Whisht man, I would have arranged things so that she didna have the chance."

The calm avowal, spoken with careless disregard for the wishes of either Caitlin or her hypothetical suitor, annoyed Rand. He had an impression of a puppeteer pulling the strings on his marionettes. "You are a cold-blooded, ruthless rogue, Glenshiel," he said.

"Aye. I'll no deny it. When a man comes to the end o' his tether, he falls back on desperate measures." Beneath the humor, his voice held a suggestion of challenge. "What was I to do? The lass is almost two and twenty. She can come and go as she pleases. There is no law that says she must obey the dictates of an aging grandparent. A husband is a different matter."

Rand grinned impudently. "And you think I am the man to manage her?"

Glenshiel was unsmiling. "Aye . . . God help her."

Rand thought about Glenshiel's words long after they had rejoined the wedding celebration. He was thinking of Caitlin and the fact that her grandfather considered him the right man for her. It was what he himself believed. With him to guide her, she would blossom into the vibrant, confident woman she had it in herself to become. At the same time, he would restrain that alarming tendency to willfullness which no man worth his salt could condone. She had a husband now. He would not tolerate a wife who went her own way regardless of her husband's wishes.

His eyes traveled the throng of dancers and narrowed when they found Caitlin. She and Fiona flanked the dashingly handsome figure of Daroch as he led them through the intricate steps of some dance Rand could not name. Daroch was a devil on the dance floor.

Rand followed their progress down the set with an indulgent eye. Daroch was not the man for Caitlin. He was a mere boy. Too young, too impetuous, too much the ladies' man, too much in thrall to himself. Caitlin could never find happiness with the likes of Daroch. Caitlin's husband must be part lover, part guardian. Daroch was in sore need of a guardian himself. He was a poor laird, and an even poorer risk as a husband. If Rand was complacent, and he admitted to himself that he was, he had good cause.

Caitlin was many things, but she was not fickle. On the night he had tried to seduce her, she had responded with such sweet abandon that Rand had known incontrovertibly that her relationship with Daroch was entirely innocent. A flick of his long, gold lashes dismissed from his mind all thought of Daroch and the insane suspicion he had once entertained.

Without volition, his thoughts turned to David. His cousin's dying breath had been of Caitlin. David and Caitlin had been friends, close friends. Rand had never been friends with a woman in his life, and he was not sure that he ever wanted to be. He supposed that if things had been different, David might have been the one to marry Caitlin. He didn't care for the subsequent thoughts that crowded in on him, and resolutely pushed them away. He had fulfilled his promise to David. He had returned to Scotland; Caitlin was now under his protection. There was a sense of completeness in the way things had turned out. He was sure David would have thought so had he lived.

Unlike David, friendship was not what he wanted from Caitlin. He could not think of her without being possessed by a near-violent ache to take her. He burned for his wife. He could make her burn for him. Few husbands of his acquaintance could make that boast. In his circles, by and large, marriages were alliances. Properties and fortunes were consolidated. Titles were bought and sold. Husbands and wives rarely found pleasure in the marriage bed, nor did they expect to.

By anyone's standards, he and Caitlin were enviable indeed. They had it all. The Randal dynasty would be strengthened. She came to him well dowered, not as the poor relation he had supposed her to be. And they were well matched. When he closed his bedchamber door on the world every night, he and his wife would know the sweetest bliss to be found this side of eternity.

There was one fly in the ointment, of course—Caitlin's ridiculous insistence that he was her brother. He wasn't. He had tried to imagine himself in that role. It was impossible. Everything in him revolted against it. He wasn't her brother. The rub was, how could he persuade his wife to his way of thinking?

He had hoped that Glenshiel could throw some light on the subject. That had not happened, not really. Everything was speculation and conjecture. It seemed that there was no way to prove who had sired Caitlin. For his purposes, it was not necessary. It was enough if he could prove that his own father could not possibly have been that man. Until such time, he was resolved to treat his wife's scruples with all the respect they deserved.

He laughed mirthlessly thinking that, on reflection, his wife had plunged him into a drama that had all the makings of a Greek tragedy.

Chapter Fourteen

The journey from Glenshiel House to Rand's estate was made in a carriage that had been decked out in ribbons in the clan plaid. In place of horses, six strapping, kilted Highlanders, all of them Randal men, were harnessed to the traces. Behind the bride and groom, the wedding guests streamed out of Glenshiel House, jostling each other for the best positions, carefully avoiding the cavalcade of riders who held aloft flaming pitch torches to light their way to Strathcairn.

"Quaint," said Rand, and waved cordially to all and sundry from his position at the coach window.

"The siller!" hissed his bride from the opposite banquette. "We cannot leave until you have performed the ritual."

"The ritual? Quite!" There were so many rituals accompanying a Highland wedding, all of them invoking the pagan powers that be for prosperity and good fortune, that Rand easily forgave himself for overlooking one of them. The only ritual that meant anything to him was one he must forgo until he had straightened out a few things. Digging deep in his borrowed sporran, a great furry goatskin affair with tassels on it, he withdrew a fistful of silver coins and made to throw them out the open window.

Caitlin clicked her tongue. "Use a little finesse." Rand looked at her blankly, and she elaborated, "Open the door. Stand up, why don't you? This is your big moment."

A crude retort trembled on the tip of his tongue. Stifling it with a teeth-grinding grin, he flung open the door and performed the ceremony with all the dignity and grace he could muster. The shower of silver went scattering in every direction to the accompaniment of cheers and thunderous applause. The young people in the crowd, and some not so young, went diving after the gleaming coins. Rand repeated the performance until he had emptied his sporran. When he slammed the carriage door, as though he had given the signal, the coach and its escort of riders moved off into the night to the accompaniment of cheers intermingled with bawdy catcalls.

In the flickering light, he could just make out the gleam of his wife's teeth. She was smiling, and that relieved his mind. During the course of the evening, it had seemed to him that she was unnaturally pale, with as much animation as a wax doll. The strain of the last few weeks had evidently taken a toll on her. It had taken a toll on him too, but of a different sort.

Smiling, he said, "That pleases you, does it?"

"What?"

"Giving me orders."

Another flash of white teeth. "I daresay the novelty will wear off with a little practice."

"Don't bet on it!" Though his words were meant to be jocular, even he detected the bite in them. Deliberately moderating his tone, he went on, "You would not be happy with a henpecked husband, Kate. No woman would."

"I would not be happy with any husband."

His attempt to smooth over his tactless remark had not been received in the humorous spirit in which it was offered. Before Rand could hit on a way of correcting this error, Caitlin seized the offensive.

"I am not one of your shrinking misses who views the single estate as a fate worse than death. I liked being my own mistress. I enjoyed being a spinster. Marriage was the farthest thing from my mind. You know all this."

Her impassioned words shattered his mellow mood. "You seem to forget that you are not the only one to suffer from a marriage that was foisted upon us. And if we are ascribing blame, you will come off very much the worse."

"What does that mean, pray tell?"

"It means that I hold you responsible for bringing us to this pass. Do you imagine that I would have conveyed you to my home, a bachelor establishment, if I had known that you were a female? I thought you were Dirk Gordon."

She sniffed. "As I remember, you were not always so straitlaced. At our first encounter, your estate was positively teeming with females."

The darkness hid the stain of color that ran along his cheekbones. "Respectable females is what I meant!"

"I suppose it's something that you count me respectable."

"That, madam, is debatable. You have been skirting the edges of ruin for a very long time now, and well you know it. You may count yourself fortunate, indeed, that your grandfather and I managed to suppress the knowledge of your double life. Nor do I hold Daroch entirely responsible for leading you astray. In point of fact, I am much more inclined to believe that Daroch was led astray by *you*."

She sucked in a breath and quickly expelled it. "You seem to think I am some sort of female adventurer. Do you imagine that I took up smuggling to ward off boredom?" Her pitch was climbing.

"Were it not for you, and those like you, I would never have taken it upon myself to form a smuggling ring. Look around you, my lord. Are you so blind that you cannot see the poverty of the common people? At the best of times, wresting a living from their small crofts is a precarious business. The Highlands are not the lowlands. There is no abundance of rich pastures and fertile fields here. And when even the little they possess is taken away from them, how are the common people to stave starvation from their doors? Smuggling at least allows them to survive."

Rand quickly sifted through her heated rhetoric and pounced on what irked him most. "So I was right! *You* are the driving force behind Daroch and his band of smugglers! And I suppose I have you to thank for plotting the attack on my coach and the petty annoyances I was made to endure when I first came into Deeside?"

Her silence was answer enough.

"Caitlin," he said, "I can hardly credit that a woman of your intelligence should be so lacking in foresight. If any of your accomplices had been captured by the redcoats who accompanied me that night, do you know what would have been in store for them? They would have been transported to one of the convict colonies in the New World."

Her tone was considerably subdued. "We were not thieves and murderers. We did not do anyone bodily harm. We only destroyed a few suits of clothes and a rowing boat that was on its last legs. Those are scarcely serious offenses."

"Oh? And do you think the authorities would have accepted your protestation of innocence? I assure you, they would not. Do you know, it does not surprise me that your grandfather was quick to make capital of finding you in my house? In his place, I should have done the same."

"You speak in riddles, my lord."

"I think you know what I mean."

"I assure you, I do not."

He debated about teasing her, and gave in to the temptation, not because he wanted a quarrel on his hands, but because he wanted to dispel any lingering traces of her inertia. Though verbal sparring was not exactly his idea of domestic harmony, in this case it served a useful purpose.

"Only consider, Kate. Your grandfather was almost at his wits' end. He had lost control of you, if ever he had it. You were a confirmed spinster. You had attained your majority and were under no obligation to heed anyone's advice. Marriage to some gentleman who was not afraid to stand up to you was the only solution to his dilemma, but how was it to be contrived? It occurs to me that your grandfather must be thanking his lucky stars that things have fallen out so fortuitously."

For a moment, she seemed to be too taken aback to answer him. Expelling a pent-up breath, she plunged into speech. "You cannot mean to suggest, seriously, that my grandfather engineered our marriage? He is not so devious!"

"I didn't say that. As I have already pointed out, it was you who precipitated this present chain of events.

Nevertheless, Glenshiel was quick to see his opportunity and seize upon it. He might just as easily have married you off to Daroch. He chose not to do so, and I know why. Daroch is not the man for you. You would soon wrest the reins from his hands. Your grandfather knows this and acted in your best interests."

Her eyes were flashing fire. "That is not the reason Glenshiel chose you over Daroch!"

He regarded her in silence, digesting her words. "There is something in what you say. Daroch is an incorrigible skirt-chaser. He'll prove an inconstant husband to some unfortunate woman. Infidelity is one thing you will never have to endure at my hands, Kate. I intend to abide by our marriage vows."

"The feud is what I meant! My grandfather would never see one of his granddaughters go to a Gordon of Daroch. He has never forgiven them for taking up arms against the Stuart cause."

Rand had a faint recollection of hearing his father mention the feud between Glenshiel and the Gordons. In those days, Glenshiel was a regular Tartar, at outs with all his neighbors. Shaking his head, he said, "Those feuds are ancient history and best forgotten. Your grandfather knows this, else he would not have allowed our marriage to go forward."

Caitlin muttered indistinctly under her breath.

"I didn't quite catch that."

"I said there are other more cogent reasons why this marriage should not have been allowed to proceed." She was thinking of the mortification of having been foisted on a man who did not want her, a man who had told her in no uncertain terms that she was completely ineligible as a wife.

Rand's thoughts were moving in a different direction.

"I am not your brother! I don't know how I am going to prove it to you, but I aim to try." Aware that his voice was gaining in volume, he checked himself. Edging forward slightly until his knees were brushing her skirts, he said softly, "You need not fear that I shall insist on my conjugal rights. Is that what it is? Is that why you are so pale and drawn? I am not an animal. Rest assured, Kate, I intend to respect your scruples." He hoped he could hold himself to that promise.

"Thank you. You have greatly relieved my mind."

Her tone was so dry, so devoid of gratitude that he sat back, folding his arms across his chest, staring at her intently for some few minutes. In the crisp night air, the words of the old love ballad which their escort was singing rose like the song of a nightingale. The coach moved slowly, swaying from side to side. Occasionally, soft masculine laughter from outside filtered into the coach. When Rand adjusted his position on the banquette, Caitlin jumped.

"Kate," he said, "if this is some kind of elaborate ploy to keep me at arm's length, I swear I shall wring your neck."

He caught the flash of her teeth in the dim light. "My lord, what other reason could I have for wishing to keep you at arm's length? I am sure I must be the envy of every woman in Deeside, if not in the whole of Grampian."

When they arrived at Strathcairn, servants came running with tureens of hot toddy which they doled out to every man in the cavalcade. As Rand moved among the men, shaking hands, accepting their congratulations and advice in good part, Caitlin slipped through the front doors. She had barely time to remove her cloak when Rand joined her.

He studied her closely, noting the high color across her cheekbones, the sparkle in her eyes, the little chin tilted at a provocative angle, and he smiled his approval. "Now that is more like the girl I know," he said. "Mrs. Fleming will show you to your chamber." And wanting to set her mind at rest, he brushed her cheek with a chaste kiss and whispered, "I shall see you at breakfast, then."

Caitlin's air of bravado was to last until she was in her night clothes, and Mrs. Fleming had finally taken her leave of her. In solitary state, she surveyed her bridal chamber. A fire was burning in the grate; several candelabra were set around the room, the light from the candles casting a welcoming glow. She could smell beeswax and lavender and the faint fragrance of newly starched sheets. It was evident that the servants had gone to a great deal of trouble to make the room comfortable. She must remember to thank them in the morning.

Lost in thought, she stared at the huge tester bed. One word from her, one hint that she had concocted the brother and sister story in order to protect her virtue, and she knew that Rand would be more than willing to share the bed with her. He had never tried to conceal his desire for her. Carnal lust, Caitlin amended scrupulously. She was the object of that lust, an honor she doubtless shared with many women. As she well knew, her husband was none too particular where he bestowed his sexual favors. Until she had plotted her course, until she could see her way clear, it would be best not to complicate matters by taking that last irrevocable step. And they would take that step if she confessed the truth to him. For the present, she would let the fiction stand.

She hoisted herself onto the bed and sat cross-legged

on top of the covers. For the first time in weeks, her brain seemed to have unfrozen itself. She was able to take stock of her position, calculate odds, set a course for herself.

Annulment. She didn't know how it could be contrived, but she knew one thing. Once the marriage was consummated, annulment was no longer a possibility. She considered the problem from all sides. An annulment seemed to be the only solution, not only for her sake, but also for Rand's. She was as aware as he of the great gulf that separated them. She knew that she would never fit into his world, that she would be the proverbial millstone around his neck. The thought of meeting his family sent shivers of trepidation dancing along her spine. She could well imagine what they would think of her and this hastily contrived marriage.

One thing was certain: Rand would never demand an annulment. His view was that they must make the best of it now the thing was done. She could applaud his scruples. What she could not resign herself to was his contempt. Oh God, why hadn't he done as he had promised and found a way out of this fix they were in?

That thought sent her to her dressing table. From a delicate porcelain dish she retrieved the ring she had worn throughout the day on the fourth finger of her right hand, the ring she had found in her mother's effects after her death.

To her knowledge, her mother had never worn this ring, and if it had any significance, Morag Randal had never explained it. Caitlin knew she would always wonder if this ring had once belonged to her father.

Her thoughts slipped away to another occasion when Morag Randal had taken it upon herself to keep her daughter to the straight and narrow. It was the day her mother had come upon a Caitlin of fourteen years helping one of the gillies with his salmon catch. The young lad had stolen a kiss, and Morag Randal had known it.

"There is nothing a lad will not do, no trick to which he will not stoop, to lure you into his bed. It's in the nature of the beast, so be on your guard."

"What tricks?" asked Caitlin. She was thinking of the kiss, wondering if it would look too obvious if she offered to help Johnny with his catch on the morrow.

"Some men have been known to promise marriage and then renege on it."

She would wait a day, she decided, before offering to help Johnny again. Absently, she answered, "But I couldn't marry without your consent."

Rather more sharply, her mother retorted, "There are ways around that! This is Scotland, lass. If a man and woman want to marry, they can pledge themselves to each other without witnesses. But mind my words; if a man decides not to honor pledges made in private, the woman has no recourse. I'm telling you this so that you will keep yourself chaste until you wed your husband in church, before the whole congregation."

Caitlin was really looking at her mother now. "Is that what happened with you and my father?" she whispered. "Did you pledge yourselves without witnesses?"

The answer was a long time in coming: "Aye. That's what happened to your foolish mother." And more than that, her mother would not say.

Caitlin was left to draw her own conclusions. It seemed to her that her parents had married secretly. It was no real marriage, but an elaborate hoax, the ploy of an unscrupulous rake to lure an innocent girl into his bed.

She studied the ring closely, the cluster of tiny opals

234

and rubies set in filigreed gold. Was this the ring her father had given her mother to persuade her that his intentions were honorable? She could tell that the ring was worth a pretty penny. Shaking her head at the impulse that had prompted her to wear it on her wedding day, she opened a drawer in her dresser and tossed it carelessly inside. She would never wear it again.

Rand's wedding ring glinted from the fourth finger of her left hand. She touched it gently, almost reverently, with the tips of her fingers. She had to give the man his due. He might be English bred and a tad too high handed for her taste, but no one could accuse him of taking advantage of an innocent young girl. In fact, if anyone had been taken advantage of, it was Rand.

Far from chastening her, this thought amused her, and she giggled. She wondered if she would be giggling when he discovered, as he must, that they were not related by ties of blood. The Randal on the rampage—now that was a sobering picture. Smiling, chuckling, she doused the candles and slipped into bed.

The following morning, Rand introduced Caitlin to all the members of his staff. For a girl in the habit of taking care of her own meager needs, the experience would have been daunting had she not had a nodding acquaintance with most of those assembled in the great hall. In Deeside, families who could place a son or daughter in domestic service with the local gentry were considered fortunate indeed. There was little else to keep young people in the Highlands. Caitlin strove to overcome the awkwardness of her position. Young men and women with whom she had once freely mingled were now as stiff and formal as though they were being presented to the queen of England. A few inquiries respecting the members of their various families soon broke the ice.

Two of the staff were unknown to her, Rand's personal valet, Hobbes, a little man who put her in mind of a dancing master, and the French chef who looked exactly as Caitlin imagined a French chef should. Gallic and temperamental, he was named Ladubec. Behind his back, the other servants called him "La-dee-dah" among other things. Knowing this, Caitlin could not prevent her lips from twitching. Her smile faded rapidly when Rand introduced her to the unsmiling man who stood next to the chef.

"My factor, Mr. Serle," said Rand.

John Serle was in his mid-thirties, of medium complexion, and he carried his spare frame with a military air. He lived in a cottage on the estate, and rarely showed his face in Ballater or its environs. He was a true lowlander, in Caitlin's estimation, dour-faced, with his nose always to the grindstone, the sort who chafed because the Sabbath was ordained by the laws of both God and man as a day of rest. Though she had never done more than exchange the odd word with Rand's factor, she knew that she disliked him intensely.

Mr. Serle was only slightly less stiff than Caitlin. As the introductions were made, his lean face thinned to a razor sharpness, and Caitlin's gray eyes lightened to a chilling transparency. Hostility seemed to vibrate between them. The encounter lasted no more than a moment or two, for Rand's firm clasp on his wife's elbow nudged her along to the next person in line.

Later, over breakfast, Rand did not mince matters, though he was careful to keep his tone light and pleasantly modulated. "Serle is my agent," he told her, "and

236

a very able one at that. I was lucky to get him. He's had extensive experience in East Lothian as well as Norfolk. I know you hold him in dislike because of the changes that have been made here, on Strathcairn. I hardly need tell you that Serle was only acting on my instructions, so if you have anything to say—anything new to say, that is—I suggest you say it to me. One thing more, it would be highly undesirable if the man's authority were called into question by my other employees, and that's what would happen if my wife were to openly display her contempt for him. A factor's position is not an easy one, Kate."

There was a long interval of silence as Caitlin's sharp teeth ground a small piece of dry toast into minuscule fragments. The Randal did not rave and rant in the manner of her grandfather, but she recognized a lecture when she heard it. Such blandishments had never been known to moderate Caitlin's thinking or conduct.

"Kate?"

"Point taken." Her little smile was as wooden as her voice.

Rand's own smile became more of a grin. "It would be more fitting if you would confine your interests to household matters. There's plenty to occupy you here." When she made no comment on this, he continued in the same conversational tone, "Nothing has been done to the house for years. I used it more as a hunting box. If you wanted to, you could fix it up, refurbish the place." A spark of interest kindled in her eyes, and Rand was encouraged to say, "You won't find me a tightfisted husband. Feel free to spend as much as you like."

She acknowledged his generous offer with a slight inclination of her head. His words had softened her a little. Testing the water, she said diffidently, "In the next little while, I thought I might ride around the estate, get to know your gamekeepers and gillies, familiarize myself with how things are run."

"And stop off at every cottage to acquaint yourself with the problems of my tenants and cotters? Kate, it won't do."

"Only a courtesy call, you understand."

"I understand perfectly. My factor, on the other hand, might consider it meddling."

"Mr. Serle is an employee, and as you once pointed out to me, an employee's services are not indispensable."

"I won't have you meddling in what does not concern you."

She flashed him a cold, brittle smile. "I see. Your domain and my domain are to be mutually exclusive?"

He pressed his napkin to his lips and regarded her thoughtfully before attempting to answer. Drawing a cautious breath, he said, "Not exactly. Though I have no wish to be a tyrannical husband—far from it—I expect to be kept informed of what goes forward on the domestic front." He shook his head at her lowered brows. "No, Kate, don't glower at me. I'm thinking of you. You know that you have had no experience in managing an establishment on this scale. This will be good practice for you. When we remove to my estates in Sussex, the responsibilities will be far more onerous. There is no question in my mind that, with a little guidance, you will prove equal to the task. You are an intelligent, capable woman with proven abilities." Injecting a little humor into his voice, he went on, "Anyone who can successfully operate a smuggling ring under the noses of a garrison of redcoats is capable of anything, if she puts her mind to it."

She leaned slightly toward him. "But don't you see, Rand, that is my point precisely? I am not averse to taking guidance on the domestic front, as you put it, because I do lack experience. However, there is not much I don't know about the land and its people. Together, we could turn Strathcairn into a model estate. Others could learn from us. Your influence could be far reaching, not only here, on Deeside, but all over the Highlands."

There was a moment when it seemed as if her words might persuade him; then he laughed and shook his head. "I already have a factor, Kate. I don't require another one. What I want is a wife."

She held his quizzical stare for a long moment, then dropped her eyes to her plate.

Rand was at the sideboard, helping himself to a succulent fillet of finnan haddie when Caitlin rose from the table. "Kate?"

Her mouth curved in a humorless smile. "With your permission, I shall ask Mrs. Fleming to show me my new domain. Before refurbishing the place, I thought we might make a beginning by taking inventory, you know, counting chamber pots and such like." Her hand reached for the doorknob. "Oh, do you have any words of wisdom to offer, my lord, should it be necessary to replace any that are cracked or showing signs of wear, any preference as to style and decoration? You'd best tell me now. I would not want to incur your displeasure at my first major undertaking."

Rand's smile conveyed only amused tolerance. "In this enterprise, I trust your judgment implicitly, my dear."

The door did not slam, but it did vibrate as she shut it smartly behind her. Grinning, Rand seated himself at the table. All in all, he considered he and Caitlin had made a fair beginning. It was not the marriage he had envisioned, but it was a start. She had his ring on her finger. She was living under his roof. That she'd had no choice in the matter was regrettable, from her point of view, but hardly of paramount significance. The women who moved in his circles were rarely allowed to marry where they wanted. The thing was done, and it was up to them to make the best of it.

He did not wander at her chagrin. She had ordered her life to suit herself for so long that any restrictions were bound to prove irksome. His Kate would not take kindly to confining her energies to the typical woman's sphere. That would soon change. What she needed was a brood of children hanging on her skirts, and—he smiled a slow smile—it was his dearest wish to give them to her.

That thought put him in mind of the obstacle that kept him from his wife's bed. His brow furrowed in concentration. The more he thought about it, the more the conviction grew that she really did believe they were brother and sister. She could not be toying with him. What would be the point? She had everything to gain and nothing to lose by ensuring that their marriage was consummated. He wasn't thinking only of the legal implications but of something he recognized as primitive and deeply ingrained in his nature. Once Caitlin had surrendered herself to him, the bonds that held them together would be strengthened a hundredfold. She and her children could look to him as their shield and protector. It was nature's way, he supposed, of ensuring the survival of the species.

Digressing, he imagined himself explaining to his bride the law of nature that made it imperative for her to grant him unlimited access to her body, and he laughed softly to himself. Caitlin would soon stand that argument on its head. He'd had many women in his time, and his wife knew it. It was only with Caitlin that he felt driven to forge a connection that was indissoluble. If it were only that, he thought wryly, he would not be consumed with impatience to get at her. He wanted her in every way it was possible for a man to want a woman. His whole body was aching from frustrated desire, and if the question of her paternity was not settled soon, he very much feared that he would take her, her scruples be damned. She might not want it, she might fight against it, but she would accept him. He was no novice where women were concerned. She was susceptible to him, more than susceptible. If he had played his cards differently, he could have had her any time these last few months. His scruples, not hers, had held him off. Sex was a powerful weapon, and he had not wanted to use it against her unless it became absolutely necessary.

That weapon had been very adroitly taken away from him. He gazed blindly at the congealing food on his plate. A moment later, uttering an imprecation, he threw down his napkin and strode from the room.

Chapter Fifteen

The glen was to remain cut off from the outside world for another month. When a westerly wind brought a partial thaw, only the road to Aberdeen became navigable. There would be no traversing the mountain passes to the south and Perthshire until the arrival of spring.

For the most part, the vagaries of the climate hardly affected the residents of upper Deeside. Few had interests or business they wished to pursue outside their own little realm. Rand was an exception. The long hours he was compelled to while away in his wife's proximity in enforced celibacy had worked a change in him. Beneath his calm exterior, he was beginning to feel like a ravening beast of prey straining at the bars of his cage, and he was appalled.

Time was wasting, and he was no nearer to removing the obstacle which kept him from his wife. If it had been possible, he would have posted down to his estate in Sussex to quiz, circumspectly, his mother and some of his father's former cronies, his uncle among them. The condition of the roads hemmed him in. When winter temporarily relaxed its grip, he seized the opportunity of pursuing a lead that had come to him by way of Jamie MacGregor. Aboyne was Rand's destination, to seek out a local celebrity, a man known to be one of the last surviving Jacobite rebels in Deeside if not in the whole of Scotland.

As a mere boy of sixteen summers, Patrick Gordon had forsworn his own clan to come out under the banner of Bonnie Prince Charlie. Rand could not have cared less about the Jacobite Rebellion. That conflict was almost seventy years past. Since then, Britain had been engaged in other, more crucial conflicts in every corner of the world. His own generation, in particular, had seen action in Spain, culminating at Waterloo. His interest in Patrick Gordon was in the man's reputation as a chronicler of events. In his time, Gordon had served as bard to the chiefs of the Clan Farquharson. He possessed an inexhaustible fund of stories on local characters and, since his retirement to Aboyne, was much in demand at weddings and wakes. He was a spinner of tales, all set to music, and all expurgated or exaggerated according to the company in which he found himself. He was not precisely an historian. In another time, another age, he might have been a wandering minstrel.

On this particular evening, Rand was feeling none too pleased with himself. The ride from Ballater to Aboyne had taken longer than he had anticipated, necessitating an overnight stay. That meant his meeting with Gordon would have to be delayed till the following morning. He had chosen to put up for the night in a very indifferent inn when he might have taken up more agreeable lodgings in Aboyne's leading change-house. The nature of his errand as well as his status as a newly married man only added to his irritation. He could think of better things to do with his time than hide himself away like some guilty truant who was avoiding his schoolmasters. At The Twa Craws, Rand hoped to avoid running into anyone who might recognize him.

All his precautions proved to be in vain. He had hardly sat down to a late supper in the tiny dining room—there were no private parlors at The Twa Craws—when he was addressed by name by the proprietor. After that, Rand could not hope to remain inconspicuous. He was waited on with all the pomp and circumstance due a reigning monarch. Nothing could have been more calculated to drive him away. Gulping down the dregs of his tea—there was no coffee to be had—he slipped into his greatcoat and exited through the back doors, intending to check the quarters where his horse was stabled.

The light from the porch lantern hardly penetrated more than a few feet from the main building. Rand had almost traversed the width of the dark courtyard when a coach and pair came careening around the corner of the inn, narrowly missing him, before coming to a shuddering halt. Having no wish to advertise his presence, Rand checked a rush of anger and stepped to the side, well out of sight.

One of the coachmen jumped down and went to the assistance of his passengers. A man struggled out of the coach, with what appeared to be a swooning woman clutched to his chest. For a moment, Rand thought he might be witnessing an abduction. He felt in his pocket for the pistol he carried whenever he was on the road.

"How is he?" asked the coachman, adjusting the loose plaid solicitously around the invalid's head and shoulders.

"He'll do until we get him to the infirmary."

Rand recognized the second voice. It belonged to young Douglas Gordon o' Daroch.

"Och, a wee tot o' whiskey will do him the world o' good." The coachman's words were punctuated with chuckles.

Daroch laughed. "It was one tot too many which led to poor Jock's undoing. God, he's a dead weight. Here, give me a hand before the redcoats find us."

Bracing their companion's weight between them, they pushed through the back doors of The Twa Craws. Rand hesitated, debating whether or not he should go to their assistance. He hardly liked to turn his back on anyone who was in difficulty. On the other hand, he had not formed the impression that there was any urgency in conveying the unconscious man to a physician. He assumed that Daroch and his friend had been drinking or wenching or both when they had become involved in an altercation. That brought back fond memories of his own salad days.

Smiling nostalgically, he continued on his errand. Though not quite up to what Nero was used to, the stable was clean and comfortable, and his bay hardly lifted his head from the pail of oats he was munching. Rand had no qualms about turning in for the night, not when his groom had found a pallet in the vacant stall next to Nero's.

There was no sign of the coach and pair when Rand entered the inn. Wondering a little at this, he mentioned it in passing to the proprietor. The landlord knew nothing of a coach and pair. To his knowledge, no one had entered his establishment later than his lordship. Certainly, no one had ordered a meal or called for a jug of ale or a tot of whiskey. Rand was more relieved than puzzled. He had no inclination to come face to face with Daroch, necessitating explanations for either's presence in such an out-of-the-way inn that evening, and he was quite sure that the young laird shared his sentiments. Bidding the landlord goodnight, he ascended the narrow staircase to his chamber.

Rand's foul humor had not improved by one iota when he rose from his bed the following morning. It seemed to him then that he was setting about the thing the wrong way. What he should have done was approach a bona fide historian, someone like Donald Randal. Who better than his wife's great-uncle could answer his questions about her parentage? Patrick Gordon did not deal in precise truths. A bard's chronicles owed far more to fiction than fact. So why had he come on this wild-goose chase?

He was here because he could not bring himself to embarrass his wife by openly stirring up an old scandal. Subtlety and finesse were called for here. A dozen times in the last weeks he had hinted that Donald Randal might give him the information he wanted. With some people, suggestions and innuendos were as effective as blowing on a bowl of cold porridge to warm it up. He could not see himself coming straight out and asking point-blank for the name of Caitlin's father as he had done with Glenshiel. Caitlin's grandfather was wise in the ways of the world. He had a thick skin. Donald Randal seemed almost fragile in comparison. Any perceived offense to Caitlin would be an offense against himself. Rand had observed that Caitlin could do no wrong in her uncle's eyes.

Patrick Gordon lived with a widowed daughter at the eastern edge of the village, and within minutes after

Rand had entered the tiny cottage, his ill humor began to fade. There was something about the old gentleman that he took to immediately. Those wise old eyes with their mischievous glint were so appealing. For all his five and eighty years, Gordon was as trim and spry as a man in his prime. He was one of those ageless types. Neither the lines on his face nor his bald pate with its thin feathering of fine white hair could detract from that first impression of youthfulness.

It was not so with his daughter. Rand was glad that he had kept his thoughts to himself until the introductions were made, for he had mistaken the lady for Gordon's contemporary. In point of fact, she looked older than her father.

Gordon lost no time in waving his tight-lipped daughter out of the room. As was to be expected in a Highland home, two tot glasses were soon produced and both gentlemen were seated in chairs which practically hugged the fire in the gate.

"Lang may your lummie reek," said Gordon, raising his glass in a toast.

Rand had only a vague notion of what the words meant, something to do with a smoking chimney, but Caitlin had explained their significance—a wish for prosperity.

"*Slainte mhaith,*" he replied at once, "good health."

They drank slowly, as was proper, savoring each droplet of the delectable liquid. At the same time, they were taking stock of each other.

Rand had rehearsed what he wished to say. Even if the old man could not help him in his quest, he still had a legitimate reason for being there.

At length, he said, "I was prevented from coming here before my marriage by the storm that cut off my place from the rest of Deeside. Still, better late than never. I have a commission for you, Mr. Gordon. I should like you to compose an ode, or a ballad or whatever you want to call it, on the occasion of my marriage to Caitlin Randal. Will you accept the commission?"

"A ballad on the occasion o' your marriage?" murmured Gordon. "Now what could be more fitting? The two warring branches o' the great House o' Randal finally united. Och, I dinna ken why I didna think o' it myself."

Rand drew a cautious breath. "It means, of course, that someone will have to fill you in on the histories of our two families. Donald Randal would be your man. He knows just about everything there is to know about the Randals of Glenshiel and the Randals of Strathcairn."

"Pshaw, man, I'll no be needing help from the likes o' that young stripling. What does he know that I don't know?"

"You tell me," murmured Rand. He was thinking that perhaps he had not come on a wild-goose chase after all.

"Did he fight at Culloden? And afterward, was he there in the hills, hiding like a terrified rabbit when Cumberland's redcoats aye, some o' them members o' my own clan, hunted us down?"

"I believe the family escaped to Holland," said Rand diffidently.

"Aye, and so began the Randal feud. Och well, it wasna much o' a feud, not like others I could name."

Though the last thing Rand wanted was to regurgitate Scottish history, politeness compelled him to make some comment. "I hear tell, Mr. Gordon, that you were

248

at outs with your own clan when the Prince raised his standard?"

"Aye, and proud o' it. Ye'll observe that to this day, I wear the Mackintosh tartan?"

Rand's eyes made a sweep of the red and black plaid draped around Gordon's shoulders. "Why is that?" he asked.

"Because I fought at Culloden under my mother's colors, long afore the Gordon tartan was ever invented."

"I assumed the Gordon tartan was as ancient as the Highlands of Scotland," joked Rand.

Patrick Gordon clicked his tongue. "Laddie," he said, "we Gordons were lowlanders. We were Normans. We arrived wi' William the Conqueror. It's only lately that we hae become Scottish, and even more recently that we hae spread out into the Highlands."

"How lately?" asked Rand, smiling in anticipation of the answer.

Gordon's eyes were twinkling. "I'd say about two or three hundred years. Ye might say that we are newcomers, just a cut above *sassenachs*. Och, it will be centuries yet afore we are truly accepted by the ancient clans."

Rand was surprised to find that he was enjoying the conversation. "And the Randals. What about my own clan?"

"It pains me tae tell your lordship, ye are no better than a Gordon."

Rand laughed at this. "After two or three centuries, who can tell the difference?"

"Och, well, some would say that Culloden separated the sheep from the goats." Detecting the interest in Rand's expression, he elaborated, "The ancient clans, such as the Mackintosh, for instance, came out for Prince Charlie, or if they didna they wanted to. The

Randals, the Gordons, the Campbells—they fought as lowlanders. Aye, they were redcoats. Can you believe that?"

Rand did not pick up this bone of contention. The men of his own Scottish regiment were also known as redcoats. "What about my wife's family?" he said. "Why did they come out for the prince?"

"Och, ye can well ken that they would do the opposite o' whatever the Gordons o' Daroch would do. They were ever at each other's throats. And after Culloden, their hatred could not be contained. Aye, has anything changed?"

If there was one thing Rand was tired of hearing about, it was the senseless blood feuds that had caused so much dissension among his neighbors. He was debating how best to pursue the subject of Caitlin's family tree when Gordon changed direction.

"I was sorry to hear about the death o' your young cousin," he said. "Such a fine young man, and a credit to the Randal clan."

"David? You knew my cousin?" Rand could not keep his surprise from showing.

"I wouldna say I knew him," corrected Gordon. "I met him once, afore he left Deeside, aye, never to return."

"David came here? To see you? For what purpose?" Conscious that his tone was abrupt, almost suspicious, Rand shook his head and then continued more reasonably. "I beg your pardon, Mr. Gordon. David never mentioned to me that he was coming to see you."

"Well now, I never said he came to see me. I met him, quite by chance, at Aboyne's ball. He was taken with the ballad I was singing."

Rand remembered the ball but not the ballad. "Oh?"

"I sang o' the duel that took the life o' the young laird o' Daroch in the summer o' ninety-two. Your young kinsman spoke to me afterward. The tale had caught his fancy."

Rand felt as though an electric current had passed through him. The summer of '92 was precisely what he was most interested in hearing about—the summer before Caitlin was born. "What did you tell him?"

"Very little. I only know what everyone else knows, that the duel was over an unknown lady and that Daroch died almost instantly from a bullet in his brain."

Rand had very little sympathy for Robert Gordon of Daroch, and it showed. "From what I hear, his fate was probably well deserved." He was thinking of what Glenshiel had told him, that in all probability, the young laird o' Daroch had forced himself on Morag Randal and then abandoned her.

For a moment, no one spoke. From the room next door, the rattle of pots and pans indicated that Gordon's daughter was preparing the midday meal. The eyes of the two gentlemen brushed and held, and a silent, humorous communication passed between them. It was very evident that the mistress of the house was not happy in her work.

Breaking the silence, Gordon said, "Your young cousin thought my ballad betrayed too much sympathy for Daroch."

Rand made a small sound of derision. "I don't doubt it. David despised men of that ilk. He was something of an idealist."

The twinkle had faded from the old man's eyes, and he was regarding Rand with a look that was oddly inquisitive, as though something in Rand's manner or expression puzzled him. Before Rand could answer that look, Gordon said, "Ye hae been listening tae Glenshiel."

"Why do you say that?"

"Daroch was not as black as he was made out tae be, but ye'll never hear a Randal o' Glenshiel admit as much."

Rand could feel his frustration growing. He still was no nearer to learning what he wanted to know. "Tell me about my cousin," he said. "What else did you talk about?"

"I told him about the man who killed Daroch in the duel, Ewan Grant."

"The name means nothing to me."

"Maybe not, but your father would have known o' him. He rented your place—Strathcairn is it?—for the hunting season. That would be the year your father didna come into Scotland."

"Not come into Scotland?" said Rand.

"Your family was in mourning."

It came to Rand like a flash of lightning bursting across a darkened sky. He was eight years old. His sister, a babe of only a few months, had died within hours of contracting a fever. His mother could not be consoled. Fearing for his wife's health, his father had rented a house in Brighton for the season. The sea air had worked such an improvement on his mother that they had lingered in Brighton well into October. After that, the children had gone to visit their grandparents in Wiltshire while his parents had opened up the house in London.

"Of course," said Rand. "My sister, Clara. I had all but forgotten that sad episode in my family's life." He didn't look sad. He looked pleased in a subdued way. "Is that what my cousin wanted to know?"

252

"No," Mr. Gordon replied cryptically, obviously puzzled if not a little fascinated by Rand's interrogation.

"Forgive me, Mr. Gordon, for putting you through this inquisition. When you mentioned my cousin, naturally I was interested. He saved my life at Waterloo, you see, at the cost of his own. I've wished a hundred times since that I had got to know him better when I had the chance. Please, finish what you were saying."

Though Gordon nodded sympathetically, the quizzical gleam in his eye had not lessened one whit. "Your cousin asked me about his father."

"His father," repeated Rand.

"Aye. Young Mr. Randal wanted tae know if his father had come into Deeside with Grant that year, but I couldna remember whether he had or no."

Behind Rand's blank stare, his mind was busily at work sifting through fragments, fitting the pieces together to make a comprehensible whole. "What happened to Grant after the duel?"

"He became a fugitive from the law. Some say he fled to America. Others say the Gordons or the lady's kinsmen caught up wi' him and exacted their own form o' retribution. No one ever saw him again. It's all in the ballad I sang at Aboyne's ball."

There was an imperceptible narrowing of Rand's eyes. After a pause, he shook his head, "That's not what my wife told me," he said, casting his line without much hope of landing anything.

"Oh well, when Miss Randal came tae see me, you might say she was not quite herself."

To his credit, Rand masked his astonishment well. "Of course," he said, "that would be when ..." He trailed to a halt, gazing off into space as though he were lost in private reflection. His ploy worked.

"Aye, right after the death o' her dear mother." Gordon sighed regretfully. "I couldna tell her any more than I've told ye, aye, and your cousin afore ye. After the duel, Ewan Grant seemed to disappear off the face o' the earth."

Rand looked into those intelligent gray eyes and realized that he was fooling no one. With most brutal frankness he said, "And my wife thinks this Grant may be her father?"

"Aye, or so it seemed to me. A thing like that haunts a body, ye ken," observed Gordon reflectively. "It's a great pity that her mother went tae her Maker without taking the lass into her confidence. She'll never stop wondering, don't ye think?"

Rand had no ready reply to make to this. He wasn't feeling sorry for Caitlin. Instead he was livid. She suspected that Ewan Grant was her father, and even suspecting it, she had called his father's honor into question. Damnation, she must have known his father had not come into Scotland for a good twelve months before she was born. From the sound of it, she had pulled the same trick on David. He wondered how many other gentlemen's attentions had been deflected by that devious ruse. But dammit all, he was her husband. He deserved better than this.

Having discovered what he wished to know, Rand did not linger. He quickly brought the conversation round to the ballad he had commissioned, and left on the understanding that it would be performed at the first gala event to take place at Strathcairn, possibly when his family came into Deeside to meet his bride. The outside door had hardly closed upon him, when Gordon was joined by his daughter.

"What did Lord Randal want?"

Gordon studied his daughter as though she were a stranger to him. He noted the sullen line of her mouth, the hair scraped back tightly in a bun, the almost hostile glare in her sharp blue eyes. There were occasions when he wondered who could possibly have fathered this dour-faced, killjoy of a woman. It wasn't a serious thought. He knew his dear departed wife too well ever to suspect her of infidelity.

"Father?"

"Whatever it was, I'm thinking that the Randal got more than he bargained for."

Chapter Sixteen

The estate of matrimony was not nearly as irksome as she had feared it would be. The stray thought flitted through Caitlin's mind, circled, returned, and captured her complete attention.

A smile tugged at the corners of her mouth. She was thinking that if she were honest with herself, she would admit that this last month she had enjoyed herself enormously, and she could thank her husband for it. Rand was not the tyrant he sometimes pretended to be. Oh, he could be stern, he could be fierce, when he wanted to be, but she knew how to get around him. No man liked to be backed into a corner. Every man liked to think he was master in his own house. So a wise woman cultivated the virtues of tact and diplomacy, and where Rand was concerned, Caitlin was coming to believe she'd become something of a sage.

Drawing her Randal plaid more securely about her, she began to descend the track which led to Strathcairn. With the thaw, only odd pockets of snow remained to hamper her progress. In another week or two, the woods and moors would be carpeted with the first hyacinths and bluebells of the year. It was only on the mountain peaks and in the passes that winter dared to linger. Soon the swallows would return from their winter quarters in Africa and the cry of the cuckoo would echo in every glen.

Checking her stride, she held up her face to the watery sun. The moors, the ancient forests, even the snow-capped mountains in the distance seemed to be at one with her. A laugh started deep in her chest, gurgled to her lips and spilled over. Then a cloud covered the sun and she shivered.

Suddenly conscious that her hound had wandered off, she put her fingers to her lips and emitted one long, shrill whistle. Moments later, Bocain came sailing over one of the dry-stone dikes which bordered the track.

"I've never seen you so restless," Caitlin scolded. "What is it, girl? Wasn't the run on the moors enough exercise for one day?"

With a snap of her fingers, she brought her dog to heel. A moment later, Bocain growled softly and would have bounded away if Caitlin had not restrained her with a sharp command. Though they were still some way from Strathcairn, Caitlin was taking no chances, having promised Rand that in his absence she would keep her hound on a tight leash. The gamekeepers, it seemed, quite unnecessarily in Caitlin's opinion, feared that Bocain might scare off game or savage the live-stock. She had promised Rand something else: she would not go far afield unless attended by one of the grooms. Her conscience was easily soothed. She was out walking, not riding. A groom's presence on a walk was entirely superfluous. What could possibly happen to her?

At one point in the track, where the trees in the valley thinned out, there was a clear view of Strathcairn House and its policies. Caitlin halted and surveyed the spectacle with unmitigated pleasure. It wasn't only the house which pleased her, though there was much to admire in the beauty of Strathcairn's graceful lines. It was a Georgian edifice to suit Scottish sensibilities, that is, the architect had made no attempt to gild the lily with ornate pediments or elaborate Grecian columns and porticoes. The solid, granite building suited its setting—noble in its stark simplicity. Caitlin acknowledged the house's appeal to her aesthetic sense, and her eyes moved on, absorbing the lingering trail of smoke from the chimneys of various cottages which, until recently, had stood empty. This evidence of prosperity was her doing.

Rand had given her carte blanche to refurbish Strathcairn, and she had held him to his offer. His former tenants were now employed in a variety of capacities inside and outside the house. Strathcairn was going to rack and ruin, she had told her husband, and had proved it to him. Used only as a hunting lodge, the house has been neglected for years. The walls were dingy; the plasterwork was falling down about their ears; the roof leaked; there was dry rot in the attics and wet rot in the cellars; the wainscoting was riddled with woodworm; and the privies were an offense to anyone with an ounce of delicacy. She very much feared that it would take an army of carpenters, plasterers, slaters, painters, and general laborers to set the place to rights. As a further persuasion, she had added something to the effect that she hoped to have the place ready by summer.

"We shall be expected to do our share of entertaining," she said, then added with a little less eagerness, "Even if your family has no thought of coming into

258

Scotland, we must at least extend the invitation to them."

Rand had looked at her in that way of his which indicated he was weighing every word and measuring every omission. Then he had smiled, a knowing smile, that warned her she was not pulling the wool over his eyes.

"Now this is something I can have my factor handle," he said. "Leave it to me. Serle shall take care of it."

She didn't trust Rand's factor, and would have argued the point if Rand had not been called away. Thinking she had lost the skirmish, she'd turned her attention to augmenting Strathcairn's meager staff. With only two persons in residence, however, she could hardly make a case for employing an army of servants.

A week later, to Caitlin's great surprise, she noticed chimneys smoking all over the estate.

"Your workers have been hired on," Rand told her. To her profuse expression of thanks, he had merely returned, "You are not to deal with them directly, but through my factor. Understood?"

She'd nodded her assent, though in truth she did not understand her husband's confidence in the dour-faced lowlander. She surmised that Rand was intent on demonstrating that she could not have everything her own way. It was a small price to pay if even a few families could find a living on the estate.

This was only a temporary measure, of course. When work on the house was completed, she would have to find another way of convincing her husband to keep on his tenants. There was no dearth of ideas in her head, if only she were given enough time to execute them.

"He really is a nice man," she told Bocain, and moments later, "a *very* nice man."

Wanting to express her gratitude in tangible ways, she

had cultivated the good graces of the three people at Strathcairn who were in a position to know her husband's tastes. With Rand's valet, chef, and housekeeper as her mentors, she had exerted herself to please. The clothes she wore, the food they ate, the regimen they followed were all calculated to please Rand. Of course, Rand had soon divined her purpose.

"If you really want to show your gratitude," he had said, "you would become a real wife to me."

"I . . . I can't."

He regarded her soberly. "Can't? Or won't?"

Her voice was stronger, more confident. "I can't. And you know why."

"You're still insisting that we are brother and sister?"

She nodded.

He didn't press her, although she could see that he was not best pleased by her answer. She hated deceiving him, but it was the only sure defense she could hit upon. She refused to allow their marriage to become a real one. Though she had long since forgiven him for the insults he had heaped upon her, she had never forgotten them. The words were branded on her heart. She was willing to allow that he had spoken in the heat of anger. All the same, she recognized the truth behind the furious words.

It was perfectly true that she would never fit into his world. Just thinking about Rand's family—their wealth, their prestige, their English modes and manners—was enough to bring on a fit of the dismals. When they found out about her, she was sure the explosion would be heard all the way to John o' Groats.

Soon, she must press Rand for an annulment. But not yet. Time and enough when Rand returned to England, as she knew he must. He was more English than Scots, while she was Highland born and bred. But oh, she wished . . .

Her eyes filled with unexpected tears, and her throat clogged. Almost at once, anger rushed in to rout her self-pity. Their marriage, she reminded herself, was not of Rand's choosing. Though he might lust after her, he had made his sentiments regarding her person and her lowly estate insultingly clear. She had too much pride to hold a man who did not really want her.

Following the steep, downhill track, she entered the home wood. Tall, stately oaks cut off her view of the surrounding countryside. The wood of these same oaks was much in demand in Aberdeen for its fledgling ship-building industry, as evidenced by the logging opera-tions all along Deeside. In summer, selected trees on various estates were felled, stripped, and floated down-stream to Aberdeen's harbor. Rand had no interest in shipbuilding or in turning his forests into a profitable operation. His moneys came from his holdings in En-gland. That was the trouble with him. Since he did not depend on Strathcairn for his living, he treated it as a rich man's toy.

Her thoughts were interrupted by the low whimper that came from deep within her hound's throat. "Be still!" Caitlin commanded, but Bocain ignored the order and halted in the middle of the path, legs stiff, hackles raised, her lips pulled back in a feral snarl. A flock of crows rose as one from their perches in the topmost branches of the bare oaks and shrilled a raucous warn-ing. As of one accord, their cries were cut off, and an unnatural stillness descended. The fine hairs on the back of Caitlin's neck rose.

They came to her so quickly, that she could never af-terward say from which direction they had sprung. Four sinister, snarling foxhounds, their powerful muscles bunched for attack, suddenly tore out of the woods and launched themselves upon her. They had not reckoned on Caitlin's deerhound.

One hundred and fifty pounds of unbridled, tooth-and-claw fury leapt to her mistress's defense. The fox-hounds checked, but only momentarily. They were bred for courage and would have pitted themselves against a bear if the command had been given.

The leader of the pack was dealt with swiftly. With little more than a shake of her head, Bocain broke its neck and tossed the corpse over her shoulder. Then three dogs rushed upon the deerhound simultaneously. Caitlin had recovered her wits sufficiently to reach for something to use as a weapon. Brandishing a stout oak branch above her head, she went after them.

"Call off your dogs! Call off your dogs!" Her words were automatic. Though she could not see who had charge of the dogs, she knew they would not be unescorted. These were not pets or strays, but prime specimens, highly bred and worth a king's ransom. There was only one pack of hounds in the whole area, only one master of hounds and that was the laird o' Daroch.

She wasn't surprised when she heard the whistle. By this time, however, the dogs were past heeding commands. They were in a state of frenzy, circling, feinting, gauging a weak spot into which they might clamp their powerful jaws. Bocain charged like a lion bringing down its prey. There was a hideous shriek and another fox-hound went flying, its jugular severed by deerhound's ferocious fangs.

Only two foxhounds remained. Before Bocain could

recover her position, they were on her, clamping their jaws into her back and neck.

"Call off your dogs!" Caitlin was sobbing in sheer terror. The spectacle was awful. A trail of blood and fur followed the dogs from the path into the edge of the wood. Stumbling in her haste to launch herself upon them, she fell headlong. At the same instant, something ripped into the trunk of one of the oaks not inches from where she had been standing. Dazed, she stared blindly at the tree before it registered that she had been narrowly missed by a bullet.

A man's shout brought her head round and she looked back along the path she had descended to see two figures approaching her at a run. Across their arms, they carried hunting guns. There was a moment when Caitlin was sure that her last moment had come; then one of the men yelled out, "Keep your head down!" and even as he called out the words, his companion stopped in his tracks and got off a shot, as though to warn off a watcher on the rise above them.

The report of the second shot startled the canine combatants sufficiently for human intervention to make itself felt. Another shrill whistle rent the air and the foxhounds retreated, growling and barking, then turned tail and loped off into the woods. Bocain would have gone after them if Caitlin had not dived for her dog and secured her by the collar.

The first wave of terror had ebbed, and fury rushed in to replace it. Even so, her teeth were chattering so hard by the time her rescuers came up to her that she could do no more than stutter incoherently.

As she dragged herself to her knees, the older gentleman, whom she recognized as Mr. Haughton, the tenant of Balmoral Castle, quickly crossed to her and offered her the support of his arm. "My son and I were drawn by the commotion," he said. He paused to catch his breath. "Those were Daroch's dogs, were they not? A most curious business."

"A most criminal business!" retorted Haughton's companion. He was scanning the woods and surrounding area. Not a thing stirred. "Some lunatic gamekeeper is going to find himself with a lot of explaining to do." He looked at Caitlin. "Before we came over the rise, we were sure we heard the report of a shot."

She gestured weakly toward the oak tree with the bullet in it, and the younger Haughton went to investigate. "Now that is what I call a close call," he said, tapping the tree with the flat of his hand, then belatedly, "I say, are you all right?"

Bocain was licking Caitlin's hand. "I'm fine," she said. "Truly, I'm fine." And she covered her face with both hands and began to cry.

An hour later, in her own drawing room, Caitlin was once again in command of herself. In large part, this was due to the necessity of playing hostess not only to the two gentlemen who had escorted her home but also to Fiona. Hearing that Rand had gone off to Aboyne on some business or other, Fiona had dropped by to keep her cousin company.

On reflection, and after consuming a large fortifying glass of whiskey, Caitlin had decided that the poor gamekeeper who had charge of Daroch's prize foxhounds was, in all probability, in a worse case than herself.

"You are letting him off too lightly," protested Fiona.

"He did try to call his dogs off," reasoned Caitlin,

more to persuade herself than from any firm conviction, and though at the time I was furious when he let fly with that shot, I presume he did it as a last resort." It was not fury she had experienced when the shot was fired, but a terror so profound just thinking about it made her skin come out in goose bumps.

The younger Mr. Haughton addressed his father. "What I can't understand is what he hopes to gain by skinking off like that. Two foxhounds lie dead. Daroch is bound to miss them. His gillie dare not concoct a story to the effect that Lady Randal's hound is responsible for the attack, for we were witnesses to the whole thing."

"The man panicked," answered his father. "There is no other explanation."

"You are sure they were Daroch's dogs?" asked Fiona.

Caitlin suppressed a shudder. "It would seem so. At any rate, Mr. Serle has sent one of the gillies to examine the corpses." She laughed nervously. "Anyone overhearing us would think a murder had been committed."

Fiona's eyes, usually so demure, were flashing. "If Cocain had not been with you, I shudder to think what might have happened." In an altered tone, she went on, "I suppose some will lay the whole thing at Daroch's door?"

"Why do you say that?" The older Haughton drained his glass and laid it aside before studying Fiona's bent head.

She shrugged, then looked appealingly into the eyes that were regarding her with a kindly light. "You know," she said, "it's a case of giving a dog a bad name. In these parts, the Gordons of Daroch are held to be responsible for all our misfortunes, from the cream curdling to . . . to . . . the Jacobite Rebellion."

"Daroch is not responsible," said Caitlin forcefully.

"Nor can I believe that any of his gamekeepers was s
craven as to leave Bocain to the mercy of those dogs.

Observing the tremor in Caitlin's hand, M
Haughton said reassuringly, "Your deerhound is in
class by itself. Are you worried about her? I shouldn
be. Mr. Serle seems skilled in what he is doing. Do yo
know, this episode brings to mind a dog I once owned
When I was in India, I was invited . . ."

As Mr. Haughton's voice droned on, Caitlin'
thoughts wandered to the interview she had had wit
Rand's factor. There was no doubt in her mind tha
Serle held her culpable for the whole sorry inciden
In his mind, she had no business to be runnin
around without an escort. And it was evident Serl
did not approve of dogs as pets, a deerhound least c
all. Not that he had said as much to her. Nor had h
displayed a shade of sympathy or regret for the har
rowing ordeal she had endured. Fortunately, her do
had fared better.

One glance at Bocain's injuries had softened th
man's tight-lipped, razor-sharp expression and mad
him look almost human. Clucking his tongue, ignorin
Bocain's bared fangs as though they were useless orna
ments, he had gone down on his knees to examine he
wounds. After one, half-hearted growl, Bocain ha
lapsed into pathetic whimpers as Serle's sure hands as
sessed the damage.

"A few stitches should do the trick," he'd told Caitli
crisply, and had called for two of his gillies to assist him

The elder Mr. Haughton had intervened at this point
drawing Caitlin away, suggesting that her presenc
might distract Mr. Serle from the work at hand.

In Rand's absence, and in the face of his factor'
coldness, Mr. Haughton's support, his gentleness an

266

concern were doubly gratifying. He was not an old man, far from it; in his late forties by Caitlin's reckoning. Somehow, his soft eyes and benevolent manner seemed almost grandfatherly. The thought of her own acerbic-tongued grandfather, so different from this quiet-spoken gentleman, made her want to laugh.

Caitlin came to herself with a start when her guests rose to take their leave.

"My husband will wish to thank you in person for your assistance," she told them warmly. That was no lie. Rand might want to blister her ears in private for wandering far and wide with only her dog for protection, but he was unfailingly punctilious in taking care of his obligations, and any service to his wife, however small, would undoubtedly be considered as such. That awareness put Caitlin in mind of her obligation to Mr. Serle for his care of her dog.

She was aware of a keen scrutiny from pale blue eyes before the elder Mr. Haughton shook his head regretfully. "This is goodbye," he said. "My business in Deeside is concluded. As soon as we may, we aim to take advantage of the thaw and return home."

She was still thinking of that curious scrutiny when she returned to the drawing room. Fiona was idly turning the pages of a back copy of *The Edinburgh Review.*

"I think he is a nabob," she said.

"Who?"

Fiona threw her magazine aside. "Mr. Haughton."

"What makes you say so?"

"He's lived in India for years. He rents Balmoral Castle, and"—her brow puckered—"I heard Daroch say as much. I wonder what business brought him into Deeside?"

Caitlin absently shook her head. Truth to tell, her mind was still preoccupied with this awful business of the dogs. Rand would be incensed, not only at Daroch's gamekeeper, but also because, against his express wishes, she had wandered off unattended. She did not see how, in this instance, the virtues of tact and diplomacy could help her evade her husband's wrath.

"Is your business concluded, Father?" The younger Haughton slanted his father a keen look. Though the old man had kept him very much in the dark respecting his business in Scotland, he had a general idea of what was afoot. The specifics of this affair, however, remained a mystery to him, and he found that irksome.

"I thought it was," replied his parent. "Now I'm not so sure."

"The attack on Lady Randal? Is that what is bothering you?"

"You must admit, it's a strange business."

The younger man frowned when his father made no further comment. "Don't you think it was an accident?" he prompted.

"One hopes so."

"Surely, it must be. What motive could anyone have for doing away with the girl?"

The elder Haughton shook his head. "It's too far-fetched to be credible."

Young Haughton was fast losing patience. "What is?"

"Oh, the thought that just occurred to me. Look, I don't care to deal in speculation and conjecture. I did so, once, a long time ago, and we both know I lived to regret it. This time, I want to make quite sure of my facts before I act."

They trudged on in silence for some few minutes, then the younger man offered tentatively, "That young man who came to see you—David Randal? When you read his name among the lists of those killed in action at Waterloo, you said you owed it to him to come into Scotland to right a great wrong?"

The elder Haughton assumed a less guarded expression. "And so I would have if it had been necessary. The thing is, my boy, the fates or Providence got here before me. If I had been the Deity, himself, I could not have arranged things for better effect."

Young Mr. Haughton snorted derisively. "What cant!" he exclaimed. "Since when did you believe that the powers that be interest themselves in the affairs of lesser mortals?"

"This could almost convert me to that persuasion," answered the older man mildly.

"What? The marriage of Caitlin Randal to the chief of Clan Randal?"

"The same. All things considered, things have worked out rather well."

"Ah, but not perfectly, else you would know for a certainty that your business here is concluded."

His ploy to draw out his father, as ever, was not successful. "That reminds me," observed the elder Mr. Haughton, "we have a number of courtesy calls to make in the district before we can take our leave. If we divide them between the two of us, we should get through them in short order."

The younger Haughton had to laugh. "In other words, you want me out of the way when you do whatever it is you feel you must."

"Your understanding is acute," allowed the olde man, and neatly turned the subject into speculatio about the gamekeeper who had charge of Daroch dogs.

Chapter Seventeen

Lifting the weight of her hair with both hands, she shook it back over her shoulders, then rotated her head to ease the tension in her neck. Downstairs, a door slammed, and her eyes went involuntarily to the reflection of the door in her dressing-table mirror. It gave onto her husband's chamber. When it remained reassuringly closed, she leaned both elbows on the flat of the dressing table, letting out a little hiccuping breath as she cupped her hands to her eyes.

Rand had arrived home hours ago, long after she had retired for the night. By this time Serle would have given him a complete report of the dog attack. He would know that her nerves were shot to pieces, and that she did not wish to be disturbed. Not that Rand would accost her in her own bedchamber. By tacit consent, from the day they were wed, this room had become her sanctuary. Rand would never dream of violating it.

She didn't know why she was so on edge. It wasn't only a reaction to the harrowing experience with the dogs. Nor was it fear of what Rand might have to say about her gallivanting all over the countryside without benefit of escort. A host of little things, inconsequential, revolved inside her head, warning her of some dire threat to her person.

It was past one o'clock in the morning. The servants, or at least some of them, were still up and about. For a long time, she had lain wide-eyed in her bed, listening to their shuffling footsteps as they crossed and recrossed the flagstoned hall to her husband's bookroom. He had been closeted there for hours, drinking himself into a stupor. She didn't know how she knew this, but she was certain that she wasn't imagining it. He was brooding about something. She could feel it in her bones.

The shattering of glass brought her to her feet so quickly that her silk wrapper flared and tangled in the legs of her stool, overturning it. More doors slammed and Rand's voice sounded, strident and imperious, issuing orders to servants. Dear God, what was going on?

She had just made up her mind to douse the candles and slip into bed when she heard him taking the stairs. He was moving at the speed of lightning. Thoroughly frightened now, she moved blindly, and in her haste, stumbled against the stool she had overturned. Clutching the edge of the dressing table to steady herself, her hand knocked a crystal bottle onto its side, spilling its contents, and the essence of lilies became distilled in the air.

Like a creature of the wild sensing danger, she held herself immobile, her ears straining for every sound. None came to her but her own rapid heartbeat and the moaning of the wind outside her window.

Scarcely daring to draw breath, she carefully restoppered the perfume bottle. After righting the stool, she crossed to the walnut washstand to fetch a cloth and hand towel, halting every few steps to listen for any sound that would give her a clue to what Rand was doing. The silence was only marginally reassuring.

She had just finished mopping up the top of her dressing table when a movement in the mirror caught her eye. The door to her husband's chamber slowly opened. She couldn't move; couldn't call out. As though rooted to the spot, she watched the reflection in her looking glass. Rand's voice broke the spell.

"The fragrance of lilies becomes you. They represent purity, did you know? Pure and virginal." He laughed softly, taunting her. "There are other kinds of purity, but you would know nothing of that."

She turned very slowly to face him, every instinct warning her not to make any sudden moves. He wore no jacket or neckcloth, and his white lawn shirt was open to the waist, where it disappeared below the band of his black pantaloons. One shoulder was propped against the doorframe. His blond hair was disheveled, as though he had combed his fingers through it only moments before. He was smiling, but without warmth. Though his eyes were heavy lidded, giving him a drowsy appearance, she knew he was as alert as a jungle cat lying in wait at a watering hole.

When he spoke, his voice was smooth and mellow. "Now what could possibly have brought that anxious look to your face? Could it be . . . a guilty conscience?" Though he paused to give her time to reply, she didn't even make the attempt. "Not conscience," he said whimsically. "Of course not. As we both know, you have no scruples to speak of."

He straightened, and only then did she notice that he held two crystal glasses in one hand and a bottle of wine in the other.

"Champagne," he said, "I believe it's customary," and he proceeded to fill the glasses in his left hand.

It took all of her willpower not to flinch when he advanced to within a foot of her. Without volition, she accepted the proffered glass. "I can explain about going out without an escort," she said.

He smiled, a slight curling at the corners of his mouth. "I don't doubt it. You are never stuck for an explanation, are you, my sweet? Well this one is going to tax even your fertile imagination."

When she opened her mouth to answer him, he cut in savagely. "I don't want to talk about the dogs your hound savaged. I don't want to talk about how you deliberately went against my wishes. If we must talk, let's talk about us, shall we, and this farce of a marriage we have entered upon."

He knew. Her mouth was suddenly parchment dry, and she swallowed convulsively. Now she understood the violence she sensed in him. He knew that she had deliberately deceived him, knew there had never been any obstacle to their marriage, and he wasn't annoyed in the way she had anticipated. This was deeper, stronger, more unpredictable. She could almost feel herself slipping toward the edge of an abyss.

He wandered around the room, examining various objects with desultory interest, occasionally taking long swallows from his glass. At length, he settled himself on the bed, one knee updrawn, his arm resting across it. Caitlin had not moved from her position at the dressing table, though she was half propped against it, as if her knees had buckled under her.

"You are not drinking, my pet."

Obedient to his suggestion, she raised her glass to her lips. She had the strongest urge to laugh, but knew that if she did, it would sound demented. Bedlam could not be more alarming than this.

"There never was a *sodger* who was courting you."

Soldier? What soldier? She groped in her mind, but there were no answers, only confusing impressions that made her more afraid than ever.

"I should have recognized your pattern even then. When cornered, you are amazingly inventive." He replenished his wine glass, and set the bottle of champagne on the table beside the bed. "Come here," he said, and patted the bedpane, adjusting his long length to make room for her.

There was an interval when Caitlin debated whether to reason with him or not; then she came away from the dressing table and slowly, reluctantly, approached the bed. She sat down gingerly, as far from him as she dared.

"Tell me about David," he said.

"David? What about David?"

His eyes were moving over her, and she itched to pull the edges of her wrapper together to shield herself from that brooding stare. In weak moments, she had indulged in fantasies of Rand making love to her. This was not love. There was no tenderness here. In his heated stare, she read possession and thwarted desire and something intensely dark and masculine which was beyond her knowing.

"You and David were friends. Pray explain this friendship to me. I really want to understand."

"David," she said cautiously, "was like a brother to me."

He laughed, not very pleasantly, and made a small, choked-off sound of derision.

She was terribly aware of the sheer masculine power

275

of him; broad shoulders, muscular arms and thighs. Through the parted edges of his shirt, she could detect the profusion of gold hair which covered his chest. This blatant evidence of his virility made her feel more vulnerable than ever.

Quickly averting his eyes, she concentrated on his hands. His fingers were long and deceptively effeminate as they toyed with the glass of champagne which he frequently raised to his lips. She knew the strength in those hands. It seemed inconceivable to her, then, that she had ever dismissed this man as a fop who could be frightened off by the empty threats of Daroch and the little band of conspirators. How foolish they had been to imagine they could play cat and mouse with Rand.

Then it came to her that he and she *were* playing cat and mouse, and the only thing in question was when he would decide to pounce.

"Rand," she began, appealing to the man she had come to respect and admire in the month since they had wed, "I misled you. I admit it. We are not brother and sister, but if you would give me a chance to explain . . ."

He captured her wrist with such force the glass in her hand went tumbling to the carpeted floor.

"Don't try to get around me. I'm not David. I don't allow females to hold hoops for me to jump through, especially not my wife. Now tell me about David. I won't ask you again."

He had shortened the distance between them by simply pulling on her wrist. Knowing that the worst thing she could do when he was in this mood was openly defy him, she had allowed herself to be dragged as close to him as she could come without being embraced. When

276

he released her to reach for the half-empty bottle of champagne, she let out a panicked breath.

None too carefully, he upended the bottle, sloshing champagne into his glass. Ignoring the droplets which had spilled down the front of his shirt, he drank deeply, then replenished his glass before setting the bottle away from him.

Stone cold sober, Rand was a formidable adversary. He had been drinking, and though he was far from inebriated, the controls he habitually placed on himself were fast disintegrating and she wondered if he intended that to occur.

Completely unnerved, she rushed into speech. "David was my friend. I don't know how else I can explain it. He entered into my feelings about things. We dared not meet openly, because of the feud and . . . and . . . well, it's just not done. You know what I mean; unattached males and females have no occasion to meet unless they attend balls . . . We went for walks, and sometimes went riding on the moors. It was all very innocent."

"What? Did you never entertain my cousin alone in your cottage?"

The sarcastic inflection was not calculated to reassure her. "It was all very innocent," she repeated, this time more desperately.

Under that considering stare, she felt the last vestiges of her control slipping away. "I swear it," she whispered.

"As you swore that we were brother and sister?" he said, and tossed off the dregs in his glass.

"Why won't you believe me?" she cried out.

"Oh, I do believe you. You wear your virginity like a badge of honor. But no longer."

Every instinct warned her that now, *now* he was going to pounce.

As he moved to set down his glass, she flung herself backward. One strong hand instantly reached for her, catching at her skirts, and there followed the sound of rending material. Frantically striking out at him, she half rose to her feet. He lunged for her, and they both went rolling on the bed. Panting, gasping, she tried to fight free of his iron grip. Immediately, the weight of his body trapped hers, bearing her back against the rumpled bedclothes. Winding his hands into her hair, he held her head steady and his lips came down on hers in a smothering kiss.

Twisting back and forth, trembling with impotent rage, she balled her hands into fists and struck out at him. Her blows fell harmlessly against his back. Raising himself, he quickly shifted position to take advantage of her movements, and pinned her with one long leg between hers. Her wrapper had fallen away, and the hem of her nightgown had worked its way up to her thighs. Her heart was pounding against her throat, as if it were trying to find a way out of her body. When she stopped struggling, he lifted his head slightly.

His expression was unreadable. Her eyes flashed fire. Bitter tears, scalding tears, welled up in her eyes and spilled over. With ravishing gentleness, he kissed them away. That one act of tenderness, coming so late, seemed more insulting than anything that had gone before.

"I shall never forgive you," she said, her voice as brutal and as bitter as she could make it.

His lips flattened. "I'm not asking for your forgiveness. Your submission is what I have in mind."

She caught her breath as if he had slapped her. Before she could marshal her thoughts, his head descended and his mouth moved demandingly over hers, forcing her lips to part, muffling her cries as his hand covered her breast.

Her capitulation was sudden. She wasn't moved by his passion, nor did she fear him. She wanted to demonstrate her complete and utter contempt for him. She succeeded, but not enough to deflect him from his resolve.

Taking advantage of her passivity, he quickly disrobed first her and then himself. She stiffened when he stretched out beside her. If he was determined to have her submission, she was equally determined to give him a hollow victory. She was going to remain as cold and unmoving as a corpse.

So she thought.

He knew better. Since she wasn't offering any resistance, he made a feast of her. He was fascinated by the slope of her breast and the engorged crest that flushed delectably when he laved it with his tongue. The valley of her waist, the indentation of her navel, and the dark veil shielding her femininity received equal homage. His touches grew more wanton as he felt the change in her.

Caitlin was fighting the battle of her life, holding her breath in an agony of suspense over what he would do next. The heel of his hand was there, between her thighs, kneading a pleasure point she had not known existed. She made a small sobbing sound and shifted restlessly, lifting herself to give him freer access.

"Yes," he said thickly. "This is how I knew it would be. Give in to me, Caitlin. Give in."

Those few words pulled her back from the brink of the sensual abyss into which she was slipping. He wanted her submission. With a strangled cry, she clamped her legs together. Rand sat back on his heels.

"Kate, I want you wet and open for me," he said. "Believe me, it will make it easier for you."

She gave him such a look that he almost laughed out loud. Ignoring that reproachful look, he parted her legs. Eyes locked on hers, with the tips of his fingers he tested her readiness to take him. When she moaned he let out a long shuddering breath, and moved to cover her. For a moment, he seemed to be on the point of saying something; then, shaking his head, gathering himself, he thrust into her.

The pain was so shocking, so intense, that she could not draw breath to cry out. In her extremity, she did no more than gasp. He thrust again, and again, as though uncaring for her agony, and she went wild. Twisting, heaving, in mingled pain and fury she tried to throw him off. Her movements only worked against her, ensuring a deeper more complete penetration of her body. She wasn't aware that for her sake, Rand was holding himself rigidly in check, gritting his teeth against the exquisite pleasure she brought him. She only knew that he was the aggressor and was refusing to retreat.

When the pain eased to an uncomfortable, stretching fullness, her struggles gradually became feebler. He was extraordinarily gentle with her now, brushing the lightest of kisses against her lips, her cheeks, and her throat. She flinched when he eased deeper, then sighed, a little breathy sound, when his movements brought her no pain.

He shuddered and went still. Caitlin's eyelashes lifted, and she studied him silently. His eyes were closed, and the planes of his face were hard with strain. His head was thrown back. She could feel the tremors begin to sweep through him.

"Caitlin," he said, "Caitlin."

One arm slipped beneath her, lifting her to him. He was sucking air into his lungs as if his heart would burst.

Thoroughly frightened, she cried out, "Rand, what is it? What's wrong?" and she raised her hands, grasping him by the shoulders to steady him.

Gasping for breath, laughing, he moved deeply, rhythmically, gathering her to his hard length. There could be no pleasure for her in the act. It was too soon. She had not allowed him to prepare her adequately for his possession. But at the end, when he spilled his seed deep inside her, they both knew she was not unmoved.

Afterward, when he had relieved her of his weight, he pulled her into the shelter of his body, her head resting against his chest.

"Go to sleep," he said, and adjusted the bedclothes to cover them both.

She didn't say anything, though she knew that sleep was the furthest thing from her mind. Even in this, however, he proved invincible. Before long, her eyes grew heavy. She wasn't aware that she had turned into him, sprawled against him in a gesture of trust, but Rand knew, and he lay awake for a long while after.

He was propped on one elbow and was looking down at her. She was too proud to turn away from the naked triumph in his eyes.

"You won," she said.

"More than you know." And to test the truth of his words, for his own satisfaction, he kissed her swiftly. When she made no move to evade him but allowed his kiss to linger, he could feel the pent-up tension gradually uncoil from the pit of his stomach. He had stormed the citadel and taken possession of his own. There could be no turning back now.

Subduing a grin, he reached for his shirt and shrugged into it. The embers in the grate were almost cold. Using tongs and poker he added a few lumps of coal to get a fire going, then padded over to the wash-stand. Within moments, he had returned with a wash-cloth wrung out in cold water and a linen towel.

He didn't ask her permission, but tugged the bed sheet out of her hands, exposing her nakedness. Not by the flicker of an eyelash did she betray that his pro-prietary mien caused her the least annoyance. Rand had witnessed this kind of pride in the aftermath of battle, among prisoners of war. They asked for no quarter, expected no favors. As with them, he assumed a matter-of-fact manner. Parting her legs, he washed away her virgin's blood, then carefully dried her.

"You hurt me," she said.

"Yes. More than I wanted to." He wasn't apologizing. He had made up his mind that he wasn't going to apol-ogize for anything, not because he had no regrets but because he deemed it politic not to betray any weakness with Caitlin, at least not until everything was straight-ened out between them.

When he laid the towel aside she picked it up and, ca-sually half turning away from him, proceeded to dry herself. There was no defiance in the gesture. There was reserve, but it was natural, not meant to provoke him. Knowing all this, Rand judiciously gave way and went to inspect the candles. They were drowning in their own wax. Having substituted fresh ones in their places, he came back to the bed and sat down beside her. Her back was to him.

Not wanting to shame her, at the same time refusing to give up the ground he had won, he carefully slid one hand into the mass of her hair, lifting it, brushing it forward to expose her naked back. When he began to trace each vertebra with the backs of his fingers, her spine went rigid, but that was no more than he'd expected. He gave her a moment or two to become accustomed to his touch, then he went further, pressing his open mouth to the nape of her neck, slipping his arms around her waist, pulling her to him. There was a moment when he thought she was going to resist him.

"Rand," she said, shaking her head, then relaxed against him.

She was accepting him. The thought blazed through him, igniting his blood, burning away the restraints he had imposed on himself. She was accepting him. Resting his forehead against her back, he breathed deeply as he took a moment to gather his control. He was so hot and hard, he longed to bury himself deep inside her and take his release. Yet he wanted more than that. This time, he would teach her that desire was a two-edged sword, that she was no more immune than he to the sexual magnetism which had attracted them.

"You're trembling," he told her, "and there's no need. This time, I won't hurt you."

He wanted to tell her that the last thing he had wanted was to hurt her, that he wasn't an unfeeling brute ruled by lust. He had been driven to take her, not for pleasure, though she had given him the sweetest pleasure he had ever known, but because in the taking of her a bond would be established which she could not easily shrug off. And that had been so.

The weight of her body was slumped against him, boneless, yielding, nestling trustingly in the shield of his powerful arms.

He moved slightly, bringing his hands up to cradle her breasts. She shifted but froze when her movement merely thrust herself more deeply into his cupped palms. With exquisite care, he brushed thumb and forefinger against her nipples, teasing them, plucking them into hardened peaks.

She caught her breath and half turned, arching her neck against his shoulder. With a harsh sound, he took her mouth, penetrating her with his tongue as he so ardently wished to penetrate her with his sex. She made no move to stop him when he parted her legs. He explored the silky thatch at the juncture of her thighs, then one finger pushed into the melting center of her femininity.

She made a small sound, a quick sob of arousal, and the banked fires in him flamed to a white-hot inferno. There was no subtlety now when he pushed her back into the covers. In one quick movement, he dragged his shirt over his head and tossed it to the floor. Kneeling over her, braced on his hands, he pressed open-mouthed kisses from her throat to her toes, lingering at her breasts, her belly, and the dark screen at her loins. He knew when her fingers buried themselves in his hair, flexing and unflexing convulsively, that she would yield whatever he demanded of her.

He kissed her knees and parted them, savoring her surprised, love-dazed expression. Her body was open to him, unresisting to each passionate caress. When her head began to thrash back and forth on the pillow, he came down on her. Overwhelming her with his virility, he pressed into her, then stilled, forcing the surge of unbridled lust to recede.

It was then that she took the initiative away from him. Whimpering, she arched beneath him, instinctively fusing their bodies with a deeper, more complete penetration. As he sank into her, he sucked air into his lungs. She cried out. Like lightning in an electric storm, passion leapt between them. His mouth fastened avidly on hers. She twined her arms around his neck. In a fever of need, they came together, straining violently for release, till the stunning, mindless climax engulfed them both, and they lay shuddering in each other's arms.

They remained so, silent and spent, for a long while after, his weight still pressing her into the soft feather mattress. Finally, raising his head, forcing himself to breathe normally, he waited until her somber gray eyes lifted to meet the inflexible blue in his.

"Now everything is different between us," he told her, not harshly, not carelessly, but with an uncharacteristic gravity which she could not ignore.

"Don't you think I know it?" She sounded a bit like a fractious child.

It was done, but she wasn't going to let him have everything his own way. Now why did that make him smile?

Pulling her to his side, he turned her into his arms. He ran his hands possessively down her spine, over her thighs, and draped one smooth leg over his flanks. Her skin was cool. Reaching down, he pulled up the bedclothes. Her head was nestled under his chin.

"*Mo gaol orist.* What time is it?" she asked drowsily.

He glanced at the clock. "Don't worry," he said, "you still have an hour or two to make up your beauty sleep."

With one hand, he tipped up her chin and kissed her softly. "Little hypocrite," he said, teasing her, "you wanted me as much as I wanted you. Tell me. I want to hear you say it."

"There wouldn't be much point in denying it, would there?"

The pout in her voice brought the smile flashing to his lips. "There would not be any point in denying it," he corrected, and laughter sparkled in his eyes.

She slapped him, not very forcefully, but not quite playfully either. "There are more important things between a man and woman than this," she said, gesturing vaguely at the unkempt bed.

"Name me one," he retorted. He was nuzzling her ear, savoring this new docility that allowed him to touch her intimately and without demur. Testing her, he pressed light kisses to her lips, her throat, and finally to the soft swelling flesh of her breasts. When she made no move to parry this tender assault on her person, but rather adjusted herself in obedience to his unspoken demands, the last of his regrets quietly slipped away.

Caitlin was frowning in concentration. "Friendship is more important . . . and . . . and affection, don't you think?" She didn't want to be completely transparent with him. The wonder of what they had just shared was so awesome, she was still reeling from the effects of it. She needed time to get her bearings, time to sift through what she was feeling so that she could discover why such pleasure would make her want to bawl her eyes out.

He pulled away slightly to get a better look at her. The smile in his eyes had cooled. "And what you shared with David compares to this?" His hand calmly took possession of one breast, molding it with gentle, persuasive pressure.

David? Why was he mentioning David at a time like this? Her mind cast about frantically, trying to recall what she had shared with David. "We were friends ... confidantes. Our minds were in tune. I don't know how else to explain it. 'Soul mates' was how David used to describe it."

The arms holding her went rigid, and his nostrils flared. "God forbid that I should begrudge David your mind." A new violence had crept into his voice. "I'll not trespass on holy ground," he went on, mystifying her, "but I'll not be denied my due either. It's too late for that."

"Rand," she murmured weakly when he pressed into her again. "Is this all you can think about?"

He braced himself on his arms, levering himself higher, holding himself above her. "This," he said, and sheathed himself inside her, "is the only thing that matters to a male. I don't envy what you had with David. If you must know, I feel sorry for him, poor devil! Soul mates! As though any man worth his salt would be satisfied with that!

"He may have been grateful for the crumbs from your table, but don't expect the same forbearance from me. You may keep your precious mind. I wouldn't know what to do with it if you gave it to me on a silver platter. I'm your husband. I won't be turned away from this."

His kiss was so violent, she thought her neck would snap. An instant later, there was the taste of blood in her mouth. Her hands splayed out against the corded muscles of his arms, trying to gentle him. And then gentleness became the last thing she wanted as he plunged her into an unfamiliar world that was primitive and unashamedly wanton, where nothing existed but the driving demand of their bodies to blend into one.

Chapter Eighteen

"England!" Caitlin spat out the word as if it were a moth she had inadvertently sucked into her mouth. "I have no desire to go to England! What would I do there? How would I pass the time?" And how could she face Rand's family, be they ever so polite, knowing the scorn they must feel for her, an interloper and a foreigner?

Her eyes were eloquently trained on Rand. His attention was not on her, but on the salvers on the long sideboard from which he was filling his plate. Having made his selection, he sat down across from her at the dining table.

"Is that all you are having for breakfast?" He indicated the small bowl in front of her. "That's hardly enough to sustain a sparrow. You would do better taking a leaf out of my book. This beef steak is not only tender, it will do you good. You could stand to gain a pound or two."

"Porridge is good for you!" She responded as though he had made an unwarranted attack on everything dear to her. "I'll have you know that during the wars with England, the Scottish army practically survived on oats in one form or another."

"Which wars were those?"

"What?" The twinkle in his eyes was confusing her. "I don't know. William Wallace and all that."

"Oh those wars! Now let me see . . . That must be all of . . ."—he gazed reflectively at the ceiling before bringing his gaze back to hers—"yes, all of five hundred years ago. That's the trouble with the Scots. Once they get an idea in their heads, they never let it go. If memory serves, and I'm trying to recall what my history masters had to say on the subject, William Wallace and his followers were hammered by the English. I don't think that says very much for your porridge."

Her nostrils were quivering. "Your schoolmasters were Englishmen!"

"Very true. Am I to understand that Scottish schoolmasters give the victory to the Scots in that particular conflict?"

"You know very well that they do not!"

"Ah!"

"But Robert the Bruce soon sent your lot packing when he became king. At Bannockburn, the Scots thoroughly trounced the English. It was a rout."

She said this with so much relish that Rand's lips quivered. When they had steadied, he said reasonably, "Robert the Bruce, like his English counterpart, was a French-Norman knight. So what it comes down to is this: the war for Scottish independence was nothing more than a dispute between two powerful Norman overlords over territorial rights."

Breathing audibly, she sat back in her chair and regarded him with a reproachful eye. Summoning her dignity, she said, "We have wandered far from the point. You were suggesting that we remove to England so that you might attend to your affairs there, and I merely pointed out that I would prefer to remain here."

"It wasn't a suggestion."

"Beg pardon?"

"I wasn't making a suggestion. We are both going to England, Caitlin, and that's final."

"You can't expect me to desert Bocain at a time like this!"

"Bocain? She's not in any danger. My factor said so. In another week or two, she'll be as right as rain."

"Serle! What does he know? He has muzzled her, did you know?"

Rand's sigh betrayed a hint of exasperation. "You'll never give the man his due, will you? Look, the muzzle is in the dog's best interest. She has sustained a number of nasty wounds. You know as well as I do that a dog's instinct is to scratch and lick its injuries. If that happens, the stitches will open and infection will set in. Is that what you want?"

"Rand," she began, trying to get around him.

He stopped her with a look. "Do you mind? I'd like to eat my breakfast before it gets cold. Eat your porridge, Caitlin, there's a good girl, else you'll have my poor chef in a passion. My valet tells me that poor Ladubec labored for hours to obtain just the right consistency for your demanding palate. Surely you don't mean to offend him by rejecting his efforts?"

Smiling faintly at the jest, she picked up her spoon and obediently began to eat. She thought it strange and rather daunting that since Rand had become her lover—was it only last night?—a subtle shift in power had taken place. It wasn't precisely that she felt like a chattel or a possession. It wasn't that Rand was any more dictatorial than he had ever been. The change was mostly in her.

Their coming together had upset all her preconceived notions about how it should be between a man and a woman. In her ignorance, she had denigrated the importance of physical love, at best assigning it a place only marginally higher than reading a good book. Rand had shown her how wrong she had been. The kind of intimacy they had shared in that long night of passion had surpassed her wildest fantasies. And herein lay the difference between them. Something inside her had softened toward Rand. He, on the other hand, had become more demanding, less giving. If she wasn't careful, she could very well end up turning into a doormat.

A picture, a pathetic picture, took possession of her mind: Caitlin Randal begging for a man to notice her. It hurt. As clear as crystal, it came to her. She was robed in the diaphanous attire, what little there was of it, of a slave girl, some woman of the East, whose only object in life was to gratify the slightest whim of her lord and master. He wouldn't care what she was feeling, what she was thinking, so long as she kept her thoughts to herself. If she never had an original idea, it would be all the same to him. Her place in his life would be negligible, while for her, he would be as necessary as the very air she breathed.

Her spine stiffened in resentment, and she glared across the table at the man she had no difficulty imagining in the role of potentate. She decided, then, that his face was too aggressively masculine for her taste. It wasn't the first time she had detected an edge of cruelty in the curl of his finely molded mouth. His eyes could be as hard as chips of sapphires, as cold as ice. No one who knew him doubted that he possessed a formidable will.

Such a man would bend a woman or he would break her.

"Hah!" The word exploded from her lips, startling her.

Rand looked up with faint alarm. "What is it?"

Her eyelashes lowered, concealing her murderous expression, "This porridge is too hot," she mumbled.

"Too hot?" He looked puzzled. "I would have thought it would be cold by now."

It was cold. Blowing on it, she said ungraciously, "Who is eating this porridge, you or I?"

"Mmm. What's got your dander up?" Recognizing that light in her eye, he made haste to head her off. "You seem to think of England as some exotic foreign country."

"It is a foreign country, and one I have no wish to visit."

"Nevertheless, a wife's place is with her husband. Where I go, you go."

"As you wish," she said, striving to emulate that expression which was peculiar to the English, evincing a certain balance between indifference and imperturbability. Inside, her Scottish temper was on a slow simmer.

His smile was not quite a leer. "I am delighted when you give in to me. But don't become too docile, my love, or I shall scarcely know you."

Her smile held. "That will be the day," she murmured.

When she rose to leave the table, he captured her wrist. "What are your plans for this morning?"

"If we are leaving tomorrow, there are a score of things I must attend to."

"If you leave the house, for whatever reason, I want you to take MacGregor with you."

She frowned down at him. "I won't go further afield than Glenshiel House."

"Caitlin," He sighed. "Just—"

"I know, I know. Just do as you say. Well, allow me to put you right about a few things, Iain Randal. You are not an Arab sheik, and I am not your slave girl. I am a Scottish lass, a Highland lass, and where I come from it's the lad who does the running, not the other way round. So don't let last night go to your head. Last night I gave in to you because I wanted to. Don't expect to have everything your own way."

As the door slammed at her exit, Rand sat back in his chair and dabbed at his lips with his table napkin. Crushing it, he flung it on the table. "Now what the devil brought that on?" he demanded of the empty room.

Rand spent the morning with his factor, going over the scene of the attack. The casual attitude he had taken with Caitlin was not evident here.

"Foxhounds don't usually attack people unprovoked," he said.

"No, your lordship, but they will set upon any stray dog that doesn't belong to the pack."

"So you think it was Bocain they were after?" When Serle nodded, he said, "How is she, by the way?"

"She's lost a lot of blood, but there's no fever that I can detect. In a few weeks, with care and rest, she should be on her feet. Yet . . ." His voice faded as he reflected on the dog's progress.

"What is it?"

Serle shook his head. "She's restless, shivery. I don't

294

know how to explain it. The slightest noise will set her off."

"After what she's been through, who can blame her?"

"Aye. That must be it."

He waited for his factor to elaborate. When Serle remained silent, Rand said, "You do realize that you will have the care of the dog while we are away?"

"Aye. There's no way ye can take her with ye. Does her ladyship know it?"

Rand was examining the tree where the bullet had struck. He nodded absently. Through his teeth he said, "If and when I find the man who fired this bullet, I think I shall set Bocain on him to tear his throat out."

Serle's hand absently went to his neckcloth. "Ye think the bullet was meant for the dog?"

Rand's head snapped round. "Don't you?"

"Aye. I suppose. Nothing else makes sense."

Rand's eyes narrowed to slits. "Where were you, Mr. Serle, when all this was taking place?"

It was a question that Rand was soon to put to several people, none of whom, to his way of thinking, had a satisfactory explanation, and some of whom took exception to the implied accusation. Daroch was one of these last.

"Where was I? Where were you—that's what I'd like to know!" Daroch's face was livid.

Having inspected the kennels, they were making their way back to the house.

"You don't deny that the dogs who attacked Caitlin were yours?" said Rand.

"I don't deny it. You heard my gamekeeper. The dogs got out. By the time he realized a number were missing, your factor was storming through our gates."

"And you were not here," pointed out Rand.

In Daroch's bookroom, they resumed the conversation. "You didn't answer my question," said Rand.

"I was in Aberdeen," Daroch answered truculently. "My solicitor can confirm it if you like. Good God, man, why the inquisition? It was an accident. I'm willing to apologize or make restitution. What more would you have me do? Here!"

None too gently, he shoved a glass of whiskey into Rand's hand. *"Slainte mhath,* good health to you," said Daroch, and bolted his drink.

Rand examined the glass. Satisfied that it was clean, unlike the rest of the house, he raised it to his lips. In the normal way of things, he would have recoiled from making observations of a personal nature on things which did not concern him, but there was a mystery to Daroch and he was resolved to clear it up.

"How can you bear to live in this squalor?" Rand said, gesturing to the mounds of dirty dishes and the piles of old newspapers stacked at random on tables or on the floor. The solid oak furniture, of Jacobean design, and the small window panes in the long windows were coated with a film of soot and dust.

"It's a bachelor establishment. It suits me," Daroch answered carelessly, without a trace of resentment.

"You are fastidious about your person. Why this laxity in your domicile?"

Daroch's expression had altered slightly. Shrugging, he said, "I've learned to my cost that female domestics are more trouble than they are worth. And my gillies would rather find anything to do than clean up the house."

A fragment of conversation came back to Rand, something to do with the young laird and the daughter

f a former housekeeper. Scandal seemed to dog
aroch's heels.

"I believe you," said Rand. "When the master is
way, there's no telling what the servants will get up to."
e brought his glass to his lips and slowly imbibed.
ithout any ulterior motive, he then asked, "By the
ay, how does your friend go on, the one I saw you
ith at The Twa Craws?"

Daroch went as rigid as a bar of iron and the color
rained out of his face.

Rand's eyes narrowed in speculation. "I remember
inking that he was in urgent need of the services of a
hysician," he observed casually.

"A physician?" Daroch laughed, a forced sound that
e quickly choked off. "Don't trouble your head about
y friend. We got him to a physician, all right. No, re-
lly, he's . . . eh . . . in the peak of condition, all things
onsidered."

No amount of clever talking on Rand's part could in-
uce him to say more.

The next person Rand put his question to was Mr.
Haughton, the younger.

"We were on our way home, descending the rise,
vhen we heard the commotion. It sounded to us as if a
ouple of lions were having a go at each other."

"What about the shot that was fired?"

Haughton gave him a long, level look. "It came from
bove us, but you must know this if you examined the
ole made by the bullet."

Ignoring this moot observation, Rand said, "I had
oped to find your father here, to thank you both for
he assistance you rendered to my wife."

"He went off this morning to keep an appointment
omewhere in the neighborhood. He should have re-

turned long since. As you can see, our boxes are packed and ready. We were due to leave before lunch

Sensing that the other man was more annoyed than anxious, Rand made a joke of it. "Ah, parents. They rarely afford their children the same courtesy they demand from us. Or is it that the older we get, the more the tables are turned?"

Haughton laughed. "I'll tell him you offered your thanks. This is goodbye, then. I don't know when we shall come into Scotland again."

"Perhaps we shall meet up in London. Do you take the season?"

"We may. I say, does this mean that you and Lady Randal are leaving Deeside as well?"

"We leave tomorrow at first light."

"'Good God! Don't say you think she stands in any danger!"

Rand was quick to nip that notion in the bud. "Not in the least," he answered emphatically. "I am convinced that the whole thing was an accident. It was always in my mind to go to England to introduce my wife to the members of my family. We shall be back in Deeside before you know it."

But it wasn't only to introduce Caitlin to his family which motivated Rand. Having begun to delve into the circumstances of her birth, he was reluctant to give up the investigation.

Investigation was too forceful a word, Rand later amended. He was merely intrigued by the name the bard of Aboyne had given him. Ewan Grant. It was possible that his mother knew of the man, and if not his mother, then certainly his uncle ought to be able to give him a clue. David's father was as often at Strathcairn as his own father had been.

It wasn't a serious investigation, Rand decided, wondering if he were trying to convince himself. Having ascertained that his own father was not involved, he had no driving interest in discovering the identity of Caitlin's father. If her sire proved to be a common footman, it would be all the same to him. He was not like those in his class to whom bloodlines were everything. As a soldier in Wellington's army, he had soon learned the value of bloodlines. They were worthless. In his opinion, some of the most illustrious titles in England belonged to incompetent blockheads who had no business setting foot within a hundred miles of a battlefield. To such as those, he gave a wide berth.

Still, his interest was piqued, that much he would allow. Ewan Grant. Someone somewhere must know what had become of him. He would make a few inquiries and that would be the end of it. Whether or not he would pass along what he discovered to Caitlin remained to be seen.

As for the dog attack upon her, Rand was quite sure in his own mind that the whole thing was unpremeditated—not that that mitigated the offense of the fool who had irresponsibly shot at the dogs. He was not surprised that the gillie who had done such a thing was too craven to come forward. If he ever learned the man's identity, he would stuff his gun down his throat.

The attack had been nothing more sinister than a horrifying misadventure; as the evening progressed, Rand became more and more convinced of it. A premeditated attack required a motive. Who would wish to harm Caitlin or her dog?

The thought circled in his mind as he quietly sipped his glass of whiskey at Glenshiel's dining table. Since this was to be their last night in Deeside for some time to come, the ladies had elected to remain at the table where the decanter and glasses were passed round. There was no port to be had, for Glenshiel eschewed that libation as something uncouth and foreign, fit only for the palates of lowlanders and others of that ilk. Rand spared a thought for his cellar at Cranley, his place in Sussex where he had laid down several casks of the finest port to be had in the whole of Portugal.

Though the subject of the dog attack had been thoroughly exhausted, no one seemed ready to relinquish it.

"Daroch's foxhounds," disparaged Glenshiel, not for the first time. "I might have known it."

Answering Fiona's silent, anguished appeal, Caitlin interposed, "Bocain is in no condition to travel. I wondered, Grandfather, if I might leave her in your care?"

Before Glenshiel had time to consider the question and all that it might entail, Charlotte Randal rushed in. "No! That is, with you gone, Caitlin, there's no saying what your dog will do. I remember the time you ran off to Aberdeen. Bocain reverted to something untamed and ferocious, like a creature of the wild."

"Whisht, woman, you're exaggerating." Glenshiel's brows were down. "The dog made a wee bit o' a ruckus, as was natural, 'tis all."

"She practically attacked me!"

"Caitlin," Rand said, "really there's no need for this. Serle is perfectly capable of looking after your dog."

It was Donald Randal who settled the argument. "I understand, lass. Bocain is more like a bairn to ye than a dog. There's a room in the stables. I'll take care o' her for ye. And never fear, Charlotte. The hound will no be allowed tae run tame in the house."

* * *

300

Bocain paused to sniff the air, then growled deep in her chest before returning to her task. For the last little while, she had been struggling to remove the muzzle from her powerful jaws, as though sensing an urgency she had not sensed before. The object of her fear and hatred was still in place, however, and her skin was rubbed raw from her efforts.

When the stable door creaked on its hinges, the dog went rigid. Her ears pricked to catch the sound of footsteps which crossed the cobbled floor to her stall. Before the door opened, the hound's tension had gradually receded, and she was back to pawing at the leather straps which bound her jaws together.

"Oh, you poor dear!" Fiona stood framed in the doorway. Setting down her lantern on the floor behind her, she went down on her knees beside the dog.

"Bocain, this has got to stop. The muzzle is for your own good. If you go on like this, you'll disfigure your beautiful face. Then where will you be?"

The dog cocked her head to one side, and looked at the girl with huge, soulful eyes.

In the same bracing tone, Fiona continued, "See what I've brought to tempt your appetite? A shank of mutton. I know it's your favorite, because you-know-who told me so." As she spoke her fingers fumbled with the buckle securing the dog's muzzle. "I daren't say her name, and you know why. Bocain, this is silly. She has only been gone a fortnight, and already you are down to skin and bone."

The muzzle was off, and Fiona dangled the meat bone in front of the dog's nose. Bocain sniffed at it disinterestedly, then licked Fiona's face. When the outside door creaked, both girl and dog went still.

"Who's there?"

The door banged, then silence, and Fiona let out a shaky laugh. "I shouldn't be here," she told the dog. "Mama would have a fit if she could see me now. She thinks you are unpredictable, can you believe it? Why, you are as safe as a newborn lamb!"

Sitting back on her heels, she studied the hound. Though Bocain's wounds had healed nicely, and the sutures were out, bald patches of skin showed up redly on the dog's back and neck. Her coat was dull, and her ribs stood out prominently. In only two weeks, she had lost more than a stone.

"Eat!" This time Fiona's voice was rough with anxiety. She pushed the bone under the dog's nose. Bocain merely turned her head away.

"You must eat." She had gentled her tone, trying to coax the dog. "How am I going to face Caitlin if you pine away to nothing?"

At mention of the forbidden word, Bocain's tail began to lash the air, and she strained against the lead that tethered her to the wall. Pitiful, almost human whimpers of distress, like the crying of a baby issued from her throat.

Fiona flung her arms around the dog's neck. "I know, I know," she said soothingly. "You miss her dreadfully. I wish there were some way I could make you understand. She isn't gone forever, you know. She'll be back. And even supposing Rand insists that they stay on in England, I have my instructions. I'm to take you there in person. Now doesn't that make you feel better?"

The hound had lost interest in Fiona. Something outside, some sound or scent discernible only to herself, had caught her attention. Her lips were pulled back, and she emitted a low growl.

"If you are not going to eat the bone I've brought

you, I should go." Fiona looked down at the muzzle in her hand. "I don't like this any better than you, but it's for your own good." She made to slip the muzzle over the dog's jaws and Bocain snapped at her. Fiona pulled back in alarm, dropping the muzzle. "Bocain!" she berated. "I'm your friend. You've never objected before."

Bocain licked the girl's face, but when Fiona picked up the muzzle, the dog growled warningly.

"Oh, have it your own way! I don't suppose there's any harm in leaving it off. See that you eat the meat on that bone before I return." She rose to her knees, then to her feet. "I'm warning you, there's going to be the devil to pay if you open those wounds."

The dog's head was up. "What is it you hear? What scent have you picked up?" Fiona cocked her head, straining to catch any stray sound that would account for the dog's unease. Everything she heard was reassuring: the occasional snort or whinny from a horse in one of the other stalls; the sound of the rain as it bounced off the roof of the stable. There were few gillies about, for most of them made up a search party that went out every day at dawn to systematically comb the countryside for Mr. Haughton. They never returned until dark had fallen.

It was a sad business. It seemed that only the day before Caitlin and Rand had departed for England Mr. Haughton had gone off on some unspecified errand and had simply vanished into thin air. Two days were to pass before his son had given the alarm. He'd suspected, hoped, that his father had had an accident while out walking and would be soon found. Two weeks had gone by, and still the search parties had not found him.

There was no hope for him now. No one native to Deeside doubted the outcome. The temperatures warmed up during the daylight hours, but at night, once the sun had set, in the mountains the cold was lethal.

She shivered. "Poor Mr. Haughton," she said softly.

Finally, with a last regretful look at the shank of mutton, Fiona left the stall, picking up her lantern as she went, taking the light with her.

Ignoring the succulent meat bone, Bocain made to follow the girl. Her head was jerked back by the short leather lead which tethered her to the wall. She gave a low growl and tried again, with the same result. Whining now, Bocain put her head back and strained at her collar, using her powerful haunches for leverage. Abruptly lowering her head, she turned and stared into the gloom. Though her lips were pulled back and her hackles were up, she made no sound.

"Bocain!"

At the sound of the hateful voice coming to her through the darkness, the hound tensed her powerful muscles, readying herself to spring. Soft laughter, barely audible, brought the dog's head up even more. When the door to her stall slammed shut, she launched herself at it. The collar brought her up short with so much force that the wooden walls of the stall began to shake.

"I thought as much," said the voice on the other side of the door. "It's uncanny that a dog should sense the change in me. No one else does." There was a pause, then, "Forgive me, Bocain. I have no choice."

Though the words were said in a soothing undertone, the dog went wild. Again and again, she rushed at the door. At each assault, the collar around her neck tightened, almost strangling her. By this time, the horses in the adjoining stalls were stamping their feet and whinnying their alarm. But this was as nothing when a sheet of flame suddenly engulfed the north wall.

Thoroughly maddened now, Bocain leapt for the door. At the second attempt, the leather lead snapped and the dog slammed against the obstruction. There was the sound of splintering wood; then the door came away from its frame, and Bocain went tumbling into the central corridor.

The exits were a solid wall of fire. Whining, tracking and backtracking, the hound frantically circled the stable, looking for an escape. The smoke was thick and acrid and though she kept her head well down, it entered her nostrils and she began to heave and choke. As each second passed, the horses became more and more panicked until they were pounding their hooves against the doors of their stalls, their ghostly screams echoing and reechoing under the wooden rafters. Outside, men were calling out to each other. When one of the beams overhead burst into flame, the dog was galvanized into action. She charged.

Like an exploding artillery shell, she went hurtling through a small window that gave onto the tack room at the back of the stable. Glass shattered into a thousand shards as the hound's momentum carried her forward, over a wooden water trough and into a quagmire of mud and water. Half-stunned by the impact, she lay shuddering in the mire, sucking fresh air into her lungs in great noisy gulps. At the sound of human voices close by, she bared her teeth. A moment later, she loped away into the shadow of one of the stone dikes and gained the track that led to the shieling.

For three days and a night, Bocain haunted the places where Caitlin's scent was still strong. Though there were plenty of people about, she never showed herself to any of them, but slunk away before her presence could be detected. Dried blood and mud covered her once glossy coat and her skin hung grotesquely in folds.

On the fourth night out, she left the environs of the shieling. As if driven by instinct, she made for the place where Caitlin had found her as a pup, taking the long way round, crossing the river at the ford, then recrossing it further up. Once there, before many days had past, starvation compelled her to hunt for her own food. Rabbits and small game were all that she could manage, until she slowly regained her former strength.

Soon, she was stalking deer. On one occasion, she crossed the river at the Inver ford and lay in wait, high up in the hills, where the snow still lingered, above Balmoral Castle. The buck she selected for her prey was fleet of foot and led her for miles over rough terrain. She was gaining on it, when some scent distracted her attention.

Growling now, Bocain turned aside and picked her way down a steep incline to the bottom of a gully. Wedged into the gully, she came upon Haughton's remains. The scent that she hated above all others was still clinging to the dead man's clothes.

Bocain worked at the loose scree and snow which covered the dead man until she had freed him. Dragging him clear, she tore at his clothes until they were in shreds and the wind had whipped them away.

Chapter Nineteen

The dowager Lady Randal was in a fine fettle. Her eldest son had sent word that they could expect him at Cranley before the month was out. Her various offspring could not help remarking the change in their mother: her step was more sprightly; she had more to say for herself; the servants were all set to clean the house from cellars to attics. But it was the gleam in her eye which gave one of them pause.

"She is up to something. You can bet your last groat on it."

The comment came from her ladyship's son, Peter, who, though only four and twenty, was affectionately if not a little provokingly addressed as "Pater" by his younger siblings, a role which had fallen to him as one by one his three older brothers had deserted the nest.

Mary Randal's fingers fumbled on the harpsichord keyboard, and she said something rude under her breath. Swiveling to face her brother, she said, "Sorry, I didn't quite catch that, Pater?"

"I wish you would give me my proper name. I am not your father, thank God. Furthermore, young ladies do not swear."

Mary threw an amused look at the only other occupant in the music room, her twin, Martha. "And he wonders why we call him 'Pater,'" she said.

Laying aside her needlework with a muttered imprecation, Martha gave her attention to her brother's words. "You're right, Pater. Mama *is* up to something, but damned if I know what it is."

Peter let out a long-suffering sigh. Tossing aside the newspaper he had been perusing, he glared fiercely at one sister and then at the other. "Kindly refrain from using bad language, or I shall be forced to take punitive action."

"What does that mean?" asked Mary, looking a question at her twin.

"You know, he'll do something nasty, like carry tales to Mama, and we'll have to forgo dancing class or some other treat."

"Pater, you wouldn't! Signor Luigi is our only diversion! We'll watch our language, won't we, Martha?"

"I'll say! Anything to ensure that the signor is not taken away from us. Well, how else are we going to learn how to flirt, and so on, when our brothers can't be prevailed upon to teach us?"

Martha was referring not only to Rand and Peter, but also to two married brothers who fell between the eldest and the youngest male Randal.

Mary nodded wisely. "To hear our brothers talk, anyone would think they were saints. We may be only sixteen, but we know a thing or two."

"Such as why our governess gave notice to quit. Poor old Miss Hadley. It was all too much for her."

"Scandalous!" Mary said the word with relish. "Harry's elopement she might have allowed. It can happen in the best of families. But when Robert eloped as well, it was just one elopement too many. I heard her tell Mama so."

"True. And poor Miss Hadley didn't know the half of it. Perry Marples told me, in strictest confidence, that—"

"Silence!" Peter's roar of rage had the desired effect. Both girls pressed their lips together and looked properly chastened. "You girls are incorrigible, do you know? I don't mind telling you, I can hardly wait till Rand gets back. Then *he* can have the schooling of you. God knows, I've failed miserably to inculcate even a modicum of decorum. You are tear-aways, that's what you are." No one thought it strange that Peter did not lay the blame for the girls' lack of decorum at their mother's door. "If all else fails, I warn you, I shall advise Mama to send you packing to one of our married sisters. Perhaps Emily or Jane can succeed where I have failed."

His threat worked on his sisters as he knew it would. "We'll mend our ways, won't we, Martha?"

"Peter, it was only a joke! Don't you know when we are funning? We wouldn't dream of conducting ourselves improperly in polite society."

Peter was far from mollified. "If you go on as you have been doing, you may *never* find yourselves in polite society. I shall see to it that you remain in the schoolroom until you are both withered old maids." Having gratifyingly robbed his sisters of speech, he made a quick exit, containing his laughter till he entered the privacy of his office.

"Well!" said Mary when she had come to herself. "What's got into him? *He's* not thinking of eloping, is he?"

Martha considered her sister's words seriously. "I shouldn't think so. He's too young." She mentally reviewed the history she had been compiling on her family, a history which her elders, in all innocence, had persuaded her to undertake in the hopes of drawing off some of the girl's excess energies. Their ploy had succeeded, but not in the way they had anticipated.

Having marshaled her facts, Martha continued, "According to all the information I have gathered, the males in our family are all quite sensible until they are overtaken by their twenty-fifth birthday. That's when all hell breaks loose, if you'll pardon the expression."

"They really are a shocking lot!"

"Oh, quite!"

"With the exception of Rand. He doesn't fit the pattern. How do you explain that?"

With the sagacity of one who has been deemed the expert, Martha patiently explained this annoying aberration. "He's been away at the wars. That must have retarded his development."

For a long interval, the twins silently contemplated what they knew of their oldest brother's amatory exploits, which was considerable.

"There was Lady Margaret," mused Mary aloud at one point. "I thought he might elope with her."

"Meggins?" Martha vigorously shook her head. "A man doesn't marry his mistress," she said.

"Doesn't he? How would you know?"

"I thought everybody knew."

This was said with so much condescension that Mary did not pursue that line of inquiry.

"Helen Fielding," she suggested.

"No, and for the same reason."

"Juliet Halliday."

"Ditto to that too."

Several names were suggested in quick succession

only to meet with the same end. Finally, in exasperation, Mary burst out, "I wish you would tell me what a mistress is so that I can hit on someone he is likely to elope with."

Martha's jaw dropped. "You don't know what a mistress is? *You don't know what a mistress is?*" She laughed disbelievingly. "I can't believe I am hearing this. Why, a mistress is beautiful. She goes to the opera. She drives in a fine carriage and is attired in dazzling gowns."

"I thought as much."

"What?"

"You don't know what a mistress is either." And grabbing for a cushion, Mary went for her sister, pursuing her around the house till their shrieks and whoops of laughter brought their brother's wrath down upon their heads.

The dowager's thoughts, no less than her daughters', were focused on Rand, and with much the same feelings of speculation.

"I blame the war," she told the portrait which hung above the marble mantelpiece in the library. Her late husband's eyes, so like Rand's, gazed down at her as though silently contemplating her confidences. "I tried. Believe me, my darling, I tried. Every time he came home on furlough, and long before that, I paraded a whole bevy of eligibles in front of his nose." She shook her head sadly. "It was all to no purpose. He would rather spend his time pursuing the dashers. Well, you would know all about that, wouldn't you?"

She took a few steps away from the portrait, then quickly returned to it. "This calls for desperate measures. Surely, this time you agree with me?"

There was no visible response from the portrait; nevertheless, after a moment Lady Randal visibly brightened.

"Mama?"

At the sound of her youngest son's voice, she spun on her heel. There was an absurdly guilty look on her face.

Peter Randal quickly crossed the distance that separated them. He looked first at his father's portrait, then at his mother. "I thought I heard voices," he said.

"Did you?" She slipped her arm through his. "As you can see, I am quite alone. Was I talking to myself again?" She clicked her tongue. "Old age must be creeping up on me."

He smiled, and his whole face softened. "You'll never be old to me," he said.

"Flatterer! You sound more like your father every day." She then asked inconsequentially, "How old are you anyway?"

Though he looked to be surprised at the question, he answered at once, "Four and twenty," then frowned at the little smile which winked at the corners of his mother's mouth.

Over dinner, the conversation was all of Rand and the letter which had arrived that morning.

"It says that he has a surprise for us," said Mary.

For a moment, a very fleeting moment, the dowager allowed her imagination to soar. No, she decided. She'd built her hopes up before now only to have them dashed to smithereens. "I expect he's bringing John Murray with him," she said.

"Or he might have purchased a stud bull for our herd." Peter's enthusiasm for the idea was evident in his voice. "We discussed it before he took off for Deeside. The Scots are getting quite a name for themselves you know. Their cattle are in demand all over England."

"Really?" said Lady Randal, dutifully summoning as much interest as she could command for a subject which she knew was dear to her son's heart. In Rand's absence, each successive son had taken over the management of the estates, until the task had fallen to Peter. Like his brothers, he had demonstrated a remarkable aptitude for the work. "Do go on, dear. How will this improve our stock?"

Peter wasn't given the chance to respond. Martha, to whom Mary had passed Rand's letter, abruptly cut in, "What's all this about a family reunion?" She quoted, "I thought we might all get together *en famille*, so to speak, and this time, Mama, I promise not to upset all your plans."

Lady Randal said mildly, "Don't interrupt when a conversation is in progress, dear. It's not polite. What Rand is referring to is the little family gathering I had it in mind to arrange for him before he took off for Scotland. With one thing and another, it had to be postponed."

"A family gathering? Yes, I like that idea." Peter had pinned each sister in turn with a playfully menacing look. "Perhaps Emily or Jane can be persuaded to invite the twins for a visit . . . A long visit," he added meaningfully.

The heated exchange that this provoked was ignored by the dowager. "A family house party," she mused, "with a few select guests. And in conclusion, a gala ball. Yes, my mind is set on it, and really, we are close enough to London that the distance can scarcely matter.

Besides, we have plenty of spare beds to put up our guests."

"Guests? What guests?" Peter demanded, baffled. "Rand said nothing about guests."

The twins were in transports. "A house party!" squealed one. "How famous!"

"And a ball! Just like the return of the prodigal!"

At this enthusiastic reception of her plans, the dowager beamed. "I'd best write out the invitations and have them delivered as soon as possible. When does Rand say we may expect him, Martha?"

As mother and daughters became involved in the intricacies of planning a house party and ball, Peter absently sipped his wine. His mother was up to something, he thought. He would bet his last groat on it.

The nearer the coach drew to Cranley, the more uneasy Caitlin became. It started when Rand idly looked up from reading his newspaper to glance out the window.

"At last!" he said. "We are on Cranley land."

"How long till we reach the house?"

"Two or three hours should do it."

For a moment, Caitlin was sure she must have misheard him. In two or three hours, their coach would cover nigh on thirty miles. "How many acres are we talking about?"

Rand had to think for a minute. "Thirty thousand, and all of it prime. This isn't a rich man's plaything, Caitlin. This is a working farm."

If Cranley had belonged to anyone else, so Caitlin told herself, she would have been thrilled at each interesting prospect Rand pointed out to her as they gradually approached the house. She took it all in. There were acres of trees, and scores of foresters wielding axes or transporting the felled logs in carts pulled by immense dray horses. The hills, which were quite low, were thick with the herds of cattle and sheep that roamed them at will. There was mile upon mile of rich arable land, and teams of oxen and men were already preparing the fields for the spring sowing. They passed hamlets and villages, all of them on Cranley land. That all of this belonged to her husband and his family was so intimidating, Caitlin wanted to turn and run for home.

The great gulf that divided them had never been more apparent to her than here, in Rand's own setting. She didn't wonder now that he thought of Strathcairn as a mere hunting lodge. Deeside could never compare to this. A pang pierced her heart.

"It's not Deeside by any means," said Rand, studying her expression.

No, it wasn't, but she wasn't going to let him crow about it. "There are no mountains," she said, peering out one window, then the other, as though she might have missed them by blinking at the wrong moment.

"Mountains? What would I want with mountains? You can't cultivate them. There's no money to be made in mountains."

"Is that all you can think about—making money?" She sounded so prudish, even to her own ears, that she winced. She wasn't prudish, leastways not about making money. She was feeling shaky and overset and in need of a little comforting. As each mile passed, the enormity of their situation was impressed upon her.

Rand ought never to have married her. It was as simple as that. A man in his position would be expected to

315

make a brilliant match. People, and his family in partic-ular, would look askance at the little nobody to whom he had shackled himself. She would be regarded as a millstone around his neck, the girl who had pulled off the coup of the century, not through beauty or grace or her irresistible charms but because she had played her cards right and had forced him into marriage.

She put a brake on her runaway thoughts. They were married, for better or worse. There was no point in cry-ing over spilled milk.

Rand's voice recalled her to the present. "As you know very well, money isn't all I can think about, not by a long shot."

His eyes were smiling at her, more than a hint of hunger behind the indulgent humor. She knew that look. He wanted her, now, at this very minute, and no amount of persuasion or prevarication on her part was going to change the outcome. So he thought.

"We've got plenty of time." He quickly pulled down the shades. "Darling," he said, and reached for her.

She scuttled along the banquette to the far corner, as far from him as possible. "Have you taken leave of your senses?" She wasn't feigning her horror. "You can't just tumble me in the coach and then present me to your family as though nothing had happened."

"Why can't I?"

He was serious. She slapped his hands away. *"Why can't you?"* She could give him a score of reasons. Be-cause a coach wasn't the proper place for what he had in mind. Because her clothes would be crushed past re-demption and her hair would be disheveled. Because his family would know what they had been up to the mo-ment she stepped from the carriage. If nothing else, her blushes would give the game away.

If there was one thing on which she was resolved, it was that she was going to make a good impression on Rand's family. Her high-waisted pink silk pelisse, trimmed at the wrist and hem with white piping, and its matching carriage dress, had been purchased in York and carefully stowed until this very morning. The high poke bonnet, which she had set on the banquette, was a delectable confection of white velvet and pink ostrich feathers. An ermine muff and white kid gloves with little kid half-boots to match completed the ensemble. And her long hair, which she could not persuade Rand to allow her to cut in the current vogue, had been professionally dressed in coronets and ringlets, all of it held together with scores of hair pins and tiny white velvet bows. She didn't care that her feet were smarting from the too tight half-boots. She didn't care that her head felt like a pincushion. To make a good impression on Rand's family, no sacrifice was too great.

Knowing that none of this would weigh with Rand, she said simply and with great dignity, "Because I don't want you to."

He had gradually eased along the opposite banquette until they were knee to knee. His broad shoulders were slumped comfortably against the squabs, and his arms were folded across his chest in an attitude of supreme nonchalance. A wicked twinkle lurked at the back of his eyes.

"I know how to change that 'no' into a 'yes,' " he said softly.

It was no idle boast. One look, one touch and she melted for him. She wouldn't have believed it possible if he had not proved it to her time without number over the last little while. It was beyond belief that she, Caitlin Randal, confirmed spinster, should burn for a man's touches. It had never happened to her before Rand. The meeting of true minds—that was what she had esteemed in relations between the sexes. Rand took a devilish delight in demonstrating that it wasn't his mind she lusted after but his magnificent body. It was true. He knew how to make her ache for him until she was screaming with frustrated desire.

But not today.

As his hand feathered along her knee, she jumped and brushed it away. "Don't start that! I don't want you to touch me, Rand! I mean it!"

At once, his hand lifted and he folded his arms across his chest. The twinkle in his eye became even more roguish.

"I can change that 'no' into a 'yes' without laying a finger on you," he said, with so much complainsance that Caitlin's blood began to heat. They both knew that she was susceptible to him, but this blatant display of masculine arrogance was not only galling, it simply wasn't merited.

"Without laying a finger on me?" she repeated, smiling through her teeth.

"I don't have to touch you, and you'll come tumbling into my arms, begging me to take you."

She gasped. She huffed. She shook her head and looked up at the carriage roof. Every gesture was calculated to demonstrate her complete and utter incredulity. It was all wasted on Rand because when she brought her gaze back to his, he wasn't even looking at her but was examining one of his beautifully manicured hands.

"What is this?" she asked, making a fair stab at imitating his nonchalance. "Is this some kind of joke?"

The eyes brightened. "Let us say, rather, a wager.

318

Yes. Let us say a wager, shall we, between a Highlander and a lowlander?"

Suspicion narrowed her eyes to slits. She had the strangest feeling that he was playing her as though she were a pawn in a game of chess. He was too casual, too relaxed, and much too sure of himself for her peace of mind. She was cautious. At the same time, she was annoyed that he would think he had so much power over her. Annoyance won out.

"A wager," she snapped, "between a Highlander and a lowlander? You make it sound as though the war for Scottish independence were still in progress."

His teeth flashed white in the shadowy interior. "Isn't it?" he murmured. "And something tells me this battle is going to be the turning point."

Insufferable, she was thinking. Smiling, she said, "I haven't said I accept your wager."

"I wouldn't, if I were you." He crossed one booted foot negligently across the other. "That was the trouble with the Scots. They were courageous, I'll give you that. But they were foolhardy. They never would admit it when the odds were stacked against them. Unlike you."

Her eyes heated. "Remind me, if you would be so kind," she said pleasantly, "exactly what the nature of this wager is."

Equally pleasant, he replied, "That I can seduce you without so much as laying a finger on you."

She wasn't being reckless, she told herself. A quick inventory had convinced her that she was as close to succumbing to his seductiveness as a wise old hedgehog to a ravenous fox. Let him do his worst. Her defenses were in place. Hedgehog, she told herself. Think 'hedgehog.'

"Sassenach," she said, "you're on," and she relaxed against the squabs, twiddling her thumbs in a manner

319

that was designed to convey her supreme indifference to his empty boasts.

The carriage rumbled along. She tensed for she knew not what. Nothing happened. Rand simply stared at her, and she stared back at him. This was going to be easier than she had thought.

Presently, he said, "I'm hot."

"Yes, it is warm in here," she agreed. "That's one thing I'll say for England. It's warmer than Scotland. I couldn't help noticing the daffodils and hyacinths along your hedgerows. It will be another month at least before . . . What are you doing?"

"I told you. I'm hot. I'm making myself comfortable."

Before her startled eyes, Rand removed first his neckcloth and then his waistcoat and his blue superfine. It wasn't the first time she had seen him disrobe, but not like this. There was a mesmerizing quality to each languid movement that brought her spine right off the squabs. He was down to his shirt and black pantaloons. Her eyes grazed his groin, then quickly lifted.

"Yes. Hot," he said, "and hard for you. A man can't hide what he is feeling from the woman he wants, especially in these skintight pantaloons. At least they stretch. If I were wearing my breeches, I don't mind telling you, I would be in agony by now."

Though his words were teasing, his eyes gave her a different message. Passion blazed out at her, invading, scorching, heating her iron resolve to make it pliable.

Bathing her in his burning gaze, he said coaxingly, "Help me remove my shirt?"

She shook her head vigorously. Hedgehog! an inner voice screamed. An image of a round ball with hard, impenetrable spines floated into her mind, but she couldn't hold it. Her eyes were trained on long fingers that slowly, sensuously, from throat to waistband, slipped each small pearl button from its buttonhole in his shirt. His movements were as graceful and controlled as those of a ballet dancer when he shrugged one arm out of his shirt, then brushed the soft material slowly, slowly, from the other shoulder and down over his wrist. When he flexed his muscles, Caitlin could feel her palms being to itch. She loved the way his muscles clenched and unclenched when her hands moved over him.

"Hedgehog!" she said.

He looked questioningly at her, and she mumbled indistinctly, then shook her head.

"Your breathing is audible, did you know?"

She stopped breathing, and he smiled knowingly. He was removing his Hessians, slipping them from his feet, stretching and bending like a graceful acrobat. Powerful muscles tensed in his things.

He was doing it to her on purpose, she reminded herself, assaulting her senses with his damnable virility. She managed a hoarse laugh. "You look like a blasted dancer. All you lack is an orchestra." She was trying to make light of it, hoping he wouldn't remark on the odd hiatus that had developed in her breathing.

He smiled in that drowsy way of his. "Listen and you'll hear what has been driving me to take you since we left our lodgings this morning."

Caitlin listened, but she could hear only the creak of the springs as the coach swayed, the muffled pounding of the horses' hoofbeats. She did not know when her own pulse began to beat in rhythm, but suddenly the coach's swaying and jogging became unbearably erotic. The heat in her loins seemed to spread, flooding her with delicious sensations. She was melting with pleasure.

In the golden filtered light of the shaded interior, their eyes met and held. Unspoken messages as old as time passed between them. She could smell the faint tang of his cologne, and something darker and more primitive—the musky scent of the aroused male. She knew he was as aware of her as she was of him.

"There's an ache inside you, isn't there?" His voice was hushed and careful. "Your body is readying itself to take mine. If I lifted your skirts and slipped my fingers inside you, now, this minute, I know what I would find. I want to. Oh God, I want to."

She moaned and turned her head away, gritting her teeth, clamping her legs together.

"And if I put my mouth to your nipples, they would swell and harden even before I could put my tongue to them. Are they hard now?"

Yes, damn him! Hard and sore and desperate for his mouth on them. She shifted uncomfortably.

"I want to come into you. Do you want me to? Don't lie to me, Caitlin. Tell me!"

His words were blotting out the defenses she was trying to muster. She was trying to think of something, if only she could remember it. Something to do with a hedge, or was it a pig?

"Tell me!"

"Yes!" she said. "Yes!" and she opened her eyes to glare at him.

Naked and unashamed, he was sprawled against the opposite banquette, his powerful arms stretched along the edge of the backrest. His arms were not the only powerful part of his anatomy that her eyes were drawn to.

"Rand," she said faintly, "Oh, Rand."

322

His chest was rising and falling as he labored to regulate his breathing, and a fine sweat had broken out on his forehead. "I've let it go too far," he said. "I'm losing control. If you don't get over here fast, and take me into you, I'm going to disgrace myself."

Her own secret parts were clenching in anticipation of the final consummation. Teetering in the balance was which of them would disgrace himself or herself first? Still, she had her pride.

"You won't crow about your victory afterward?"

"I promise!"

"And no snide remarks about Highlanders and lowlanders or the War of Scottish Independence?"

"You have my word on it."

"And—"

"Caitlin!" he roared. "I haven't got time for this."

It was all the encouragement she needed. Though she was somewhat at a loss, he showed her how it could be contrived. Astride his lap, holding her skirts out of the way, she came slowly down on him.

"Now ride me," he said.

It was an intoxicating experience. Rand was holding to his promise not to touch her, and his arms were firmly welded to the backrest of the banquette. She was the one who, by default, had freedom of movement. She was the one who could determine the pace. She became a snail, exulting in his tortured entreaties and the stifled groans of agony which her slow punishment elicited. And then the coach hit a pothole, sending him deep into the recesses of her body, and the game came to an explosive end. Caitlin gasped, then cried out, and her body took over. Sobbing his name over and over, she became a wild thing, bucking, twisting, writhing, until the last wave of pleasure left her weak and spent.

She was slumped against him in languorous repletion. It was some time before she realized he was still inside her, and still very virile. Not to put too fine a point on it, he was enormous.

Groaning, she lifted her head from his shoulder and looked down at him, ready to pounce at the first wrong word.

His eyes were bright with laughter. "After that little bout, I'd say I deserve to be mentioned in dispatches for my heroism. I did not know I possessed such control. No, my darling Kate, I am not gloating. I'm not even going to mention the War of You-know-what. All I wish to point out is that you lost our wager, and now it's time to pay your forfeit."

"You cheated! You know you did."

"Now that is simply untrue. I *was* close to disgracing myself. But I am a more experienced duelist than you. While you writhed in the throes of your passion, I gritted my teeth and concentrated on ways of draining the south pasture."

Her head drooped to its comfortable rest in the crook of his shoulder. "Damn all hedgehogs to perdition," she said, and closed her eyes.

He shook her awake. "You're forgetting your forfeit."

"What does that mean?"

"It means, my pet, that I can have my wicked way with you, and we shall begin by removing all your clothes."

She hadn't the energy to argue with him. She was so completely spent that she just wished she could go to sleep. She almost did fall asleep when he began to disrobe her. But when he stretched her out on the banquette with her knees raised, and he pushed into her, she didn't feel like sleeping at all.

When it was all over, she said, drowsily, *"Mo gaol orist. What time is it?"*

"Hush. Go to sleep. I'll wake you in good time."

"The carriage has stopped! We've arrived!"

"What?" Caitlin roused herself from her husband's arms and the pink pelisse which covered her nakedness slipped from her shoulders to pool on the floor beside her abandoned gown.

"Quick! Lock the doors." Even as he spoke, Rand heaved himself up, dislodging Caitlin from his lap, and he quickly secured both carriage doors. Impatient now. "Don't just kneel there like a postulant taking holy orders. Dress yourself!" Already he was skimming into black pantaloons and reaching for his shirt. "Do you hear that?" He jerked his head, indicating the buzz of voices outside the coach. "That's my family waiting to welcome us. If they catch a glimpse of you in that *dishabille*, they'll think I've brought one of my doxies home with me."

With dawning horror, Caitlin stared up at her husband.

"Hurry!" he barked.

She moved with the urgency of a wild thing caught in a forest fire, and all the while, the doors were rattling and the voices outside the coach were raised stridently, demanding to know why there was a delay.

"Just one more time," she quoted savagely under her breath, wriggling into her lace-edged drawers, dragging her chemise over her head. "Just one more time and then we shall call it quits! I could murder you for this. I wanted to make an impression on your family."

"You'll make an impression all right, but not the one you were hoping for." The humor in the situation was beginning to act on him. In nothing but her frilly underthings, she looked so adorably tragic as she surveyed the crushed bonnet with its limp and broken ostrich feathers—a casualty of the combat which had occupied them so pleasurably for the last hour or two—he couldn't resist dropping a quick kiss on the nape of her neck.

"I'll buy you a dozen bonnets. Here, let me help you with your hair."

There was nothing for it but to comb his fingers through it, dislodging as many hairpins and ribbons as he could manage. "I prefer it loose anyway," he told her soothingly when he noticed that her bottom lip was beginning to tremble.

When she finally hobbled from the coach at Rand's back, she wanted to weep her eyes out. It was just as she had known it would be. Her garments were crushed beyond redemption; her bonnet was ruined; her elegant coiffure had the look of an abandoned robin's nest; and she was blushing like a guilty schoolgirl.

She had to blink her eyes against the sudden glare. A figure stepped forward in a swish of skirts, and Caitlin was conscious of the fragrance of a garden in full flower after a shower of summer rain. A voice to match the fragrance addressed her husband.

"Rand, darling, if you could only see the look on your face!" Then, with a backward glance at the interested spectators, "I think we surprised him!"

In a voice that Caitlin had never heard before, Rand said, "Lady Margaret! What are *you* doing here?"

The mist lifted from Caitlin's eyes the instant before a blond vision in white gauze stepped into Rand's arms and laughingly pulled his head down for an intimate, open-mouthed kiss.

Chapter Twenty

Caitlin studiously tipped her soup plate at the correct angle, slightly away from her, and plied her silver soup spoon in the manner polite usage prescribed. She was excruciatingly self-conscious, as was to be expected. She was playing hostess to a distinguished group of about thirty people, all of them either Rand's family or friends, and all eyes were on her. She wasn't imagining it, though the glances were covert. Suspense seemed to hang on the air, as if their guests were waiting for the moment to arrive when she would finally disgrace herself and run screaming from the room.

Sometimes, such as on the present occasion, the temptation to do just that was almost irresistible. They had put her down as a northern barbarian, strange and unpredictable, and she longed to prove them right. For two pins, she would throw down her napkin and pick up her soup plate, put it to her lips and suck it dry with as much gusto as her hound emptyied a drinking trough. It was what everybody expected her to do. Only one thing stayed her hand. No one would blink an eyelash. No one would comment upon it or laugh or show the slightest discomfort. It was enough to drive any sane Scot to murder and mayhem.

She had discovered that one of the distinguishing characteristics of the English aristocracy was the knack of turning a blind eye to any social solecism committed by one of their number. If she were to strip naked, right this minute, she could almost predict everyone's reaction. There would be a slight hiatus in the buzz of conversation. Rand would call for more champagne, and as the servants hastened to do his bidding, the conversation would resume. He would thereupon rise from his place at the head of the table, converse easily with various guests as he made his way down to her, and before a minute had passed, his dark coat would be around her shoulders, covering her nakedness. She would then be escorted to her chamber by one of the footmen. On returning to his place, Rand would look around at the assembled guests and say in that easy way of his, "Now where was I?"

The English hated scenes, and their way of dealing with them was to act as if they had not happened. She knew all this because she'd had ample proof of it in the few days since they had arrived at Cranley, beginning with the moment she had stepped outside the carriage and had come face to face with her husband's mistress. It wasn't until this very morning that the dowager had taken her aside and had complimented her on her presence of mind, saying something to the effect that it was all a regrettable misunderstanding and she never would have invited Rand's mistress to Cranley if she had known that he was a married man.

Mistress! It had never occurred to Caitlin that Lady Margaret was Rand's mistress! She was too patrician, too well bred, and much too refined for that role. Good grief! She was an earl's daughter and the widow of a gentleman who had left her a considerable fortune. When Caitlin thought of mistresses, she thought of Doris at The Fair Maid, or the more exotic Nellie—vulgar women who painted their faces and tarted themselves up to advertise their profession. Lady Margaret was a vision of loveliness.

In Caitlin's ignorance, on first having set eyes on her and witnessed that lingering embrace, she had assumed that the poor woman was Rand's betrothed or near enough as made no difference. She'd felt guilty as sin for stealing him away from her, which was why she had stood there like an abandoned, battered portmanteau waiting for someone to claim it. And when that passionate embrace had played itself out and Rand had made the introductions all around with his usual aplomb, she'd stifled her jealousy, allowing the dowager to lead her into the house, conscious that Rand and the vision of loveliness had turned aside for an intimate *tête-à-tête*. She'd felt, then, that it was the least she owed them. When she had discovered this morning in what relationship the two stood to each other, she had wished she could go back to the moment she had stepped down from the carriage. If she had known then what she knew now, she would have thrown such a temper tantrum that Lady Margaret would have thought herself lucky to escape with her life.

Naturally, the first thing she did was tackle her husband about it.

"I never said I was a monk before my marriage," Rand said, dismissing her allegations with a wave of his hand. "Margaret, that is, Lady Margaret, need not concern you. She is my mother's guest. That's all you need to know."

330

"Your former profligacy is not what is at issue here." This wasn't precisely true, but she did not want to appear irrational in the face of his reasonableness. "Surely you must see how improper it is?"

"It's a little awkward, I grant you. But there is nothing improper about it. We are not involved in a *ménage à trois*. My whole family is in residence. What could be more proper that that?"

His eyes were dancing in that roguish way which never failed to raise her hackles. "If 'Meggins,' " she said pettishly, remembering the twins' nickname for the lady, "had an ounce of breeding, she would pack her bags and make some pretext for returning to London."

"That is where you are wrong," corrected Rand. The humor had faded from his eyes and he was watching her speculatively. "If Lady Margaret were to do anything so precipitous, tongues would begin to wag. Before you know it, it would be bandied about all over London that there had been a falling-out between my mistress and my wife. The gossips would make capital of it."

"So let them! What do I care what a few gossips want to make of it? Anything is preferable to living under the same roof as that woman."

"You are not the injured party here. My relationship with Lady Margaret hurt no one. Neither of us was married at the time."

His logic, of course, was unimpeachable. She tried a different argument. "Do you suppose I enjoy those avidly curious looks everyone is slanting at me?"

"Who is looking at you?"

"Your sisters!" she snapped.

Again, she wasn't being as scrupulously honest as she might have been. It was Lady Margaret's looks which bothered her the most. The woman had a trick of making her feel small. It didn't help that she *was* small in comparison to all the females in Rand's family. She felt like a dwarf set down in a tribe of Amazons; albeit handsome Amazons. Tall, willowy blondes, every last one of them, including Lady Margaret. Only one of Rand's sisters-in-law broke the monotony. She was a redhead. Even so, Caitlin envied Frances her inches.

And they were all so sophisticated. Their fine clothes, their manners, their cultured accents, their conversation—everything about them intimidated her. With Lady Margaret, however, it was calculated. When that woman widened her beautiful eyes and allowed her gaze to linger on Caitlin's coiffure, or on the hem of her gown or wherever, Caitlin itched to find a mirror and set herself to rights. Anyway, how could she not feel all the disadvantages of her position when Lady Margaret's conversation was all of the Prince Regent and of the illustrious personages who moved in her circles? Caitlin could not compete, and she had the sense not to try. Even to return some commonplace had become a trial when Lady Margaret lost no opportunity in drawing attention to her "quaint" Scottish accent.

She had allowed Lady Margaret to have her petty revenge out of a sense of guilt. The information that the lady was not a jilted fiancée, but in fact her husband's mistress, had touched Caitlin upon the quick. She was incensed, not only at Lady Margaret but at the whole tribe of Randals for subjecting her to an insult no bride should be made to endure.

They were a queer lot, these English Randals, and as like to her as creatures from another world. She had not been with them a day when her own abigail, Maisie, had regaled her with such scandals as would set the Highlands back on its heels for a long time to come.

Elopements and forced marriages seemed almost *de rigueur* in this strange family. It was no wonder that not a soul had looked askance when Rand had introduced Caitlin Randal as his bride. Nothing could shake them. If Armageddon suddenly exploded around their heads, she wondered if any of them would lose the thread of conversation or do more than politely remark on it in passing. Of course, in her husband's case, she knew that his public face was not the one he wore in private.

"I don't like the way your sisters watch me," she had elaborated, driving home her point. "I feel as though they are waiting for the fireworks to go off."

He had taken her words as a jest. "You must mean the twins. Their manners leave much to be desired. I shall have a word with them."

She *had* meant the twins, but she wasn't going to allow him to make light of it like this. "It's not only the twins. Everybody is watching me. Oh, they are too polite to do it openly, but they are watching me just the same."

"You are imagining things. Why should they watch you?"

Because they wondered what Rand had seen in her when his mistress surpassed her on all suits. "Because you and your mother have put me in an intolerable position. They are waiting for me to make a fool of myself."

His eyes were searching, probing; and it required all of her powers of concentration to give him back a clear-eyed look. He spoke carefully. "As I said, it's best to do nothing. Lady Margaret and I are of the same opinion. She feels the awkwardness as much as you do. In another day or two, after this infernal ball is over, we can all go our separate ways."

His words astonished her. "Am I to understand that you have discussed this with Lady Margaret while I, your wife, whom it concerns most nearly, have not been taken into your confidence?"

He answered her in the same infuriatingly reasonable tone. "In the first place, I did not know you were aware that Lady Margaret was once my mistress. The last thing I wanted was to embarrass you by divulging the nature of that relationship. In the second place, there is nothing here to excite this exaggerated passion. The affair is long over. My mother hoped to revive it. She knows now that she made a blunder. For everyone's sake, we must put a face on it and act like civilized people."

Exaggerated passion; civilized people. The English were masters at delivering the veiled insult, and Highlanders were masters at translating it into their own tongue. They should be. They'd had centuries of practice. In short, he was telling her that she was little better than a savage governed by unruly passions. So be it! Bloodless he wanted, bloodless he would get.

Across the width of the table, her idle glance chanced to catch her mother-in-law's eye. A silent exchange took place, and a moment later Caitlin signaled the servants to serve the next course. She was at the foot of the table in the place that rightly belonged to the dowager. That first night, she hadn't wanted to usurp the woman's place. She would have been more than happy to lose herself somewhere in the middle of that endlessly long table with thirty or so guests seated around it. Lady Randal, herself, had insisted that Rand's wife take precedence. The gesture, however unwelcome, had touched Caitlin. But that was before she had known that Lady Randal had invited Rand's mistress to Cranley in the hope of reviving their affair. What kind of mother, she asked herself, would invite her son's mistress to her home, where her innocent young daughters were likely to strike up a friendship with the woman?

Innocent my eye! some inner voice remonstrated. Martha and Mary could probably teach Rand's mistress a thing or two, and that was no exaggeration. They ought to be able to. They'd made a study of their brothers' scandalous careers, as Caitlin was to discover when she'd agreed to go for a walk with them that afternoon over the downs. There was no malice in them. They were merely as inquisitive and as mischievous as young puppies and could nose out a scandal faster that Bocain could nose out a fox.

A shiver passed over her. Bocain. Her thoughts drifted to Scotland, and to the snow-capped mountains towering over the lonely moors. She could see herself as clear as day, with Bocain at her heels, striding out over the Larich Gru with a knapsack containing bread and cheese and a bottle of her own spring water to break their fast. It was inconceivable that even here in the bosom of Rand's family, with the intimate buzz of conversation going on all around her, she should be pining for the moors of Scotland and the wild calls of curlews on the wing as they circled overhead. What was wrong with her? Dear God, what was *wrong* with her?

She made a sound, a small, inarticulate murmur, and her eyes flew down the length of that interminably long table to collide with Rand's. He had not heard her. She *knew* he had not heard her. But he sensed the beginnings of the hysteria that was beginning to ravage her composure. She had to get a grip on herself. *Bloodless.* That was what he wanted her to be, *that* and the freedom to use her body whenever it suited him.

She had been drinking too freely. She was not used to champagne, or the servant at her elbow who watched like a hawk and made to replenish her glass as soon as it was half-empty. She was slightly tipsy. Raising her glass in a silent tribute to her husband, she drank lustily, uncaring of the brooding we-shall-get-to-this-later look Rand's eyes burned into her consciousness. His cool composure was slipping, and that did not disturb her one jot.

Bloodless. They would see who could best carry off *that* game. She turned to the gentleman on her right. Sir Henry was in his mid-sixties and, as she recalled, a former crony of Rand's father. He was snoring softly into his cravat, but from where Rand was sitting that could not be seen.

"Tell me, Sir Henry," she said, smiling down the length of the table at her husband, "What was your first impression of my husband's house?"

The question raised a few eyebrows in the vicinity, but Caitlin did not trouble herself about that. Her husband would see only that his wife was exerting herself to overcome her shyness and make herself agreeable to his guests. And really, it was no labor. Sir Henry would not judge her and find her wanting because her accent was as thick as a Scottish mist. With Sir Henry, there was no possibility that she could fail to please. It made her quite the coquette.

Leaning slightly toward the elderly gentleman, she said, so that no one else could hear her, "Do you know, that was my first impression precisely? I don't mind telling you, the population of Ballater could fit quite nicely into Cranley, yes, and with room to spare."

As though Sir Henry had plenty to say on the subject, she tilted her head at an angle and listened intently. After a suitable interval, she went on, "Do you know, I am of the same mind as you? I know that Cranley is reputed to be a family dwelling, but really, what family has need of four wings and over one-hundred bedchambers." Warming to her subject, she continued, "Cranley, as you must know, was conceived and constructed at one stroke between seventeen thirty-four and seventeen sixty. Yes, you are quite correct, Sir Henry, when you say that it is a great Palladian *palazzo*. But, do you know, in spite of the luxury to be found here, in spite of 'Capability,' Brown and his magnificent natural landscaping which owes nothing to nature, I hanker after my own little shielding in the shadow of the Cairngorms and Grampians?

"What is a shieling?" Her eyes grew misty. "A shieling is what we Scots call a but-and-ben, that is, a two-room cottage. Happiness, you see, does not depend on the opulence of one's surroundings. Deeside . . ."

After dinner was completed most of Cranley's guests trooped off to bed, while a few of the gentlemen engaged in an unexciting game of billiards. Rand was enjoying a solitary smoke on the terrace when he was joined by Lady Margaret. He made no move to evade the lingering kiss she pressed to his lips.

"Your bride is charming, Rand. My heart is quite broken."

He chuckled softly. "Your heart is not so fragile, Margaret, as we both know."

She smacked him playfully on the shoulder with her closed fan. "Speak for yourself, rogue! You know how fond I am of you."

When he made no reply to this, but merely stared out

over the sweep of the gardens and lawns, she went on archly, "We shall all miss you when you return to Scotland."

"That won't be for some time yet."

She had his full attention now, and she made the most of it. With a slow, languid movement, she reclined gracefully against a stone pillar, arching her back slightly. The pose set off her magnificent figure to advantage. Rand's eyes were warmly appreciative. Her own eyes reflected his admiration. She knew that they would make a stunning spectacle to anyone observing. They were both tall and with hair like spun gold. He was all in black; she was a picture in pale diaphanous muslins that floated around her long legs.

She smiled. "From something your wife said, I understood that you were considering taking up permanent residency in Scotland." She cocked her head at a provocative angle. "Somehow, Rand, I just can't see you as a Highlander in kilt and plaid and all that."

His steady gaze was unreadable. "What has Caitlin been telling you?" he asked pleasantly.

"This and that. I think the poor girl is homesick, and she has hardly been here a week!"

He smiled. "Everything is unfamiliar to her. It's no easy task, taking over as mistress of Cranley."

Lady Margaret's smile hardened at the edges when she thought of how close she had come to snatching the prize for herself. But Cranley was the least of it. If she could not have Rand with his ring on her finger, and she had hardly dared hope for so much in spite of the dowager, she would take him any way she could get him.

She was sure that her confidence was not misplaced. It was not unusual in their circles for a man to marry for

338

heirs and take a mistress for pleasure. Lady Margaret thought she had fathomed the intricacies of the match Rand had made for himself. To her, it seemed a dynastic alliance between the English Randals and the Scottish Randals. There was nothing to fear there.

Nor did the girl excite her envy. If she felt anything for her it was a tepid pity. When Rand had introduced them, after that first electrifying shock, she could hardly believe her eyes. So much pink and white put her in mind of a frothy dessert. The girl's taste was atrocious. Only the bonnet was stylish, and it was ruined beyond repair. This girl did not know enough to present the semblance of a woman of taste and fashion, a woman who cared about herself. No one had ever seen Lady Margaret with a hair out of place. *That* was the way to keep a man interested.

She smiled benignly into the night. Keeping her voice low and intimate, she murmured, "If you are not returning to Scotland—and I could scarcely credit that you really meant to desert Cranley so soon—do you plan to take in the season in London?" As they both knew, she would be in London, and though it was many months since he had made use of it, Rand still had the key to her house in Mayfair.

"Caitlin taking in the season? I can't quite see it."

"Oh, I don't know. She has it in her to cut quite a dash. With the right hair and clothes, and your mother to guide her, she might surprise us all."

She didn't know what she had said to annoy him, but suddenly she was aware that his eyes were as hard as flint. Hoping to retrieve her position, she went on hurriedly. "She'll charm the birds right out of the trees with her quaint Scottish accent. Her voice is soft and melodious and . . . and really quite musical."

"Yes," he said. "I could listen to it for hours on end and never grow tired of hearing it."

There was a silence; then she let out a breathy laugh. "So that's the way of it, is it?"

He did not pretend to misunderstand her, nor was there a hint of apology in his voice. "Yes. That's the way of it." A moment later, he fished something out of his coat pocket. "I've been meaning to return this to you." He pressed a key into her open palm.

Her hand closed around it automatically. Never was she so close to breaking one of her own cardinal rules. At the end of an affair, when it was time to let go, it was best to do it gracefully. But then, she was the one who usually brought the thing to an end. Looking at that finely molded mouth and the vivid blue eyes that she knew would darken in passion, she experienced such a sense of loss that she feared she was on the verge of creating a scene.

Blinking to dispel her tears, she lifted her head a fraction. "She's a fortunate girl," she said lightly.

"Thank you." The reply was grave and lacked warmth. "But it's customary, I believe, to congratulate the gentleman on winning the lady and not the other way round."

She hardly heard his words. This coldly polite stranger, she thought wildly, could not be Rand. He used to tease her and act the gallant. The little Highland upstart had got her claws into him good and proper, had set him against her. Well, two could play at that game.

On the point of moving away, she pivoted to face him. "Oh, now I recall what it was that Caitlin told me. We were in conversation with Peter. He offered to inveigle an invitation to Cokes's place, Hokham in Norfolk I

340

think it is, and she said . . ." She frowned in concentration.

"Yes?"

Her smile was unconvincing. "She said that there would not be the time, that there were matters begging her attention in Scotland and that to delay could prove disastrous. It was all farm talk, so I'm afraid most of it went over my poor head. But it did seem to me, Rand, that Cranley and her duties here did not weigh too heavily with your young wife." And on that parting shot, she floated away.

Rand threw the end of his cigar into the shrubbery and inhaled several long breaths, trying to get command of his anger. "Venomous!" he said under his breath.

Such condescension! Such thinly concealed contempt! And what struck in his craw was that none of it was deliberate, or at least, it had not started out that way. Her tactlessness came, rather, from a proud and unfeeling disposition. As if he wanted to make Caitlin over into a pale copy of the fashionables who thronged Mayfair! Caitlin, who had more genuine feeling in her little finger than Lady Margaret had in her whole body. As if his wife required guidance from anyone on how to conduct herself in polite society! As if it mattered! Good God, if Lady Margaret only knew of the life Caitlin had pursued in Scotland she would be horrified. She had judged Caitlin and found her wanting, and that proved to Rand how small-minded she was. The wonder was, he had not perceived it sooner.

Caitlin had it in her to be and do anything she wanted, as she had proved since coming to Cranley. He was well aware of the strain she was laboring under, and he was tempted to throttle his shatter-brain mother for the trick she had pulled on him. It was bad enough that

Caitlin had to go through the ordeal of presiding over a houseful of guests almost as soon as she had set foot inside the door, but that one of those guests should be her husband's former mistress was appalling. It didn't help that his mother was trying to make up for her awful gaffe. Mothers should not meddle in the affairs of their grown-up children. She should have known that if he had wanted to marry Lady Margaret, he'd had ample opportunity to offer for her.

When he'd stepped from the coach and his eyes had alighted on his erstwhile mistress, he'd felt like a tall oak suddenly struck by lightning. He'd been on tenterhooks, thinking that Caitlin might know of their connection, and he'd hardly drawn breath till those first few minutes were safely over. It wasn't that he minded Caitlin in one of her rages. It was simply that he didn't want his family's first impression of his wife to be that she was a virago, and she would have been a virago if she'd known that he'd been introducing her to his mistress. He wasn't forgetting the night she had thrown her dirk at him when she'd found him in bed with one of the barmaids at The Fair Maid.

A grin spread across his face, and he chuckled softly. He was congratulating himself on the way he had handled his wife's ire when she had finally confronted him with the knowledge of his relationship with Lady Margaret. How he had longed to tease her, to set spark to the dry tinder of her temper and watch the flames go up. He dared not, for the simple reason that there were thirty-odd people in residence at Cranley and he wasn't quite sure what form her revenge would take. He wouldn't put it past her to dose his soup with a powerful purgative, or worse, gunpowder. She liked nothing better that to take him down a peg or two.

Gradually, his smile faded. He was thinking of the blunder he had made in letting slip that he had consulted Lady Margaret about what was best to be done about the fix they were in. Under the circumstances, he did not see what else they could do. He was thinking of Caitlin. In view of their forced marriage, any rumors were bound to reflect on her. People would say that he had been an unwilling bridegroom and that he was looking to resume his affair with Lady Margaret. Nothing could be further from the truth on both counts. Nor would he tolerate Caitlin's name being bandied about by ill-bred louts, be they male or female. Caitlin was right in saying that it was an intolerable situation, but there was no easy way around it.

This last thought put him in mind of Lady Margaret's parting shot. He recognized spite when it stared him in the face. That was the worst of affairs. No one could predict what a woman would do when a gentleman tried to extricate himself from the relationship. Some were avaricious; others were spiteful. Few were gracious. He had expected better from Margaret.

He idled his way into the billiard room and was not surprised to find Peter there. When he left him, Rand went immediately in search of his wife.

He turned her into his arms with all the confidence she had come to expect of him. He must have known from the rigidity of her spine that she was feigning sleep and that he was not exactly in favor this evening.

"I won't have you brooding," he told her. "I know everything is strange to you. That will pass. The house, my family and friends—you will soon be comfortable with them."

The champagne had befuddled her thinking. She had to concentrate very hard to make sense of what he was saying. As from a great distance, she heard her own voice, *"Mo gaol orist.* What time is it?"

"Don't pretend you were sleeping, because I know that you were not. It will get easier." He said the words fiercely, and she turned her head on the pillow to look up at him. More gently, he went on, "I know that England seems strange to you. That will pass. You have not had the time to make a life here for yourself yet. When you do, your thoughts will turn less and less to Scotland. You are mistress of Cranley. How can Strathcairn compare to that?"

"Mistress of Cranley? That means nothing to me." She did not notice that he had recoiled as if she had slapped him. Her thoughts were still on Lady Margaret and her own appalling inadequacies when she compared herself to that paragon. She waited hopefully, willing him to say something that would reassure her.

"You are determined to despise everything English. Well, you married an Englishman. Your children will be English."

"You are chief of Clan Randal," she cried out. "You are Scottish too."

"Scotland means nothing to me," he retorted. "I could not care less if I never see it again."

"But . . ."

He stopped her words with the fierceness of his kisses. She sensed the violence in him, but did not understand its origins.

"Rand, it's all right, it's all right," she murmured, and tried to gentle him with little kisses pressed to his throat and shoulders.

He didn't want her gentle. He wanted her wild for

him, as hungry for him as he was to take her, and he told her so graphically, with no attempt to pretty up his words.

Between deep harsh breaths, his voice almost savage, he said, "I'll make you forget Scotland. I'll make you forget everything but this. I am your husband, and in English law, that means something. You are mine, Caitlin, to do with as I please. No, don't turn away from me." He wrenched her back. "And *this* is what pleases me."

He used her as he had never used her before, revealing that dark and primitive side to him that never failed to win an answering response from her. Again and again, he brought her to the brink of fulfillment, then prolonged the moment until she was sobbing with her need for him.

"You are mine," he told her again. "Mine." And he plunged into her, sending them both hurtling to their first climax.

Before she had time to recover her breath, he was turning her in to him, his lips and hands beginning to work their familiar magic. It wasn't the first time he had tried to initiate her into things she wanted no part of, but it was the first time he refused to take no for an answer.

"There is no shame in what passes between a husband and wife in the marriage bed," he told her. "I want to know your body as intimately as you are going to know mine."

She was allowed no modestly as he remorselessly explored every inch of her. "No," she moaned when his hands cupped her hips and his tongue sank into the secret place between her thighs. Then rational thought slipped away and her feeble protests became pleasure sounds. She tried to warn him that it was all too much for her, but he wouldn't listen. Before she could prevent it, her body contracted and the crisis overtook her in a flood of sensation.

Breathing hard, still dazed with the force of her release, she was given her next lesson. Eyes holding hers, he showed her the touches that could drive him crazy for her. Modesty was forgotten when she took the lesson one step further and used him as he had used her. She was rocked back on the bed with such violence that the breath was knocked out of her.

"Rand," she cried out. "What is it?"

He laughed triumphantly. "Little wanton! I know, now, how to hold you. This is the only thing that matters." And he buried himself deep inside her. "I want to hear you say it."

He got his wish. In the clear light of day, however, it was not the passion that Caitlin remembered but the vague threat that Scotland might be lost to her forever.

Chapter Twenty-One

Caitlin reverently unwrapped the layers of tissue paper and removed the ball gown from its box. To little feminine oohs and ahs around her chamber, she shook out the soft folds of the creation she had spied in the shop window of Tunbridge Wells's foremost mantua maker. With only slight alterations, the gown of primrose satin had been made to fit her like a second skin.

"The color becomes you. It does something for your complexion." At the shy compliment, Caitlin flashed the speaker a grateful look.

"I am indebted to you for your advice, Frances. I know little of fashion. If it had not been for you and Dorothy, I would have had to make do tonight with the gown Rand picked out for me."

This brought mingled groans and hoots of laughter from all the ladies.

"Did you really allow Rand to choose your wardrobe?" The dowager's eyes gleamed with laughter.

Caitlin made a rude sound. "How was I to know that all the Randal men are notoriously inept about ladies' fashions? I am not experienced. And it always seemed to me that Rand was immaculately turned out. I thought he was a fop."

This last brought a scream of derision from the twins.

"My dear," said the dowager when the uproar had subsided, "he has Hobbes. If it were not for their valets, Rand and his brothers would go about looking like scarecrows. It's the Randal women who keep them right."

As the chatter went on around her, Caitlin sat back in her chair and surveyed her companions with a degree of satisfaction. In the space of only a few days, all her reservations and misgivings were laid to rest. These were the Randal ladies, either by birth or through marriage, and they were as close as any clan in the Highlands of Scotland. If it had not been for the unfortunate circumstances surrounding her arrival at Cranley, she would have known it sooner. Fearing her reaction to the dowager's ill-advised scheme for Rand and Lady Margaret, the Randal ladies had approached her with caution. When it appeared that their fears were groundless, that she had not taken umbrage, they had welcomed her as one of their own.

When she thought of it, there was no family in England that could have suited her better. These were not toplofty English sophisticates who thought themselves superior to other people. They were a collection of oddities, something like herself. Guided by their own inner lights, they felt if the world judged them and found them wanting, the world knew what it could do about it.

Her eyes touched on the various ladies present, and it was all she could do not to shake her head. Only the twins had not been touched by the taint of some scandalous event. Not that the English Randals ever admitted their conduct was anything less than scrupulous. In their view, if they flaunted society's unwritten codes, then either society or its codes—or both—were far off the mark.

Contrary to appearances, they had their standards, and these were high. They had nothing to do with the minutiae of correct etiquette, everything to do with loyalty and looking out for each other and closing ranks when any one member of the clan came under attack. In Caitlin's own case, she had had occasion to be grateful for this family solidarity whenever she and Lady Margaret had exchanged the odd word over the last number of days. For some reason known only to herself, Lady Margaret had turned downright spiteful. The Randals had soon got wind of it, and were there in force to carry Caitlin off or to distract Lady Margaret. It was mainly Rand's doing. She had seen with her own eyes how, at a slight nod from him, one of his brothers would casually drop what he was doing and close with the enemy. Nor was Caitlin the only person to benefit from her husband's shepherding. In particular, the dowager's two daughters-in-law also come in for shares of his attention.

As she'd heard tell, these gently bred, respectable girls had done the unthinkable. Each, in her turn, had gone against a guardian's wishes and had eloped with a Randal man. Had they not done so, one of them would have been a marchioness today and the other a countess. Whatever Rand may have said to his brothers in private, and she'd wager it was plenty, in public he'd adopted the view that in choosing Randal men, his sisters-in-law had demonstrated the superiority of their intellect.

In such company as this, Caitlin had no fears that her own background would excite pity or disgust or more than a passing interest. She was a Randal who had married a Randal man. What could be better than that?

That evening, when she took her place in the receiving line with the other members of her husband's family, her heart swelled with pleasure. These long-limbed, lean, fair-haired Randals had the appearance of a pride of tawny lions. She felt quite dainty beside them, dainty and *soignée*.

She hadn't known she had it in her to be so vain, but since she had donned her yellow satin ball gown and Rand had fastened a necklace of diamonds and pearls at her throat, she had hardly been able to tear herself away from the looking glass in her chamber.

Smoothing her hands in their white kid gloves over her skirts, she chanced a quick look down. There wasn't a furbelow or a piece of piping to be seen. Nor was there one bow in her hair. *The simpler the better when one is as dainty as you.* How right the dowager had been. And how Caitlin treasured the word "dainty." She wasn't small. She was dainty. What a difference a word could make to how one felt about one's self. It did not hurt either, that Rand's eyes held a special glow whenever they chanced to alight on her, which was often.

"You are lovelier than moonlight on Loch Morlich," he said.

Eyes downcast, she bobbed him a curtsy. She was becoming a little more comfortable with the extravagance of English compliments. "Thank you, kind sir," she said.

A moment passed. He huffed, he coughed, then said in a mock sorrowful tone, "Don't I rate the courtesy of a compliment too?"

Her smile flashed. "What I think of you dare only be said in the privacy of our bedchamber."

His eyes flashed, then darkened. "I'll remind you of that when this deuced ball is over."

"However, I will say this: you, sir, have the mien of a great chieftain. Your proper setting should be the Highlands."

"What's this about the Highlands?" Robert Randal had arrived late, and was edging into line between the dowager and his wife.

Caitlin obligingly elaborated. "Rand is the chief of Clan Randal. You might not know it to look at him now, but when he wears the ancient Highland dress, he is quite the Scottish laird."

"Rand in a kilt?" Robert slapped his thigh and let out a great shout of laughter. "Did you hear that Harry? Peter? Our big brother, the baron, has taken to wearing skirts. I say, do tell! Is he a true Highlander or does he, you know, cheat?"

Caitlin's dainty nostrils were quivering. "There is nothing to laugh at in the ancient Highland dress. If you English Randals would only condescend to show your faces to your clan once in a while, you would know it."

No one paid the least heed to Caitlin's umbrage.

"I'll bet he scared all the girls with those hairy legs of his."

"Not to mention his bony knees."

"Can he toss the caber?"

"The what?"

"You know, it's a felled tree. That's the test of a true Highlander, not the ... hmmm ... other."

"I don't dispute that tossing the caber is the test of a true Highlander. Where you are wrong, Harry, is when you say that it is a felled tree. Madam Caber, as I understand, runs the local ... ah ... hostelry."

The dowager was beginning to look quite distracted.

The receiving line had disintegrated entirely, and this when her footmen were waiting for the signal to open the glass doors to admit their guests. From the sounds of the banter, which was becoming louder by the minute, she very much feared that before long her sons would be embroiled in a vulgar brawl. She knew the signs.

She flashed a look of acute apology at Caitlin. Rand's young wife had taken it into her head that they were a close-knit family, and she had done nothing to disabuse her of that notion. In point of fact, she had basked for a little while in the girl's adulation. The sorry truth of the matter was that she wasn't much of a mother. She was a bit of a shatter-brain, and had never been able to enforce discipline. There was hardly a time she could remember when her children were not at each other's throats. They weren't just naughty. They were *beastly.* And now that they were grown up and beyond squabbling, they had invented new ways to torment each other. Though she loved them all dearly, sometimes she wished they lived at the end of the world. The pity of it was, no sooner did she get her wish than she was pining for their return.

"Children!" she scolded, to no effect. She had just opened her mouth to ring a peal over the lot of them when a sudden silence descended.

"What did you say, Kate?" she asked in amazement.

Caitlin tossed her head. "I said that I'll wager anything you like the Scottish Randals can outmatch the English Randals in any test of skill or strength you care to name."

"Those are fighting words," murmured Robert, looking a question at Rand. "Do we go to Scotland to find out?"

Rand's eyes were narrowed on Caitlin. "Which do

352

you consider yourself?" he asked in a tone of voice that made his brothers shift uneasily.

"Beg pardon?"

He spoke pleasantly, and his posture was relaxed. "Come now, Caitlin. I think you understand me. Are you a Scottish Randal or are you one of us?"

When she fumbled for an answer, Peter, recognizing the look in Rand's eyes, rushed in to defend her. "We are all of us Scottish Randals whether we acknowledge it or not. Where does our name come from? Where is our clan? Where is your barony, Rand? Scotland, that's where. Do you know, Caitlin has given me the notion to visit the land of our forefathers?"

Rand's smile conveyed amused tolerance if not a little boredom. "Caitlin would. But I think not. You did not ask yourself the most crucial question, Peter."

"Which is?"

"Where does our wealth come from? And of course, it comes from Cranley. No, we'll not go to Scotland for a long time to come. There's more than enough to do here."

He waited momentarily, as though anticipating further argument. When there was none, he signaled to the footmen, and the glass doors were duly opened to admit their guests.

The dowager was in a nostalgic humor. "I met your father at a ball, you know," she told her eldest son. What she refrained from telling him was that she was betrothed to someone else at the time.

"I know," said Rand gently as he led his mother to the edges of the dance floor. The next set had yet to be called, and people were promenading about as the musicians tuned their instruments. He held a gilt-edged chair for her as she sank into it, then he seated himself beside her.

"It was love at first sight." Her thoughts slipped away to another time, another place. Coming to herself, she sighed and looked at Rand curiously. "Was it like that for you?"

In the act of straightening one shirt cuff, Rand's fingers stilled. He glanced up sharply, with such a look that the dowager cried out, "Rand, what is it? What have I said?"

The look faded, and he was able to smile. "It's of no consequence. You asked me a question, but I wasn't paying attention. I beg your pardon. What was it you wished to know?"

The dowager shook her head. "I don't remember. Something to do with Caitlin. She is a delightful girl and not unlike her mother in looks."

This was more the sort of thing Rand wanted to hear. "Did you know her mother? I understood that you hardly ever went into Scotland."

"I went when I could, which was not often when I was a young married woman. Then, I seemed to be in a perpetual state of breeding. Traveling was out of the question."

"What was she like?"

"Morag Randal? It's so long ago. She was very beautiful, in a Celtic way. I remember thinking that she was very proud." The dowager played with the slats of her fan as the recollection came back to her. "Robert Gordon, yes, that was the young man's name. But they didn't call him Gordon, they called him . . ." She shook her head.

"Would it be Daroch?"

354

"Yes! The laird o' Daroch. He was smitten with the girl. Nothing could come of it, of course, because of the feud."

Carefully edging the conversation along, Rand said, "I never did understand the nature of that feud."

The dowager shivered and carefully adjusted the tissue scarf at her shoulders. "It was horrible! After Culloden, Cumberland's forces came into Deeside hunting down rebels."

Very gently Rand said, "I'm aware that Glenshiel's mother was raped by redcoats who were afterward hanged from the rafters of Strathcairn's great hall."

"Yes, well, what you may not know is that those same redcoats were of the Clan Gordon. Their commander was the old laird o' Daroch."

"Are you saying that the laird o' Daroch was one of the rapists?"

The dowager looked as if she would prefer to discuss a less harrowing subject, but answered with composure, "Certainly not. The laird had died at Culloden. These men were rabble."

"Ah." Taking pity on his mother's pained look, Rand changed direction. "What about the young laird o' Daroch, the one who was smitten with Morag Randal? Did he find favor with her?"

"It seemed to me that he did. In fact, it would not have surprised me if he had carried her off and married her in spite of her grandfather's opposition. They can do that in Scotland, you know. The laws are very different from the ones we have here." She gave a little laugh. "But your father said that it was all in my head. And it seemed that he was right. The following year, Daroch was killed in a duel over another lady."

"By Ewan Grant."

355

"Who?"

"The gentleman to whom my father rented Strathcairn for the season when we went to Brighton."

"Yes, so we did."

The conversation was interrupted when the dowager turned aside to compliment her daughter, Emily, on the gown she was wearing. This led to a general discussion on the qualities of various muslins. Rand patiently bided his time.

When Emily moved away, he said, "I'm sure my father must have reproached himself a hundred times over for renting Strathcairn to a stranger."

The dowager's eyes took a moment to focus on her son's face. "You may be sure that he did. But that was as nothing to the regret your uncle experienced."

"My uncle?" Rand had only one uncle, and that was David's father. "What would my uncle have to regret?"

"Mmm?" The dowager's roving gaze had come to rest on her son, Peter. The boy's face was animated, and his eyes were vivid with admiration. Her eyes moved to his partner. Caitlin was no less animated. The two of them seemed to be oblivious to the people around them.

"Mama!"

Rand's impatient tone brought her head round. "Ewan Grant," she said, "was your uncle's particular friend."

Rand made no comment. His gaze was riveted on the couple on the dance floor who had eyes for no one but themselves.

Caitlin felt just the tiniest bit guilty for slipping away from the ball. She was, after all, the hostess, and her first duty was to her guests. She remembered another ime and another ball, and how graciously her husband had presided there.

As though reading her thoughts, Peter Randal said, "They can spare you for five minutes or so. That's all it will take."

Reassured, she passed through the door to his office. While Peter went to the bookcase behind the massive flat-topped desk, Caitlin looked about her with interest. There was no elegant furnishings here. The room was all leather and parquet flooring, very masculine and businesslike, and surprisingly neat.

She wandered around idly, taking cautious sips from the long-stemmed glass in her hand. According to Peter, this was really Rand's domain. He was the one who had developed what their father had started and had made the estate what it was today. Even his stint with the Scots Greys had hardly deflected his interest. Long letters had passed back and forth from Cranley to British lines in Spain. As Peter told it, the job was an easy one. In Rand's absence, he and his brothers were merely trustees of an estate that practically ran itself.

"Rand a farmer!" She laughed softly to herself. "I can hardly believe it."

"Oh? Well, what did you think he did with his time when he wasn't away soldiering?"

"I thought he spent it . . . in London." That was as much as she would permit herself to say.

Peter's fingers had found the folder for which he was searching. Tossing it down on the flat of the desk, he gave her a roguish look, very much in the manner of his oldest brother. "That too," he said. "Well, it stands to reason. London is only a few hours away." When her lips tightened, he laughed. "Haven't you heard? The

357

Randal men are boringly reformed once they finally settle on one female."

"Are they indeed?" Observing Peter's uncertain look, she forgave his thoughtless jest. "What about your brothers, Harry and Robert? Are they farmers too?"

"If either of them wanted to, he could make a living as an estate manager. Their interests lie elsewhere."

"Oh?"

He was flipping through the folder, searching for something particular. "With Harry, it's horses. His stud farm is making quite a name for itself. As for Robert, he is our business manager. There's not much he doesn't know about markets and investments. Ah, here it is." He smoothed out the folds of a newspaper cutting and then stepped back, inviting Caitlin to read it.

"What about you, Peter? Do your interests lie elsewhere, or are you content to remain at Cranley?"

"I love it here. However, I can't help feeling, sometimes, that it lacks challenge. Everything has already been developed. Sometimes I wonder if that's why Rand went off to war. When all one's ambitions are met, one looks around for something else to do."

Caitlin snorted. "If it's a challenge you want, I could tell you where to go."

"Scotland?" He was smiling.

"The Highlands! It would break your heart . . . Oh, never mind that now."

Positioning the candle to get the best light, she began to read. It was exactly as Peter had described it. In England, there was a Board of Agriculture which promoted farming of an experimental nature.

"So you see, Caitlin, there is nothing new about crop rotation or improving the fertility of the soil by adding manure."

"What's this word here?" she asked, and pointed.

Peter bent his head close to hers. "Where?"

This was how Rand found them when he finally tracked them down. Rand did not speculate, did not weigh consequences, did not hesitate. He pounced. At the sound of that quick tread, Caitlin jerked back in time to see Peter go sprawling across the desk with Rand on top of him. In a clutter of loose papers, pens, and ink pots, the two went rolling to the floor.

"Rand! Peter!" Caitlin dived for an ink pot and caught it before its contents spilled. "Stop this at once, do you hear?"

She was answered by a series of grunts as each men strained to lock the other in position. Peter's elbow connected with Rand's eye, and in the next instant they had separated and were springing lightly to the balls of their feet.

Half-crouched over, they circled warily.

"Now what's brought this on—as if I didn't know?" taunted Peter, and quickly sidestepped Rand's furious lunge. "This time you are not going to have everything your own way, big brother. At last we are evenly matched."

Rand snorted. "What? You think you are ready to take me? Halfling, you are still wet behind the ears."

Peter's eyes narrowed shrewdly. "Is that so? I don't think Caitlin would agree with you. Why don't you ask her?"

Caitlin's eyes moved between them. There was a recklessness here that made her tremble. The indolence which she had taken to be a characteristic of all the English Randals was no longer evident. "Please," she said. "Please."

Both men charged at the same moment. Locked together, they crashed into a small table, overturning it, and Caitlin let out a shriek. Eyes staring, fist to her mouth, she watched them in horror. Peter had his knee in Rand's back and was pounding his brother's head against the floor. Frantically looking around for some way to stop the fight she ran to the hearth and fetched a poker.

"Please," she begged them, "this has got to stop!" And she waved the poker helplessly in front of her face.

With a heave and a shove, Rand reached for his brother's leg. The edge of his hand caught it such a blow that Peter let out a howl and rolled over onto his side, clutching his kneecap.

"You hurt him!" Caitlin wailed.

"God, I hope so!" grunted Rand, and sprawled on top of him. Breath coming through clenched teeth, he locked Peter in position, face down, one arm twisted behind him, his head pulled back by the force of Rand's free arm.

"Don't hurt him! My God, if you don't stop, you'll break his neck!" She was sobbing with fright, hopping from one foot to the other.

Her words only aggravated the situation. Rand's hold tightened. Through his clenched teeth, he grated, "This is what you may expect, halfling, when you make up to my wife."

Peter's only answer was a choked-off gurgle.

Caitlin raised the poker high above her head. "Rand," she pleaded, "don't force me to hurt you! Please!"

"Don't be so dramatic . . ." He broke off as Peter's open palm hammered the floor, the signal that he was conceding defeat. Rand let him go at once.

Breathing hard, both gentlemen pushed themselves

up to sit cross-legged. Peter's hands were at his throat and his jaw worked. Caitlin was clutching the poker in a death grip as she waited in terror to see what they would do next.

It was Rand who extended his right hand first. "You are getting quite adept," he allowed generously.

Peter grimaced as he clasped Rand's outstretched hand. "Tell that to my sore throat."

Aware of a sudden stillness, they both looked up at Caitlin. Stomping her foot, she emptied the ink pot over both blond heads, then went stomping out of the room.

The ball was long over, and Rand and Caitlin faced each other across the width of their bedchamber. Only moments before, Rand had dismissed Caitlin's maid. His eyes were wary. Hers were simmering.

"I believe I owe you an apology," he said.

He sounded faintly uneasy. Good. She was going to make him *cringe* before this was over. "I suppose you think it amusing, terrifying the life out of me like that? I thought you meant to kill each other."

"No, did you? We always settle arguments with a wrestling bout."

"Someone might have told me." Her voice was frigid.

His was placating. "Couldn't you tell that it was only playacting—more or less?"

"You came within a hairbreadth of having your brains bashed in by a poker."

His eyebrows lifted. "I don't think so."

"It's what you deserved!"

Smiling, he touched his fingers to his swollen eye and the bump on his forehead. "I think I got more than I deserved, certainly more that I bargained for. Peter is getting to be quite skillful. And you had your revenge with the ink pot." He combed his fingers through his wet hair. "I'm going to have your mark on me for many a long day. The stuff is almost impossible to wash out."

"What I can't understand is what set you off. You didn't ask any questions. You didn't wait for explanations. You charged in there like a bull on the rampage. Why?"

He shrugged carelessly. "Peter is at a bad age. You know how it is."

She looked at him blankly, but he did not explain himself. "It was all very innocent," she assured him.

"Yes, I know. You were discussing . . . manure."

His smile won no answering smile from her, but rather ignited her temper. "We were discussing Scotland," she snapped.

At the mention of Scotland, the laughter in his eyes went cold, and suddenly Caitlin did not care about taking a petty revenge for the fright he had given her. Other things of far more significance must be settled between them.

Breathing deeply, choosing her words with care, she said, "When you brought me here, Rand, it was on the understanding that we should divide our time between England and Scotland. It seems to me you have had a change of heart?"

"No. Let us just say you assumed too much."

Her eyes went wide, and she curled and uncurled her fingers. "I assumed too much?" she said faintly, then rallying, "But, Rand, you must see that I have responsibilities in Scotland. I can't turn my back on them."

"What responsibilities?"

"Fiona for one. She's just at an age when—"

"Fine! We'll have her come to Cranley, give her a season in London, if you think you are up to it."

Nothing in her expression betrayed that his barb had found its mark. "My grandfather is not getting any younger. Is he to come to Cranley too?"

"Your grandfather is as strong as an ox. If his health were to break down that would be a different matter entirely."

Her brows were knit, and she was studying him as though he were a stranger whose face she could not quite place. "In the past, you used to visit Deeside every year for the hunting season."

"I may do so again, if the fancy takes me."

A sudden involuntary movement of her hand sent the chair toppling to its side. Ignoring it, she advanced upon him. The words burst from her passionately. "I thought you were coming round to my way of thinking. Rand, you are chief of a great clan. You bear a proud and honorable name. You can't just turn your back on Scotland. There is so much to do there. Peter said so himself. Everything here is perfect. Your life lacks challenge. Don't you see, in Deeside you would find that challenge?"

"Ah. At last we come to the crux of the matter."

His arms were folded across his chest; his smile was not quite a sneer. Shaking his head, he said softly, "Tell me, my sweet, do you really suppose that I am such a slave to your beauty, your wit, and your delectable body that I will allow you free rein to order my life to suit yourself?"

Herein lay his chagrin. When his mother had questioned him, oh so casually, on the nature of his feelings for Caitlin, the truth had hit him with all the velocity of a runaway carriage. He had loved her almost from the

363

moment he had set eyes on her. Not that he had known it. Like most of his sex, he had never been in the habit of searching his emotions, trying to identify what he was feeling. He wanted her. He delighted in her. She stirred something in him, an odd mixture of tenderness and possessiveness that no woman had ever touched. He had not looked beyond that until his mother had prodded him.

The knowledge that he loved Caitlin did not make him happy. He burned to know what she felt for him. She had never said the words to him, words he had heard from the lips of a score of women in his time, words he was very adept at turning aside. No woman had ever heard them from him.

This was not the only cause for his chagrin. The suspicion was growing in him that the only thing Caitlin loved, was capable of loving, was a tract of rocky land in the Highlands of Scotland—Deeside. Peter had confirmed Lady Margaret's poisonous remarks, and if that were not enough to convince him, David's avowal that he meant to return to Scotland if he survived Waterloo confirmed it. Caitlin's devotion to the Highlands of Scotland was almost fanatical. There was nothing she would not do to draw others to her cause.

How differently now he viewed his former indulgence of her—the free hand he had allowed her in setting Strathcairn to rights. With Caitlin, that had been only the first step in her campaign to make his Scottish estates into a showplace. If she had given him the only words he wanted to hear, he would have laid the world at her feet. Without them, every word, every look, every inflection must be minutely examined. Scotland had become the testing ground.

"A slave of my what?" She gave a small gasping

laugh. "Rand, you must be confusing me with another lady, or you have taken leave of your senses."

"Do you deny that you are using me for you own ends?"

Guilty color stole up her throat, into her pale cheeks. "Why, whatever do you mean?"

"That innocent stare may work very well with Peter, but I am alert to all your wiles. There is nothing you will not do, no trick to which you will not stoop, in order to get your own way."

"Are we talking about Scotland?"

"You know very well that we are. Well, let me tell you, you overreached yourself this time, my pet. Throwing down the gauntlet to my brothers with that barefaced wager! Filling Peter's head full of ideas about the challenge that awaits him in Deeside! What next will you try? Is my mother to become your next target, or perhaps one of my sisters? One thing is certain: you won't find me as easily duped as I once was. The Highlands of Scotland, and Deeside in particular, will no longer be at issue between us. As far as I am concerned, they are not worth the price."

She stared at him for the space of several heartbeats while the blood in her veins turned to ice. "What are you saying?" she asked hoarsely.

His eyes raked her. "A mistress barters her beauty and sexual favors for money. My dear, you missed your calling. Need I say more?"

She wasn't hurt. She was furious. After everything that had passed between them! The torrid nights! The long, intimate conversations! The shared laughter! After everything she had done for him! Giving up her home in Scotland! Trying to fill the role of mistress of Cranley! Accepting his crazy family as if they did not belong in

Bedlam! And this was how he saw her! He thought she had prostituted herself for a few acres of land.

"You won't try to pretend, I hope, that you love me?" His voice was strained and there was a stillness about him that mystified her.

"Love," she said scornfully. "That is a word that does not exist in my vocabulary any more than it exists in yours. Do you know what your trouble is, Rand? You don't know how to be friends with a woman. Friendship ... affection ... Oh, what's the use—we've had this conversation before."

A muscle in his cheek clenched, but he spoke without heat. "Are you, by any chance, holding David up to me again?"

"I'm not saying David was a paragon, but he knew how to be friends with a woman."

"A soul mate, in fact." His lip curled.

She glared up at him. "He was wrong about you. He thought that once your days with Wellington were over, once you had done your duty to your country, you would remember the duty you owed to your clan. But you don't really care a straw about the Clan Randal, do you?"

"In a word, no."

Swiftly moving to the bed, she pounded her pillows the way she wanted to pound his head. "You won't be sleeping with me tonight, so don't even think it," she told him.

He smiled nastily. "How like a woman! A headache, my sweet? Don't despair, I have just the remedy to cure it."

She allowed him to get one knee on the bed before, smiling sweetly, she said, "It's the wrong time of month, and if you can cure *that*, I and women the world over will be forever in your debt."

With a stream of muffled profanities, he slammed into his own chamber.

Chapter Twenty-Two

When the house party broke up the following morning, and Cranley's guests had departed to go their separate ways, most of them to their townhouses in London, on the spur of the moment, Rand made up his mind to follow them.

"I shall expect you to join me in a week or so," he told his startled family over luncheon. "That should give you time to pack your bags and do whatever it is you need to do for a prolonged stay in town. I shall take a small contingent of servants with me to open up the house. Once it becomes known that Caitlin and I are to take in the season, I've no doubt there will be a flood of invitations waiting for your attention."

His words were received with mixed feelings. The twins were in transports, the dowager was stoic, Peter was faintly puzzled, and Caitlin was downright aghast. Rand scarcely gave them time to come to themselves before he was off.

The Randals' townhouse was in Berkeley Square, in the very heart of Mayfair. In short order, Rand had informed his resident butler, Willis, what was afoot, and after washing away the dirt of his journey and changing his garments, he quit the house and made for his club in St. James.

For three days and nights he tried to blot out what he was thinking by giving himself up to the pleasures of drinking and gaming in convivial masculine company. When that did not work, he took to putting in an appearance at dos and parties where he knew he would be welcomed with or without a gilt-edged invitation card.

Here, he thought to himself, surrounded by the most beautiful and sophisticated women in the whole of Europe, he would be able to put what he felt for his own little wife into its proper perspective.

And the London scene was like a breath of fresh air. Caitlin could not hold a candle to these alluring women of the world. Their hothouse beauty pleasured his senses, their practiced flatteries made him feel ten feet tall. It amused him inordinately to try to introduce subjects which were of the keenest interest to Caitlin, such as crop production at high altitudes, or whether or not horses produced the most superior manure. As was to be expected, these sophisticates looked at him as though he had insulted them. Every night, he fell into bed laughing his head off.

A full week was to pass before it was borne in upon him that the most beautiful and sophisticated women in the whole of Europe bored him to tears. It came to him suddenly when he was sitting in his dining room in Berkeley Square, having just consumed a most delectable dinner which his French chef had prepared. He knew it was delectable because Ladubec would have cut his own throat before he would have served up anything that was less than a masterpiece.

Rand looked at his empty plate, and for the life of him, he could not remember what he had just eaten.

Groaning, he threw his napkin on the table and leaned back in his chair, gritting his teeth. It seemed he had lost his taste for everything but the society of one impossible witch.

In one last, superhuman effort to break her spell, he shut his eyes and tried to recall his first impression of Caitlin. It was useless. It seemed to him he had been lost from their first encounter on his last night of furlough on Deeside. It was irrational. He had not even caught a glimpse of her face, had not exchanged more than a few words with her before David had spirited her away. But he had kissed her, and even then the magnetism that always drew him to her had come into play.

It was not so when he had returned to Deeside to find the witch who had ensnared him. He'd taken one look at her in Crathie Church and had put her down as a mouse. It was what she had wanted him to think, what she had wanted all men to think. It had not taken him long to sniff out her true nature. He had sensed and responded to the depths of passion which lay dormant just beneath the surface. He had wanted that passion for himself.

He had known about David, of course, but in his usual, unthinking way, he had discounted whatever might have been between the two of them. David had been a mere boy. He was a man. He would be the one to awaken her and teach her what it meant to be a woman. And he had done it, and had had more joy of her than he had ever had of any woman.

Then everything had begun to lose its savor. In that part of him he never cared to examine he had guessed, no, he had *known* that the relationship was unequal. Without understanding his resentment, he had become hard and demanding, as though by mastering her he could most truly possess her. It was nothing to him to make Strathcairn a showplace and develop the estate as Caitlin dreamed of doing. What had begun to prick his pride was the suspicion that in the sweet giving of herself, she had an ulterior motive. Strathcairn and Deeside were all that truly mattered to her.

The knowledge that his love was unrequited made him writhe. If she ever discovered it, she would pity him, as he had pitied former mistresses who had bestowed a love he had neither sought nor wanted. How pathetic their attempts to force the words from him! How wearying their jealous rages over trifles! And how relieved he had been that he could be shut of them with a quick kiss and a fat purse to soften the blow to their pride.

The future pattern of his days with Caitlin passed before his eyes. The picture revolted him. He saw himself as a lovesick suppliant begging for her favors. She didn't know it yet, but she had it in her power to make him do almost anything she wanted. Sooner or later, he was bound to betray himself.

He took that sobering thought to bed. In the morning, when he awakened, the notion had become fixed in his mind that he needed time to master himself before coming face-to-face with Caitlin. Over a solitary breakfast, a number of schemes came to him and were rejected. Though he had almost lost interest in delving into Caitlin's background, he finally decided to pursue the lead his mother had given him on Ewan Grant.

Penning a quick note to the effect that he had gone into Dorset to inform his uncle of his nuptials, he gave it into his butler's hand with the information that he hoped to return within the week.

* * *

As he approached Dorchester, Rand had time to reflect that the journey, more rash than wise, was also open to misinterpretation. Cranley was not so very far out of his way. It would have delayed him by only a day to stop off there, advise Caitlin of his change in plans. Then again, it would seem churlish to her if he did not invite her to go along with him. He could hardly tell her that he was avoiding her in the interests of self-preservation.

The trip itself, he did not regret. It was more than time that he sat down with his uncle and gave him an account of David's last days. When he was last in Dorset he had found his uncle so sunk in grief that he had abandoned the attempt. He might have expected to see Eric Randal at Cranley making up one of his mother's house party, if the old boy had not been in Shropshire visiting a married daughter and her children.

As his closed chaise bowled along the avenue that led to the house, more and more, Rand found his thoughts focused on David. He remembered another time and another carriage ride, when he had traveled to the Highlands, and how he had been consumed with guilt and a vague determination to make everything up to his cousin for what he had lost at Waterloo.

He remembered that the girl had been uppermost in his mind. The girl had mattered to David, and he, Rand, was going to take care of her. He grimaced and looked out for a moment at the tranquil scene, lush lawns and horse-chestnut trees bursting into leaf. In the Highlands of Scotland, the snows in the hills and mountains would be melting and the rivers would soon be in full spate, but he doubted if the trees would be in leaf.

He sighed and slumped against the banquette, closing his eyes. He was thinking that on Deeside he'd picked up the threads of his own life. Caitlin Randal had soon deflected him from his resolve to find out what his young cousin had wanted of him. The irony was, if he had only listened to Caitlin, he would have known what was on David's mind. He knew that now.

He'd made a royal fool of himself, accusing Caitlin of bartering her sexual favors for his patronage. She was his wife. He could take her any time he wanted. Besides, it wasn't like that between them. He knew it wasn't. He'd been fishing, hoping that she would not only deny his vile accusations, but go one step further. He'd come by his just desserts.

He made a resolution right there and then that he was going to return to Deeside with Caitlin and give her a free hand in the management of his estates. It would be a costly and unprofitable business in his estimation, but that did not weigh with him. He owed it to David to do right by him. He owed it to Caitlin to make up for David's loss, a loss from which he had profited.

David and Caitlin. Both had denied that their friendship was anything but platonic. *Soul mates.* There was a time when Rand would have sneered at that word. It was so unmanly. He wasn't sneering now. He was beginning to think he didn't know the first thing about how to appeal to a woman of Caitlin's sensibilities.

In the act of alighting from the coach, he paused for a moment to take in the house and its setting. Stands of oaks, elms, and beeches cast pools of dappled shade on the lawns and driveway. The house itself was Georgian, though on a more modest scale than Cranley. Its walls were covered with ivy, and its red-bricked facade was mellowing with age. He had an impression of something pastoral and tranquil and unreservedly English.

It put him in mind of another regret which had troubled his mind. He again wished that when he'd had the chance he had taken the time to get to know his cousin better.

By the time the covers were removed and Eric Randal had poured out two glasses of his prize port, Rand was more than ever glad that he had come into Dorset. His uncle was very much improved since he had last seen him. Where before, Eric Randal had been careless about his appearance, he was now immaculately turned out. Looking at that shock of carefully combed silver hair, a leonine mane, Rand had an impression of how he, himself, would look in another thirty or forty years. Though Rand could hardly recall the lady, he knew that David had taken after his mother.

It was time well spent, decided Rand, for though there was still a sadness in those vivid blue eyes, not only was his uncle able to speak with composure about the death of his only son, but he was able to reminisce about the past with humor. Rand was coming to have a much clearer picture of his cousin.

"I had no idea that David suffered from asthma when he was a child," he said, remarking upon something his uncle had said earlier, accepting the proffered glass of port.

"It started up when his mother died. As a child, his health was very delicate. If you did not know it, it was because David tried to hide it from you. He was ashamed. Well, you know how boys are. You and your brothers were robust little fiends. David had a hard time keeping up with you whenever we visited Cranley. You must have wondered why he spent so much time indoors, when the rest of you were outdoors riding hell-

374

for-leather across the downs, or involved in one of your interminable wrestling matches?"

"I don't remember. David was so much younger than I. If I thought about him at all, I thought of him as Peter's friend."

"David and Peter? They might have been friends, I suppose, if David hadn't felt so self-conscious about his infirmities. As I recall, you were always kind to him."

"I could afford to be. He wasn't my brother," said Rand, and both gentlemen laughed.

"Well, he grew out of the asthma before he went up to Oxford, thank God." Eric Randal stared at the ruby red liquid in his glass. "He was so proud to be serving with you, Rand. The boy hero-worshiped you, do you know?"

This was so unexpected that Rand did not know what to say, but almost in the same breath, his uncle went off on another set of reminiscences about his grandchildren, and the moment passed.

From there, the conversation moved to Scotland, and before long, Rand's uncle was asking about mutual acquaintances. Rand seized on the opportunity of introducing the subject of Ewan Grant.

"An old scandal was resurrected," he said casually. "Do you remember the duel between Ewan Grant and the laird o' Daroch?"

"A terrible business! At the time, I was so incensed I wanted to call Ewan out myself. He was my friend, you see. It was because of me that your father was persuaded to lease Strathcairn to him. I should have known that his sister would cause murder and mayhem wherever she went. It's not the first duel Ewan fought to protect her honor, such as it was, but it was the first time he had ever killed a man over it."

"His sister?" asked Rand neutrally.

"A regular baggage if ever I saw one. That's the reason he took her to the wilds of Scotland. There was some unsavory business in London. I swear she fell into one scandalous scrape after another. She threw herself at Daroch then cried rape when he refused to marry her. Not that that was generally known, of course. It was a terrible tragedy, a terrible tragedy."

It took Rand a moment or two to marshal his thoughts. "You seem very well informed! Surely, you were not there?"

His uncle let out a snort of derision. "I most certainly was not. You would not catch me sharing a roof with Sally Grant. For all her angelic looks, the girl was poison. No. Ewan wrote to me before he sailed for India. Of course, I read between the lines. If it had been anyone else but Daroch, Ewan would have thought twice about his sister's story."

"I suppose Daroch's reputation told against him?"

"Quite. But it wasn't only that. Someone corroborated the girl's story, someone who swore he had seen Sally and Daroch together. I don't know who. Ewan never told me. Poor Daroch. As it turns out, he was innocent."

"Oh?"

"It all came out later, quite recently, in fact, after Sally swallowed a great dose of religion. The Methodists got to her, don't you know?" He laughed, an ugly, grating sound. "The bitch was a scorned woman, and in her spite she turned on the poor devil who had scorned her. There wasn't much Ewan could do to make restitution. By the time she wrote to him, confessing the whole, Daroch was in his grave and Ewan was in India. One good thing came of it, I suppose. Aboard ship, he

376

met the lady who was to become his wife, a widow woman with a young son."

"And he is still in India?"

"Good Lord, no! Didn't you know? The Grants are my neighbors, Ewan came home a rich man, oh, all of eighteen months ago."

Rand hardly knew what reply to make to his uncle's revelations, and he covered his silence by offering to replenish both empty glasses.

When this was done, his uncle took up the conversation. "Look here, Rand, something is going on and I should like to know what it is."

"Why do you say that?"

"Because I don't believe in coincidence. You see, David asked me things, much the same as you, when he was last here."

"Idle curiosity," said Rand easily. "That's all it is."

His uncle grunted. "I could not get a straight answer from David either."

Suddenly, Rand had the strangest impression that he was looking over David's shoulder. He had always had the feeling that he was following in David's footsteps. It was, after all, David who had sent him into Scotland to find Caitlin. One thing had led to another, culminating in his presence here, quizzing his uncle about the gentleman who was, in all probability, his wife's father, Ewan Grant. It seemed to him now that he should have taken all of this a mite more seriously. It was uncanny, but he sensed an urgency that he had not felt before.

Setting down his glass, he said baldly, "If you can arrange it, I should like to meet this Mr. Grant."

His uncle blinked, then nodded. "At the moment, he is in London, I believe. But in the morning, I shall send a footman to Mrs. Grant for his direction. Their place is only a mile or two along the road to Dorchester."

Another delay. Rand tried to contain his impatience. His uncle's eyes were avidly curious. "Thank you," he said; then, with an abruptness that left his uncle staring, Rand changed the direction of the conversation. "All of London is agog with the news of the betrothal of Princess Charlotte and Prince Leopold of Coburg," he said.

His uncle took the hint. "That will cost the British taxpayer a pretty penny, I'll wager."

Rand smiled. "You would win your wager. The Commons voted the young couple a grant of sixty thousand pounds a year, in addition to other allowances."

"Mmm. I suppose we shouldn't grumble. After her father, the Prince Regent, she is the heir apparent to the throne."

"It won't surprise you to know that public feeling against the prince is running very high at present."

And by these means, Rand steered the conversation away from speculation about the man who had fathered Caitlin.

The following morning over breakfast, Eric Randal had a particular favor he wished to ask of his nephew. "It's David's things," he said. "Someone has to go through them and decide what to do with them. I tried, but . . . well, you know how it is. I don't want strangers or servants going through his effects. I know it's a lot to ask of you—"

Rand quickly interrupted, "You could not ask any favor of me that I would not undertake. No, really, I would deem it a great honor to be entrusted with the task."

His uncle looked away, blinking. "Thank you, dear boy. There's no hurry. Whenever you are ready."

"I'm ready now."

David's suite of rooms was one floor up, with a splendid view over the park and shrubbery. Through a gap in the trees Rand could just make out the spires of Dorchester. His uncle did not linger, and Rand could see why. The rooms looked as if David would return to them at any moment. A coat was tossed inelegantly over the foot of the bed. A pair of muddied top boots were thrown in a corner. The soap on the washstand was half worn away from frequent use. A torn neckcloth lay in a discarded heap on the floor. Rand understood the apparent disorder. In much the same manner, when he had left Cranley to rejoin his regiment, his mother had preserved his chambers. It was as if time could be made to stand still.

He took a moment or two to look around the place. He couldn't remember the last time he had entered these chambers, yet he felt no sense of strangeness. The blue curtains at the windows with matching bed draperies put him in mind of the chamber he had occupied at Cranley before his marriage. There were other similarities: the dark oak furniture; a certain Spartan atmosphere; the model of Drake's *Golden Hind* which he, Rand, had built with his father when a boy. A vague recollection came back to him. He had outgrown his interest in sailing ships, and he'd carelessly passed his model of the *Golden Hind* along to his young cousin. Evidently, David had treasured it.

For a long time, Rand stood crouched over that model, tracing the masts and rigging with one finger, lost in memories of a happy boyhood and of a father who had entered into all his interests. He was smiling when he pushed into the little dressing room which had served as David's bookroom.

There was no sense of familiarity here, for David's store of books were of a far more literary bent than Rand's. The Greek dramatists were well represented. Rand opened a volume of Sophocles and quickly shut it when the Greek letters jumped out at him. He had not looked at Greek since his Oxford days. David was clever. Rand could remember his mother saying so, now that he thought about it. He supposed that a boy who could not enter into the games of other boys must find other ways to occupy his time.

On top of David's desk, he came across a well-worn copy of Byron's *Childe Harold*. There was nothing to interest Rand there. One drawer down, he found a gentleman's monogrammed driving gauntlet. There was no mate to it. Beneath the gauntlet, in the same drawer, was a letter written in a feminine hand. Rand stared at that letter as if debating with himself. Finally, as though it would crumble into dust at the first touch, he gingerly withdrew it.

Hardly breathing, he smoothed out the one-page epistle, and read.

Oh, my dear,

Forgive me for what I said. I did not mean it, not one word of it. Come back to the Highlands. Come back, and we shall see if there is not something we can do to ease this hopeless passion of yours. I pray for your return.

There was no signature. None was necessary. Rand would have recognized Caitlin's hand anywhere. Colors seemed to leap before his eyes, and the pain in his chest was so acute, he feared he might faint. *Caitlin and David.* He crushed her letter into his balled fist. For one demented moment, he was fiercely glad that David was dead and no longer a threat to him. But that thought had sprung from the worst part of him. There was another part, a better part, which rushed in almost at once to draw off the poison.

He was shaking and was hardly aware that someone had entered the room. Fighting to find his control, he passed a hand over his eyes. A cough brought his head round. Just inside the door, a footman stood waiting respectfully to attract his attention.

"What is it?" asked Rand.

The look of concern was replaced by a mask of well-bred indifference. "The master begs a moment of your time, your lordship. You may find him in the library."

Rand gave himself a few minutes before he made his way downstairs. When he entered the library, two gentlemen rose to greet him. Rand's eyes passed over his uncle and fastened on the younger gentleman.

"Mr. Haughton!" he exclaimed, going forward. "What brings you here?"

Haughton colored hotly and stammered before getting out, "I'm afraid I'm the bearer of very sad tidings. Your friend, Mr. Murray, has missed you, it seems."

"John? John Murray of Deeside?"

"The same. We parted company in London. He went on to your place in Sussex, and I came on here."

Rand was aware of a sudden release of tension. Whatever the sad tidings, they did not immediately concern his wife. "Why don't we sit down?" he said.

When they were seated, Haughton said at once, "It's your wife's grandfather. He has suffered a stroke. Obviously, it's serious or your wife would not have been sent for. I'm sorry I know so little about his condition, but I did not expect to find you here. Murray could tell you more. There was a fire, you see—oh, not the house but the stable! All the horses perished. It was too much for Glenshiel."

Rand fired a few questions at Mr. Haughton, but there was little more to be learned. Then he remembered that Caitlin's dog had been tethered in Glenshiel's stable. The question in his mind was answered by Haughton's next words.

"The deerhound managed to escape the conflagration."

Eric Randal's voice was very grave. "Don't cavil, man! Tell him the whole of it!"

Rand looked from one sober face to the other.

Haughton coughed to clear an obstruction in his throat. "You may remember, Lord Randal, that my father was missing?" When Rand nodded, he continued in the same strained tone. "His body has been found. At the inquest, the verdict was that it was an accident, that he had lost his step and had fallen down a gully. There are some, however, who are blaming his death on your wife's dog. It seems almost conclusive that he was savaged by your wife's dog."

"That is preposterous! Bocain would not attack anyone unless that person were to attack Caitlin. I beg your pardon, Mr. Haughton. Naturally, I am shocked to hear of your father's death. But if there was not an accident, there must be some other explanation for it."

Haughton sounded unutterably weary. "I don't know what to believe. All I know is that my father's body was not a pretty sight when I identified it. However, I assure you, whatever the truth of that matter may be, your wife's deerhound has become the terror of Deeside. She has reverted to something wild and unpredictable, so much so that there's a bounty on her head."

A suspicion was beginning to grow in Rand's mind. "What I can't understand is what brings you into this neck of the woods, Mr. Haughton? It is Mr. Haughton, is it not?"

The hot color returned to the young man's cheeks. "My name *is* Haughton. However, I think it is my father, my *stepfather,* whom you have found out. He was, as you must know, Ewan Grant, and as for what brings me here, I have brought his body home to my mother for burial."

Rand was still trying to grapple with so much confusion when his uncle quietly interposed, "I did not know that my friend had gone into Scotland, or I would have told you. To my knowledge, he was in London, attending to business."

"There was nothing sinister in it," cut in Mr. Haughton. "For reasons you must understand, my father did not wish to use his own name. He was afraid that the Clan Gordon would take their revenge for the duel which resulted in the death of the laird o' Daroch so many years ago."

"Those feuds are a thing of the past," Rand answered shortly. "No one, nowadays, carries a vendetta to such extremes."

"You are wrong there," replied Haughton. "At all events, it was what my father believed." He looked away and made a helpless motion with his hands. "I thought it best not to reveal my father's true identity. As far as everyone on Deeside knows, it was Mr. Haughton, the senior, who met with a terrible accident."

A number of things were going through Rand's mind. He was thinking of something his uncle had said the night before, namely that he did not believe in coincidence. No more did Rand.

There had been two separate accidents on Deeside within the space of a few weeks, one involving Caitlin and the other involving Ewan Grant. They were presumed to be accidents, because there was no apparent motive for murder. If these accidents were not accidents, Rand reflected, then what had set them off and what connection did one have to the other? More to the point, who was behind them?

"What did your father hope to gain by going to Scotland?" asked Rand.

"As to that, I'm not sure that my father was clear in his own mind. Before your cousin went off to Brussels to join his regiment, he came to see him. I was not present at that interview. And later, when it was known that David Randal had fallen at Waterloo, my father became restless. I know he had an agent in Deeside, someone who spied out the land. I've come across his reports among my father's papers. They make interesting reading, but there is nothing sinister there either. I don't really know what my father hoped to gain. All I know is that he hoped to right a great wrong."

Though Rand was listening intently, his brain was functioning at another level. Fragments of this and that were beginning to fall into place, forming something so incredible that he was reluctant to accept it.

When there was a prolonged silence, he said, "Mr. Haughton, I should like to see those reports, if I may."

Rand was certain of one thing. He was not going to allow Caitlin to return to Deeside. He was sorry about her grandfather, more than sorry. He wished that things were different, but as they stood, he was not going to chance his wife's life.

Mr. Haughton had erred when he had said there was nothing sinister in the reports his father's agent had sent. The irony was that the man had gathered all the information without understanding its significance. Rand remembered his conversation with Patrick Gordon, the Bard of Aboyne.

That put him in mind of something else—the uncanny feeling that he was following in his cousin David's footsteps. It was David who had sent Ewan Grant to Scotland, and even if Mr. Haughton could not fathom the reason for it, Rand knew why. David must have told Grant that Caitlin believed he was her father.

But Grant wasn't, could not be, for if he had been, there would have been no reason to do away with him—and no reason for the attack on Caitlin.

Everything always came back to the laird o' Daroch. It always had, and Rand was cursing himself now for not having seen it sooner.

When he stepped down from his chaise outside Cranley's front doors, he steeled himself to meet tears and entreaties. The doors were flung open, but it was not Caitlin who ran down the steps to welcome him home; his mother and the twins greeted him. It took him some time to make sense of their excited babble.

It seemed that his brothers were chasing him down all over the south of England to give him the news about

Glenshiel, while Caitlin and Murray had set off for Scotland on the understanding that he would follow almost immediately.

They had almost a week's head start.

Chapter Twenty-Three

"I'm verra pleased with ye, Sir Alexander." The physician patted the inert hand which lay upon the counterpane. "With plenty o' rest and good food to nourish ye, we'll soon have ye on your feet." He bent over the bed and gave those staring eyes a straight look. "Ye must have patience, sir. Everything will come back to ye in time. Ye'll be roaring at these soncy granddaughters o' yours afore ye know it."

Outside the sickroom, Dr. Innes's prognosis was more restrained. "It could go either way," he told Caitlin.

"There must be *something* we can do for him."

"Aye, it's hard to let nature take its course, but when the patient has suffered a stroke, it's the only way. There is no cure but patience."

She shook her head. "I feel so helpless. I can't just sit there and stare at him all day."

"Then talk to him. Make him want to talk to ye."

"He does, but it's without form or substance, and he gets so frustrated when I can't understand him. It's painful watching him make the effort."

"That he wants to talk is a hopeful sign." He patted

387

her awkwardly on the shoulder. "With ye here, it will make all the difference in the world."

At the bottom of the stairs, Daroch was waiting for them.

"He's doing as well as can be expected," the physician told Daroch.

Daroch nodded, as though knowing to a nicety what those few noncommittal words might mean. "It's a slow business," he told Caitlin, "but there is every hope that your grandfather will recover."

"I know. I know." She said the words automatically. Speculation was useless, as Daroch and Innes had been quick to point out in the short while she had been home.

The door to the library opened, and Donald Randal appeared just inside the room. "Ye'll have a wee dram, Dr. Innes? Daroch? And ye'll both break bread with us too."

"Now that is uncommon kind o' ye, Mr. Randal," replied Innes. "It's been too long since you and I sat down and enjoyed a good chin-wag."

When the three gentlemen entered the library, Caitlin turned on her heel and retraced her steps to her grandfather's room. Daroch breaking bread at Glenshiel's table! Glenshiel would never have allowed a Gordon o' Daroch over his threshold! But then, her grandfather could not know how much they had all come to depend on the young laird. He was quite literally a godsend. He never made demands, never needed to be entertained. He was there in the background, a bulwark in a time of trouble.

It was through his good offices that Dr. Innes had been able to consult with an eminent physician from Aberdeen, a certain Dr. Simpson, who was attached to the university. He was the best to be had, according to Dr. Innes. How Daroch had persuaded so notable a person to make the long journey to Glenshiel House was a mystery to Caitlin. There was more to Daroch than she would ever have believed, and one day, she hoped her grandfather would thank him for all he had done for them.

"Oh, Rand," she cried softly. "Please, *please* come to me." For the two days since she had arrived home, she had felt as though all the cares of the world had been thrust upon her shoulders. The tragedy of the fire as well as her grandfather's stroke coming so soon upon it seemed to have robbed everyone at Glenshiel of their wits. Her aunt, Charlotte, went around like a sleepwalker, Fiona had turned into a watering pot, and Donald Randal spent hours staring into the coals in the grate. That he had bestirred himself to offer hospitality to Daroch and the physician, she counted as a small miracle.

When this was over, if and when her grandfather recovered, she was going to read the riot act if he dared to say one unkind word about Daroch. It was Daroch who had sent John Murray down to Sussex to fetch her; it was he who had taken charge in the aftermath of the fire, setting men to clear the debris and rubble. It was he who had organized the search parties that had finally found the remains of poor Mr. Haughton.

A shiver passed over her, and her steps faltered. She was thinking of Bocain. It wasn't true. She *knew* it wasn't true. Bocain would never attack anyone unless provoked past bearing, and from what she remembered of Mr. Haughton, he would not have provoked a fly.

The search for her dog had turned into a witch hunt. Every day, the men of the glen went out tracking with hunting dogs. There was more to it now than the death of one man. If a lamb lost its footing and tumbled into a ditch, it was Bocain's doing. If a pony came home lame or with an injury that could not be explained, that, too, was blamed on Bocain. Gamekeepers, crofters, poachers—no one had a kind word to say for the hound. Children allowed their imagination free rein. From as far as Aboyne to the Braes o' Mar, they swore that they had narrowly escaped an attack made by the vicious deerhound, and everyone believed them. In men's minds, Bocain had turned into a monster. The locals waited in fear for some poor child to be carried off and devoured.

She was terrified to step outside the doors of the house, not for her own sake but for her hound's. They must think her blind not to see that men were loitering about, waiting and watching for Bocain to find her. Then what would they do? Caitlin shivered when the answer came to her.

"Rand," she said, and wanted to weep her eyes out. Pinning a smile on her face, she pushed into Glenshiel's room.

Fiona was sniffling into a handkerchief.

"What is it?" Caitlin asked in alarm, then quickly crossed to the bed. She searched her grandfather's face for some sign of change.

He returned her look with an expression she was coming to know, something between frustrated rage and fear. "It's all right," she soothed, smiling reassuringly. "You heard Dr. Innes. Soon you'll be roaring at Fiona and me in your usual style." She knew how hard it must be for a vigorous man like Glenshiel to become as helpless as a babe, depending on others to take care of his most personal needs. His womenfolk nursed him in shifts, but it took two of the gillies to turn him in bed or lift him to the commode.

Fiona turned her tear-streaked face up to Caitlin. Between sobs she got out, "Grandfather said a word. As clear as day he said 'fire.' He blames me for what happened. It's not true. I didn't leave the lantern behind me. I took it outside and extinguished it before hanging it on its hook."

"I'm sure Grandfather isn't blaming you. Besides, faultfinding serves no useful purpose."

"But it isn't true! I didn't leave the lantern burning inside the stable. I swear I didn't. One of the stable boys must have lit it again and left it there for Bocain to knock over."

Caitlin had heard it all before. This wasn't the time or place to go into it. "Go on downstairs," she said. "Uncle Donald could do with a little company." She flashed a silent message with her eyes.

Fiona's tears gradually dried, and moments later she had exited the room in search of Daroch.

Caitlin pulled her chair close to the bed and stared for a moment into her grandfather's eyes as if she were a mind reader. Finally, she said, "Well, you gave Fiona a word. I expect no less of you, Grandfather. What word do you have for me?"

His mouth worked, and syllables which made no sense to Caitlin poured out of him.

"Easy," she said, and covered his hand with one of her own. "Now try again, but this time more slowly. I don't expect you to talk in sentences, you know. One word will do."

Without volition, her own lips formed the word with him. She nodded her encouragement. Eyes closed, jaw working, he strained to get the word out. His hand lifted from the bed.

"Go . . . go!" he said, and opened his eyes to stare at her.

It was the look coupled with the words that wiped the smile from her face. There was anguish there and a fear which bordered on terror.

Dinner that evening was a stilted affair. Caitlin sensed undercurrents that made the hair on the back of her neck rise. She tried to tell herself she was being fanciful, that her grandfather's strange sense of urgency had put her on edge, but when everyone's eyes seemed to be avoiding her, the suspicion grew that something secret and sinister was afoot.

The conversation had turned to Rand, and how soon he might be expected to put in an appearance.

"I thought he would have been here by now," she replied in answer to her aunt's question. Laying aside her cutlery, she asked, "It's Bocain, isn't it?" Her eyes were on Daroch, appealing to him. "You are planning something. What is it? I have a right to know."

When Fiona burst into a fit of weeping and ran from the room, and when Charlotte followed her daughter's example not moments later, Caitlin felt her nerves stretch taut.

Donald Randal tried to placate her. "Now, now, Caitlin. Nothing has been decided. We were only talking in general, ye know."

Her eyes never left Daroch's. "Fine," she said. "Then tell me what you have not yet decided upon."

A muscle in Daroch's cheek twitched. He too, set down his cutlery. "We are debating," he said, "whether or not my foxhounds could accomplish what our hunting dogs have failed to do."

Caitlin had a vision of foxhounds tearing their quarry to pieces. She remembered the vicious attack on Bocain which had been halted by Mr. Haughton and his son. There was no point in arguing that Bocain was as gentle as a lamb. She could not convince them.

"If your hounds catch up to her," she told Daroch, "she will decimate your pack before they can finish her off."

"I am aware of that."

"Daroch, don't *do* this."

"As your uncle said, nothing has been decided."

She saw that her entreaties could not sway him. Her one hope was that Rand would arrive before any action could be taken. Rand would not see anything happen to Bocain. She held onto that thought as Dr. Innes made an effort to fill the silence. The poor man, Caitlin was thinking, must feel as though he had walked into Bedlam. This thought put her in mind of Rand's family. It was a different kind of bedlam at Cranley, and one she longed to enter into again.

Later, when Caitlin heard the front doors close upon Daroch and the physician, she left her grandfather's bedside and went in search of her uncle. She found him in the library, nursing a tot glass of whiskey.

"Don't be too hard on him," were his first words to her. He rose and poured out another glass of whiskey.

"Daroch?" Wearily she sank into a chair and gratefully accepted the glass he offered. "I think he is misguided, but I don't blame him. He has been a tower of strength these last days. Sometimes, I have to look at him twice to make sure he is the same reckless boy I knew before I went off to England."

"Aye. He may do very well for Fiona, if only Glenshiel will stoop to accept a Gordon into the family."

"You know how he hates all the Gordons o' Daroch."

Donald Randal sighed. "Aye. I've tried to persuade him that there is no' a drop o' Daroch's blood in the lad. Glenshiel will no' listen tae reason. The lad was raised a Gordon. Your grandfather canna see past that."

Very gently, Caitlin said, "Uncle Donald, you have hardly been in to see grandfather since I got here. I think he would like to see you."

Tears filled his eyes. "It's only—"—his voice cracked—"it's only that I canna bear to see him look so frail. But if ye think—"

"I do, oh, my dear, I do think so!"

They ascended the stairs in silence. When they entered Glenshiel's chamber, Caitlin said softly, "He's been so restless that the doctor prescribed a few drops of laudanum to give him a good night's sleep. If he seems tired, it isn't your doing."

Her uncle nodded, and Caitlin turned aside to the little dressing room, where a cot had been set up for her. She busied herself with trivialities, not wishing to spoil the moment for the two brothers who had been inseparable since they were infants. Donald Randal's voice, low and earnest, went on for a long time. When there was a silence, Caitlin glanced toward the bed. Her uncle was on his knees crouched over, and Glenshiel's hand was resting on his brother's head.

It was the baying of the foxhounds that awakened her. Caitlin leapt out of bed and moved quickly to the open window. It was barely light, and in the distance, the hills and mountains were shrouded in mist. Below, a stable boy was holding the reins of two fresh horses. The only horse at Glenshiel House was her own little pony which she'd had brought from Strathcairn. All the others had perished in the fire. Grabbing for her robe, she moved to the bed. As though aware of her presence, her grandfather opened his eyes. That look was there again. He labored to speak, and though sounds erupted from his lips, they were unintelligible to Caitlin. Patting his hand, she said, "I'll send your gillies to you. Don't fret. It will all come back in time."

On the gallery, she looked over the banister and saw her uncle with John Murray. That alarmed her, for Murray's place was a long way from Glenshiel. Someone must have sent for him the night before, or something had occurred at Inverey.

"What is it?" she cried out. "What's happened?"

Her uncle said something to Murray, and the younger man strode out the front door before Caitlin's foot had touched the bottom step.

Donald Randal came to meet her. "It's Serle," he said, looking very grave. "Last night, they found his body near Murray's place. It looks as if he has been savaged by a wild beast. Don't say anything yet to the others. I don't want Glenshiel to get wind of it."

All the blood rushed out of Caitlin's face. "I don't believe it," she whispered. "Bocain would not attack Serle. He doctored her injuries! And she allowed it! Bocain trusts him!"

"Lass, the dog has reverted to her natural state. She is wild and untamable, just as her dam was—a great beast o' prey. How do you think she has managed to live these last weeks? She hunts deer and game and any stray lamb that comes her way. She's tasted blood now. She'll never be the same."

Caitlin looked up at him with huge, frightened eyes. "But foxhounds! I don't want her to die that way! Oh God, it's a horrible death!"

"Aye. If she were my dog . . ."

"What?" she whispered, knowing what he was going to say.

"I would kill her myself afore I would let that happen to her."

Her eyes locked on his. "But how?" Her tones were hushed as if she were a conspirator to murder. "How shall I find her?"

"She must have a lair."

"The old quarry. It's where I found her as a pup."

"I must go." He pried her fingers from his sleeve. "They need every man. Take care. She may turn on ye at the last."

No sooner had she seen him mount up, than she went tearing back up the stairs.

Bocain lifted her head and sniffed the air. Rising from her haunches, she took a few restless paces forward, then halted, hackles raised, teeth bared. The baying of the hounds was coming nearer, but there was something else in the air that the dog seemed to recognize, a scent that made her careless of the approaching pack.

She was whining now, eyes staring straight ahead at Glenshiel House. Suddenly she barked, and her tail began to lash. Panting, ears pricked, she looked expectantly at the house. Then she saw the dogs, and she was off and running.

The dry-stone dikes were no obstacle to her. Bocain sailed over them with room to spare. Then, at a safe distance, she would turn back to watch the progress of the foxhounds as they scrambled over them as best they could. Though she was leaner than she had ever been, she was in the peak of condition. She was used to hunting for her own game now, and her physique showed it. Where Donald Randal had erred was in assuming that she ravaged the flocks and herds in the hills. For a canine, Bocain had a highly developed understanding of right and wrong. Caitlin had dinned it into her when she was a pup.

"Would you look at that!" John Murray reined in beside Daroch. "If I did not know better, I would say that that dog is thumbing her nose at us."

They had reined in to give one of the marksmen a clear shot at the deerhound. The gun went off, and dirt and turf were kicked up not a yard from Bocain. Snarling, barking, she showed them her heels.

"What she thinks she is doing," said Daroch grimly, "is leading us away from Caitlin. She is protecting the girl. That's what she is doing."

"Oh, God! I wish we didn't have to do this!"

"Don't we all?" Daroch was looking toward the hills. "What is it?"

"A Highland mist, wouldn't you know it? If we don't get her soon, we shall have to call in the dogs."

The horn sounded, and riders and dogs rejoined the chase. At the ford leading to Balmoral, near Rand's boathouse, the leader of the pack caught up with Bocain. The fight was over in a few seconds. At the sight of those powerful fangs tearing out the foxhound's throat, men swallowed convulsively, thinking of Haughton's fate.

Though the river Dee was not yet in full spate, the level of water was rising daily as the snow in the hills melted. Bocain crossed the ford without mishap. Again, she moved away to a safe distance and waited for her pursuers to catch up with her. She had a long wait, for both horses and hounds balked at the first attempt to cross the ford.

As the first dogs came out of the water, Bocain took off. Skirting the old castle, she led the way through bog and pine forest to the higher ground, where the trees thinned out and birse and heather covered the hillsides. On a grassy knoll, she halted, looking back the way she had come. When the foxhounds came racing from cover she barked furiously. The hounds sighted her and went wild.

Up she went along a narrow deer track, till the heather gave way more and more to bare rock. From a high rocky promontory, she looked down on the Dee valley.

Below her, pandemonium reigned. The foxhounds had discovered that the grassy knoll from which the deerhound had taunted them was, in effect, a badgers' set. Bocain's scent was forgotten as badgers and foxhounds went at each other in mortal combat. Horses and riders were milling around in utter confusion. Men were cursing, and trying to bring order to the chase.

Bocain lifted her great head, her sensitive nostrils quivering as a light froth of mist floated around her. Ears back, she leapt from her rocky lookout and bounded away.

For three miles, she pushed on, keeping close to the bank of the river. The mist on the hills was sinking lower, blanketing the fields and pastures of Balmoral in a ghostly shroud. Bocain's pace never slackened. When she came to the ford at Inver, she sank into a patch of wild rye. Her tongue was lolling, and she was panting hard, her ribs moving rhythmically with each harsh breath. Many minutes were to pass before her breathing had evened. Something caught her attention, a rustle of dead leaves beside a fallen log, and she cocked her head. An adder slithered across a rock and disappeared into a patch of heather. More minutes passed, then Bocain rose and shook herself vigorously, untensing the muscles along her back and shoulders.

Whining now, she sniffed at the water's edge. There were stepping stones here, but the water had risen to cover them. As daintily as any lady, Bocain stepped gingerly from stone to stone. At the last, with a great bound, she leapt clear to the opposite bank.

At this point, the Feardor Burn ran into the Dee. Bocain left the river and followed the burn, upstream, over bog, through stands of birch toward the North Deeside Road. She was moving in a circle, returning to Glenshiel House by a roundabout route. As she neared the road, it was evident that some sound or scent in the air was agitating her. Several times, she pulled back her lips and growled threateningly.

Beneath the Feardor Bridge, where Caitlin had once lain in wait for the English laird, Bocain seemed to lose her bearings. Whining, barking, she turned in circles, moving off in one direction, only to turn in her tracks and peer into the mist, as if unsure of herself. Something seemed to bring her to a decision, for she suddenly bounded up the steep incline to gain the road.

The man on horseback was unaware that he was being stalked. All at once, he was seized by an unholy premonition and he pulled on the reins. He reached for his pistol at the very moment that Bocain broke from the cover of pine trees which edged the road. With a great lunge, she leapt for both horse and rider.

Someone or something was following her. Caitlin turned her pony in a half-circle and looked back over the moor. The mist came as a surprise to her, so intent had she been on her thoughts. "Bocain," she said softly, wondering if she could go through with it.

As the mist eddied in front of her, now thickly, now clinging to her like threads of cobwebs, she had a flash of recall. Just so, she had turned her pony to face Rand, when he was pursuing her across this same moor. But it wasn't the same. Then, she had had only a dirk for protection. Now she carried her grandfather's pistol, a great silver affair that was so heavy she didn't know how she was going to manage with it. She couldn't go through with it. She *knew* she couldn't go through with it. Then she heard the dogs, far down the glen, and she steeled herself for what must be done.

At the entrance to the quarry, she dismounted. She couldn't see very far in front of her face, but it hardly mattered. She knew where she was going. There were no trees here to tether her mount. With Morder, however, tethering was unnecessary. Caitlin had trained her pony to come at her whistle.

She moved carefully, watching each step, not because she was afraid that Bocain would attack her, but because the pistol was primed and ready and she was not used to handling firing pieces. In her whole life, she had only had a couple of lessons, and that was at her grandfather's insistence. He believed that a woman who lived on her own should be able to protect herself, but that had been before Bocain had reached her maturity.

Birse and heather thinned out; then there were only lichens clinging to rocks. Then there were only rocks, and huge granite boulders. She knew there were no tinkers or Gypsies. They never stayed in one place for long.

When she came across the bones, she averted her eyes. Not far into the quarry, she found Bocain's lair. It wasn't a cave or anything like it. It was simply a dry space under an overhanging ledge.

She was weeping now. Dashing the tears from her cheeks with the edge of her plaid, she sat down to wait, her back pressed against the buttress of rock. It was inevitable that her thoughts would turn to that far off day when she had found the pup.

The rustle of something close at hand brought her head up. "Bocain?"

There was a ghastly sound, as of labored breathing. Caitlin's skin came out in goose bumps, and she lifted her pistol. A horse whinnied. She heard a soft step, then another, and a figure came out of the mist.

"Uncle Donald!" Relief surged through her, then quickly ebbed. Hoarsely, she got out, "Don't say that Daroch's dogs got to Bocain?"

Donald Randal was leaning heavily on a shepherd's staff. "I couldna say. I think not. I turned back at the ford at Balmoral. The dogs will keep her out of the way for a good while yet."

His tone was so odd that she squinted up at him. He was smiling, looking up at the sky as though he could see through the mist to the clear ether above. When he looked down at her, she could tell that he had been weeping too.

"I wanted to thank ye for last night," he said, "for bringing us together. I thought my brother hated me, but he doesna. He didna say anything—well, he cannot, can he? All the same, he forgave me. When I looked into his eyes, I knew he understood."

She wasn't alarmed. She was at a loss. "Glenshiel forgave you for what, Uncle Donald?"

He looked at her as though she had asked him a foolish question. "For setting the fire; for his stroke. He tried to stop me, ye know. He shouldn't have done that. I had to get rid of the dog, don't ye see? She knew too much. She wouldna let me come near her. Everyone remarked on the change in her. It was awkward, don't ye know?"

By this time, Caitlin was alarmed, but her fears were all for her uncle. "It's all been too much for you," she said. "When this is over, when Glenshiel recovers, you'll see things in a different light."

As though she had not spoken, he went on, "I told him everything. I told him about Ewan Grant."

At the name her head came up. "What about Ewan Grant?"

He blinked and his brow puckered as though her question or her tone of voice puzzled him. "I had to kill him. I told Glenshiel all about it, and he forgave me."

"Then tell me!" She wasn't thinking of the present. Her mind went back in time to the duel with Daroch, wondering if there had been another duel of which she knew nothing.

"All these years, I thought he was the father of your babe. But he wasna, was he, Morag? It was Daroch all the time."

The words seemed to come to her from someone else. "How did you find out that Daroch was the father of my child?"

"Och, Morag, ye were together in the shieling. I saw ye. My mistake was in thinking it was that other woman

402

who was with Daroch. But it wasna her. Grant told me himself, or Haughton, as he called himself latterly."

Her throat felt as though she had swallowed a mouthful of sand. "You killed Mr. Haughton?"

"Why did ye do it?" The anguish in his eyes was genuine. "Ye knew about the feud. Ye knew that the Gordons and Randals are mortal enemies. Yet ye lay wi' a Gordon! Have ye no shame? Did I not tell ye what they did to our mother, what they did to me?"

Though horrified, she was only half persuaded that he knew what he was saying, and a long way from thinking that she stood in any jeopardy. In the voice she might have used to comfort a distraught child, she said, "Don't think about it, Uncle Donald. You know full well that my moth—that I would not have looked twice at Daroch. I had too much pride to become just another of his women. You wrote it all down in your history of the Gordons o' Daroch—don't you remember? I read it myself. Daroch wanted my mother, all right, but she would have none of him. It was Ewan Grant she preferred."

He brought his staff down hard on the buttress, closer to her head, and she jumped. "Ye were playacting to throw Glenshiel and me off the scent! Don't lie to me! I saw his ring on your finger. The night o' the Randal's ball, ye were wearing Daroch's ring. Ye were not just another of his women! He married ye, didn't he? And had I not told Ewan Grant I saw Daroch with his sister, had there been no duel, ye and Daroch would have left the glen and set up house somewhere far away where I couldna reach ye."

Her eyes were wide, and she was staring at him as if he were a creature from one of her nightmares.

"Ye married him!" he said, demanding that she answer him.

She moistened her lips, remembering that she had worn her mother's ring on her wedding day, a ring that no one had remarked upon. "How can you be sure it was Daroch's ring? No one else mentioned it, not even Glenshiel."

"I knew! It was the ring his mother wore. If ye had read my history o' the clan more carefully, ye would have known it too!"

For the first time, she experienced real fear. "Uncle Donald, don't you know me? It's Caitlin. My mother has been dead these many years."

"I'm truly sorry." He was shaking his head, moving in closer. "I'm truly sorry."

The same moment she cocked her pistol, he lunged with his staff. Her head jerked back, and the staff smashed into the overhang, missing her by inches. She had time to get off a clear shot. Her fingers trembled, and she discovered that she had not the will to pull the trigger. When he lunged for her again, she rolled to the side and quickly scrambled to her feet.

Backing away from him, with the pistol aimed threateningly, she got out, "It was *you* who set Daroch's dogs on me! It was *you* who fired that shot which missed me by inches."

"I thought ye would have worked it out long afore now."

"And you really did murder poor Mr. Grant!" She was sobbing in terror. "But why? If he wasn't my father, it doesn't make sense!"

"I wish to God he had been your father! The Grants' blood is no' tainted. Our clan has no quarrel with them."

404

"Then why did you do it?"

As the conversation went forward, she continued to retreat one step at a time, well aware that her uncle was also edging himself into position.

"He threatened to expose me! After the attack on ye? He was almost sure that it came from me, and that Daroch was your father. I didna want to kill him! As God is my witness, I didna want to kill him! It was forced upon me."

"As you were forced to kill Serle!"

He laughed, still advancing upon her, staff swinging in an arc. There was a wily look in his eyes. "I tricked ye, lass. The last I saw of Serle, he was crossing the ford at Balmoral, by the side o' the young laird o' Daroch. Aye, and who do ye think persuaded Daroch it would be a mercy to rid Deeside o' your dog?"

"You could not be so devious," she breathed. But he was—terribly, terribly dangerous. "Keep back," she cried out, "or I'll blow your brains out!"

He stopped for a moment, head angled to the side, assessing her. "I think not," he said.

She couldn't take in what was happening. Everything about him was endearingly familiar and, at the same time, so horribly strange. "You love me," she said, sobbing in her anguish. "You know you do. You taught me so many things. We both love history . . ." She jumped back as the staff came at her again.

"Then ye should remember the lessons ye learned," he said fiercely. "Have ye no' heard Glenshiel tell ye that Gordon blood is bad blood? We'll no have it tainting our family."

She was forcing herself to converse with him as she backed out of the quarry. Soon, she would be within reach of her pony. "The young laird o' Daroch," she said, "Fiona's beau? You don't dislike him."

"Why should I? There not a drop o' Gordon blood in the lad. If there were, I would not see Fiona go to him. I would kill her first."

She whistled and though Morder whinnied in answer, she did not appear.

"I tethered her to a rock," he said gently.

He swung at her with the staff, catching the pistol such a blow that she thought her wrist would break. As the weapon went rolling over rocks and scree, she dodged away. She stumbled, and her ankle turned under her. He came at her again, and she leapt away, into the dense fog.

Chapter Twenty-Four

She did not get far. Her ankle would not hold her. Moving blindly, using her hands to guide her, she stumbled over rocks and boulders. She was holding her breath, bracing herself for the blow that would end it all. When it did not come, she knew it was the mist that saved her. Once it lifted, she would become an easy target. When her hands closed around birse and gorse, she rested. Her blood was pounding in her ears, and her lips were pressed fiercely together to deaden the sound of her breathing. She had reached the entrance to the quarry.

The silence was harrowing. She strained to catch every sound. There was nothing. No creatures were stirring. No birds were singing. The only sound she was aware of was the thundering of her own panicked heart.

When a horse whinnied, her head jerked round. Her pony was close by. If she could only get to it, she could save herself. Hardly had she risen to her haunches when she sank down again. It was what he would expect her to do. He was lying in wait for her. She sensed it in every fine hair on her body.

The whole thing seemed so unreal that she had the

strongest urge to call out, as if she were a child again, say she was tired of the game and she wanted to go home. Her mind was reeling with a confusion of thoughts, none of which made much sense to her. Of one thing, however, she was no longer in any doubt. The man who was stalking her, a man she had loved and trusted all her life, was in the grip of some murderous dementia. It had all been too much for him—the fire, Glenshiel's stroke, and now the conviction that her mother and Daroch had wed in secret. He was reliving the old feud.

She was horribly afraid. Fighting down her panic, she made an effort to take stock of her position. She must do the unexpected, take him unawares. He would expect her to choose the easy route, head down toward the Feardar Bridge. Closing her eyes, she traced in her mind the path she must take to escape him. She must go up, up to the top of the quarry and over the open moor. Carefully, soundlessly, she rose to her knees.

A pebble came tumbling from the crags above and she let out a startled sob of alarm. To her left, she heard his tread, and she was on her feet and moving. Her gait awkward, foundering on rocks, she pushed herself to her limits. She knew she was out of the quarry when she felt the wind on her face, the slope of the ground beneath her feet. The heather muffled every sound as she turned to the right, up the slope into the swirling mists. When she found the path which led around the quarry, relief washed over her in waves.

She was shaking and her clothes were wet through with a mixture of perspiration and the dew from the mist. But it was her foot which caused her the most anxiety. The swelling was straining at the confines of her boot, and the pain was excruciating. She could not go on like this for much longer.

"Morag. Ye cannot escape me."

That ghostly voice, coming, as it seemed to her, from right behind her, renewed her strength. Ignoring the stitch in her side and the pain in her foot, she forced herself to go on. Up, up, stumbling, half-crouched over, she threw herself into the kindly mist as though she were throwing herself into a lover's arms.

She could hear sounds now, the lonely call of a golden eagle from its eyrie high in the mountains, and nearby, the song of a thrush and the answering warble of its mate. But the sounds which pushed her to the limits of her endurance were the soft footfalls of the man who stalked her, his harsh breaths as he labored to overtake her.

She came out of the mist so suddenly that it took her a moment or two to adjust her eyes to the glare. On one side of the path, thickets of brambles and gorse hemmed her in. On the other, the ground fell away and the sheer granite face of the quarry disappeared into the gray mists, dropping sixty feet or so to its rocky floor. The breeze was blowing the mist down from the hills into the valley below. At this elevation, the mist would soon clear.

Comprehension flashed into her brain, and she spun around to face the sound of those sinister footfalls. Eyes staring, breath coming in sobs from her exertions, she slowly backed away. She cried out when the mist parted, like a door opening, and he emerged. Then the mist closed behind him, and they were the only two people in the world.

He looked so much the Highland gentleman. His trews were of the Randal tartan. His dark coat was draped with a Randal plaid that was indistinguishable from the one draped around her own shoulders. On his head, he wore a black bonnet with an amber Cairngorm set in silver. He was leaning on his staff, recovering his breath. Tears glistened on his ruddy cheeks.

"Why?" she moaned. "Why do you hate me so?"

"Ye know why! Did Daroch's men no' rape my mother in front of my very eyes?"

"But that was a different age! Different people! You must let the past go."

His eyes were staring at a point above her shoulder, and she knew that he had ceased to listen to her.

He was weeping openly, making no attempt to dash away the tears that flowed so copiously. "I was only a boy," he said brokenly, and in that moment he sounded like a bewildered child, crying for a mother's comfort. "Yet that did not stop them. They took me, in front o' my mother, using me as a man uses a woman. Can ye wonder that I hate the whole tribe o' Gordons?"

She was weeping too. "I didn't know! How could I have known? But they paid for what they did! They hanged for it!"

His breathing was easier now. "Aye. Glenshiel saw to it. He always took care o' me. Now I must be the one to take care o' things. Ye have sullied our blood. Ye, too, must pay the penalty for your iniquity."

"You won't get away with it! Everyone will know that you are a murderer!"

"How will they know?" He spoke softly, gently, as though he were explaining something to a difficult child. "Have I not arranged things to make it look like a mis-adventure? When they find ye, there will be no marks on ye that could not come from a fall from a great height. They will think ye fell into the quarry while ye were searching for your dog. Or they will think the hound herself has savaged ye."

Her voice came out thin and breathless. "Is that what happened to Mr. Haughton?"

He smiled, and it made her blood run cold. "Near enough. We went for a wee walk up toward Lochnagar. I hid his body in a gully, never thinking it would be discovered. It was sheer chance that your dog found him and tore the clothes from his body. Och, well, it all worked out for the best."

He brought his staff up, holding it in both hands. Her eyes were darting around, frantically searching for a way of escape. She feinted to the right, as though she meant to dash through a thicket of brambles. The staff flashed out, breaking branches as if they were straws. He came at her again, and she dodged out of the way. She was getting perilously close to the edge of the quarry.

Without volition, she glanced behind her, trying to gauge her position. He acted quickly to take advantage of the incautious impulse. The staff caught her across one shoulder, and she went staggering to her knees in a paroxysm of pain. He moved in for the kill.

Towering over her, he raised the staff high above his head. Her hands went out automatically to ward off the blow. She saw a slight hesitation, a relaxation of his muscles, and her thoughts raced about, trying to make sense of it. He was listening to the silence. Her own ears strained to catch every sound.

All her senses were heightened. Like a deer in the chase, she lifted her head. Instinct warned her of the approach of the beast that stalked her. Something was out there, something that hunted them both.

Joy burst through her, and the word tore spontaneously from her throat. "Bocain!" From the floor of the

411

quarry, her cry was thrown back, echoing eerily from rock face to rock face.

He wheeled around, searching the mist with his eyes. Cautiously rising to her feet, she began to inch away. She could hardly keep herself upright. The chill mountain breeze caught at her plaid, and her teeth began to chatter. Hugging herself, one step at a time, she increased the distance between them.

When he turned back to her, his breathing was as ragged as hers. "Your hound comes too late."

"Bocain will tear you to pieces if you harm a hair of my head." It wasn't a threat. She was pleading with him.

Her words made no impression. "We'll go together," he told her, almost as though he regretted having to hurt her. "Glenshiel will grieve for me, but soon we'll be together forever."

She cried out hysterically, "Aren't you afraid to meet your Maker with my blood on your hands?"

"No," he said. "Why should I be? This is fitting. A Randal and Gordon—what better way to end the feud for all time?"

She wanted to scream at him that it did not matter a straw to her whether she was a Gordon or a Randal. She didn't care if she was a *sassenach*. What mattered were the glen and its people, not some ancient blood feud. The present and the future counted, not the past. She stared at him miserably, without hope, knowing that he would never understand.

Beneath their feet, the earth began to tremble and a pheasant was flushed from her cover. Even as Caitlin's startled glance lifted, a voice seemed to float at the edges of the mist.

"Caitlin! Hold on! I'm coming. *I'm coming!*"

Rand's voice! Her first rush of elation gave way to dread. She listened intently, peering into the wavering mist. Hoofbeats! He was on horseback, making for the dense hedge of brambles. He was moving too swiftly. There would not be time to check his mount before they made the jump. One misstep and horse and rider would go plunging over the edge of the quarry.

Out of the mist, a shape took form. It wasn't a horse and rider. A huge beast of prey silently bore down upon them. Muscles rippling along her broad back, powerful shoulders tensed and straining, she came at them like lightning.

At the same moment that Donald Randal leapt for Caitlin, Bocain soared into the air. Man and beast came together in a sickening shock of flesh on bone. A hand clutched wildly for Caitlin, tearing the plaid from her shoulders, then the momentum carried both man and dog over the edge of the quarry.

In the next moment Rand was there, snatching Caitlin into his arms, hauling her across his mount's back. As his horse came to a quivering, stamping halt, she turned her face into his chest and wept.

It was a long time before Caitlin could bear to lift her head from the comfort to be found in her husband's arms. "I thought you would go over too! I thought you would go over too!" Between sobs and moans, she repeated those words over and over, reliving those last, terrifying moments.

"No chance of that," he said, trying to console her. "I'm an excellent rider. And I learned the trick of clearing those bramble bushes from you. Don't cry, my love. You're safe now."

She was suddenly aware that they were not alone. Twisting in Rand's arms, she saw three young men kneeling at the edge of the quarry. Their horses were on the other side of the thickets.

"My brothers," said Rand. "We all came together."

Peter Randal looked up at that moment and called out, "The dog is safe, though I think she may be injured. She landed on a ledge. I can just make her out. If we get a rope, we should be able to haul her up. There's no sign of the man. This infernal mist is obscuring my vision. It's possible that he is safe too."

He didn't sound as if he believed his own words. Caitlin practically threw herself from the horse's back and went racing to the edge of the quarry. Her eyes scoured the veil of mist. It wasn't a ledge that had saved Bocain, but the scree.

"What is it?" asked Rand, perceiving her look of astonishment.

"The scree slope," she said, looking to him for confirmation. "It's right here."

"You didn't think I'd make the jump at any other point?"

"You knew?"

"Well, of course I knew. Didn't you?"

"No. The mist was so dense I didn't know where I was." She looked about her, shaking her head. Laughter bubbled up, but she cut it off when she heard the edge of hysteria in it. "Do you think that my uncle . . . ?" Her words dwindled as she saw Harry signal silently to Rand with a shake of his head.

"We'll see," said Rand. "Harry! Robert! Peter! You three go on down and see what you can find out. Caitlin and I will get the dog up."

When his brothers had moved off to do his bidding,

Rand went to fetch a rope from one of the saddlebags. A bark and a long unearthly groan brought him racing back to the edge of the quarry. Bocain's great head lifted to look up at him.

"Come on, girl," Caitlin pleaded. "You can do it."

At the sound of that feminine voice, Bocain let out a furious bark. With a great bound, she cleared the lip of the quarry and leapt for the girl.

Caitlin's arms were around her dog. Rand's arms were around his wife. They were sitting on a patch of heather near the base of the quarry, sheltering against a buttress of rock. Rand's coat was around Caitlin's shoulders. From the quarry entrance, from time to time, one of Rand's brothers would call out. They had still to find Donald Randal's body. The dog might have helped in their search, but nothing could induce Bocain to leave Caitlin's side, and Rand refused to allow Caitlin to enter the quarry. Caitlin had momentarily come to the end of her recitation of that morning's harrowing events.

After an interval, she said, "Now it's your turn. What I can't understand is how you knew where to find me."

"I didn't," answered Rand. "We were making for Glenshiel House with all speed when Bocain found us! I don't mind telling you, when she jumped for my horse's head, I thought it was all up with me. I didn't recognize her, you see. My first panicked thought was that she was a lion that had escaped from a menagerie."

Caitlin allowed herself a small smile, though laughter was the farthest thing from her mind. She knew what Rand was doing. He was trying to distract her from thinking of what his brothers would find on the floor of

415

the quarry. She shut her eyes for a moment, then made an effort to help him.

"And she made a great to-do until you turned your horses around and followed her?"

"Nothing of the sort! She turned the horses for us. They almost bolted! My brothers are not particularly struck with this shaggy canine specimen at the moment." As he spoke, he prodded Bocain with the toe of his boot. She rolled over and let out a long contented sigh.

Caitlin shivered. "Thank God you came when you did!"

Rand made no answer to this, but hugged her a little closer to him. He was thinking that never had there ever been a cavalry charge like the one just past, when he and his brothers had ridden with whip and spur over the mist enshrouded moors, not knowing where the quarry was, trusting implicitly in the dog's instinct to lead them. Nor did he ever want to experience again that annihilating sense of terror that had gripped him when the mist lifted to reveal his wife poised on the edge of a cliff with a madman leaping for her. He had lied to Caitlin when he had told her he knew that the scree was right behind her. He had not wanted to add one iota to the terrors were bound to haunt her dreams for some time to come.

"You told me to hold on!" She turned her head to look up at him. "Your voice came to me through the mist. You knew that something like this might happen, didn't you?"

"Yes."

"How? You weren't even here."

In a matter of a few minutes, Rand had related almost all that he had found out from his uncle and young Mr. Haughton when he had posted down to Dorset.

"And you suspected my uncle?"

"Yes." He wasn't going to tell her how close he had come to suspecting her grandfather, until he had remembered that Glenshiel had always believed that the laird o' Daroch was Caitlin's father. As long as her uncle had not known it, Caitlin was safe.

"It all added up," he said. "When Daroch's dogs attacked you and someone shot at you, I could not see any motive for it. Then, with Grant's death, and with everything that his stepson and my uncle related to me, it all became clear. The answer was not in the present, but in the past."

"In the old blood feud, in fact?"

"Yes. It was all in the reports from Grant's agent. Your uncle lived in the past. It colored all his thinking. He rewrote history, did you know? Someone once told me so, but at the time, I didn't realize it was significant." He was thinking of the Bard of Aboyne. "In short, what Grant learned was that your father, that is Daroch, was not the debaucher of innocents he was made out to be. Your uncle blackened his character, not viciously, not openly, but with sly hints and innuendo. He gave all the Gordons of Daroch a bad name, and it stuck."

"His mind was unhinged by what he and his mother had suffered at the hands of the old laird's clansmen after Culloden?"

"Yes, and all of that happened almost fifty years before Morag Randal fell in love with Robert Gordon. It's . . . incredible."

She moved restlessly. "Who was Grant's agent?"

His smile was so fleeting, she did not see it. "He was

417

. . . is . . . your grandfather's physician. It was Dr. Innes who attended Daroch after the duel. Grant wrote to him, asking in general terms about all the principals involved. Dr. Innes became more involved than had been intended. His interest was piqued, you see. And of course, he had occasion to meet with your uncle every time he called on Glenshiel." What he did not tell her was that Innes had garnered enough information on Caitlin and the present laird o' Daroch to have them both sent to the colonies for a long time to come.

She ruminated silently for a moment or two, then said, "I can't think why Mr. Grant had need of an agent. Why not simply come in person?"

"He wasn't a paid agent or anything like that. It was merely one acquaintance writing to another and asking for information. For some reason, Grant delayed coming into Scotland. And as I said, Innes became more involved that he was meant to be."

"You've seen him?"

"No. It's what Haughton told me. I came straight on here."

There was a silence as Caitlin assimilated his words. At length, she said, "I knew how much my grandfather hated all the Gordons of Daroch, but my uncle always seemed so reasonable.'

"With your grandfather, it was all bluster, and everyone knew it. No one really listened to him. With your uncle, the hatred was deep seated, like a slumbering volcano. As I said, he wasn't overtly vicious with it. When he spoke, people listened to him. And when Grant came into Deeside trying to atone for the past, he stirred things up."

"And the volcano erupted?"

"Yes. Your uncle thought, as everyone did, that the

Daroch line of Gordons had died out. The present laird, Fiona's Daroch, didn't count. He was a stepson. Then Grant came into Deeside, and your uncle realized that there was one Gordon of Daroch remaining. You. I don't think that is what enraged him so much as the thought that the Randal blood was tainted and would remain so for all future generations unless he put a stop to it."

"Did Grant know I was Daroch's daughter? My uncle said something—"

"He must have suspected it. It was in his mind, I believe, to tell you so; then he decided against it."

"What changed his mind?"

"From what his son told me, it was our marriage that decided him against saying anything. Grant felt that Providence had worked things out remarkably well, and that to intervene might do more harm than good. My own feeling is that he was more than happy to leave well enough alone. You must remember, he was the man who had killed your father. No, I should not think Grant was eager to have the past raked over unless it was absolutely necessary.

"After the attack on you, he was suspicious. What he ought to have done was take his son into his confidence. He didn't do so because, as he told me, he had acted once before on hearsay and speculation, and he did not wish to call a man's integrity into question unless he had something to go on."

She shivered, and his arms tightened about her. "Cold?"

She shook her head. "It's not that. It's . . . oh, I can't explain it. Clans and feuds, and I don't know what all. They have left a terrible mark on the Highlands. When I think of my mother . . ." Her voice broke and she took a moment to come to herself. "I think she really believed Daroch had betrayed her, that the duel was over another woman, someone he was taking up with."

"Yes. And from what I have heard of your mother, her pride must have been crushed. She would not want anyone to know she had made a fool of herself over a man who cared so little for her."

"And all these years she misjudged him!" Caitlin cried out passionately.

"I'm afraid so. Don't be too hard on her. Your uncle was at some pains to ensure that everyone misjudged the Gordons of Daroch."

"And my grandfather! For the first time, I really begin to understand why my mother left the big house and moved to the shieling. She dared not confess that Daroch was the father of her babe. You know, at the end, when she was dying, I thought she would tell me my father's name. Even then she could not bring herself to do it! She was so ashamed! She truly believed all the tales my grandfather and uncle spouted. I tell you, I could weep for that poor girl."

Rand brought her face up and kissed her swiftly. "Don't let the past make you bitter."

"Oh, I won't!" she answered passionately. "I may have done so once, but never again. I thought I was born out of wedlock, and it blighted my life. Now, it seems likely that Daroch did not deceive my mother, that he really did mean to honor their secret marriage. We shall never know. And do you know what?"

"What?" asked Rand softly.

"It doesn't matter one whit to me. I'm not going to be like my uncle. I'm not going to allow the past to rob me of living life fully and richly. I'm going to . . ." Her breath came out in a rush, and she turned into Rand's chest and wept bitterly. "I feel heart sorry for him, do you know? It was such a waste of a life! He never married, never thought of such a thing. He was only a shadow of the man he might have been."

When the bout of weeping had run its course, she lay quietly in his arms. Eventually, shifting slightly, she said, "There is still so much I can't quite grasp."

"That is because you have not had the time to reflect on it."

"And you have?"

"Oh yes. I've been reflecting on things since someone took a shot at you. And when I learned that Haughton was Grant, and that he had met with an untimely end, everything began to fall into place."

She glanced briefly up at him. "Poor Mr. Grant! It would have been better for him if his sister had not confessed to her iniquitous conduct. Then he would never have come into Scotland, and he would be alive today."

Rand shook his head. "Not so," he said. "Did I not tell you that David went to see him? It was David who set this chain of events in motion."

"How did he do that?"

"It's my guess that he told Grant *you* thought he was your father. I think that's when Grant began to put two and two together."

"But . . . I never asked David to try to discover who my father was. At least . . ." She looked at him with huge stricken eyes. "Not in so many words, I didn't. I told him I didn't care *who* my father was, but he must have known that deep down, I did care. He saw things that no one else could see. How I wish he had left well enough alone! I blame myself for—"

"Don't!"

She recoiled and he instantly softened his tone. "You

must accept that these things happen. I'm inclined to believe, in this case, it was inevitable. If David had not set events in motion, then I would have done so. Almost from the first, I have had the feeling that I have been following in David's footsteps. Caitlin, this was meant to be. A great wrong has been righted. There is a certain justice in all of this. You must believe that."

"The mills of God grind slowly, but they grind exceeding small?" she quoted.

"Where did you hear that?"

"It's something my mother used to say."

"She was right."

There was a shout from within the quarry, then another. Some time was to pass before Peter appeared. "We've found him," he said. "Caitlin, I'm so sorry. His neck is broken."

Donald Randal was brought home to Glenshiel House in one of Rand's carriages. It was Peter who was sent to fetch it. He returned with Serle and the intelligence that Daroch's dogs had been called off and Bocain stood in no danger.

If Serle was surprised at Caitlin's reception, he gave no indication of it. Smiling, crying, she kissed him on his thin cheeks and told him repeatedly how happy she was to see him and how well he looked. Her dog's reception of Rand's factor was no less warm. Rand stood by, smiling, yet very grave.

While Rand's brothers and Serle waited with the carriage in the old stable block, Rand, Caitlin, and Bocain climbed the stairs to Glenshiel's chamber. Bocain was ill at ease with some scent she caught in the air, but by this time she seemed to recognize that the threat to Caitlin had been removed. On her mistress's command, she settled herself outside the door, ignoring the starts and stares of servants who took one look and hurried away.

Inside the chamber, they found Dr. Innes, with his patient, and Charlotte Randal standing nearby, wringing her hands. As they entered, Innes looked up.

"I'm glad ye are here," he said simply and without emphasis. "He has been asking for ye and Mr. Randal."

Charlotte Randal was not so reserved. Her bosom was heaving and her breath came in sobs and starts. "He has been like a man demented. Dr. Innes tried to administer laudanum to help him settle, but he refused to swallow it. Caitlin, where have you been? We sent everywhere for you. You seemed to have vanished off the face of the earth."

At this point, she was beginning to take in her niece's appearance—the tumbled hair, the filthy and torn garments, the tear-streaked face. She opened her mouth to make some comment, but Caitlin quickly pushed past her to cross to the bed.

She seized the gnarled hand that lifted toward her. "I'm here, Grandfather," she said, and brought his hand to her lips, pressing a kiss to it.

The wild look in Glenshiel's eyes gradually abated. His breathing became easier. For a long time he simply looked at Caitlin, as if he wished to memorize every dear feature, every hair on her head. Finally his eyes lifted to Rand.

Responding to the ardent question in those wise eyes, Rand said gravely, "I'm afraid there has been a terrible accident, sir. Your brother—"

"Rand, no!" Caitlin cried out.

His hand closed around her shoulder. "Don't you see,

he already knows? We must tell him the whole of it, or there will be no peace for him."

"But . . ."

Dr. Innes's look silenced Caitlin. "He knows or senses that something is amiss. Your husband is right, Lady Randal. There will be no peace for him if he thinks ye are concealing something from him."

When Rand was satisfied that Caitlin's objections had been answered, he inhaled a long breath. "It was like this, Sir Alexander," he said. "Caitlin and your brother went out looking for the dog. They thought they knew where she was to be found—the old quarry. I think you know the place? They became separated when the mist came down. Donald Randal lost his footing and fell to his death. He died instantly."

Charlotte Randal began to sob uncontrollably into her hands. Rand's eyes never left Glenshiel's. The old man blinked and seemed to shrink into the bedclothes. His jaw worked spasmodically, and Rand had to bend over to catch his words.

"It . . . it is . . . for . . . the best," said Glenshiel.

During the night, Rand called Caitlin and Fiona to their grandfather's bedside. Not long after, Glenshiel slipped away.

Chapter Twenty-Five

The laird's lady and her factor rode out to inspect the estate, the hound, Bocain, trotting placidly at their heels. Some months had passed since the tragic misadventure which had taken the life of Donald Randal, months that had seen many changes in the glen. People shook their heads and said regretfully that it was a pity Glenshiel and his brother had not lived to see this day. They would have been proud of the offshoot—and that a female!—who had brought the English Randals back into the Highlands and in so doing had brought the promise of prosperity to the whole of Deeside.

Caitlin listened respectfully to Serle as he explained the superior technology of the new, lighter, iron plough which was to replace the unwieldly monstrosity which required twelve oxen to draw it.

"At these higher altitudes," he said, "and on the smaller, hill farms, the advantage of a two-horse plough will be enormous."

Caitlin nodded her agreement and allowed her eyes to roam. From below, came the sounds of foresters at work, felling trees which would be floated downriver to Aberdeen for the shipbuilding industry.

Following the progress of her eyes, Serle commented, "It takes years to grow a tree. Lord Randal knows it. Some foolish lairds have already lost whole forests to greed."

"That won't happen here," said Caitlin quickly.

"It will not! Lord Randal has ordered new forests to be planted. He understands the land. There is no better soil for raising timber that that of Deeside."

Caitlin sighed. "But it is not so conducive to the cultivation of crops?"

Serle's look was veiled. "Much can be done to preserve the soil with the rotation of crops, and with manure to fertilize it, the yields will be improved."

"Yes, I know."

She was thinking of all the other improvements her husband had instigated with the help of his brothers. At Glenshiel, Harry was in his element, rebuilding the stables from scratch, setting up a stud with a nucleus of his own prize horses. The sheep on the hills were no ordinary sheep, but bred for the luster of their coats. This was Peter's doing. The wool trade was lucrative, and Robert, with his contacts, had found markets for the cloth that was not only spun and woven by local cotters' wives, but also dyed with their own recipes which were a closely guarded secret.

There was more work to be had on Deeside than they could find laborers and skilled craftsmen to do it. To Caitlin, it was like a dream come true. Rand was turning his estates into a showplace, a model from which other Highland lairds could learn, just as she had always wanted him to do.

Yet, she had not asked him for any of this. On the contrary, remembering the words that he had flung at her, that she would go so far as to prostitute herself for the Clan Randal, she had made it a point to show an interest in Rand's English holdings. She had resigned herself to making her home in Cranley. Rand wouldn't hear of it. There would come a day when they would divide their time between Strathcairn and Cranley, he told her, but for the present, he wanted to make up for lost time. And he had given her to understand that David, and the debt he felt he owed to him, played no small part in his decision.

"David." She said the word softly, soundlessly, as if it were a mere breath on her lips. David would not be surprised to see all the changes Rand had effected. He had told her how it would be, if only Rand could be induced to take up the challenge. She should be sublimely happy. Instead, she was bewildered.

There was a change in Rand, a new reserve which she could not understand. He never teased her, never flirted with her, never shocked her with the ardor of his lovemaking. She could not even provoke him into quarreling with her. Life of late had become very tame. He was so gentle and tender that there were occasions when she wanted to run screaming from the room.

She was with child, but that was not the reason for his restraint. Before she had ever told him he was to be a father, she had sensed the change in him. Her pregnancy merely gave him an excuse to hold her at arm's length. Not that he did not exercise his conjugal rights. Rand had too passionate a nature to live the life of a celibate, and too many scruples to turn to other women if he had become bored with his wife. Sometimes, when she was feeling particularly low, she suspected that that was what had happened. Theirs was not a love match, but a forced marriage. More and more of late, the thought had come back to torment her. She wondered if he had come to repine for all the freedoms he once enjoyed, the many women who had once warmed his bed. When she thought of Lady Margaret, she ground her teeth together.

Serle said something in passing, and Caitlin gave him her complete attention. As factors went, Serle was superlative. She knew that now. Her former prejudice had been based on a misunderstanding of where his loyalties lay. He was Rand's man. It was only latterly that she had discovered Serle's younger brother had served with her husband in the Peninsular Campaign, and that Rand had been instrumental in saving the boy from some serious scrape. If she had only trusted her dog's instinct, she would have recognized the man's sterling worth long before now. She had made life very uncomfortable for poor Mr. Serle, but that was all in the past. She had come to rely on his judgment as much as Rand did.

Later, as they approached Strathcairn, she turned to Serle with the question which had been hovering at the back of her mind. "My husband is spending a fortune in making his estates into a showplace. When will he see a return on his investment? That's what I want to know."

Serle's reply was more diplomatic than truthful. "He is the chief of Clan Randal. To a chieftain, profit must always be of secondary importance."

And with that, Caitlin had to be satisfied.

Rand was in the library performing an office that fell to him in his role as chief of the clan. The laird o' Daroch had this minute asked him for the hand of Miss Fiona Randal in marriage. The stags' heads looked down upon the scene with mute absorption.

Both gentlemen were ill at ease; Daroch because this was the first time he had ever found himself in such a position, and Rand for much the same reason. Though it was true that he had two married sisters, both of them had wed without so much as a by your leave. He was beginning to see how lucky he had been, for the role of guardian was not one he relished.

Clearing his throat, Daroch said, "Those jaunts to Aboyne and Aberdeen? They were nothing at all! You know how people exaggerate! They make mountains out of molehills. If I'd had all the women who are attributed to me, I would be a veritable Turk with a harem." He laughed, not very convincingly.

"In short," said Rand, smiling, "your reputation is wholly undeserved? You see, I am familiar with the sophistry. I've employed it myself when the occasion demanded it. But it is not to me you should be making these protestations, but to Fiona."

Daroch straightened in his chair. "Fiona needs no persuasion. She knows that she is the only woman I have ever loved, will ever love. I don't know what I can say to make you believe that I am not now, nor was I ever, a libertine, upon my word as a gentleman of honor."

"But I do believe you."

"You do?" Daroch's look bordered on incredulity.

"Certainly, for the simple reason that I know the real reason for all those jaunts to Aboyne and Aberdeen."

It had all been in the reports to Grant from Dr. Innes, not that Innes was finding fault with Daroch. He took the view that the boy was an idealist. As for himself, he had surprised the young laird red-handed, only he had not known it at the time. His thoughts shifted to the night Daroch's carriage had come clattering into the courtyard of The Twa Craws, and he could not help smiling. Daroch had taken his friend to a physician, all right. The boy had not lied to him. But Rand doubted if his friend had made a recovery. If he had, it would be a miracle on a par with Lazarus rising from the dead.

"If you are referring to my smuggling activities," said Daroch stiffly, "naturally those will come to an end. They already have."

"Oh, naturally," replied Rand affably.

Daroch's look was fierce, but he preserved his silence.

Rand leaned forward in his chair to give his words due emphasis. "Dr. Innes tells me there is an acute shortage of cadavers to be had for the study of anatomy by the medical students at the university in Aberdeen?"

Daroch moistened his lips. "Yes," he said hoarsely.

"And that the members of the Chirurgical Society are not above securing their own specimens?"

"So I've heard." Daroch's eyes were unblinking.

"Grave-robbing is a criminal offense, no matter how noble the motive."

Silence.

"But we have digressed. I only mentioned it in passing because I know you to be a man of science. Now, to get back to your jaunts to Aboyne and Aberdeen. Am I to take it that you have decided to settle here on Deeside and make something of your estate?"

Daroch nodded vigorously.

"And there will be no more jaunts to Aboyne and Aberdeen, at least not in the dead of night?"

"You have my word on it!"

"And what about your interest in medicine? Does that go by the board?"

The color was coming back into Daroch's face. "I never thought of it as my life's work. It was more in the

430

nature of an avocation. I had friends and I wanted to help them. That is all."

"Fine," said Rand, rubbing his hands together. "It seems we have come to an understanding."

"You mean, I can speak to Fiona with your blessing?"

"So eager," Rand murmured. "Yes, you may speak to Fiona, but only after we have dispensed with settlements and so on. First, however, you'll join me in a wee dram?"

Thirty minutes later, Rand watched from his library window as Fiona and Daroch met on the front lawns and entered into a rapturous embrace. He had just admitted a sometime smuggler and grave-robber into the ranks of the family. He shook his head, wondering if he were mad, or perhaps if there was more of his mother in him than he had ever suspected. As his glance lingered, the couple on the lawns broke apart, and their words reached him through the open window. "I love you," they said in unison. Rand turned away, then climbed the stairs to the bedchamber he shared with Caitlin.

As had become her custom in the last week or two, she was taking an afternoon nap, resting fully clothed beneath the top coverlet. Her dark eyelashes made fans along the sweep of her cheeks. They fluttered as he approached the bed, but her eyes did not open.

"*Mo gaol orist,*" he murmured.

"Hush. Go back to sleep."

She turned slightly, and Rand edged one hip on the bed, staring down at his wife with a hunger he was careful to conceal when she was watching him. She was four months along and more lovely to him than any woman he had ever known. No doubt the poets would tell him

431

it was his love for her that made him think so. Love. He was still uncomfortable with that word.

He had wanted to give her time to get over her lost love. Her condition had afforded him the perfect pretext to keep his distance. He might have suggested that they sleep in separate chambers, as many couples did when the wife became pregnant. Once or twice, the words had slipped onto his tongue. But he could not utter them. He could not deprive himself of the feel of her, the scent of her, and the little sobbing cries of arousal she made when he came into her. If he could not posses her heart, he would have as much of her as she would allow.

Had she noticed the difference in him? he wondered. A blind man must see it, and Caitlin saw more than most. He was forbearing of all her little foibles; sensitive to all her moods. As for his restraint, the saints in heaven must be lauding his praises. He didn't know what more she could ask of him.

He'd sunk thousands of pounds, tens of thousands, into her little domain. His factor had looked at him askance, but was obliged to keep his thoughts to himself. His brothers were under no such obligation. A walking charity, they called him, to pour his capital into a venture from which there would be no return for a least a hundred years. They had relished tormenting him.

That was before they had listened to Caitlin. She had made converts of them all. They were investing in people, she had told them, in posterity. It was not immediate profit that should guide their endeavors, but the improvement in men's lives. With all their advantages, all their experience, the English Randals had it in their power to do something really worthwhile for future generations of the Clan Randal.

432

God, he had heard recruiting officers spout much the same rhetoric! And it worked! His brothers were no more immune to his wife's blandishments than hopeful young men with dreams of heroism attending to the words of a veteran soldier. They were no more immune than he.

She had worked such a change in him that he hardly recognized himself. He was Iain, Lord Randal, chieftain of a great and noble clan. He cared about posterity and future generations of clan Randal. But sometimes, just sometimes, he wished Caitlin would look a little closer to home. If she wanted to improve men's lives, she had a husband who wouldn't be averse to a little improvement in his lot. No man had ever done as much as he to win the woman he loved. He couldn't go on like this for much longer. He was ready to explode.

The marriage of Fiona and Daroch was what the natives called a *braw* affair. Rand gave the bride away. Highland dress for the gentlemen was, naturally, *de rigueur*. Kilts, in all the bonnie tartans of Deeside, were in splendid profusion, and none more than of the clans Randal and Gordon.

The English Randals were there in force. The dowager was quite taken with the spectacle of her sons in kilts. There were a few obscene comments when they beheld the sporrans their chief had procured for them, but the dowager hardly noticed. When it suited her, she could turn as deaf as a door.

Fiona, in her borrowed wedding gown, her cousin's, brought gasps of admiration from the assembled guests. She scarcely thought of her own appearance. Her eyes were trained on the darkly handsome laird with the finely etched features who waited to claim her. When she placed her trembling fingers in his, and he smiled at her, all her apprehensions melted away.

Caitlin was wearing a gown in the Gordon tartan, her father's tartan, and on the fourth finger of her right hand, she wore Daroch's ring. If she had wanted to proclaim her patrimony, and she did, she could hardly have chosen a more obvious way, unless she had sent a notice to the papers. Those seeing her hardly blinked an eye. Had they not always known that the lass had the look of a Gordon? They understood, none better, why that knowledge had been suppressed until the right moment had presented itself. With the passing of Glenshiel and his brother, an era had come to a close. The old blood feud was finally over.

In the wee hours of the morning, after the bride and groom had left for their own home with the customary Highland escort, Rand gave the signal to the fiddlers for the commencement of a special entertainment he had arranged for his guests.

Patrick Gordon, the Bard of Aboyne, stepped forward, and a hush settled on the great hall of Strathcairn House.

"Why, what is this, Rand?" asked Caitlin.

He drew her hand into the crook of his arm. "You'll see," he said, and shook his head when she opened her lips to say more.

It was a hauntingly romantic tale of two star-crossed lovers, Robert Gordon o' Daroch and the love of his life, Morag Randal. It told of their secret marriage and of the terrible blood feud that kept them apart. Though the bard was correct in the essentials of his story, some things were glossed over. It was not part of Rand's design to reveal the scandal of Donald Randal and the hatred that had warped his mind.

When the bard related the events that led to Daroch's death and told of the secret his young wife had carried with her to the grave, there was not a dry eye in that great hall. Gordon reached for Randal and vice versa, and swore undying friendship or Scotland's honor would be forever tarnished.

Caitlin swallowed her own tears. Her head was held high, and her hand was wrapped tightly around the crook of her husband's arm. All at once, the bard clapped his hands and stamped his foot, and the tempo of the music changed to something gay and rollicking. The words that tripped from his tongue were in the Gaelic.

Rand sat up straighter. "What this?" he asked Caitlin.

Her eyes were sparkling, and her lips curved. "It's the story of how Daroch's lass brought the feud to an end."

"Oh? And how did she do that?" His eyes were smiling too.

"She snared the chief of Clan Randal," she answered saucily.

Rand sat back to enjoy the entertainment. This was more in the style of a bothy ballad. The assembled guests clapped their hands and stamped their feet in time to the music. Before long, they were singing the refrain. These were words that Rand recognized. *"Mo gaol orist,"* they sang, and he, too, sang with gusto.

When the ballad was ended, and the thunderous applause had died down, he observed, "That's a peculiar refrain," then looked again at the rosy blush which spread from his wife's throat to her hairline. His eyebrows climbed.

Mumbling something indistinct, Caitlin made her excuses and slipped away.

"What is so peculiar about the refrain?" asked Peter, who sat on the other side of Rand.

Rand had to think for a minute. He'd heard those words from Caitlin countless times. "I must have misunderstood their significance," he said absently. He was still thinking of Caitlin's furious blush. "Do you happen to know what they mean?"

Peter chuckled. "You must be getting past it, Rand," he said. "Think back to when you were a young man, a man about my age. What were the first words you familiarized yourself with before setting foot in a foreign country?

"What?"

Peter shook his head at this abysmal show of ignorance. "Sometimes I wonder if you were ever young."

"Halfling, if you don't tell me directly, I swear I shall break your neck."

"I'll give you a clue, shall I? *Je t'aime, ich liebe dich, te amo . . .* !" Before he had quite finished, he was left talking to thin air.

Caitlin bolted down the front steps and took off as though the hounds of hell were pursuing her. With no clear idea of where she was going, she struck out along the first path she encountered. Rand caught up with her before she got very far. It was Bocain who led him to her. He caught her by the wrist and swung her to face him, then ducked as her fist came at him, missing his handsome nose with only an inch to spare.

Bocain looked from one to the other. She knew this game. It always ended the same way. Yawning, unheeding of her mistress's furious curses, she sauntered back to the great hall, then burst into a gallop when she sighted the twins.

Rand didn't waste time on argument. Taking care not to hurt her, he hoisted her over one shoulder and brought the flat of his hand down smartly on the softest part of her posterior. Caitlin struggled wildly, and Rand gave her more of the same until she went limp against him.

Through the great hall he carried her, stopping to chat amiably with various acquaintances on the way, up the great staircase to their bedchamber. On the gallery, he halted and looked down at the sea of faces that were turned up to watch the spectacle.

"Well, what did you expect?" he said. "I'm a Randal, she's a Gordon; I'm English bred, she's a Highlander; I'm male, she's female." He turned away but had only taken a step when something seemed to occur to him, and he returned to the balustrade. A wicked grin spread across this face. "I won, and she lost. That's the most important thing," he said.

The laughter was spontaneous, as were Caitlin's shrieks of outrage.

Hardly had the couple disappeared from view when men began to ponder the significance of the Randal's remarks. There was more at stake here than a squabble between husband and wife. Pride of clan came rushing to the fore and Gordons and Randals began to glare at each other with smoldering eyes. The Earl of Aboyne was the first to make a move. Leaping onto one of the trestle tables, he looked around the great hall with a challenging posture. Swaying alarmingly, he said, "There isn't the Randal born who can best a Gordon in any contest of skill or strength ye care to name."

437

At these fighting words, all the Gordons present let out a mighty yell. The Randals folded their arms across their broad chests and glowered.

"Oh no!" said the dowager faintly. "What about Scotland's honor?" No one listened to her

Robert Randal swaggered to the table and sneered up at the earl. "I accept your challenge, ye cocky wee Gordon!" he said. His speech was slurred. "Let it be a wrestling match! And the loser"—he had to think for minute—". . . and the loser must kiss the winner's sporran."

To hoots and howls, they went at it, overturning chairs, smashing crockery and fine porcelain ornaments that got in their way. The spectators could not contain themselves. Before long, it had degenerated into a free-for-all.

Upstairs, in their bedchamber, when Rand set Caitlin on her feet, she stomped to the window and wheeled to face him, her arms crossed over her breasts. Her eyes were wary.

He had adopted much the same pose as she, except his eyes were smiling. "A Highlander," he said, "has more pride than a flock of peacocks. All these months, you've given me the words I longed to hear, and I never knew it. Why?"

"Because you are an English Randal. If you had put yourself to the trouble of learning our language, you would have known what the words meant." Her heart was pounding, but it wasn't with temper. Every nerve was vibrating with hope.

He moved in closer. "That's not the reason. If you had thought, for one minute, that I had known the language, you would never have said those words to me." He held up one hand to silence the rush of words as they began to tumble from her lips. "For God's sake, let go of your false pride! There's been too much of that around here already."

Her eyes faltered beneath his hard, unsmiling stare, then steadied. "How could I tell you? Ours was a forced marriage. You didn't love me. Why should I love you?" She cried out passionately, "I *never* wanted to love you, because I knew it was hopeless. Don't you think I knew the sort of women you preferred? Beautiful, cultured sophisticates who moved in your own circles. You told me so. I knew you could never love me."

"Beautiful, cultured sophisticates bore me to tears." He paused, giving her time to absorb his meaning. "And it's been a long time now since I've come to think of you as the most beautiful and fascinating woman of my acquaintance."

Her eyes were very wide, and she swallowed audibly. "Why did you never say anything?" she whispered.

He let out a sound that was not quite a laugh, not quite a sigh. "Because of David. Can you imagine what I have been made to suffer, thinking that you still loved him? I have been so gentle with you, so restrained, so forbearing." He brought his hand down sharply on top of the dresser, and Caitlin jumped. "It's enough to make any sane man sick to his stomach! I've been lovesick, that's what I've been! And the cure was beyond my reach, or so I thought."

She was shaking her head, smiling through tears. "I told you there was never anything between David and me. We were friends, nothing more."

He made a furious notion with his hands. "Don't lie to me! Not now! I read your letter to him. I *know!*"

"What do you know?"

"That you quarreled! That he believed his passion for

439

you was hopeless, but you relented and begged him to come back to you. Yes, I know. It wasn't very gentlemanly of me to read your letter. But I was consumed with jealousy. I had to know."

Tears flooded her eyes. "You misunderstood. It was never me David loved. It was someone else. You were jealous for no reason.'

"But . . . at the end, at Waterloo, it was you he spoke of. If he had loved someone else, wouldn't he have mentioned her name?"

"What did he say? You never told me this."

Rand touched one hand to his forehead, smoothing away his frown. "He asked me to go to you. 'She's a Randal of Glenshiel,' he told me."

"And that's all?"

"No. When I asked him why he had turned back to save me, he said he had done it for Randal and for Scotland."

She gazed at him mutely for a long time. "What can I say?" she asked finally. "All I can repeat is that David never loved me in the way you mean, and I never loved him. We were friends, nothing more."

"Soul mates?" His smile was twisted.

"That was David's word, not mine."

His eyes were passionate upon her face. "I don't know if I have it in me to be the friend to you that David was, but I aim to try."

She had to swallow before she could find her voice. "Friend, husband, lover—you are more than I ever thought to find in any man."

He looked into her eyes and knew that she spoke the truth. "Say the words to me!" he said roughly. "Say the words to me!"

She smiled. *"Mo gaol orist.* What time is it?"

He closed his eyes and gritted his teeth. "Caitlin!" he warned.

"I love you," she cried out. "At last I can say it. *Mo gaol orist.* I love you." And she threw herself into Rand's arms.

Crushing her to him, kissing her feverishly, he then spoke the only words she wanted to hear.

She awakened at dawn with the feeling that someone had just walked over her grave. It wasn't an eerie feeling, but more the brush of a friend's fingertips on her shoulder. Unclasping Rand's arm from around her waist, she slipped out of bed and moved like a shadow to the window. She was thinking of David and of his hopeless passion for Rand. She stood there staring out blindly for a long time. Though there were tears in her eyes, her lips were curved in a smile.

"Caitlin?" Rand moved restlessly, then hauled himself up. "What are you doing?"

She padded back to the bed. "I was remembering old times and old friends."

"David?"

She didn't try to deny it. "Yes. I was thanking him for saving your life and for sending you to me."

He hugged her fiercely. "I've been thinking. If our first child is a boy, I'd like to name him for David." He pulled back and tried to make out her features in the dim light. "It's only a suggestion. Perhaps you have already decided to name the child for your father?"

She kissed him lingeringly. "No. My mind is the same as yours. I think we should call our first son after David. David Randal. That's a good name."

441

"Our *first* son?" He cocked one eyebrow. "How many sons are you planning on giving me?"

She laughed. "I have a premonition," she said, "that by the time we are finished, we'll have run out of names for all our boys."

He smiled and pulled her closer. "Careful! Those sound like prophetic words," he said. And they were.

AUTHOR'S NOTE

There is no Clan Randal. In the interests of my story, it was necessary to invent it. Everyone in Scotland knows who the chiefs of the various clans were in 1815, and whoever does not, can soon find out. I wanted my hero to be the chief of a great clan, hence the Clan Randal came into existence.

Everything else is as accurate as I could make it, including the smuggling and the grave-robbing. I am indebted to historian and author, Fenton Wyness, for his excellent books on the northeast of Scotland, and in particular, *Royal Valley*.

For those readers who are interested, Balmoral Castle was acquired by Queen Victoria upon the death of her consort, Prince Albert. In the 1850s he built this magnificent castle, and ever since, Balmoral has been the Highland retreat of the British Royal family. It is reputed to be Queen Elizabeth's favorite residence. When in residence, the Royal family worships at the church of Crathie.